The Last Priestess
of Malia

D1522047

Laura Perry

Potnia Press

Potnia Press

Diogenes font © Apostrophic Labs.

Cover illustration and design by the author.
Malia bee pendant illustration by the author.

LauraPerryAuthor.com

Dedication

To the Minoans of ancient Crete, and to the gods and goddesses they loved. May Ida's children live forever.

Also by Laura Perry:

Non-fiction:

Labrys and Horns: An Introduction to Modern Minoan Paganism
Ariadne's Thread: Awakening the Wonders of the Ancient
    Minoans in Our Modern Lives
Deathwalking: Helping Them Cross the Bridge (anthology editor)
The Wiccan Wellness Book: Natural Healthcare for Mind, Body,
    and Spirit
Ancient Spellcraft: From the Hymns of the Hittites to the Carvings
    of the Celts

Fiction:

The Bed: a novel of angels, demons, ghosts, and old furniture
Jaguar Sky: an adventure in the land of the Maya

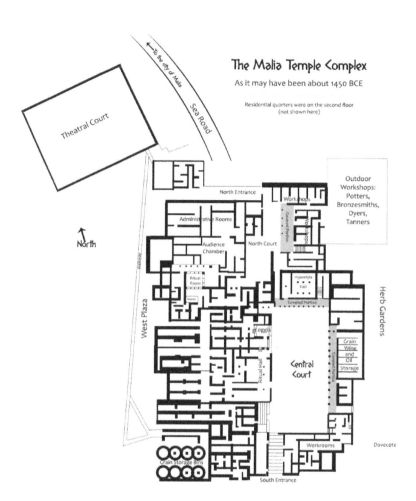

The Malia Temple Complex

As it may have been about 1450 BCE

Residential quarters were on the second floor
(not shown here)

To the city of Malia

Sea Road

Theatral Court

North

West Plaza

North Entrance

Administrative Rooms

Audience Chamber

North Court

Ritual Room

Adyton

Loggia

Ritual Hall

Central Court

Workshops

Covered Portico

Workshops

Hypostyle Hall

Covered Portico

Covered Portico

Grain Wine and Oil Storage

Outdoor Workshops: Potters, Bronzesmiths, Dyers, Tanners

Herb Gardens

Workrooms

Dovecote

Grain Storage Bins

South Entrance

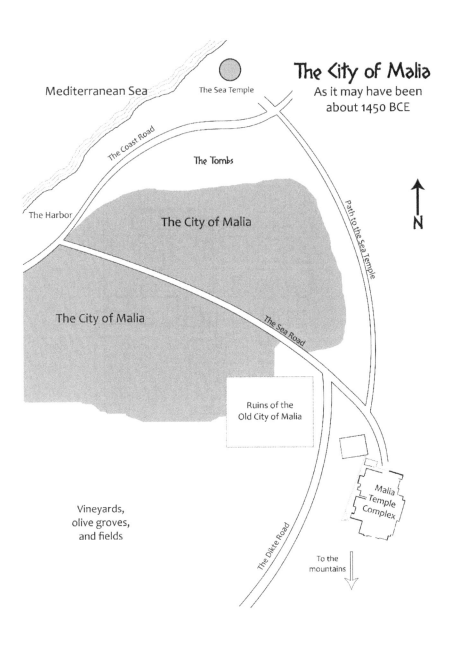

Mediterranean Sea

The Sea Temple

The City of Malia

As it may have been
about 1450 BCE

The Coast Road

The Tombs

The Harbor

The City of Malia

Path to the Sea Temple

N

The City of Malia

The Sea Road

Ruins of the
Old City of Malia

Malia
Temple
Complex

Vineyards,
olive groves,
and fields

The Dike Road

To the
mountains

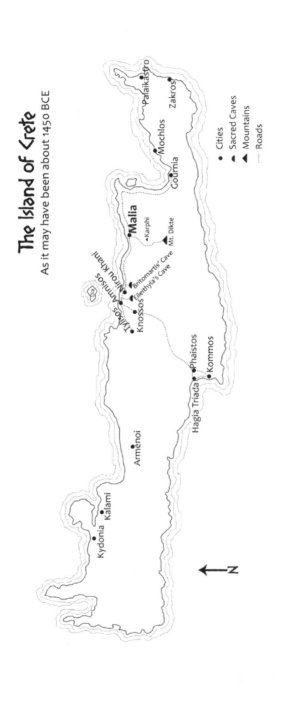

The Island of Crete

As it may have been about 1450 BCE

Cities •
Sacred Caves ▲
Mountains ▲
Roads ......

Kydonia
Kalami
Armenoi
Hagia Triada
Phaistos
Kommos
Tylisos
Amnisos
Nirou Khani
Knossos
Eileithyia's Cave
Britomartis' Cave
Karphi
Mt. Dikte
Malia
Gournia
Mochlos
Palaikastro
Zakros

N ←

This page left intentionally blank.

Contents

This page left intentionally blank.

Author's Note

Though the people in this story are fictional characters, and therefore the products of my imagination, the places in the novel—the cities, the temples, the farms—are very real, or at least, they were many centuries ago. They were a part of the world the Minoans knew. The Minoans were a Bronze Age culture centered on the Mediterranean island of Crete. Many of the details in this story come from archaeology: home furnishings, ritual ware, clothing, food and drink and the likely methods of preparation. The rituals are my own creation, with the inspiration of the Great Mothers and the other gods and goddesses of the Minoan pantheon.

The cover art includes some "hat tips" to Minoan art, artifacts, and iconography as well as references to events that occur in the story, and one quiet bit of homage. The details: The temple in the background was inspired by the image on the Master Impression seal from Chania (ancient Kydonia). The date palm trees beside the temple are in the style Minoan artists used to depict them. The boulders are a reference to the baetyl rituals found on Minoan stone seals and seal rings. The priestess' clothing looks like that found on female figures throughout Minoan art. The cup she is holding is similar to actual vessels found at Knossos, which are like the ones in the Camp Stool fresco, also from Knossos. The bronze dagger she is holding is like several found at Malia. Her necklace is the Malia bee pendant, a beautiful piece of gold jewelry found in the tombs near the temple at Malia. The spiral border at the bottom of the cover is inspired by a similar one on a fresco from the temple complex at Knossos.

In case you might think the cup and dagger in the priestess' hands are references to Wiccan ritual tools, allow me to dispel that notion. Both items are representations of specific ancient Minoan artifacts. They refer to rituals in the story that use them as sacred tools, but not at all in the manner of Wiccan practice. They also play a prominent role in the story's ending (don't worry, I'm not giving out spoilers here). And finally, they are a quiet homage to Riane Eisler's excellent book *The Chalice and the Blade: Our History, Our Future*. It was one of the first books I read in my search for information about the Minoans, way back in the 1980s. Dr. Eisler's work continues to inform both my spiritual path and my way of being in the world. I chose to include a cup and blade on the cover both because they were common items in Minoan Crete, and because I want people to think about the fact that we can't automatically ascribe meaning to objects based only on our own life experience. We always need context in order to understand artifacts. Here, the context is not Wicca, a modern Neopagan religion, but the Bronze Age culture of the Minoans from about the year 1450 BCE.

Be sure to take advantage of the Glossary at the end of the book. It can help you understand unfamiliar terms and pronounce the character names. I created the Glossary, along with the maps, to help you along your journey in the world of the ancient Minoans. I hope you enjoy reading it as much as I enjoyed writing it.

L.P.

Chapter 1

"Hold still, child. Your fidgeting is making the ringlets slip out of the bands."

"I am not a child," she muttered. "Not anymore."

"Then stop acting like one," her mother said, softly enough that it wasn't a proper rebuke. The two were, in fact, the same height, and the girl's figure was only a touch narrower than her mother's.

The girl held very still until the last of the chased gold bands was in place among her short, curly black locks. Then she reached for her mirror, a circle of polished bronze with a slim handle, and scrutinized the hairdo. She twirled a finger in one of the ringlets, glossy from the scented oil she had applied after her ritual cleansing bath. The soft fragrance of labdanum wafted from her hair as the locks shifted with her touch.

"Could we not have waited until my hair grew out more?" She made a face and set the mirror back down. "At least I no longer need submit to you shaving my head every few days as if I were still a child."

"No, we could not wait," came a voice from the doorway. "The auguries say we must do it today."

"My Lady." Startled, the girl straightened up and made the sacred salute, her back arched and the back of her fist against her forehead. The Head of the College of Priestesses stepped into the

1

room, smiling.

"Daipita, welcome," the girl's mother said, also making the salute but then embracing the older woman and kissing her on the cheek. Daipita returned the embrace and the kiss.

"Now, my dear," Daipita said, turning to the girl, "you have had your first blood-time. That ceremony is three Moons past and it is time for you to take the next step, if you wish. You have been a good novice, most dedicated." She slipped a finger beneath the girl's chin and tilted her head up so their eyes met. "I must ask you one last time if this is your true choice, made freely and honestly before all the gods."

The girl's face grew serious. "Yes, My Lady."

"You do not wish to learn a craft or become a merchant or trader?"

"No, My Lady."

"You do not wish to join your kinspeople's household in the city and have your life free for yourself?"

The girl took a deep breath and forced herself to meet the older woman's gaze. "No, My Lady. I have given you my answer. I will be a priestess like Mama." She glanced sidelong at her mother, who stood silent, waiting.

"And you know what it means to be a priestess?" Daipita asked.

"Of course." The girl nodded, beaming. "I have grown up in the temple, and you have approved all of my novice work. I will learn all the rites and serve the Great Mothers with honor."

"You know," Daipita said, "there is more to being a priestess than rites and festivals. There is labor to be done, a temple to run, and a city full of people to deal with. It is not all chants and visions, bells and incense."

"Yes, My Lady," the girl said, her brow furrowed. "But I have done all that is required of novices. Now I can be a real priestess."

The older woman sighed, an indulgent smile crinkling her face. "Very well. It is good to have enthusiastic new clergy in these uncertain times. You and the other novices give us hope."

The girl looked askance at her superior. "It is not dangerous to be a priestess, is it?"

"No, it is not. And gods willing, it will not be so as long as I am alive."

"Then I shall be the best of priestesses and perform all the rites properly so the Great Mothers will keep us safe from all danger," she said, squaring her shoulders.

"Are you prepared?"

"I have fasted and taken a ritual bath. I have dressed." She smoothed a hand down the front of her long tunic, the simple garb of the new initiate. The fine, undyed linen covered her shoulders but left her breasts bare. The front was fastened with small ties just below her breasts, and the two overlapping sides of the garment's skirt were held in place by a soft cord that wrapped around her waist. "I am ready for the rite."

"Then let us begin." She looked at the girl's mother. "Inia, you know what to do. We shall await you."

Daipita embraced the girl and gave Inia a kiss on the cheek before turning to leave the room. Alone again, the girl and her mother stood in awkward silence, avoiding each other's eyes. At last the girl spoke.

"It is my own choice, Mama. Free and honest, like Daipita said."

Inia tidied the cosmetics containers and put away the jewelry box. "You could still see Rhea any time you like, even if you move in with your brother in the city. You do not have to become a priestess like her just to be together."

The girl folded her arms across her chest and huffed out a breath. "This is not about Rhea, Mama. This is what I need to do. The visions at the ceremony for my first blood-time were clear."

"You and your visions. I never had visions."

The girl turned toward the door. "Daipita says they are real and I should heed them. She says the High Priestess proclaimed they were foretold at my birth auguries. If the Head of the College and the High Priestess both tell me to take them seriously, then so I shall." She picked up the ritual veil, a long rectangle of plain soft linen, and draped it around her shoulders. Her mother eyed her skeptically. "I have lived my entire life in the temple, Mama. I know what it means to be a priestess."

"Once it is done, you may not change your mind," her mother warned. "The oath is breakable only by death."

"I happily give my life to the gods," the girl said. She set her jaw and waited. After a few moments, her mother heaved a sigh and brushed past her, heading out into the corridor without looking back to see whether her daughter was following.

Their bare feet made no sound as they strode through the residential wing to the staircase, then down to the main floor. The stairway let out into the stone-paved north court, a feature unique to the temple complex at Malia. The temples in the island's other cities had only a single central court. The scent of food cooking—meat roasting and bread baking, the girl realized as her mouth watered—drifted through the air from the nearby kitchens. Her stomach rumbled. Three days of fasting had strained her patience and her self-control.

They crossed the court in silence, the girl following a step behind her mother and keeping her gaze lowered so she would not be tempted to speak to any of the people she saw or make eye contact with them. Though Malia was not as large as Knossos, the temple was still a busy place. Priestesses and priests, artisans and visitors made their way around the public areas all day long.

Inia led her daughter through two doorways and into a columned walkway that skirted the reception area. Here the High Priestess Eileithyia and the Consort Belisseus appeared in the audience room, mediating disputes and receiving messages and offerings. Here the Heads of the Colleges—Daipita and her male counterpart in the College of Priests—gave their regular reports to the High Priestess and asked her advice about their responsibilities. Here also, the temple scribes recorded the public's offerings on clay tablets. Later on, they transferred the information onto papyrus scrolls that were stored for the long term. Then they wiped the soft clay tablets smooth and started again.

Though the scribes—specially trained priestesses and priests—held positions of high regard within the temple, they were of no interest to the girl. What they did was ordinary, mundane. She supposed they never had visions. At the very least, few of them led

4

any of the important rites, like the one she was about to undergo.

Of course, this was the same area of the temple where the High Priestess and her Consort held audience with high-ranking visitors. Where the Heads of the College of Priests and the College of Priestesses made their reports to the High Priestess and the Consort. Where the power flowed in and out of the temple. These people did, in fact, lead the important rites. They had visions, like the girl had. Perhaps that room was something to aspire to after all.

As she and her mother stood in silence, waiting, the girl examined the wall in front of them. It was made of wooden panels punctuated every few paces by a square pillar built into the wall. The girl knew that the wooden panels were, in fact, pairs of doors, any or all of which could be opened to give access to the chamber beyond. There were several rooms in the temple that were built this way, but the girl had never been inside this particular one, never even seen inside it. As she was trying to guess what lay beyond the doors, one pair of them swung open.

Inia gave her daughter a gentle push, and the girl stepped up to the dark opening, raising her veil to cover her head but not her face, as was her people's custom. She squinted, doing her best to gaze into the room, but her eyes were adjusted to the sunbeams streaming in from the high windows above her, and she could see nothing. A fully veiled figure appeared just inside the room, shrouded in darkness, unidentifiable.

"Are you prepared?" the figure said. The voice was not Daipita's or any other she recognized. A shiver of fear ran down the girl's spine.

"Yes," she managed to croak out through a suddenly dry mouth. "My Lady," she hastily added.

The figure beckoned and the girl took a step toward the doorway, then glanced back over her shoulder at her mother. Inia shook her head. Swallowing hard, the girl stepped into the darkness alone.

The doors shut behind her, and she stood in the shadowy room, her heart pounding. She could not get her bearings. Small oil lamps flickered here and there, dancing spots of flame hovering in the darkness, with no light thrown on any wall. The sound of crackling coals met her ears, a sacred fire in a brazier somewhere in the depths of the room. The veil cut off her vision to the sides and she dared not turn her head to look around. How big was the room? Who was here? What were they going to do to her?

Panic rose, squeezing her chest and tightening her throat, but she forced it back down with a deep breath. If she wanted to be a priestess, she would have to behave properly during the initiation.

Goosebumps rose on her arms as she felt the faint breeze of people in motion around her. With the next deep breath, incense smoke swirled in her lungs and she coughed, unable to stop as more smoke billowed around her. The scent was sickly sweet, like flowers and musty soil combined. The taste of it lay heavy on her tongue as she struggled to inhale. A few choking breaths later, the smoke began to clear, but now the flames danced in fuzzy multiples—two, three, and four—as her head spun and a buzzing sounded in her ears.

A veiled figure stepped in front of her, silhouetted in the faint glow of an oil lamp. Whether this was the same one who had invited her into the room, the girl could not tell.

"Do you give yourself to the temple?"

The girl opened her mouth to speak, but no sound came out. She tried again and managed a croaking, "I do."

"Do you give your life to the temple?"

"I do."

"Do you give your life to the gods?"

In spite of the drugged incense, the girl began to tremble. Did they know this was to be a priestess initiation and not a sacrifice?

"Do you?" the veiled figure demanded again.

"I do," the girl replied, her voice shaking. She felt a cup being pressed into her hands.

"Then drink."

Swaying and slightly dizzy, she squinted into the darkness, trying to make out the other women in the shadows. A priestess' initiation would involve only women, just as a priest's initiation would include only men. Her mother was not there, that she knew.

The few figures she could see in the faint light of the oil lamps were all fully veiled, their faces covered. None spoke. None moved. They were waiting for her to follow the command she had been given. She lifted the cup to her lips, inhaling the aroma of sweet wine but something else as well, something musky, earthy, like the scent from the incense.

I am to be a priestess, she reminded herself. Then she squared her shoulders and drained the cup in one long, slow draught. She swiped at a dribble of wine that had run down her chin and found herself falling, falling... and then she was flying through the darkness, borne aloft by thousands of hands, the spirits of the dead reaching out and carrying her along toward the World Below. Her eyes were wide open, but all was blackness, not even any oil lamps any more, with groaning and creaking and the feeling of motion as she was carried down and down and down.

Dead. I am dead. They have killed me.

She was beyond crying, beyond speaking, beyond thinking. All she could do was hear the whispers of the dead, smell the funeral incense, feel the cold hardness of the stone tomb as they laid her body in it.

For half an age she lay there, unable to move, her body still and cold as she listened to the murmurs and hisses and sighs of the dead. There was no time, only being, as she hovered in the dark nothingness. She did her best to determine where she was and whether she was a spirit now, what she was supposed to do, but her thoughts were muddled and fuzzy. Eventually she gave up trying to think and just allowed herself to float in the darkness, a spirit in the Great Mother's cave, silent and dead and no more substance than the morning fog. Then slowly a soft, pale light began to dawn above the tomb, and a drumbeat began, the double-beat rhythm of the human heart, pulsing slowly.

The girl drew in a shaky breath.

Breathing. I am breathing.

The heartbeat rhythm sped up, growing louder as the light increased. The girl's vision was still blurry, but she could see dark silhouettes, veiled figures surrounding her, leaning down over her, helping her up. She could not quite feel her body, or perhaps it was someone else's body, since she did not seem to be quite fully inside it.

Gentle hands lifted her to standing then guided her, trembling, slowly up the steps and out of the adyton. When she reached the top, the hands steadied her until she stopped swaying, then all the figures stepped back to allow one among them to come forward.

"You died," said the veiled figure, "and yet you live."

The girl swallowed, her head swimming.

"The life you have now," the veiled figure continued, "belongs not to you but to the gods."

Unable to speak, the girl nodded, and her body swayed with the motion. *Not mine. Theirs.*

A whispering began, but this time it sounded different from the murmurs and sighs of the dead. Sounds threaded through the whispering, echoes of meaning that her mind could not untangle.

The whispering grew louder as she heard fuzzy fragments of words, snatches of speech: *ah, ra, ah, dah, ra, neh, ra.* Then the fragments began to assemble themselves into larger pieces, until she recognized a name within the swirling sound: *ah-ra-da-neh.* The name of the goddess, holy precious Daughter of the Three-and-One: Ariadne.

Ariadne, came the whispers. *Ariadne. Ariadne.* A murmuring chant, the name repeated over and over again. The voices grew louder, surrounding her, hissing and buzzing in her ears.

"Who are you?" the veiled figure asked through the buzzing drone of the whispers.

The girl stood mute, panicking. She shook her head, but that did not clear it. Surely they could not mean her to speak that name as hers. Perhaps she was meant to make an invocation. Priestesses did that. They made invocations to goddesses.

"Who are you?" the veiled figure said again, insistent.

When the girl remained silent, the veiled figure stepped forward, looming over her, a low growl reverberating from her throat. "Who are you?" the figure shouted, raising her arms as if to strike a double blow.

The girl jumped back, her heart pounding. "Ariadne," she dared to whisper, her voice cracking.

"Who?" the figure demanded.

"Ariadne," she said a bit louder. The hissing whispers grew louder, repeating the name over and over again, an insistent drone that filled her head until she felt that it would lift her off the floor.

The girl drew in a deep breath. "Ariadne," she said firmly, her voice echoing in her head. "I am Ariadne."

The room fell silent.

Chapter 2

"Have some bread," Daipita said, pressing half a small barley loaf into Ariadne's shaking hand. "You must eat now to relieve the effects of the rite."

Effects there were, in abundance. Though she was seated on a sturdy bench, leaning her elbows on a solid table in the dining hall, she still felt as though the room was swimming and she was not quite all the way inside her body. The flickering flames of the oil lamps blended with the twilight that seeped in through the high windows, and she could not help but think she must still be back in the ritual chamber, still dead, still waiting.

When people spoke to her, the voices echoed in her head. She took a bite of the bread, reminding herself how to chew. The process felt complicated and awkward. The bread tasted like something else, not food, and the scents coming from the dishes on the table made no sense to her addled mind.

The rest of the women who made up the College of Priestesses, as well as the High Priestess herself, were gathered around the long tables, eating and chatting. This was both the recovery meal from the rite and a celebration of a new member's induction into the College. Daipita floated from one group to another, making sure none of her priestesses felt left out. Inia had hugged Ariadne when they entered the dining hall but had quickly moved away to talk with her friends. Ariadne knew they were leaving her be until the effects of the sacred substances had worn off, but that did not keep her from feeling terribly alone.

"I am here," Rhea said softly as she slid onto the bench beside her friend.

"Were you there?" asked Ariadne as she continued to work out how to chew and swallow.

"You know we are not allowed to divulge who takes part in the rite." She reached for a platter of fruit and chose a date. "It has not been that long since I underwent it myself."

"I am not... am I still me?" She shook her head to try to clear it, but that only made the fuzzy feeling worse.

"Of course you are still you, silly," said Rhea, planting a kiss on her dearest friend's cheek. "But I am not sure I care to call you Ariadne," she said, speaking the goddess' name in a whisper. "That name has a power that makes me tremble sometimes."

"You cannot use my old name. She is dead." Her mouth full of fig, Ariadne fought back tears, doing her best not to choke on the food.

Rhea reached her arm out and held her friend's hand in a warm grip. "I shall call you Aria. That is a beautiful name, and you are a beautiful priestess."

Aria nodded and held still for Rhea to dab the tears off her cheeks. Then Rhea lifted up their hands, still clasped together, and kissed Aria's knuckles one by one.

"Will you show me how..." Aria hesitated. "How to be a priestess?" She ducked her head, ashamed. Her visions had shown her many wondrous things. But none of them had taught her what it means to live as a priestess all day long every day, dedicated to the gods and the goddesses, to the Three-and-One and all their children.

A hand squeezed her shoulder, and she looked up to see Daipita standing over her, smiling softly. "I will teach you, my dear. And so will all your sister priestesses, and Our Lady as well." She nodded her head toward the High Priestess, who sat at the end of a nearby table. "The most devoted among us never stop learning.

All the gods ask of us is that we do our best, no matter the situation." She drew the platter of fruit closer to Aria. "Eat some more, and when you have recovered, we will discover some new things together."

It took a cluster of grapes, a piece of soft cheese, another half-loaf of barley bread, and two cups of well-diluted wine before Daipita pronounced Aria fit enough to rise from the table.

"And now my dear, I have something to show you." The older woman retrieved an oil lamp from one of the sconces on the wall and beckoned to her newest priestess.

Aria was relieved to discover that she could stand and walk without trouble, though she felt dreadfully tired. Flanked by Rhea and Inia, and clasping Rhea's hand for reassurance, Aria followed the Head of her College up to the residential quarters. Halfway down a corridor, Daipita stopped and drew aside a curtain from a doorway. Aria peered inside, puzzled.

"This is your room now," Daipita explained, motioning Aria into the small chamber ahead of her. Rhea followed them into the room while Inia stood in the doorway.

In the lamplight Aria could see that her small trunk had been moved from the novice priestess' dormitory. Now she understood why her mother had insisted that day that they put all her things — her comb and mirror, her clothes and the few pieces of jewelry she owned — in the trunk and latch the lid. Now it stood at the foot of a simple bed. There was just enough space for a small table and a stool, but the room was not altogether plain: the walls were bordered with a fresco of red and yellow rosettes and the window frame was painted in red to match.

Aria glanced sidelong at Rhea then turned to Daipita. "I am to sleep here... alone?"

"Every priestess has her own chamber," Daipita explained. "But whether she sleeps there every night by herself is purely her own concern."

Aria ducked her head and held her hand out to Rhea, who took hold and squeezed gently.

"For tonight, however," the Head of the College continued, "it is best you get plenty of good sleep… alone. Come morning you will feel much better, much more yourself."

"Myself. Whoever she is," Aria muttered.

Flashing her new priestess a look of understanding, Daipita embraced her gently then motioned for them all to go. Aria gripped Rhea's hand as her friend made to leave.

"Thank you," she whispered.

"Always," came the reply as Rhea's fingers gently traced Aria's jawline. They held each other close for a long moment then said their goodnights with a sweet kiss.

When the others had left, Aria slipped out of her clothes and slid under the covers in her new bed. She could feel that the mattress had been freshly stuffed with clean wool, plush and comfortable. The softness lured her quickly into a deep, deep sleep.

Chapter 3

"Here, Aria, set this with the other supplies."

She hefted the flagon full of wine and carried it to the table that held the necessities for the First Crescent Moon rite. A few Moons into Aria's tenure as a full-fledged priestess, Daipita had finally invited her to participate in the ritual instead of just watching. Eager to display her ability, Aria followed Daipita's instructions exactly and forced herself to listen more than she spoke. Next time, she might be allowed to do even more. She rejoiced at the opportunity for real priestess work instead of the tedious tasks she had been assigned so far. She was beyond tired of cleaning ritual ware, memorizing chants and sayings, and carrying messages from one part of the temple to another.

Tonight's ritual was an open temple ceremony: all the priests and priestesses were allowed to observe, initiate and novice alike, though lay people were not invited. The people were already beginning to gather on the flat rooftop while the ritual team set up. Aria knew few of the professional clergy who lived full-time in the temple, and even fewer of the part-timers who came in from the city for the larger rites. But it looked like most of them had come up to the roof for this ceremony.

No rites of any sort were allowed during the three days when the Moon was dark. To hold a ritual during that time was to invite terrible misfortune on the people, just as rites during the rare shadowings of the Moon and the Sun were also forbidden. But now that the Moon had begun its cycle of light again, they gathered to await the visions for the upcoming days.

Aria's bare feet pressed against the plastered roof, the surface still faintly warm from the sunny day. But the breeze that brushed against her skin carried a chill. She hoped the rite would be finished before the night grew too cold. Like the other priestesses, she was dressed in thin linen, not the warm wool they would don once winter began, and of course none of them wore shoes, not during a sacred rite.

To keep her mind off her discomfort, Aria watched Daipita at work. The Head of the College was arranging the items on a shrine bench. Its top sat level with the base of the sacred horns that ran all the way around the roof edge. Kaeseus, the Head of the College of Priests, supervised two young men who carried each item to Daipita as she requested it.

The Sky-Watchers had seen the first faint sliver of the new crescent Moon in the dimming sky shortly before sunset earlier in the evening. Aria recognized Orestas, who had recently become the temple's Chief Sky-Watcher, as he sighted the Moon in alignment with the horns on the western side of the temple roof. Diktynna's Bow was riding low in the darkening western sky. When it touched the top of the mountains in the west, Orestas would signal the High Priestess, and the rite would begin.

Aria studied the arrangement of objects on the shrine bench: two pairs of sacred horns, a bronze figurine of a worshiper making the Moon Salute with both her hands shading her eyes, two fine ceramic cups, and a matching pair of wide bowls, painted black inside and out. At the end of the bench stood a copper brazier full of hot coals. The cups and bowls would soon receive the wine that Aria had set on the small table near the shrine bench. Though the wine in the pitcher was just that—plain wine—Aria knew that Daipita and Kaeseus had put a small amount of opium powder in each of the cups on the altar.

Aria's gaze swept the shrine bench and she sighed. She would not be adding the incense to the coals or pouring the wine tonight, and she would certainly not be performing the scrying. Her task was to help set up and then witness the divination, whatever the gods had to say to the people for the upcoming month. The High Priestess and the Consort, along with the older priests and priestesses, would interpret what the diviners said and did. But it was always a good idea to have many eyes and ears available to make certain of their words and actions. The human memory is a fallible thing, after all.

At the far end of the bench stood a sturdy table with decoratively carved legs, a wide bowl sitting on the rooftop beneath it. Aria knew what would soon lie on that table, but she decided not to think about that just yet.

Giving a satisfied nod toward the shrine bench, Daipita moved over to where Aria and a handful of the other clergy were waiting. A frown creased her face as her gaze swept the growing group of spectators.

"Can you believe it?" she hissed to the High Priestess. "He has the gall to come up here tonight and watch us." She jerked her head toward the edge of the small crowd, where one man was standing apart from the rest. In fact, it looked to Aria as if most of the others were avoiding him. His skin was pale, not the honey-brown color of Ida's children. But his hair was that honey-brown color, contrasting with all the glossy black hair around him.

"He is an initiated priest, Daipita. He has every right to take part."

"But he is a mainlander, one of *them*. They are all pale and tall and strange. Kaeseus should never have accepted him."

The High Priestess drew in a slow breath and let it out again. "*They* live here, just as we do. Some of their families have been here for generations, and some of them practice their trades in our temple workshops. The one you complain about was born on this island, so in a sense he is not a mainlander at all, but one of Ida's children." Aria could just make out, in the dimming light, the High Priestess narrowing her eyes at Daipita. "Your College includes the daughter of a trader from the Two Lands, yet you make no complaint about her."

Daipita sniffed. "She is different. She understands our values. And she looks like us."

The High Priestess smoothed her skirt. "Most of the mainlanders understand our values, even if they do not look like us. It is the newer ones who have come down from the mountains to the north who are the real problem. They are greedy and warlike and have no respect for women or goddesses. Thankfully, most of them keep to Knossos."

"And what happens when they wish to expand their reach?"

"Let us not make problems where none exist."

Orestas stepped up to the High Priestess and tilted his head toward the western horizon.

"Shall we begin?" she said. She nodded to the two young priests, who lit the oil lamps in the ritual area. As the flames burst to life, the spectators fell silent.

The clergy all took their places, with Aria and the other witnesses standing near one end of the shrine bench, where they would be able to hear the diviners clearly and see them reasonably well in the lamplight. The Chief Song-Priestess lifted the triton shell to her lips and blew three short blasts, signaling the beginning of the rite.

One of the young priests spooned incense powder onto the hot coals in the brazier. The smoke rose, pale in the darkness, and Aria tasted myrrh and labdanum on her tongue. The priests fanned the smoke until it lay like a pall over the shrine bench, then they moved away toward the stairwell.

Her arms upraised in the ancient goddess pose, the High Priestess intoned the First Crescent Moon chant:

The Huntress draws her bow
As the Moon begins
The silver crescent rides low
As the Moon begins
The people pay what they owe
As the Moon begins

All will be well here below
As the Moon begins

A slow drumbeat began, accompanied by the hissing of sistrums, as the two young priests who had assisted in the setup appeared out of the stairwell carrying a goat. Its head lolled to one side, but it was not dead, only drugged, its most recent meal a tasty porridge laced with opium. As the young men laid the creature on its side on the table, its rope-bound feet dangled over the edge.

Bare-chested and wearing the animal hide skirt of the sacrificial priesthood, Kaeseus stepped forward, a narrow bronze blade glinting in his hand. Aria had seen several sacrifices now. She knew this was a much easier end for the animals than the perfunctory, undrugged slaughter that most of them experienced in the yard behind the temple kitchens. But the act still disturbed her. *We must never allow the taking of life to become easy,* Daipita had told her. Aria was certain that for her, it never would.

His arms raised in blessing and benediction, Kaeseus dedicated the sacrifice: "The blood of the Horned One to feed the gods, the goddesses, the Three-and-One; blood to feed the spirits of the ancestors; blood to feed the Sight of the Diviners on this First Night. The body of the Horned One to feed the bodies of those who belong to the gods, the mortals of the temple. All is sacred. None shall be wasted."

With a quick caress of his hand over the goat's head, Kaeseus soothed the animal and covered its eyes. Then he plunged the tip of the dagger into the back of its neck, metal grating on bone. The creature shuddered once and was still. The drums and sistrums fell silent.

The priest drew the blade out and shifted the goat so its head hung halfway over the edge of the table, directly above the wide bowl. Then he sliced the edge of the blade along the animal's neck, just below its jaw, and the blood gushed out. He stepped back to avoid being hit by the spatter. The blood was for the gods and the spirits, not the humans. Taking any of their promised gift, even by accident, boded ill for anyone who knew no better than to back away.

When the blood finally stopped dripping, Kaeseus moved closer to the table once again. Aria saw that he was now holding the two black bowls that had sat on the shrine bench. With practiced care he knelt in front of the sacrificial table and dipped a ladle into the blood, spooning a small amount into each of the scrying bowls. Then he stood back up, set the bowls on the shrine shelf, and backed away. He would not be performing the divination tonight. He was overshadowed by the power of the sacrifice, so his visions would not be clear. He stayed to one side, waiting silently for the rite to end. He would neither touch nor speak to anyone, nor make eye contact, until he had gone below and bathed with purifying herbs. Next Moon, it would be Daipita's turn to take the animal's life.

The High Priestess gestured to Rhea, who approached the altar carrying the flagon of wine Aria had set among the supplies. First Rhea raised the pitcher to the sky, then she tipped a small amount over the edge of the rooftop into the gardens below, a libation to the spirits of the land, to the Great Mother whose body the island was. Next she slowly poured wine into each of the black bowls, taking care not to splash as the wine mixed with the blood. She also filled both of the cups then picked each one up and swirled it gently, dissolving the opium powder that was already in each cup with the wine she had just added.

With luck, Aria would be promoted to this duty soon, added into the rotation with the other young priestesses. As it was, she watched while Daipita and a priest approached the shrine bench. They would perform the divination for the rite. In preparation, they had both fasted from food and physical pleasure for three days. That way, their spirits would be less firmly attached to their bodies, and they could reach out into the unseen realms for knowledge and aid.

The diviners each lifted a cup and drank the wine from it. Then they turned to face each other, and Aria saw the priest clearly for the first time. He was beautiful. Curly black locks spilled down over broad shoulders and a bare chest, his skin beautifully brown. A simple linen kilt hugged his hips. Her eyes traveled down shapely thighs and calves to bare feet that pressed against the rooftop. He was perhaps ten years her senior. Aria stole a guilty glance at Rhea, but her girlfriend appeared to be equally entranced by tonight's male diviner and hadn't noticed Aria's staring at all.

Now the High Priestess moved over to the diviners and raised her arms up, holding her hands palms downward over their heads. The onlookers as well as the witnesses raised fists to foreheads in the salute, the acknowledgment of the power of the divine. Once again the High Priestess' voice rang out in the night air.

> We call to the Three
> The Great Mothers whose realms make up the world
> Kalliste, Fire of Heaven, First and Last
> Posidaeja, Grandmother Ocean, Womb-Water of the world
> Ida, Mother-of-Us-All, Sacred Soil beneath our feet
> And to the One, Mother-of-Darkness-and-Stars,
> Source of All
> Please grant to these your children
> Their eyes may be opened
> Their thoughts may be pure
> Their words may be clear
> So we may serve you all our days
> In the blessings of your love

The drum and sistrums began their slow rhythm once again. Daipita and the priest each picked up a scrying bowl and walked past the shrine bench to stand directly in front of the sacred horns that lined the roof's edge. Daipita shifted until she was centered in front of one pair of sacred horns, looking out toward the setting sliver of crescent Moon, her bowl held directly in front of her face. The priest did likewise in front of the adjacent pair of sacred horns.

The two stood still, staring at the surface of the blooded wine. One by one, the stars slowly glimmered to life in the darkening sky and reflected in the bowls alongside the shining crescent Moon. As the drum and sistrums continued their insistent beat, Daipita and the priest began to sway gently back and forth, just enough that the liquid in their bowls shifted and shimmered in the light of the Moon and the stars.

"Soon," came Daipita's voice, and Aria leaned forward to catch the priestess' every word. "Soon Lovely Tresses will walk upon the high place. Consult the auguries. She must bear the weight. Endure the darkness. The pain will be hers."

Aria drew in a sharp breath. Lovely Tresses was an epithet for the goddess Ariadne. But of course, Daipita had meant the goddess and not Aria. She must have. It took a great deal of willpower for Aria to turn her attention back to the diviners and away from the thoughts that swirled in her head.

The priest was swaying more strongly now, but his bowl remained balanced so the wine barely moved at all. "The rats from the northern mountains," he said, his voice slurred. "The rats have come down and will plunder more than just grain. They will eat their own kind and those who stand in their way. The winds will blow cold and hard among the living. Even the spirits of the dead will cry out in agony."

Several spectators gasped, but no one dared move or speak.

"No..." Daipita moaned, and Aria's attention snapped back to the priestess, who appeared to be fighting against the trance, shaking her head and doing her best to look away from her bowl.

Now the priest, too, began to groan. "Do not put this upon me," he cried out, wrenching his gaze away from the surface of the dark liquid.

A gust of chill wind whipped across the rooftop, and the oil lamp on the end of the shrine bench blew out. Darkness fell on the diviners' faces. Aria heard them both draw in ragged breaths, but neither moved.

"Oil the grapevines against the small insects, and the crop will do well," the priest said, his voice now a dull monotone. "An invitation sent to Zakros will do much to encourage friendship."

Daipita drew in a slow breath. "Counsel the merchants and artisans," she said in a flat voice, "but let them also counsel you. Temple and town each has its own value."

The assembly stood still and silent, waiting. After several long moments, the diviners carried their bowls back to the shrine bench and set them down. Their shoulders drooped and their feet dragged as they took their places next to Kaeseus. Though Aria had witnessed several of these rites, she had never seen the diviners look so exhausted afterward.

The High Priestess stepped in front of the shrine bench and raised her arms, intoning the final portion of the rite in a level voice:

The gods have spoken
Their voices in our mouths
Their fire in our heads
Their Mysteries in our hearts
The rite is ended
Go in the Mothers' peace

The Chief Song-Priestess lifted the triton shell to her lips and blew three short blasts, and suddenly the rooftop was buzzing with murmured conversation. Aria leaned toward the crowd in an attempt to pick out individual words and phrases. The spectators were milling around, slowly making their way back down the stairs, giving the mainlander priest a wide berth.

"Since when do the Children of Ida behave in such a way?" the High Priestess snapped. "You and you," she motioned to a priest and priestess standing near the shrine bench, "accompany him downstairs." She pointed to the mainlander priest. "See that he has pleasant conversation at supper as well. I will be watching."

Scowling, the High Priestess turned her attention back to the remains of the ritual. As Kaeseus watched in silence, taking care not to make eye contact with them, the young priests hauled the goat's carcass down to the kitchens. Now that the rite was ended and the animal's blood was drained, it was nothing more than meat. Daipita poured the contents of the diviners' wine bowls into the larger bowl of blood. Casting a look of concern at the High Priestess, she hefted the container of sacrificial liquid and carried it away.

"Now my people," the High Priestess said to the witnesses, "did you hear the divination clearly?" They all answered in the affirmative. "Very well. You may go downstairs to your supper. I will assist the diviners with their ritual cleansing."

Aria's eyebrows shot up. Usually, the High Priestess had each witness recount what they had heard so she could be certain of the divination. Doing her best to be subtle about it, Aria glanced around at the older priests and priestesses. They looked as surprised as she felt.

As the witnesses moved toward the staircase, Aria and Rhea delayed, shifting toward the back of the group. The High Priestess stepped over to them.

"Have no fear, my dears," she said, setting a hand gently on each one's shoulder. "I will take care of the situation."

"But..." Aria swallowed. "Was that a mistake, what happened tonight?" she dared to ask.

"There were no mistakes," the High Priestess said. "It is possible to enact every step perfectly and still not receive the outcome you desire. That is the way of things. Now go on down to supper with the others."

The young priestesses nodded but hesitated. Rhea slipped her hand into Aria's, and the two found themselves dragging their feet, casting furtive glances at the handful of clergy standing near the altar.

The High Priestess gave them a knowing smile. "His name is Lexion. And yes, he likes women as well as men. Now go." She gave them both a push, and they headed for the staircase, Aria silently thanking the dark night for hiding the blush that was creeping up her face.

Chapter 4

"Wake up, little sister."

Rhea's voice floated through Aria's dreams. Then she was blinking the dawn light out of her eyes while her friend drew their covers off.

"We will be late for breakfast," Rhea said. "You know Daipita dislikes it when we sleep too long in the morning." She stumbled out of bed and bent over the basin on the small table to splash some water in her face. "I had best go get dressed."

By now Aria was up, sitting on the side of her bed, wishing the dawn did not come so early in the summer. "I will see you in the dining hall," she said, stifling a yawn. "And then I am sure Daipita will have all sorts of amusing tasks for me to accomplish."

"Do not fret," Rhea said, bending to give Aria a kiss. "We must all begin in the same place. I am sure you will rise to great heights one day."

"Of course," Aria said, scowling as she drew a comb through her curly locks. "I will be the best dish-washer in the whole temple."

With a laugh, Rhea stepped out of the room, leaving Aria to wonder which annoying, tedious task the Head of the College would assign her today.

* * *

"Are you finished yet?"

At the sound of Rhea's voice, Aria lifted her head and set her rag down. "Yes, finally." She made a face at the shelves full of cups, bowls, pitchers, and offering stands. "I know the ritual ware is too sacred for the servants or even the novices to clean…"

"But?" Rhea perched her hands on her hips.

"I just wish," Aria sighed, "I could be done with this kind of work so I could do some *real* priestessing. How am I supposed to safeguard our traditions if I am not allowed to take part in them?"

"I have something to help your time go faster." Rhea held out her hand, and Aria took hold as she happily left the storeroom behind. "Out here." Rhea led her friend toward the east entrance.

"Where are we going?"

"The Ibex Brotherhood is practicing their spear-throwing."

"It will just be a field full of old men showing some boys how to handle a spear." Aria rolled her eyes, plodding along as Rhea tugged her forward.

Rhea cast a mischievous glance at her friend. "Lexion is teaching them today," she said.

A few moments later, the two young women were standing in the hot sunshine at the edge of the field by the temple's sacred grove of date palm trees. Holding hands, they watched a group of young priests take instruction from three grown men, including Lexion. His short, sleeveless linen tunic, barely long enough to cover his buttocks, clung to his sweaty chest and back as he showed the young men the best way to throw a spear. His spear flew straight and long, landing firmly upright in the ground at the far end of the field. Then he switched from demonstrating to teaching, his enthusiasm visible as he helped the young men find the best stance so their throws would rival his.

One of the young men became upset as his throws curved off to the side again and again. The others were careful not to make fun of him, but still he grew distraught, tears gleaming in his eyes as his spear landed sideways once again and toppled over into the dry grass. Lexion set a hand on his shoulder, offering comfort. In moments the young man was sobbing as Lexion enfolded him in strong arms, speaking quietly to him. When the young priest had finally spent his frustration, he wiped his cheeks and turned back to the field, determination clear in his face. Lexion spent some time helping him learn how to position his shoulders and hips properly, until finally he could throw the spear in a nearly straight line. The whole time, the midday sunlight beat down on the field, heating the air and the people alike.

As Aria and Rhea watched, Lexion stepped back from the group and stripped off his tunic, wiping the sweat from his chest with the fabric before tossing it to the side. Clad only in a loincloth and sandals, he continued to instruct the younger members of his brotherhood.

"He certainly is… talented," Aria said, a little breathless.

"My brother says he has an excellent sense of humor." Unlike Aria's brothers, who had taken to the sea as soon as they came of age, Rhea's brother had remained in the temple and joined the priesthood.

"We should stay until they have finished," Aria decided. "Then we can tell him how much we appreciate the time he dedicates to our brother priests."

"I agree," said Rhea, stifling a giggle.

They endured the hot sunlight for a while longer, watching the young men's skills improve as Lexion and the other priests worked with them. Just as they were about to finish, one of the temple servants hurried up to Aria and addressed her.

"I have had such trouble finding you! You were supposed to be in the storage rooms. Daipita insists that you see her right away. She is in her workroom."

"Tell her I will be right there," Aria said, and the servant hurried away. Sighing, Aria turned to her friend. "Give Lexion my compliments, please. I hope Our Lady does not have more dishes for me to wash!" With one last longing glance at the sweaty priest, she turned and headed back into the temple.

* * *

"My Lady," Aria said, bowing her head to Daipita as she entered her workroom.

"I take it you enjoyed the Brotherhood's spear practice?" Daipita said, looking up from her seat at her work table.

"I had already finished cleaning the ritual ware," Aria said. "I was not shirking."

"I did not say you were, my dear. Come, sit." She patted the empty spot at the end of her bench.

Aria perched on the bench and looked over the cluttered work table: some clay tablets and a stylus, several stacks of papyruses, a brush and an ink pot, the box that held the Head of the College's official seals.

"What are those?" Aria dared to ask.

A square of saffron-dyed linen lay in the center of the table with several pieces of dried clay scattered on top. Each lump of clay bore the impression of a seal stone. A cord lay to one side and the fabric was wrinkled as if the pieces of clay had been tied up in it.

"Those," Daipita said, scowling, "are a problem that has come from the mainland, via Knossos."

She reached out and folded the edge of the linen over the seal impressions, covering them. Then she let out a tired sigh. "You have heard tales of the Great Darkness, of course."

"That was the time when Kalliste destroyed her sacred island in a great explosion, and the whole world was like winter for more than a year. The Sun did not even shine."

She grimaced at the thought. Everyone knew how dangerous the Sun-and-Fire goddess was, how she had blasted to smithereens the very island Ida's children had dedicated to her. They called her Kalliste—the most beautiful—to appease her, though her proper name was Therasia.

Once the Fire-Mother had destroyed her sacred island, she convinced Posidaeja to lash the shores all around with enormous waves, demolishing many coastal cities including Malia and Knossos. Ten generations later, they still did not understand what they had done to deserve such a cataclysm, though Aria's teachers always insisted the goddess was sending a message, not wreaking vengeance, and her people should do their best to heed that warning.

"Even now," Daipita said, "most people refuse to set foot on the remains of Kalliste's island, for fear that it is cursed. But I have heard that some people have settled there again, and some ships stop there to trade, so perhaps it is no longer a place of misfortune."

"How can anyone say that? What if there is another time of Great Darkness?"

"Now, Ariadne, that is only superstition. The Great Mothers are not vengeful. They love their children without measure." Aria gave her teacher a doubtful look but did not contradict her. "I mentioned the Great Darkness because the time just after it is when the mainlanders came here to stay," Daipita explained. "Before that, they had only stopped off to trade, as the people from the Two Lands and places like Byblos and Tyre do. But we needed the mainlanders—their manpower, their resources—to rebuild, just as we needed help from the Two Lands. So many of our people died back then, from the cataclysm itself and the famine that followed."

"The mainlanders who came then, I thought..." Aria picked at the trim on the hem of her sleeve. "They learned our ways, I heard, and lived among us as friends. Their descendants live here now, most of them at Knossos."

"It is so." Daipita flicked another corner of the fabric over the seal impressions. "Just in my lifetime, though, new people have come down from the mountains in the north of the mainland. They are a warlike and greedy people with no respect for women or the sacred. They have already overrun the mainland. When they could not find enough riches to take there, they came over the sea to us."

Aria squinted at the cloth covering the seal impressions. "What do they want?"

"Whatever they can get: grain, oil, livestock, gold... Goddess grant that they may go back where they came from, as the worst of the old mainlanders did."

"As long as we keep to our ways, all will be well," Aria said with confidence. "The Three will protect us."

"May it be so." Daipita made the sign of propitiation then pushed the collection of seals to the far edge of the table. "But I did not call you here to talk about the mainlanders."

"Then what?" Aria said, giving the Head Priestess an eager look.

"Our Lady has asked me to discuss a possibility with you."

"Real priestessing?" Aria practically bounced up and down on the bench.

"Tell me, have you yet lain with a man?"

She shook her head. "Rhea and I…"

"Yes, my dear, I know about Rhea."

Aria's eyebrows shot up. "You heard me calling her 'little sister'?"

"I hear many things," Daipita said with a smile. "So… Rhea but no men?"

"It is so."

"Do you like men?"

Aria nodded.

"And you tell me truthfully, there is no chance you might already be pregnant?"

"None, My Lady."

"There is a rite we may ask you to take part in soon. It involves coupling with a man. Is that an act you would be willing to undertake?"

"A rite?" She met the Head Priestess' gaze, awe and fear in her eyes. There were many public festivals where lovemaking was part of the celebration—Aria had been conceived at the autumn planting rite—but only a handful of private rituals, all of them formidable, some of them dangerous.

"A most important one. We must do it soon. The High Priestess herself will oversee it if you agree to participate."

She squared her shoulders. "Of course, My Lady."

"You understand," Daipita said, laying her hand atop Aria's, "the purpose of the rite is to get you with child." Aria drew in a sharp breath. "If that is not something you wish…"

"No, I do. I just thought I would be… older."

"It must be done now, not in a year or two. The sacred calendar waits for no one."

Her brow furrowed, Aria pressed her lips together. "If you think I should do it…"

"You must walk into the decision yourself, my dear. Some choices, the gods make for us. But this one must be of your own free will."

"And the baby would be… one of the priesthood?"

Daipita shifted in her seat. "If the rite succeeds, the child who grows in your womb would one day be a Consort."

Aria gasped. "I will do it," she said, goosebumps rising on her arms. "This," she whispered, "was among my visions. I am to be a Consort-Bearer."

"I see." Daipita narrowed her eyes at Aria. "You understand that visions do not always show us the whole story, but only a portion of it."

"I know what I saw," Aria insisted. "Some of my other visions have already come true."

The older woman relented with a sigh and a fond smile. "You are as stubborn as I ever was at your age. May the gods grant you a path easier than mine has been."

"Will you allow me to take part in the rite? Will you tell Our Lady that I accept?"

"I will." Aria beamed, and the Head Priestess continued. "I expect you know the requirements regarding the ones who bear Consorts?"

"Yes, My Lady." She counted off on her fingers the details she had memorized during her training. "The baby's spirit will be called during the rite, so it will be ensouled from the very beginning. That means I may not change my mind once the ceremony is completed and go to the Medicine-Priestess to get rid of the baby. You—and the diviners—will choose the priest for the ritual. After the rite, I may not lie with anyone, man or woman, until after the baby is born. And I may never again lie with the priest who takes part in the rite." She drew in a breath, taking a mental tally to be sure she remembered all the requirements. "I will not be allowed to name the baby or give him his milk-and-honey blessing. The High Priestess will give him the name he will use until he becomes the Consort, and the midwife or some other woman will give him the blessing. He will be raised in the temple and trained to be a Consort when he reaches the right age."

Daipita considered a moment. "How do you think you will feel to be the mother of a Consort?"

"I would love…" Aria stopped and shook her head, correcting herself. "I will not be his mother. The Consort has no human mother or father. He is born of the gods. The priestess is only a vessel, and the priest is only a tool."

"You know you will not be the only one who performs the rite."

Aria nodded, her face grave. "Not all pregnancies end in healthy babies."

"Or living mothers," Daipita reminded her. "And still you consent?"

"Of course. This is important. This is real priestess work. Keeping our ways."

The older woman drew in a slow breath. "Very well. I will tell Our Lady that you accept. And I will notify you when it is time to prepare."

"Thank you, My Lady," Aria said, failing to suppress a broad smile.

"In the meantime, you know where the herb garden and the Medicine-Priestess' workshop are." Aria nodded. "Tell her you are to learn the ways of the herbs."

"Yes, My Lady," Aria said as she rose from the bench, making the salute to her superior, all seriousness again.

"Oh, come here," Daipita said, drawing the young priestess down into an embrace. "You need not be so grave all the time. There is enough in the world to be serious about. Let us find joy where we may."

Chapter 5

With only a small oil lamp to light her way, Aria stepped carefully down the stairs and into the darkness. She was clad in a plain short-sleeved tunic, open in the front to bare her breasts and held closed with a cord wrapped around her waist. The thin linen did little to keep the cool dampness of the basement from her skin. It was the Spring Equinox and the building had not yet warmed up from the growing Sun, though the rooms in the basement never quite lost their chill even at the height of summer. As the lamplight flickered around her, the golden yellow of the saffron dye that had colored her garment alternately glowed and dimmed.

Her bare feet made no sound as she approached the doorway. In fact, she could hear no noise at all, not even when the door swung open to reveal the room beyond. Swallowing past the lump in her throat, she stepped over the threshold and set her lamp down on a table. The room was barely brighter than the corridor she had come down, lit as it was by two more small oil lamps.

A quick glance around the room revealed a fallow deer trussed on a sacrificial table and a handful of people waiting in the shadows, none of whom Aria could identify. Then the High Priestess stepped into the light, handing Aria a cup and motioning for her to drink the contents. It was wine, undiluted and with something added, a musky flavor like the drink they had given her at her initiation. The flavor must be opium, she decided, since that was what the temple used for such purposes.

Someone in the shadows sprinkled incense over hot coals, and the scent swirled around Aria. Her heart kicked in her chest. It was the same odor that had surrounded her during her initiation, the same incense blend. She choked on the wine, her hand shaking as she wiped the drips off her chin.

"Have no fear, my child," came the High Priestess's voice as her hand settled on Aria's arm. "We are here today for living, not for dying. Now finish the wine."

Aria did as she was bidden, then set the cup down. The hissing rattle of a sistrum started up. A second one joined it, the sound of the two twisting around the stone chamber like the writhing of invisible serpents. The shadows jumped and turned. Aria wobbled and took a step to keep her balance. Then she felt the High Priestess' hands on her shoulders, pushing her toward the sacrificial table.

Two stumbling steps and she was standing in front of the drugged deer, a gleaming bronze dagger in her hand. Even after the wine, she found it difficult to perform the required task. Of course, both Daipita and the High Priestess had given her detailed instructions. The animal would not suffer. Still she hesitated. The young buck's small antlers hung off the edge of the table, and the pale spots on its hide glowed and danced in the flickering lamplight. At that moment, more than anything, she wanted to stroke its coat and unbind its legs and let it run away, and herself along with it, back along the darkened corridors and up into the light.

She lifted her head and looked around, but the High Priestess had receded into the shadows. It was as if Aria was alone in the crypt, just her and the deer and the waiting spirits. They were all counting on her: not just Eileithyia, Daipita, and the other priests and priestesses, but the unborn baby as well. The whole temple, in fact. And it was blood that would draw the spirits up from the World Below to assist with the rite.

The light was dim enough that Aria had to lay her trembling palm on the deer's neck to find the right spot. The animal twitched at her touch but did not struggle. The sistrums hissed and rattled around her, the voices of the ancestors bidding her to do her job, fulfill her vow. With one hand she held the deer's head still; with the other she poised the point of the dagger above the animal's spine. She set her jaw, leaned in, and pushed the dagger home. Metal scraped on bone as the animal tensed, shuddered once, and then went limp. The sistrums fell silent.

Shaking, she levered the blade loose from the deer's vertebrae. A glance told her that, as she expected, a wide bowl sat on the floor beneath the sacrificial table. With difficulty she maneuvered the animal so its head hung half off the edge of the table, directly over the bowl. Recalling the earlier instructions, Aria made a careful cut along the neck. Then she watched as the blood welled up and dripped out, pouring down into the bowl and seeping sideways into the soft pelt at the edges of the cut. The salty-metallic tang of the blood rested on the back of her tongue, flaring with every inhalation. She stood there, mesmerized, watching the blood flow while time itself stopped. Then someone touched her arm.

Startled, she whipped her head around to see the High Priestess gazing at her, then had to grasp the edge of the table to keep her balance as the room spun. The older woman tilted her head toward the deer. With difficulty Aria focused her gaze on the animal and saw that the blood had stopped dripping. The edges of the cut were beginning to crust up. The High Priestess gestured toward the flagon of wine on the table. Aria drew in a slow breath, working hard to remember what she was supposed to do next.

Clutching the edge of the table to maintain her balance, she knelt down and dipped the first two fingers of her right hand in the bowl of fresh blood. The thick fluid still held a faint trace of the animal's heat as she stroked it on her bare chest, drawing the ancient figure of the labrys, the soul-symbol of the ancestors and the World Below that would draw the baby's spirit to her. It took a moment for her to struggle back up to standing—she noted with vague annoyance that no one stepped forward to help her—and heft the flagon of wine. Clumsily she turned the pitcher around until its spout faced her and splashed some of the wine on her chest, enough to blur the symbol, to wash it from the physical world into the world of the spirits.

She set the flagon back on the table with a thump and reached for the ladle that lay nearby. Again gripping the edge of the table to maintain her balance, she stooped and dipped the ladle into the bowl of blood. Taking care not to drip, she brought the ladle up and poured the blood into the pitcher of wine, immersing the ladle into the liquid to stir it.

Now the room began to blur and sway. Setting her jaw, she forced her mind to work, to remember what she was supposed to do next. It took several long moments to recall the instructions, but in the end she staggered over to the nearest pillar. The square stone column rose out of a depression in the floor and disappeared into the darkness above Aria's head.

Aria pressed the length of her body against the clammy stone, embracing it. A moment later she felt liquid trickling through her hair. One of the others was pouring the flagon of blooded wine over her head. The sacred fluid ran down her face, her neck, her back, coating her bare breasts, soaking her tunic, and dripping off into the little moat that surrounded the pillar's base. From there its essence descended into the World Below, alerting the spirits there of the ritual's intent.

Clinging to the pillar, she waited as she had been instructed, though she wondered how she was supposed to know when the spirits had risen up. Just as she was beginning to think she had done something wrong, a sharp chill shot through her body, and she shivered all over. She felt as if winter-cold water was rising from the floor, up her ankles, to her knees, up her thighs. Panic rose in her along with the icy chill, and she struggled to shift away from the pillar. But she was frozen in place, unable to move as the frigid sensation flowed through her groin, up her torso, over her shoulders. She flung her head back and tried to scream, but no sound came. Then the freezing cold engulfed her head, and she could no longer breathe.

The next thing she knew, two pairs of hands were supporting her, guiding her to a bench as her legs collapsed beneath her. She leaned back against the wall, trembling. Then the High Priestess's face loomed above her in the flickering lamplight.

"I am Eileithyia, priestess of the Great Mothers," the High Priestess declared. "We have called to the spirits of the dead to ask their aid. We have made a sacrifice, a gift of blood and wine. Will the Queen of the Dead deliver a soul for the next Consort?"

Aria's brow furrowed. Her vision and her thinking were blurry. She did not understand the question, yet she knew the answer. "Yes," she managed to say. She heard the word echo as if someone else had spoken it.

"Do the Three-and-One approve of this vessel?" the High Priestess asked, motioning to Aria where she sprawled on the bench.

"Yes," the younger woman said again, the answer coming without her volition.

"Do we have the blessing of the Melissae, the guardians of the spirits of the dead, for this rite?"

A cacophony of voices buzzed in Aria's mind, and she flung her head back and forth, up and down, trying to clear away the sound, doing her best to hear the answer. When she tried to focus her gaze on the High Priestess's face, the whole room swam and blurred. Something was in her head—no, someone was in her head, many someones, and she did not like it. She wished they would go away or at least be quiet.

The High Priestess knelt down in front of Aria, reached out, and touched her fingertips to the young priestess' cheek. "Great Ladies," she said, "we are at your service. We wish only to follow your ways as best we know how. Do we have your blessing for this rite?"

Aria was silent for several long moments, listening, waiting. Then finally, "Yes." The High Priestess moved to stand back up, but Aria gripped the older woman's arms, holding her in place. The voices in her head were still speaking. "Take good care with the one to be born," she said, her voice a little slurred. "He will be one of the last."

Once again hands slid beneath her arms, helping her stand and move through the darkness back to the pillar, leaning her face-first against it as she wrapped her arms around the cold stone. Vaguely she recalled Daipita telling her that this was how she would receive the baby's soul, through the pillar, the same way she had received the spirits of the dead. She felt those spirits recede, the chill draining away from her and down into the earth below, and a slow warmth growing around her, behind her. Then she felt him.

A warm body pressed against her, and strong arms wrapped around the pillar on top of hers, clasping her hands. Hot breath caressed her neck, and a deep voice whispered in her ear, "I will be gentle with you, I swear it."

She twisted her head as far as she could without letting go of the pillar, and what she saw stunned her. Those dark eyes that were twinkling in the lamplight, gazing at her so gently: they were Lexion's eyes.

Her whole body went hot and cold all at once, and her head swam.

Wine-damp fabric clung to Aria's hips as Lexion lifted the hem of her tunic, sliding the garment up to her waist. She felt his big, warm hands skimming across her skin, down her belly, between her legs, stroking, caressing the way she and Rhea had done so many times. He kept on until she was panting, gasping with desire, until she was overcome and cried out with her pleasure.

"Get on with it," a woman's voice muttered from the shadows.

"I will not hurt her," Lexion insisted, taking his time to stretch Aria with his fingers before positioning himself behind her.

Leaning his full weight against her, he pressed into her slowly, relentlessly. She gasped as her body burned, pleasure and pain swirling together in rhythm with Lexion's movements. His hands gripped her hips, and she swayed, dizzy with the drugs and the sensations and the way her heart was brimming over with emotions she could not even name.

Clinging to the pillar as Lexion moved against her, Aria struggled to think clearly. But her body overrode her mind, and all she knew was that the gods had given him to her, and her to him. And from their union would come a holy child, the greatest gift of all. A Consort, born at Midwinter, to carry on her people's sacred ways.

She had no idea how much time passed as the lamplight flickered and she and Lexion moved in rhythm with each other. But the moment he cried out with his pleasure, clutching her as his body spasmed, she felt a heat rise up the pillar and into her body. And she knew she had received the baby's soul.

She felt his lips on her shoulder, a soft kiss, and then he moved away. When she tried to lift her arms from the pillar and take a step back, everything went black.

Chapter 6

"Here you go," Rhea said as she handed the basket up into the ox cart. Aria leaned down to take it, hefting the container of food into the space behind her, next to two jugs of well-diluted wine. Aria arranged the few other items—a bundle of clothing and a basket of toiletries—then settled herself on the bench, smoothing the fabric of her tunic over her round belly. She stifled a yawn. It was barely light out; the Sun had not yet risen.

"Say hello to Lexion for me," Aria said, trying for levity, though she could not hide the sadness in her voice. Since the rite in the pillar crypt, she had only been close enough to speak to him twice, and both times were at rituals where she could not indulge in casual conversation. The temple complex was not that large, so she supposed he had been avoiding her. That only made sense. He had coupled with her in the pillar crypt. The two of them could never lie together again.

"I have stayed away from him," Rhea replied. "I would not do that to you." She looked away then back at her friend. "Besides, I have heard that he prefers lovers closer to his own age."

"I may not lie with anyone, man or woman, until the baby is born," Aria grumbled, clasping Rhea's outstretched hand. "I miss you." She kissed her friend's knuckles.

The cart's driver finished checking the oxen's harness and

climbed up onto his seat in front. A moment later, Inia came out of the building with Aria's brother Ytanos.

"You will want this," Inia said, handing Aria a cushion and tossing her own onto the wagon's bench before settling down next to her daughter. Aria arranged the cushion beneath her as Ytanos took a seat on her other side.

"Ytanos," Rhea said, "you are going as well? This is a pilgrimage for women. You are not even a priest."

"I am accompanying my mother and my baby sister for their safety." He pursed his lips. "We have heard tales of bandits along the roads in some places. These are uncertain times. Luckily, I have some time free while the crew is loading my ship with new cargo. I have left my partner in charge so I can come along with my family. It looks to be a lovely day, good for traveling."

"So..." Rhea's gaze shifted to Aria. "All is well?" She gave a pointed glance at Aria's swelling belly.

"Everything is fine," Aria said. "It is more than four Moons now and no problems. No more being sick in the mornings, thank the Mothers."

"I will keep them safe," Ytanos said, "and I promise not to intrude on my sister's rites. Though I do not think she needs the goddess' help. She is already as big as a brewer's cookpot." He leaned over and nudged her with his shoulder. She gave him a gentle shove in return, and they both laughed.

The cart-driver snapped the reins and called to the oxen, and they began the slow, creaking journey to the sacred cave. The cart moved west along the Coast Road, the travelers sharing each other's quiet company as the Sun slid up over the horizon and the day warmed.

This late in the summer, near the time of the grape harvest, mornings were warm and midday was always hot. Though most of the island was crispy-brown and dry this time of year, a constant sea breeze kept the travelers comfortable until the Sun had climbed well up into the sky. Then the two women dug into their bag of clothing and drew out lengths of lightweight linen cloth, wrapping it loosely over their heads, breasts, and arms to shield themselves from the sunshine. Though their skin was naturally golden brown, the women were not used to spending a great deal of time outdoors. Kalliste's heat and light would turn their skin an angry red if they did not protect themselves from her power.

Ytanos' body was already burnished to a dark brown from all the time aboard his ship. He was a successful trader with a ship of his own, and he dressed the part when he was in port. But once they were out at sea, he often stripped down just like his sailors, for comfort and convenience, exposing himself to the fierce Sun.

The ox-cart bumped and creaked past farms and small villages, past unpaved roads that ran south to farther-off settlements. After a while, Inia rummaged in the basket and drew out some dates and figs. Aria gladly accepted the food. Her appetite was increasing daily to keep pace with the baby growing in her belly.

About three-fourths of the way to their destination, they neared a road that turned off south from the one they were traveling. Aria squinted down the pavement. It ran toward some low mountains nearby.

"Down that way is Diktynna's cave," Inia said, gesturing toward the road. "I made a pilgrimage there when I was about your age."

Aria stared at her, wide-eyed. "You wanted to be a Huntress? A priestess of Britomartis?"

"You did not know?" Ytanos said. "Our mother was a force to be reckoned with."

"Was?" Inia gave him a hard stare.

"Is," he said, covering a grin with his hand.

"I had the strength and the swiftness of the best hunters," Inia said. "I could outrun most of the boys and throw a spear as far as the best of them."

"What happened?"

"The diviner," Inia sighed. "I made the offering and performed the rite at the cave shrine. But when the diviner read the auspices, it was clear I was not meant for any of the Horned sisterhoods. So I remained a regular priestess." She turned to look at her daughter. "It took me a long time to accept that this was my place, that I could better serve the gods by doing what they wanted than what I wanted, even if what they wanted seemed rather... ordinary. Though I suppose being a priestess in the first place is not exactly ordinary to most lay people."

The cart creaked on along its way as Aria considered the alarming idea of being turned down by the gods, having to do something commonplace, ordinary. Inia did not have visions, that Aria knew. But at least she was still a priestess.

Shortly after the turnoff for Britomartis' cave, they passed the edge of a settlement that ran down to the shore, where there was a small harbor. Here a large villa sprawled across the land with two ceremonial courts adjacent to it. Aria peered around at the handful of smaller buildings nearby—artisans' workshops, mostly, and a few grain storage shelters—and the fields and groves that surrounded the place.

"Is this Amnisos?" she asked, thinking they had reached the small port city that served Knossos as well as the other nearby settlements.

"We will not be going that far," Ytanos said. "This is Nirou Khani."

"Oh yes," Aria said, eager to show off her knowledge. "They are a sacred house that serves the Sun Mother."

"And well it is so," Ytanos said, a sharp edge to his voice. "Those in charge at Knossos would happily take over our entire island if we allowed it, and turn her out of every temple, as they have from theirs."

"They cannot do that," Aria said, folding her arms across her chest. "Kalliste would have her revenge on them."

Inia shook her head. "There are those who say the Sun Mother is angry and vengeful. They have said so since the time of the Great Darkness when her sacred island was destroyed. But it is not so."

"Did she not destroy her island to show her anger? There are people in the market square who still shout just such things. Even if it was not revenge, it was certainly dreadful. Though I suppose it was a long time ago."

"Not so long ago," Ytanos said, "as the gods reckon time. Kalliste is fierce, and she makes us listen to her even when we do not wish to. The Great Darkness was a message, one we are doing our best to heed… unlike those at Knossos, who prefer to ignore the Great Mothers and honor only the gods who tell them what they want to hear."

"But I thought Nirou Khani had priests and priestesses from Knossos."

Inia nodded. "They do. Just like the temples, they must replenish their staff one way or another as the old ones pass back to the Great Mother. And they do not have so many priestesses who care to bear children." Her gaze flicked down to Aria's belly, and she gave her daughter an indulgent smile. "But they bring in only select individuals from Knossos, from our own temple, and sometimes from farther away. Those who will keep our ways and not allow them to deteriorate. I know a few there who came from Phaistos."

Aria eyed the settlement nervously. "And how does Our Lady decide which of our people she will send there?"

"They decide for themselves," Inia said, patting Aria on the knee. "And if the leaders at Nirou Khani agree and Our Lady gives permission, they go."

"Oh."

"We will stay there tonight, and you can meet them then."

The three travelers and their driver continued a short distance down the Coast Road, with cicadas buzzing in the heat and vultures circling overhead. When they turned off south down a side road, Aria watched several small lizards skitter over the rocks. The mountains loomed to the south as the wagon creaked onward. And then they were at the cave.

The driver pulled the cart to one side of the grassy area in front of the cave, away from the other visitors, and unhitched the oxen so they could graze. Inia climbed down, and Ytanos began handing her things: the basket of food, one of the jugs of wine.

"Are we not going into the cave?" Aria asked.

"Soon," said Inia, shooing her daughter down off the cart. "First we will eat." She glanced at the small crowd gathered around the cave entrance. A woman was organizing the people into groups and guiding them into the cave a few at a time. "Perhaps most of them will be done and gone by the time we have finished eating."

As Aria watched the crowd, she realized the priestesses could be identified by their clothing: they were all dressed in golden yellow, the midwife-goddess Eileithyia's sacred color, the color of honey and of bees. The special dye that made fabric look like sunshine came from the stamens of the saffron crocus. The temple at Malia had their own fields of this sacred flower that blooms in the autumn when the rains come, when the Daughter returns from her sojourn in the Underworld.

The golden-clad priestesses ushered one group of visitors into the dark cave mouth as another was emerging. In this cave, the goddess Eileithyia was born to the Great Mother Ida, and here mortal women sought her aid in child-bearing. Just beyond the cave entrance, Aria could see the small structure where the resident priestesses lived, a simple house much like those in every city, town, and farmstead across the island.

The three travelers found a spindly pine tree whose meager shade afforded some relief from the strong midday sunshine. With a sigh, Aria leaned back against the tree trunk, thankful for the support for her lower back. She was too hot to want to eat much, so she picked at the bread and cheese. The wine-and-water mixture, though, was refreshing even though it was warm from sitting in the sunshine on the long ride. As they ate, Inia and her son chatted quietly about Inia's visits to the cave shrine over the years, when she was pregnant with her four children. Their voices washed over Aria, and she let her head tilt back against the tree, her eyes closing.

"Wake up, Aria," Ytanos was saying as he gently shook Aria by the shoulder.

Aria's eyes slid open and she looked around, drawing in a slow breath. "I did not mean to fall asleep."

The corners of Ytanos' eyes crinkled as he grinned at her. "You must be sleeping for two now as well as eating for two."

With some effort, Aria got herself up off the ground and straightened out her clothing. She saw that the other two had already packed the food back in the cart. The three travelers took turns walking around behind a nearby boulder to empty their bladders. Then they washed their hands and faces with herbal water from one of the jugs in the cart, a brief purification before they entered the sacred cave.

"Here, my dear," Inia said as she handed Aria two small jars. Honey and poppyseeds, Aria saw as she peered into them. Her offerings for the goddess.

They had also brought offerings for the priestesses who served Eileithyia here: a jug of good wine, a sack of barley, and a large flagon of olive oil. It was up to the patrons to support the priesthood, Aria knew, and without the priesthood, who would keep the sacred rites that had maintained the peace and prosperity of Ida's children for so long?

Ytanos stretched out beneath the tree to rest. "May the goddess bless you with all good things," he said to Aria, quite sincerely, then laid an arm across his face and closed his eyes.

Laden with their containers, Inia and Aria approached the cave entrance. A small group of women was just coming out, and no one else was waiting. Moving over to the outdoor altar area, Aria and her mother presented their offerings. Before they could identify themselves, one of the resident priestesses came over and greeted Inia with a hug.

"I did not expect to see you here, my sister," the priestess said to Inia.

"But I expected to see you," Inia replied. "Aria, this is Psoreia, daughter of Daipita. She is one of our own from Malia, come to tend the goddess' cave. Psoreia, this is my daughter Ariadne, come to seek the goddess' blessing."

"Ariadne, eh?" Psoreia said, giving Aria a significant look.

Not knowing how to respond, Aria kissed Psoreia's cheek. That was a polite—and therefore safe—choice for a fellow priestess.

"Aria, you should know," Inia continued, "we send some of our people to the cave shrines and mountaintop sanctuaries as well as the sacred houses like Nirou Khani." She swept her hand around to indicate the nearby region. "The places that need trained clergy to run them. We stay connected, weaving the Mother's web for her. We share people as well as food and goods."

"Why do I need to know these things, Mama?" Aria whined. "I am no administrator. I am a priestess."

"There is more to being a priestess than just visions and rituals," Inia replied, her eyes narrowing at her daughter. "Come, let us do what we came here for."

The resident priestesses directed the two women toward the cave mouth. They walked between two large boulders and down a path of shallow stone steps, ducking to avoid hitting their heads on the low ceiling. Aria was glad for her sandals on the rough stone. Though the cave shrines were sacred, outdoor rites allowed shoes for safety.

In the flickering lamplight Aria could see a few people gathered around the central altar. She recognized one woman as a native of the Two Lands by her dress, and two others as mainlanders by their speech, but the rest appeared to be Ida's children. She waited with Inia until the others were finished and had begun to file out. Then she accompanied her mother over to the altar, where a priestess greeted them.

Aria held up her little jars of honey and poppyseeds. The priestess gestured to a large stone that sat on the altar, a round stone with a hole in the middle, just like the hole all people pass through when they are born into this world.

Though Inia had explained the ritual to Aria the day before, suddenly she could not remember what she was supposed to do. They had not rehearsed this the way they practiced the temple rites. So many words, so much memorization. The work was tedious, and few of the ceremonies were as interesting as her dreams and visions. But she did the work anyway. A real priestess must master all the rituals she is qualified for.

Aria forced her thoughts back to the rite she was about to perform. Though her belly qualified her for this one, it did nothing to help her remember what to do. And it did not aid her concentration to have her mother breathing down her neck in the close confines of the cave.

She felt the weight of the jars in her hands and drew in a slow breath. Lifting the jar of honey up above the stone, she spoke, forcing her voice to remain steady.

"Mistress Eileithyia, midwife to goddesses and women, I taste the sweetness of your presence." She dipped a finger into the honey and touched it to her tongue. "I offer you golden honey, a gift of the bees that are sacred to you. As the sweet honey pours through the hole in this stone, so may my sweet baby come swiftly and easily through birth and into this life." She upended the jar, drizzling the honey through the hole in the stone and onto the altar beneath it. Then she held up the other jar and sprinkled the poppyseeds over the stone and into the hole. She turned and handed the empty jars to Inia, then stepped over to the holiest part of the cave, running through the ritual procedure in her head, hoping she remembered it all correctly.

In the flickering lamplight she saw the Trinity: three stalagmites, pillars of stone made of the cave's very substance, two larger ones and a very small one. The largest one stood in the middle, its rounded side protruding like the belly of a pregnant woman, a small dimple in the stone in just the right place to be the woman's navel: the Mother. Behind that stood a stalagmite of similar height but slender: the Midwife. And in front of the pregnant stone pillar, the small one. The newborn baby. The Child.

Beside each stalagmite was a small pool of water: three depressions in the stone floor, each the size of a shallow bowl. Recalling the words her mother had taught her, Aria positioned herself in front of the Midwife and spoke.

"Mistress Eileithyia, midwife to goddesses and women, I have made a sweet offering to you. Please watch over me and my unborn child. Keep us both safe and sound as this baby grows large in my belly and is born into the world." She saluted and made the sign of blessing, then moved to the middle pillar: the Mother.

Here she did not speak, but knelt down and leaned over toward the rounded side of the stalagmite. She untied the front of her tunic and spread the edges, baring her belly. Then, holding onto the stone for balance, she pressed her palm to the rounded side of it and rubbed her belly on the stone: her navel to its navel, goddess to woman, sacred to sacred.

A great warmth suffused her, and she felt herself surrounded by a golden glow. She knew, at that moment, that all would be well with her child. Relaxing into the sensation, she allowed herself to enjoy the feeling. Safety. Caring. Unconditional love.

A cool breeze brushed her cheek, and she drew in a sharp breath. Shivering, she shifted back so she was no longer touching the stone. She glanced around. Inia had moved and was now standing in a different spot. How long had she knelt there in front of the Mother?

Quickly Aria tied her tunic back in place and shuffled on her knees until she was in front of the Child, with its little pool of water. In the dim lamplight, the water looked like a spot of black against the grey cave floor. It took some effort to get her thoughts to focus again, but after a few moments she remembered what she was supposed to do next.

"Mistress Eileithyia, midwife to goddesses and women, I have made a sweet offering to you. Please grant me a vision of the baby who will soon be born from my belly."

Balancing herself with her palms on her thighs, she leaned over until she was peering down onto the surface of the water. She had learned to scry along with all the other young women who trained in the College of Priestesses. She had done it in water and in wine and in fire, indoors and out, but never like this: never just her, with no one to tell her whether she was doing it right or wrong, no one to interpret what she saw. She was not supposed to tell anyone about these visions, though like all mothers-to-be who visited the cave, she was allowed to share them with her child when they were old enough to understand.

She tilted her head until the lamplight no longer shimmered on the surface of the water, until it was solid black. A black mirror of water. Then she relaxed her eyes, letting her vision soften until it blurred.

She could feel her heart beating, hear the echo of the drip-drip-drip from the stalactites on the cave ceiling. But she saw nothing but swirling blackness.

Her heartbeat sped up, pounding in her chest. She was going to fail. There would be no visions for her, and she would have to smile at her mother and pretend. But it would all be a farce. This goddess was not speaking to her, in spite of all the other visions she had received.

She heaved a sigh and blinked, watching the blackness swirl before her eyes. Then, just as she was ready to lift her head up with a smile plastered on her face, the night-dark swirls shifted and resolved into another kind of blackness: shiny waves of long hair, lustrous as obsidian. The hair flowed back and she saw a face. Handsome, tawny: a young man.

So I will have a boy. The rite in the pillar crypt has worked.

Then the image shifted again, and she saw the flowing locks, the handsome face, the noble head lying on a table, the dark eyes lifeless, blood dripping from the muscular neck.

"No!"

She shoved herself back from the stone, struggling to get to her feet, wavering and off balance. Inia rushed to help her up, her strong hands beneath Aria's arms. Panicking, Aria made to run from the cave, but her mother held her tight.

"You must finish," Inia insisted. Inia held her daughter beneath the Breasts, the tiny stalactites on the ceiling that dripped a milky liquid, Eileithyia's own elixir, a liquid blessing. Inia steadied her daughter as her whole body shook, holding her in place until the liquid had coated Aria's swelling breasts. Then Inia helped her back out into the daylight.

Chapter 7

They reached Nirou Khani as the Sun was tipping over toward the western mountains. Aria did not speak as they came out of the cave and packed up the wagon. Her silence continued as they rode back to the villa in the center of the settlement, and her two companions left her to it. She broke it only for a few murmured pleasantries when Inia introduced her and Ytanos to their hosts at the villa.

"Welcome, Ariadne, daughter of Inia, and Ytanos, son of Inia," Nestia said. "I am the presiding priestess of this sacred house."

Leaving the driver to tend to the cart and the oxen, Aria and the others followed Nestia across the east courtyard. They passed the altar with its ever-burning flame and its sacred horns, its bowls of blood-red wine in which floated the magical black rocks that fell from the sky during the Great Darkness. The large bronze mirror that hung above the altar was covered with fine cloth, hidden until the next rite. They stopped briefly to salute the Sun-Mother in her sacred place, then moved on. Aria glanced around, taking in the whitewashed walls and brightly-colored blue and green trim. The place was like a miniature temple, complete with blood-red columns and flashes of gilding here and there.

They moved through a series of rooms and up a stone staircase. After a short walk down a whitewashed corridor, Nestia ushered them into a spacious guest room. "Please refresh yourselves and rest from your journey. I will send someone to let you know when it is time for the evening meal."

The three travelers took turns washing their faces, hands, and feet in the basins of fresh water the villa had provided. As Aria was drying her feet on a linen towel, her head lowered to her task, she watched Inia and Ytanos out of the corner of her eye. The two were having a silent conversation, gesturing to each other but not speaking, casting looks at Aria over their shoulders. When Aria sat up, Inia glanced at her daughter and shrugged at Ytanos, shaking her head. Ytanos stepped through the curtained doorway onto the room's little balcony. Silently he stood there, looking out over the harbor and the sea, his back to the room.

Inia dropped onto the bench next to Aria. "My dear," she said, placing her hand over Aria's. "I am sorry the cave rite did not go as you hoped."

"You do not understand," Aria snapped, drawing her hand away from her mother's.

"But I do," Inia said. She touched two fingers beneath Aria's chin and turned the young woman's face toward hers. She smiled softly, a bit sad, then her look turned stern. "You knew what your child would be. You agreed to bear a Consort. Never forget that you undertook this of your own free will." With that, she stood up and began tidying her hair, preparing for dinner.

Though she would have liked to scream and tear the towel to shreds, Aria did not wish to appear childish. She was a priestess now, a representative of her temple. She settled for grinding her teeth and twisting the towel some more.

A short time later, the three travelers emerged from their room with fresh clothing, glossy hair, makeup and perfume and jingling jewelry. They made their way downstairs with Inia in the lead. Turning a corner, they found that the small dining hall was already full. Aria was wondering where they were going to sit when she saw Nestia gesturing to them, and to the empty space next to her.

Though two or three servants brought the food in from the kitchen, the people at the tables passed the dishes among themselves and poured each other's wine cups full. Sitting in silence, Aria helped herself to the bread, dried fruit, and roasted onions that came her way. She would like to have refused the food—her anger at her mother's words was still burning bright—but the baby growing in her belly had given her an appetite she could not ignore. A few bites into her fish stew, fragrant with coriander and thyme, she decided it would be more productive to be social than to sulk. She looked up just in time to see her mother make a face.

"They can do as they like," Inia said, lips tight, "but we will stick to the old ways. Our Lady will see to that. I hope you will do likewise. We must be strong."

Nestia nodded, her look grim. "We do our best. As long as they do not close us down..."

"By Ida, they cannot!" Ytanos declared. Then, more calmly, "Surely they do not want to lose your donations."

"It gets harder for us with every passing Moon," Nestia said. "They have threatened to close the road so no one reaches us from there if we do not pay. And they insist on a higher amount every time. This is not sharing. It is extortion. And we are hurting." She looked down, and when she raised her head, there was a deep sadness in her eyes. "They disrespect not just women but also the goddesses, the Mothers. I fear the Sun-Mother's light will go out one day, if she is pushed out of all the sacred spaces."

"The threat is real," Inia said, giving Nestia's hand a squeeze. "But I do not know what we can do about it."

Ytanos nodded, his look grim. "I have heard about the displays they put on, huge ranks of armed men strutting across the sacred plaza, showing off their might like so many angry animals. They pretend they are performing rituals to the gods, but the powers they worship are not the ones I know."

"Who?" Aria asked, suppressing a shudder. She had seen visions of an army at Knossos, or at least, that was what she thought she saw. Now Ytanos' words made her worry that this one had already come true, just in time for her and her fellow clergy to become targets. She hoped she was not too late in coming to the priesthood. It was the clergy's job to protect the people from misfortune.

The others at the table turned to her as if they had just noticed her presence.

Inia narrowed her eyes at her daughter. "You had best learn the details. My concern is about Zephyra."

"The High Priestess at Knossos?" Aria asked. Inia nodded. "Is she a bad woman?"

"Bad, no. Weak, yes." Inia sighed. "Her parents were mainlanders, and there are enough of the backward ones, especially within the College of Priests there, to keep pressure on her all the time. Pressure to do the wrong thing."

"They are greedy," Nestia said. "For wealth and power. They take and take without sharing, without kindness or compassion. They pay no heed to the warning Kalliste sent us all those generations ago. They think that if they are rich enough, they will be more powerful than the gods. Their wealth has addled their minds."

"Surely they cannot close you down," Aria insisted. "Every sacred house is independent, from the largest temple to the smallest villa. No one rules you."

"They do not rule us only so long as we can keep paying what they demand to keep their armed men from our door. They have already taken over some of the smaller sacred houses along the North-South Road."

"They want an empire," Ytanos spat. "Ruled by men alone, with nothing sacred except war and greed. I have seen their kind in other places during my travels."

Inia reached over and touched Nestia's hand. "How can we help?"

"Send people to us—worshipers, travelers in need of lodging—when you can. Every donation helps, and the company of like-minded people is reassuring." She shook her head. "But you already do those things. And I know you have little to spare yourselves."

Inia gave Aria a sidelong glance before replying. "We manage. We have long since repaid the people of the Two Lands for their aid during the time of the Great Darkness. A few of them even settled in Malia to stay, and their descendants are part of our city."

"But…"

"But the mainlanders at Knossos say we still owe them, though our debt to them was discharged long before I was born."

"They have not threatened you, I hope?" Nestia said, her eyebrows raised.

"Not yet, but they may if we ever balk at paying. Every year, they say we owe them even more. Their calculations are… creative. Their greed has no end, and apparently their gods conveniently agree with them."

Aria scowled. "Is that why Our Lady gets so angry when the messengers from Knossos visit?"

"They do not understand what is sacred," Inia replied.

Nestia nodded. "Knossos has long been the pre-eminent temple on this island, but that is a sacred matter, not one of government or power. Each sacred house gives a larger offering to Knossos than to the other temples because of this. But the people who have recently come into power there see it otherwise."

"We may differ in our focus," Inia said, gesturing to indicate herself and Nestia as representatives of their respective sacred domains. "But no matter which gods and goddesses each temple or shrine focuses on, we all still honor the same principles, the same values of respect and compassion and generosity. Every one of us, all over the island, except Knossos. They have taken our gods, our skilled crafts, our trading ties. But they have discarded what is truly sacred, like so much rubbish on a midden."

"In spite of all the gods they worship," Nestia said, "I think the only things they truly hold sacred are wealth, power… and war."

Chapter 8

Aria doubled over with the force of the contraction, as far as her enormous belly would allow. Gritting her teeth through a groan, she fumbled to light the oil lamp on the table beside her bed before she began pacing again. She tried to convince herself that these were the practice contractions the midwife had told her about, the ones that would prepare her body for the eventual birth many days later. Then she felt a sudden release of pressure, as if she had emptied her bladder, and liquid gushed down between her legs, soaking her tunic. There was no denying it now: this baby was coming, whether she wanted it to or not.

Even folded double and double again, her small linen towel did little to stop the stream of liquid that insisted on dripping down her thighs. She shivered, glancing over at the brazier in the corner. Its coals were still glowing, but they were not sufficient to stop the chill of the weather, so close to Winter Solstice, now that her tunic was soaked. Soon she was unable to stop the sounds that came out of her mouth as her body clamped down, pushing the baby toward this world. So it was no surprise when the midwife knocked on her doorframe and drew the curtain aside.

"Come, dear, let us find you a dry garment. I have sent a servant to bring Our Lady to us."

By the time the midwife had swathed Aria in a fresh tunic of soft wool, warm and dry, and pressed a much larger folded towel between her legs, Aria's room was full. The High Priestess had come. She had to be there, had to witness the birth in order to verify the child as a Consort-to-be. On her way, she had woken up Inia. Now three women crowded around Aria, who held her arms out against them.

"I cannot breathe," she groaned.

The others shifted as far back as the small room would allow, and Aria held as still as she could while the midwife slipped soft leather boots on her feet. Then, with the High Priestess' blessing, the midwife hurried out to prepare the birthing area. Inia clasped Aria's hand, wincing as her daughter gripped tightly in the throes of another contraction.

"Was it this hard for you?" Aria gasped out.

"It is like a footrace or a long session of spear-throwing," Inia answered. "Your body knows what to do, but it is tiring. And it always takes longer than you wish."

The High Priestess draped a long cloak over Aria's head and shoulders, arranging it so her face was hard to see, and Aria looked the question at her. "We must keep you warm," Eileithyia said. "And no one must see who you are."

"But everyone will know which room I came out of, and I am the last one still pregnant from that round of rituals."

The High Priestess shook her head. "The Consort has no human mother. We choose not to see. It is our way."

Then she helped Aria to the doorway. The three women moved together along the corridor, down the stairs, and across the north court, stopping for Aria's contractions. Then the High Priestess directed the group out the north entrance and onto the Sea Road that ran north through the city, toward the harbor.

Aria peered into the darkness, squinting at the few, faint lights of the city and the harbor as they moved slowly along the way. A short while later, the other women directed her toward the paved path that ran east from the Sea Road.

"Are we not going back to the midwife's chamber in the temple?" Aria asked, her voice trembling from fear as much as from the chilly night air.

"Do not worry, my dear." Eileithyia patted her hand. "We will not leave you alone in the night. The Consort must be born in the Sea Temple."

"The Place of Living and Dying," Aria gasped, finally understanding the official name of the small building down by the shore.

The group began the slow trek down the path in the dark. The way curved around, skirting the edge of the cemetery where the temple clergy had buried their dead before the time of the Great Darkness. Some of the priesthood still went down there at certain times of the year to make offerings to the spirits of the dead. Eileithyia made sure of that. Aria knew the burials were there, but she gave little thought to them as she passed, needing to spend her energy and her focus on simply walking forward between the contractions.

The three women took their time, stopping more and more frequently as they went. Every now and then, Eileithyia offered Aria a sip from a small skin of water. Aria grew tired, her movements gradually slowing the closer they came to their destination. But when the women offered to support her and help her along, she shooed them away.

"It is too much," she said, "to have hands on me. Too much sensation."

They moved at Aria's pace along the worn flagstones through half the night as the stars slowly wheeled through the sky above them, the sound and the scent of the sea growing stronger with every pace.

Finally they reached the Sea Temple. It was a simple building, a circular stone floor with columns standing around the edge, supporting a narrow roof that was open in the middle. In the moonlight, the royal blue columns with their gilt edging looked silvery-blue, like the moonlight on the sea. The small building stood just up from the high tide line, at the edge of the solid land. As they neared, Aria saw that there were oil lamps hanging around the temple. The midwife was standing next to a small table, folding a length of linen.

"Let us see how you are getting along," she said, motioning the group into the temple. Eileithyia and Inia slipped their shoes off. Then Eileithyia lifted the cloak off of Aria and set it aside, helping her unfasten her boots. Even though birthing was a practical activity, this was still sacred space: no shoes allowed.

The midwife drew Aria over into the lamplight and peered at her face, scrutinizing her eyes in particular, then lifted up the hem of her tunic and felt her belly. "Close indeed," she said. "What do you think, My Lady?"

Eileithyia moved over to join them. She pressed her fingertips against Aria's belly, feeling the shape and position of the baby. "Very soon," she said, eyes twinkling. Aria stared at her, confused. "My dear," said the High Priestess, "how do you think I came by my name? I was a midwife here long before I was the Lady of this temple. Surely you knew I attended your mother at your birth."

Eileithyia and the midwife engaged in quiet discussion as they arranged several cushions along the edge of the floor, in front of one of the pillars. By the time they were finished, Aria was groaning and panting, bent over with her hands on her knees, with almost no time between contractions to catch her breath. She was only managing to stay upright because her mother was supporting her.

"It is time," said the midwife. "My Lady, would you care to do the honors?"

Eileithyia nodded and the midwife sank down onto the cushions, her back against the pillar, her legs spread wide. Inia helped her breathless daughter shed her tunic. Then the midwife reached her arms out as the High Priestess and Inia helped Aria down into the space between the midwife's legs, with Aria's back to the midwife's front. The midwife slipped her arms around Aria between her breasts and belly, supporting her. Inia knelt to one side, holding her daughter's hand, as Eileithyia knelt between Aria's legs.

"Let us be sure you are very clean for the baby," the High Priestess said. She dipped a folded piece of linen into a cup filled with an herbal brew and washed Aria's vulva. Aria writhed, biting back a moan, as another contraction rocked through her. "There is no need to be quiet, my dear. The birthing woman cries out with the voice of the Great Mothers themselves." She arranged Aria's legs with knees bent, the soles of her feet pressing against each other. "Now with the next contraction, push for me. This is your first baby, so it may take a while."

Aria bore down again and again at the High Priestess' behest. Though Eileithyia kept insisting it would not be long yet, Aria was exhausted. "No more," she panted out.

Inia squeezed her hand. "Your eldest brother was like this for me. You are strong. You can do this."

Aria shook her head. Tears gleamed in the corners of her eyes.

"You must keep on," Eileithyia insisted. "Your child will be the Consort when he is grown. He will bear the sacred name Belisseus, just as my Consort does now and every Consort has for more generations than anyone can remember. There is none other for your son's year, for his part of the cycle." Aria gasped. "Out of those who were conceived in the special rites last spring, one miscarried and one was stillborn."

Inia tilted her head toward the High Priestess. "I thought one was born alive a few days ago."

"He died last night, along with his mother, of the childbirth fever, in spite of all our precautions."

Eileithyia touched Aria's cheek and their eyes met. "This is priestess work of the holiest kind. You had a vision of this, remember?"

Aria drew in a deep breath and pushed with all her might. Her teeth ground together. Her face turned purple. And the top of a tiny head appeared out of the folds of flesh between her legs.

"Once more," the High Priestess demanded, and Aria obliged, grinding out a loud groan as she pushed her son's head out into the chill midwinter air.

A few moments later he was lying on a length of linen, mewling softly, and the High Priestess was washing him down with a fresh cloth she had dipped in the cup of herbal brew. She tied off the cord and cut it, then wrapped him up against the night air. Then, before

Aria could even reach out to ask for him, Eileithyia was walking away, out of the temple, carrying her baby.

"No!" she cried, fighting to get up while the midwife held her in place.

Inia put her hand on Aria's shoulder. "He is a Consort-to-be, not yours. We must deliver the afterbirth."

Aria's shoulders rocked with soft sobs as her mother attended her, as her body forced one more mass out of the tender, swollen folds between her legs.

"Now let us get you cleaned up," the midwife said.

The midwife got up, and the two women arranged Aria among the pillows, half sitting, half lying. They cleaned the blood off her vulva and thighs, then pressed fresh folded linen between her legs.

"I want him," she sobbed. "Give me my baby."

But she was exhausted from the birth. She could do no more than curse quietly and cry as the two women wiped the sweat off her skin and dressed her in the woolen tunic again, draping the cloak over her for warmth.

"Drink this," the midwife said, offering Aria a cup of herb tea.

"What is it?" She narrowed her eyes at the dark liquid.

"It will dry up your milk and slow the bleeding," the midwife explained.

Aria wrinkled her nose but took a sip anyway. The flavor was odd, a bit earthy and faintly bitter but not unpleasant, and suddenly she realized how thirsty she was. A few moments later, the cup was empty.

"Very good. You will rest here for a while. Your mother will keep watch until you are well enough, then she will help you walk back up to your room."

With a tearful sigh, Aria lay back, clutching one of the cushions to her breast as if it were an infant. Her eyelids grew heavy. A moment before she fell asleep, she realized what the odd flavor in the herbal tea had been. They had given her a sleeping draught.

Chapter 9

Aria shifted to allow the Consort to exit, bowing her head to him as he passed. Then she stood in the doorway to the High Priestess' workroom. "You wished to see me, My Lady?"

Eileithyia looked up from her spot behind a broad wooden table. "Yes, my dear. Come in."

She motioned to a bench and Aria took a seat, doing her best not to stare at the jumble of items on the table.

"Running a temple is a messy business," Eileithyia said, smiling. "You are welcome to look."

At that, Aria took the opportunity to examine the objects on the worn tabletop: stacks of clay tablets separated by small rectangles of thin linen; a handful of reed styluses; sheets and rolls of papyrus in varying sizes, some empty and some written on right up to the very edge; a flagon and a cup with the dregs of some wine still standing in it; and several small wooden boxes, plain but finely made.

"What is in those?" Aria dared to ask, gesturing toward the boxes.

"Those are the temple's seals," Eileithyia explained. "The ones for official business. Belisseus and I use them here, and the clergy who represent us on official visits to the other temples take them for identification."

Aria nodded, then clasped her hands together to avoid fidgeting. She was used to talking with Daipita. The Head of the College gave the priestesses their assignments and met with them regularly. The High Priestess, however, was an unknown quantity, and she did not want to offend.

Setting her stylus down, Eileithyia turned her full attention to Aria. "I would like to discuss a new arrangement with you, Ariadne." Aria shifted in her seat. "I see you are not used to hearing your full name. I know most of the people here call you Aria, and that is certainly acceptable for casual conversation. But you are named after a goddess."

"The Daughter," Aria said. "The Labyrinth-Weaver. Walker between the Worlds."

"Yes. You have a name to live up to." Aria's eyes widened. "And I would like to help you do just that."

Aria tried to reply, but the words stuck in her throat. How was she supposed to live up to the name of a goddess, the Daughter of the Three-and-One?

"The auguries at your birth were indeed special," Eileithyia continued. "I have been keeping an eye on you as you have come along in the temple. I have spoken with Daipita about your progress. The Head of the College has taught you well, but I am making a change in your instruction. I will give you your assignments now."

Aria's eyebrows shot up. "You will?" Though Aria knew the High Priestess occasionally worked with one or another of the clergy on certain projects, she had never heard of one sidestepping the Head of their College entirely.

"Have no fear, my dear," Eileithyia said, patting Aria's hand. "Daipita will not be offended by the change. She agrees with me."

Aria's brow furrowed, and she wondered if the High Priestess could read her mind.

"It is time for you to do more in the temple, my dear, learn more skills and take on more responsibility. It will do you good to be busy." Eileithyia touched her fingertips to Aria's cheek. "You have wallowed in grief long enough. Now you must throw yourself into your work."

Aria swallowed hard. "Yes, My Lady," she said, her voice shaking. "Are you removing me from the College?"

"No, no, not at all. You will still participate in all the rites you are qualified for. You will still live with your fellow priestesses." Eileithyia offered her hand and, after a moment's hesitation, Aria took it. "This is not a punishment, Ariadne. You must understand that. Sometimes the gods single us out, and we must work hard to live up to their desires for us."

"Daipita says Lady Fate is fair but not gentle."

"Exactly. Understand, you will come to me here in this workroom for your assignments from now on."

"Yes, My Lady." Perhaps this was what it meant to be a real priestess, to help safeguard Ida's children by keeping the ancient ways.

"And here is your first assignment. You are to go to the priestess Thalamika in the scribal rooms. She is our new Chief Scrivener." Aria nodded. "You will tell her she is to instruct you, at my request."

"I am to learn to write?" Aria's face lit up.

"Indeed. And you will come tell me of your progress every day so I know how hard you are working."

"I will, My Lady."

"Go on, then," Eileithyia said, shooing Aria up from the bench and toward the door. "Get to work."

"Thank you, My Lady!" Aria called as she hastened from the room, grinning from ear to ear.

Chapter 10

Tugging her shawl tighter around her shoulders, Aria shifted in place, doing her best not to disturb the other priests and priestesses clustered around her in the corner of the theatral court. Though the winter rarely got terribly cold this close to the coast, this Winter Solstice morning was chilly enough that Aria would rather have been indoors near a large brazier, drinking a cup of heated wine. Instead, she huddled with a group of her fellow clergy on the stone pavement while the stepped seats that surrounded the court filled up with the local townsfolk, all bundled up for the weather.

The theatral court was almost as large as the temple's central court, though it was closer to square in shape while the central court was long and narrow. The theatral court lay outside the main temple building, just north of the temple walls along the west side of the Sea Road. All four sides of the court were bounded by rows of stepped seats, enough to accommodate most of the city's population. The openings between the sections allowed the spectators to access the seats. But the clergy also used those gaps to enter and leave the court during rituals, and to bring in the necessary items to set up beforehand.

The High Priestess and her Consort had already led the private solstice rites in the temple that morning, lighting Therasia's sacred fire in the altar in the central courtyard. That ritual had begun before dawn and culminated with the sunrise. Only the priesthood and a few privileged lay people were invited to attend. Since Aria was a priestess, she had witnessed the ceremony, but she was not allowed to participate yet: she was not experienced enough, not yet trained in all the ways of the temple.

But now that the Sun had climbed partway up into the sky, she took her place among the novices and young initiates, male and female, for her part in the public solstice rites. Rhea waited nearby in the same group. In previous years, Aria had made a point of standing with her friend during this rite, quietly holding hands. But the required separation during her pregnancy and her unpredictable moods after the birth had driven a wedge between them. Aria's heartache for her baby, tangled up with the loss of intimacy with Rhea, left her with a deep emptiness.

She glanced over at her friend, only to find Rhea looking at her with concern. Irritated at Rhea's constant efforts to cheer her up or take her mind off her troubles, Aria turned away without bothering to smile. She was here for a ritual, after all, so she should concentrate on that, even if her toes were freezing.

She was glad for the pale morning Sun and its faint warmth. She turned her face up to the light as she waited, giving silent thanks to the Fire-Mother. Next to her group stood a number of older clergy holding drums, sistrums, flutes, and lyres, taking care to keep their instruments still and silent.

The Chief Song-Priestess and Priest had led Aria's group onto the court a short while earlier and now stood with them. Their place in one corner of the broad court mirrored the altar area in the corner diagonally opposite, with its heavy table laden with ritual paraphernalia. Incense smoke wafted from two large braziers that sat at opposite ends of the table, wreathing around the figurines and offering stands before floating off across the court to mingle its pungent scent with the crisp morning air. The table was flanked by a pair of sturdy pillars as tall as a man's shoulder. Each was topped with a wide bronze bowl full of olive oil mixed with precious essential oils and resins.

The clergy had prepared the ritual area the previous evening.

Once again, Aria had not been asked to assist. The setup was a job for experienced priests and priestesses. It involved not only organizing the altar area and all the sacred items that would be needed for the ritual, but also cleansing and consecrating the theatral court with herb-water and incense smoke. While every priest and priestess learned early on how to purify themselves with water and smoke before a rite, the related methods for purifying ritual spaces were more complicated, varying depending on the situation. Aria had not learned those yet, and she wondered when she would be allowed to do so as she gazed at the incense smoke threading its way around the court.

Days earlier, the servants and clergy had joined in decorating the temple building. Aria had delighted in being allowed to help collect the broad lengths of fabric from the temple storerooms and organize them by color before the others assembled them and hung them up. The Winter Solstice decorations were numerous and substantial. All hands were needed to prepare and place them every year.

Aria tilted her head and looked up at the trimmings of deep purple, gold, and blood red that hung from the horned edge of the rooftop. The colors represented the two Winter Solstice miracles that took place in the island's sacred caves: purple and gold for Dionysus' birth to the Great Mother; blood red and gold for Kalliste's self-rebirth. The gold, of course, was from the sacred saffron dye—stamens of deepest red that magically turn to gold in the dyepot. The bluish-purple came from grape skins from the temple vineyards, Dionysus' purview. And only the holy murex dye was special enough to represent the color of Kalliste's power. The dye was, in fact, sacred to her, crafted only under the auspices of the priesthood.

Along the temple's rooftop, enormous swags of purple-and-gold alternated with swags of blood-red-and-gold, their colors deep and vibrant against the whitewashed walls. Between the swags, lengths of purple and blood-red fabric hung down nearly to the ground, huge columns of color that declared to the community that one of its most sacred times had come. And now the people had come, filling the seats around the theatral court, sitting in quiet reverence as they waited for the rites to begin.

Out of the corner of her eye Aria saw the Chief Song-Priestess lift the triton shell trumpet to her lips, so she did not jump when three blasts from the shell rang out across the court. The people in the seats, however, startled as they turned their attention to the courtyard. When the Chief Song-Priestess lowered the shell, she and her male counterpart began the call-and-response opening chant. Aria and her fellow clergy joined in, as did many of the laypeople in the seats surrounding the court. Most of them had attended this rite every year since childhood and knew all the songs by heart. The musicians began their part, their sistrums and drums keeping time while the flutes and lyres played a chiming counterpoint to the melody.

In light of dawn
We gather together
On Solstice morn
We gather together
The Sun new-born
We gather together
The temple adorn
We gather together

As the chant repeated, Aria heard the distant sound of more sistrums and drums keeping time with the singing. They were outside the court, moving toward it from the south along the processional way that bordered the temple's west plaza. The sound grew louder until a group of clergy appeared in one of the gaps between the rows of seats and strode onto the court. Their clothing shimmered from the threads of real silver and gold that had been woven into the fabric and the tiny polished stones that were sewn onto the garments. There were twenty or more people in the group, men and women both, some of them playing instruments and all of them singing. Though certain ones of them were dressed alike for their parts in the rite, they mingled together in such a way that they looked like a living, moving rainbow, glittering in the solstice morning sunlight.

Once the procession had entered the court and the group had arrayed themselves along the center of the pavement, the Chief Song-Priestess gave the signal: the singers and musicians fell silent. The crowd stopped singing and focused their attention on the courtyard.

One of the men stepped forward, and Aria saw that it was Kaeseus. He wore the diagonally-wrapped formal robe of the priesthood, each edge of the pale green linen decorated with saffron-dyed fringe. Threads of real gold shimmered just above the fringe, their pattern of sacred numbers and symbols woven directly into the material. He spread his arms wide and turned around slowly, taking in the gathered crowd, welcoming the people. Then he addressed them, his voice ringing out across the court.

"We are Ida's children!"

Aria's group responded, along with many of the people in the crowd, speaking the familiar formula: "May Ida's children live forever."

"May Ida's children be blessed," Kaeseus continued. "Tell me, children of Ida, what happens on this day?"

Aria's group responded as one: "The Great Mother Ida enters her cave."

The group of clergy in the center of the court parted to reveal three priestesses standing close together, all of them wrapped in cloaks of deepest brown, the color of the island's rich soil. The three women moved a few steps apart from each other and lifted up a broad length of dark woolen cloth the same color as their cloaks. They held one edge of it up high so it resembled the entrance to a cave.

From behind the group of priests and priestesses, Eileithyia emerged, the deep golden yellow and blood red of her garments intense in the morning sunlight, sparkling with tiny beads in the colors of the fabric. Her yellow bodice, edged in dark red bands, was open on top, revealing her breasts: the sign of the priestess — though the fashion had long since expanded into the lay population, among wealthy women who did not need practical clothing for their daily work.

The tiers of Eileithyia's skirt alternated yellow and red, with tiny dark red lilies embroidered all over the yellow panels. The waist of her skirt was tied high, just under her breasts. The fabric had been stuffed underneath so her belly appeared huge and round, as if she were pregnant about to bursting. She ran her palms up and down that swollen belly, moaning like a woman in labor.

"Sanctuary!" she cried out. "Where is my sanctuary? It is time!"

She turned toward the women holding the dark cloth and shook herself, as if she were seeing the cave for the first time. Then she made her way the short distance toward it, miming the act of climbing a mountainside. She bent her head and stepped into the cave. The drums and sistrums began a slow rhythm as she settled herself on a cushion in the darkness, continuing to moan.

The rest of the gathered clergy slowly circled the cave, moving in time with the rhythm of the instruments. As they stepped around, they turned their heads toward the cave and chanted:

Through the Mother
Come to us
Come to us
Come to us
Bless the day
Bless the year
Come to us
Come to us

Aria's group picked up the chant, then she heard echoes of the familiar tune coming from the seats around the courtyard. The rhythm sped up. The circle of priests and priestesses kept time with the instruments, grasping each other's hands and moving around faster and faster until they were almost running. The Great Mother's moans from within the cave increased as well, growing louder and more frequent until she finally gave one great, powerful cry. The clergy froze in place and the instruments and voices fell silent as the sound of a baby crying rang out through the courtyard.

Aria choked back tears as she sang along with the others, along with the whole gathered community, the song of Dionysus' birth.

Come from darkness into light
Come from spirit into life
Blessed Dionysus
Blessed Dionysus
Whose coming lights up the world
Whose coming lights up the world
Child of the Mother
Child of the Mother
Draw your first breath
In peace

The familiar song went on for some time, the sound swelling around the courtyard as the people expressed their love for the Great Mother and her holy son. As the melody reached a crescendo, the circle of clergy broke apart, and Eileithyia stepped out of the cave holding an infant snugly wrapped in layers of fine white linen shot through with gold.

Aria wondered if they had used her son, her tiny infant son, for this purpose three years earlier, when he was born so close to the Winter Solstice. She would not have known him if they had, would not have recognized his face or his cry, she realized with horror. Her voice cracked as she forced herself to repeat the song one last time. Then the gathering fell silent. The last words of the chant echoed around the courtyard as the infant in Eileithyia's arms made faint mewling sounds, wriggling in his soft swaddling.

Six priestesses dressed head to toe in saffron yellow, like the ones who tended Eileithyia's cave, separated themselves from the rest of the clergy. They swept around the courtyard with arms outstretched as the sound of sistrums buzzed through the air. Then they gathered back together, clustering around the Great Mother and her newborn son, tiptoeing in place like hovering bees. One of them lifted up a small alabaster jar and removed its lid.

"Honey for the Mother's child," Aria's group chanted as one. "The blessing of the Melissae on his lips now and forever."

The Melissa-priestess dipped her finger into the jar and touched it to the infant's lips, the gesture of blessing that the midwives made to every one of Ida's newborn children. The honey connected each child back through time to all the ancestors, all of Ida's children back through the generations. And it sealed the newborn's soul into the body, the soul so generously transmitted by the ancestors from the World Below.

Aria could not remember. Had the midwife honeyed her newborn son's lips? Or had the High Priestess done it later on, after she had stolen him away from his mother? But she was not his mother, Aria reminded herself, only a vessel for the Young God to be born into this world. Little good the reminder did, though, as she watched the Melissa-priestesses sweep away from the infant and back into the group of clergy behind Eileithyia. At least this year, Aria did not have to fight back tears. The wound was slowly healing.

Now Daipita appeared from within the cluster of priests and priestesses behind Eileithyia. She wore the rough wool and leather garments of a goatherd, her top wrapped closed over her breasts, the hem of her plain skirt stopping above her boots, a practical length for those who work outdoors. She walked cautiously to avoid spilling the contents of the jar she held balanced on her hip. Aria could see that it was full to the brim with milk—goat's milk, of course, for this was Amalthea, come to nurse her sister-twin's child.

Aria spoke her line in unison with the rest of her group: "Milk for the Earth-Mother's child. The blessing of the Horned Mother on his lips, now and forever."

Daipita drew one side of her top open to expose her breast. She dipped two fingers into her jar and dabbed the milk on her nipple, then leaned over and pressed her breast against the baby's mouth. He sucked briefly, taking in the few drops of goat's milk. This was the second blessing every one of Ida's newborn children received, either from its own mother or, if she was unable or had died in childbirth, from the midwife via a jar of milk until a wet-nurse could be found.

While the honey-blessing sealed the infant's soul to its body, the milk-blessing fixed the baby's body to the Earth, the World Above. Once a newborn had received both blessings, it had to be raised as a beloved member of the community and could not be rejected. This requirement was a new development among Ida's children. Though the double blessing itself was an ancient practice, in the times since the Great Darkness, the native women of the island had found it necessary to use it more openly in an attempt to stem the cruel practices the mainlanders had brought with them. The newcomers considered infants in general, but especially female ones, disposable. The slopes of the mountains south of Knossos were littered with the remains of the newborns they had exposed in recent years.

Shaking herself, Aria returned her attention to the courtyard as Daipita disappeared back into the cluster of clergy behind the High Priestess. A slow drumbeat began and two groups of people emerged from behind Eileithyia, one on each side of her. To her left were five women dressed in long, coarse tunics dyed the earthy color of fresh clay. Their hair hung loose and wild, and each one carried a small terracotta pot with some water in it, along with a short wooden rod. To the right of the High Priestess stood five men also clad in long tunics of rough wool, but theirs were dyed the brighter color of freshly polished bronze. Each one of them held a small bronze disk that dangled from a short cord, as well as a small wooden baton.

These were the Hekaterides and Daktyls, the embodiment of the hallowed skills the Great Mother had taught her children: pottery and metalsmithing, the art of turning the Earth itself into something precious and beautiful through the touch of human hands and the magic of fire. The old story said that the Great Mother had dug her fingers into the soil of her sacred cave as she birthed her son. Her very finger-marks had risen up and formed these ten magical beings. Now those who practiced the Mother-crafts were called by the same name as the beings who rose from the finger-marks:

Hands of Great Skill.

The old tales also spoke of the Hekaterides and Daktyls dancing and playing their instruments for the Great Mother's newborn son. The mainlanders said this was to protect him, to hide the sounds of his cries from his vengeful father, their god Zeus. But Ida's children knew that Dionysus had no father, only a mother. And her creations, the Hands of Great Skill, danced to delight her and to show her infant son the wonders his mother had wrought.

So the Hekaterides and Daktyls danced around the theatral court, around the Great Mother and her son: quick-quick-slow, step-step-leap, the dance that Rhea herself had taught them, every motion done in her honor. The sound of their sticks rang against terracotta and bronze, the voice of the Mountain Mother as she speaks through the substances of her body. As the five women and five men stamped around the court in time with the beat of their craft-instruments, the Chief Song-Priestess signaled to Aria's group. Aria drew in a breath and, along with her fellow priests and priestesses, began the song in time with the dancers' beat. In just a few moments, the whole arena was ringing with the people's voices, all sharing the joy of the day, all proclaiming the Great Mother's delight in her many acts of creation.

Ring the bell,
Sound the chime,
Dance for the Mother
At this special time.
She gives us all—
Her children bless
In life and love
And happiness.

The song sped up and swelled and rang out through the courtyard. Aria saw the people in the stands swaying in time with the beat. Then she realized that she and her fellow singers were doing the same, everyone standing shoulder to shoulder, celebrating the miracle of the Great Mother and the Winter Solstice.

The Hekaterides and Daktyls swung faster and faster around the courtyard, beating the rhythm on their instruments and crying out with joy. Finally they all leapt into the air with a great shout and the people in the stands rose from their seats and cheered, waving their hands above their heads. After several long moments, the crowd quieted and the people sat back down. By the time the courtyard was silent again, the central area was empty except for Aria's group and the musicians. The High Priestess, the dancers, and the other clergy had disappeared through one of the gaps between the stands. Now the people sat silent in the stands, awaiting the second part of the rite.

A gong rang out, three strikes, and two of the clergy strode back into the courtyard: Kaeseus, still in his priestly robes, and Daipita, now dressed in the open-front linen tunic and tiered skirt of the priestess. Each of them carried two flagons, one in each hand. Sistrums hissed as the Heads of the Colleges approached the altar. They stopped in front of a double-bowled stone libation table that sat among the sacred items on the tabletop.

"To the Earth-Mother," Daipita declared, "Ida, the mother of her people. Rhea Pandora, the All-Giver. You give yourself and your precious gifts to us. It is only fitting that we should give back to you from the very best that we have."

She raised one flagon and slowly poured milk from the temple's herds into her side of the libation table. The creamy-white liquid streamed down and pooled in the stone basin, the last few drops trickling out as the pitcher ran empty. Then she lifted up the other flagon and poured its contents into the stone bowl, a precious gift from the temple's hives and hence, from the ancestors. The morning was chilly, so the honey flowed slow and thick, creeping over the pitcher's lip and stretching down to puddle in the center of the milk. Patiently Daipita waited for the last globules of the viscous golden substance to ease over the flagon's edge and drip down into the milk. Then she lowered the vessel and nodded to Kaeseus.

"To the Son of the Mother," Kaeseus proclaimed, "Adoneus the infant, Iacchus the youth, Dionysus the grown one. You give yourself and your precious gifts to us. It is only fitting that we should give back to you from the very best that we have."

He lifted one flagon and tipped it over his half of the libation table. A stream of pure water poured out, splashing gently into the bowl. Aria knew that this water had been gathered from the underground lake in the sacred cave at Mt. Dikte, the place of Dionysus' birth, and stored in the temple for this very occasion. When that vessel ran empty, Kaeseus raised the other flagon and poured out wine of deepest red, the vintage crafted from the temple's own grapes and reserved for rites such as this one. The blood-red liquid flowed into the basin of water, the two fluids swirling together until dark and light mixed into pale red.

The offerings completed, the Heads of the Colleges set their empty containers on a small table that stood to one side. Then Daipita slipped around behind the altar to stand quietly in the shadows. Kaeseus drew in a deep breath and spread his arms as he had before, addressing the crowd.

"Children of Ida," he said, "we have seen the Earth-Mother birth her son this Winter Solstice morning. Tell me, who else lies within the sacred cave on this day?"

Aria's group answered as one: "The Sun-Mother Kalliste, the Burning One."

Sistrums hissed, and goosebumps rose on Aria's arms. Tilting her head to see over the shoulders of her fellow clergy, she watched as an odd image appeared in the gap between the stands. The three priestesses clad in dark brown were carrying their cave-cloth once again, but this time they held the front of it closed so no one could see inside the cave. Together they edged into the courtyard, holding the cloth so its lower hem dragged the pavement. The sistrums played a rattling beat to match their slow footsteps. When the women reached the spot where the cave had stood earlier, they stopped. The sistrums fell silent, and a gong chimed three beats.

As the sound of the gong echoed around the courtyard, the priestesses drew their fabric apart to open the cave mouth, revealing a figure swathed head to toe in purest white, crumpled forward in a near-fetal position, with the head tilted down and the face hidden. This pose was eerily reminiscent of the way the people arranged the bones of the dead in the burial pithoi, folded up like babes in the womb.

Aria knew the figure was actually Eileithyia, dressed for her new role in the rite. But no woman, not even the High Priestess, dared to show her human form when she appeared in ritual as the Sun goddess, Fire of Heaven, whose power the people adored and feared in equal measure.

The Sun-Mother crouched in the cave mouth, unmoving, just as the Sun stood unmoving for three days at Winter Solstice. The Head Song-Priestess signaled, and the instruments began a steady beat. Then she turned to Aria's group, leading them in the first part of the song, the words and tune so familiar that the crowd joined in before the first line was finished.

Falling, falling
Into darkest night
Falling, falling
Out like a light
Time for Fire of Heaven
Like every soul we mourn
To complete the circle
To die and be reborn

The people repeated the last two lines over and over, with the drums and the sistrums driving their words onward: "To complete the circle... to die and be reborn... to complete the circle... to die and be reborn..."

Slowly the white-clad figure shifted and unfolded, one bit at a time, finally standing tall, facing the back of the woolen cave. As the chant repeated, the figure turned around to reveal a bronze mirror where the face should be. Within the depths of the cave, the mirror hardly shone at all. The figure edged forward bit by bit, slowly enough that Aria could feel the frustration of the people as they tried to chant faster to make the figure move more rapidly. But the Sun progresses as she will, and no human can change her timing.

When the mirror-faced figure reached the opening in the fabric, a gong rang out and the chant stopped. Now a cadre of dancers swept into the courtyard, all garbed in bright yellow fabric shot through with gold threads and trimmed with shiny beads of pure gold. These men and women—the ones who had danced as Melissae, Daktyls, and Hekaterides earlier in the rite—now pranced around in front of the cave, skipping and frolicking to a new rhythm. The sistrums and drums picked up a faster beat while the flutes and lyres chimed a joyful melody. Then Aria's group, and soon the whole crowd, joined in the song:

Come, come
Come the Light
Bless us with
Your presence bright
Shine, shine
Shine the Light
Come the morn
And banish night

After a few rounds of the song, Aria noticed that the figure in the cave mouth had begun to move. Slow as the sunrise, the white-clad figured edged forward, bit by bit, until it was entirely outside the cave. Then, as the song reached its final line once more, the figure tilted its head up so the morning sunlight gleamed on the mirror, reflecting brilliant sunbeams around the courtyard.

As one, the crowd rose to their feet and cheered, shouting with joy. Aria's group cried out as well, and the musicians put up a clamor with their instruments. Flames blazed up at one end of the altar, then the other as Daipita touched a burning brand to the bowls of oil: the fire offering to the Sun-Mother at her rebirth. As the fire grew, the cheering waned, until the courtyard was quiet once again. Then Kaeseus spread his arms one last time, addressing the assembled crowd.

"We have seen the sacred cave today, the place where the three realms meet, the holiest abode of the Earth-Mother, the Fire-

Mother, and the Water-Mother. This is the source of all mysteries, including the greatest one that we encounter only when this life ends." The clergy and crowd together made the signs of blessing and propitiation. "We must keep and honor the sacred days, following the paths of the Star-Mother's lights as they turn and turn above us. And we must share our bounty with one another, as the Great Mothers have taught us. Today we share our bounty with you. Come feast with us and celebrate the community of Ida's children!"

The triton trumpet sounded three blasts, then Aria's group began the final song. All the other clergy joined in, and then the crowd began to sing along as well, their words swelling the familiar tune, sharing the Mothers' love for their children and their children's love for each other, for their community.

Hand in hand
We sing their songs
And share the bounty they give
The Mothers provide
Their children dear
With all they need to live
We all give thanks
This blessed day
For rite and feast and games
We dance the dance
We sing the songs
And praise their holy names

As the crowd sang, the mirror-faced goddess turned and began to walk toward the nearest gap in the stands. The cave-priestesses folded up their fabric and fell in step behind her, followed by the dancers, then Daipita and Kaeseus. Still playing in time with the song, the musicians joined the procession. When the Chief Song-Priest and Priestess took their places behind the last of the musicians, Aria's group followed.

Singing and playing, the clergy processed out of the courtyard.

The crowd in the stands began to rise from their seats and make their way across the pavement as well, clustering behind the clergy. The people of Malia, priesthood and laity alike, sang their way out of the theatral court and down the processional way that led to the west plaza, where they would feast together and celebrate the day and the season.

As Aria came out of the courtyard and onto the processional way, she saw Eileithyia, still swathed in white, disappear into a doorway in the side of the temple building. The rest of the procession continued on, singing and chanting, until the people were crowded along the walkway that ran the length of the plaza where it flanked the west wall of the temple complex. The musicians created a clamor with drums, gongs, and sistrums, and the singing devolved into happy chatter as the people spread out across the plaza to feast.

Along the west wall of the temple, beneath the colorful drapery that decorated the building, stood rows and rows of tables laden with food. Aria knew the temple's kitchen staff had spent days preparing, roasting goat and beef and mutton, baking bread, and cooking vegetables and fruit. There were enough wine jars lined up alongside the tables to fill the hold of a good-sized ship. Now the temple's bounty was laid out for all to share.

The aroma of food greeted Aria, and her stomach rumbled. She fell in line behind the other clergy, waiting their turn alongside the laypeople, to serve themselves a solstice meal. Aria had to wait for a bit, since it was customary to allow the musicians to go first. That way, they finished their meal before everyone else did and were able to take up their instruments again for the dancing afterward.

Looking along the laden tables, Aria saw that there were stacks of bowls and cups for the temple folk. The townspeople brought their own dishes to these public feasts, unless they had none, in which case the temple provided. Aria served herself some mutton, soft cheese with herbs in it, stewed chickpeas, and a piece of barley bread. She topped her dish with several small onions stewed with thyme—her favorite. Her bowl in one hand and a cup of wine in the other, she went to find a seat.

While Aria was making her way through the crowd, searching for friends to sit with, Eileithyia emerged from the temple. Her white wrapping and the shiny bronze mirror were gone. She was no longer wearing the red-and-yellow ritual outfit, either, but one in shades of blue and green, with a soft wool shawl wrapped around her shoulders. Aria knew that the High Priestess had stored the white linen and the mirror safely in the temple, ready to use again next year.

The red-and-yellow ensemble, however, was not within the temple storerooms. It was hung up on a special stand in the theatral court. Aria had seen the ritual before: the people would walk in a few at a time, slowly, reverently, and make the salute to the garments that were draped on the tall stand. Then they would approach the stand and touch the hem of the fabric, asking the goddesses for healing and blessings. The clothing had touched the Great Mother and was now imbued with her power. But the people would wait to approach the sacred garments until after they had feasted, so they could adore the clothing as the last act of the day and carry the blessings home with them.

As it was, the feast was only just beginning. The long rows of tables and benches that lined the plaza soon filled up with people eating, chatting, and visiting with each other, the clergy scattered among the townspeople. Aria found a spot next to Ytanos, his partner Yassib, and their friends, men and women both, all traders and sailors of one sort or another. For a while she listened to their banter, their talk of trade goods and sea-going adventures and bargaining challenges in foreign lands and on their own island.

"Do you not grow bored during the winter?" Aria asked her brother.

"You think that, because we cannot safely sail again until the Flock-of-Doves rises with the Sun in the springtime, we have nothing to do?" He laughed. "Winter is a season of hard work and no fun."

"Oh, there is fun," Yassib said, nudging Ytanos with an elbow. The deeply tanned man from Byblos was not just Ytanos' lover but also his first mate and business partner. Many traders and sailors ended up pairing with foreigners, and no one thought anything of it. People who lived with Grandmother Ocean were different from those who lived inland, Aria reflected.

Ytanos smirked but ignored the bait. "Aria, we are like farmers. Though we cannot ply our trade during the winter, we are still busy. We must repair the ship and its rigging, make sure we have enough sailors for the next season, and make plans for our upcoming travels. When I am not patching canvas and pressing beeswax into wood, I am busy reviewing the previous season's activities, deciding where to trade again next year and which places, and people, to avoid. We all," he gestured to the other people at their table, "spend the dark months talking with each other, making plans, and sharing what we have learned so we can do better next season."

"I did not realize," Aria said.

"You thought I spent the winter with my feet up in front of a brazier, swigging wine?" Yassib gave him a pointed look. "All right, that is some of it. But most of it really is work. You are not the only one who is productive year-round."

Aria reached for her cup of wine, and her bracelet slid around her wrist, one of the pendants clinking on the edge of her bowl. Yassib peered at the small engraved stone, a quizzical look on his face.

"You are... a Consort-Bearer?" he asked, awed. Heads turned along both sides of the table, the people eyeing first Aria's bracelet and then the rest of her. "Ytanos, why did you not tell me?" Though he did not stand up, he made the hand-gesture portion of the salute, the back of his fist to his forehead. In his time with Ytanos, he had learned the ways of Ida's children, while Ytanos had also learned the ways of Yassib's people in Byblos.

Aria pulled the edge of her cloak down over her arm.

"She has visions as well," Ytanos said, the pride clear in his voice. "Always has, since long before she was initiated. She has seen many things that have come true."

"My Lady," Yassib said, "I would hate to think that someone of your great esteem might be alone on this sacred day." He tilted his head, his eyes directing Aria to their friends gathered around the table. "I am sure we can find someone worthy to help keep you warm tonight." More than a dozen friendly smiles and warm looks greeted Aria as she gazed down the table.

"If you will excuse me," she said, picking up her dishes in haste, "I think I would like some more food."

Refusing to look back at Ytanos and his friends, she made a beeline for a table loaded with dried fruit and nuts, choosing some dates, roasted almonds, and raisins. Then she stood off to one side, picking at the food. While she waited, the musicians who had played during the ritual reassembled in an open area along the edge of the plaza and began to play again, more festive songs this time. As people finished their meals, they gathered in front of the musicians, holding hands and dancing in circles and in twisting, snaking lines, the dances everyone knew that told the stories of the gods and the goddesses.

"Will you dance?"

Aria's head whipped around as she felt a tap on her shoulder. "Rhea."

"Here, put your dishes down," her friend said, pulling the bowl and cup from Aria's hands and depositing them on the corner of a nearby table. "Stop moping and come dance."

She grasped Aria's hands and drew her across the pavement. They joined up with several townspeople who were just approaching the dancing area. They circled slowly and then faster, stepping around in time with the music. After a few moments of grudging participation, Aria allowed herself to float on the beat of the drums, the rattle of the sistrums, the chiming melody of flute and lyre.

She and Rhea swirled around as the people moved tables and benches out of the way to make more room for the dancing. More and more people joined in, men and women and children, clergy and lay people, farmers and city-dwellers, forming circles large and small. Everyone danced the dance of the gods, the dance that celebrated the turning of the year and the sacred cycles of life and death.

The group next to hers swayed close to Aria, and she had to lean back to avoid bumping into them. As she twisted around to see where she was going, she caught sight of Lexion dancing with a group of men, his fellow members of the Ibex Brotherhood.

She watched as he moved around the circle in time with the music, his movements agile and fluid. Even wrapped up in sturdy boots and a long tunic, he was lithe and handsome. The man next to him said something to him, and he laughed, his head tilting back with the joy of it. Then he leaned over and kissed the man, both of them smiling. They broke off from the circle dance and walked away hand in hand, disappearing into the temple by a side door.

There was no formal rite of love at the Winter Solstice. The weather was too cold for outdoor abandon, either in the field beside the plaza or in the grass down by the Sea Temple, the two usual places for such rituals. But many people celebrated in private anyway, taking their activities indoors. Aria bit the inside of her cheek, letting the pain drive away the images of Lexion and his friend that were rearing up in her mind.

Rhea squeezed Aria's hand and pulled her around the circle faster as the music sped up. Aria danced, her feet moving in time with the beat, but it was as if someone else were dancing and she was only watching, cold and numb and far away.

Chapter 11

"Like this," Thalamika said. "You need to improve your grip. You have become careless in the way you hold the stylus."

The older woman held her reed stylus upright and made slow, careful marks on the soft clay tablet. Aria did her best to copy Thalamika's hand position and proceeded to write the word for barley.

"Well done," Thalamika said.

Aria sat back and massaged her hand. She had spent all morning in one of the scribal rooms writing the signs for the sounds over and over: filling up her little clay tablet, no bigger than her hand, smoothing it clean, and starting again. After many days of practice, she finally had all the signs memorized and could draw them to Thalamika's satisfaction. Now the older priestess was beginning to teach her whole words.

"Do you know why Our Lady wants me to know how to write?" Aria asked. "It is so difficult to learn."

"She did not give me any specifics."

"Certain jobs in the temple require writing. And so few people learn how. My mother does not know how to write." Aria twirled her stylus on the table top. "The Head of the College of Priestesses must know how to read and write."

Thalamika patted her hand. "I am sure Our Lady has plans for you. So you had better apply yourself."

Aria stroked her fingers across the clay tablet, smoothing away her work to begin again. She wrinkled her nose at the residue of clay on her fingertips. The whole room smelled of fresh clay, a damp, earthy scent that reminded Aria too much of the pillar crypt in the temple's basement. "When will I be allowed to write on papyrus?"

"Not until you have mastered the art. Papyrus cannot be reused, and it is expensive."

Aria sighed and slumped down on her bench. "I practice and practice, and still I am not good enough."

"Then you must work harder."

"Even if I do, there are only certain things we are allowed to write down. Some things must be shared from mouth to ear only. It is so hard to remember them all."

"This island is full of weakness and complacency, people who do not know how to be strong, how to forge ahead."

"And who is strong?"

"The mainlanders, of course," Thalamika sniffed. "Since the Great Darkness, our people have taken the easy way out. Our temples refuse to change, to move with the times."

Aria's eyebrows shot up. "But we have our traditions! Our Lady says we must not change them, but respect the sacred and keep it safe. That is why I became a priestess."

"I would not go against her, of course," came the quick reply. "But I know many people in the city. They send their children to me to learn how to read and write. And they tell me things about the mainlanders. How they are moving ahead in the world, gaining in wealth and power. We do not have to change our rites to enrich the temple. We should not be giving so much away, and the people should offer us more than they do."

Aria shrugged. "The mainlanders are not Ida's children. We have our ways, and they have theirs."

"We could learn a thing or two from them. We deserve to be as wealthy as they are."

"Bronze, silver, and gold cannot buy the gods' love," came a voice from the doorway.

Aria looked up to see Rhea watching them. "Of course the priestess who is named after one of the Mothers would say that."

Rhea stepped into the room, laughing. "You are one to talk, named after the Daughter of the Three-and-One."

Aria shifted on her bench.

"Perhaps," said Thalamika, rising from her seat, "you would like to help Aria with her writing. She is doing well, but I have other matters to attend to."

Rhea dropped onto the bench next to Aria as Thalamika disappeared out the door. "What," she said, "no hug from my little sister?"

"Must you still call me that?" The endearment was a common one, but it implied an intimacy the two had not shared since before the rite in the pillar crypt.

"We are under no prohibitions now. You could come to my room, or I to yours, any night we please."

Aria pressed her lips together, forcing an amount of composure she did not feel. "Being with you would just remind me of how things used to be."

"Is that so bad?"

"It is when it forces me to think about how different my life is now."

Rhea held her arms out, waiting.

With an exasperated sigh, Aria accepted her friend's hug, though she was stiff in Rhea's arms and pushed away after a brief moment.

"How is your little boy?" Aria said, returning her gaze to her clay tablet.

"He is well. I wish you had been there when we marked his second birthday. The children love their little celebrations." Rhea drew back and scrutinized her friend. "Your son is well, too, I am sure. He must be, what, four now? You know that all the temple children are loved and cared for."

"He is not my son. I have no children." Her voice was cold, tired, with a hard edge. "Will you teach me to write the words for the offerings?"

"Of course." Rhea poised her stylus over the clay tablet Thalamika had been using. "Here is the way to write *olive oil*."

In silence Aria copied the word once, then again and again down the tablet until it was full.

"I have not lain with Lexion," Rhea said as Aria was writing.

"So you keep telling me, year after year."

"I rarely even see him, and he was not at the ritual where my son was conceived. You should attend some of the rites. He is not often there, and you would have your choice of partners." She set her hand on top of Aria's. "You could get another child."

"With any man except him." Aria drew her hand away from Rhea's and swiped her fingertips along the surface of the tablet to wipe it clean, digging them in until the edges of the clay curled up.

"Why are you still angry with me?" Rhea demanded. "After all this time."

"I am not angry with you. I am just..."

"Angry."

Aria curled her hand into a fist and pounded the tablet flat. Then she picked up the stylus and began writing 'olive oil' again, hard enough that the stylus pierced almost all the way through the clay to the tabletop.

"If it is a woman you prefer," Rhea said softly, "I would not mind. I make no claim on you. I never have."

"Right now, I prefer no one," Aria said through gritted teeth.

Rhea sat silent for a while, watching Aria write with her head tilted down close over the clay, concentrating on her task. As Aria worked, her movements became less vicious and more measured, the signs less jagged and more comely.

"Our Lady must have ambitions for you, if she wants you to learn to write," Rhea said at last.

"You can write, too," said Aria. "Better than I can."

"But only because I have been doing it longer."

"It is hard."

"Yes, but you and I both know that eventually you will be better at it than I am." Aria lifted her head up and met Rhea's gaze with a look of concern. "Oh, Aria, you have always been a better priestess than me, even if you are a little younger. What is more important to me is that you are my friend."

With that, Aria relented and gave Rhea a real hug, clinging to her and blinking back tears.

Chapter 12

The stones clattered as they tumbled into the basket, chunks of raw lapis lazuli piled against wicker in a corner of the small storeroom.

"Be careful!" Rhea said. "Daipita will know who did it if those are broken. And so will Our Lady."

"Sorry," Aria mumbled. She adjusted the cord, tying the seal impression onto one of the basket handles. That way, the wealthy merchant who had given the stones to the temple would be credited for her generous donation. "I just want to be finished."

Rhea adjusted a stack of wooden boxes. "We should be thankful the offerings continue to come in. Our Lady says the leaders at Knossos are neither patient nor kind when waiting for their seasonal donations from us."

"There," Aria said, sliding the basket back against the wall. She turned to a set of shelves full of stacks of papyrus sheets. "Now we are supposed to store the records from this season's offerings." The new papyrus sheets slipped around in Aria's hands as she gathered them up. "They should go on top there..." She indicated the spot with a nod of her head. "Since they are the most recent."

Rhea took the sheets two or three at a time and slid them in on top of the previous stack. "I think there are more pages here than it looks like. How far back do you think these records go?"

"Back to the time before you were born," Eileithyia said as she stepped into the small room. "Here, you see?" She indicated one of the low shelves. "The sheets of papyrus flatten out over time until each one takes up very little space. Of course, every time there is a fire, we must start all over again. Thank the Mothers, there has not been a major fire here in more years than you have been alive." She made the sign of propitiation.

Aria and Rhea eyed the stored papyrus, taking in the information.

"You have done good work," Eileithyia said. "I have spoken with Thalamika, and she agrees that you have both mastered writing."

"Does that mean we get to use papyrus now?" Rhea said.

"Indeed it does. Well done, both of you."

Smiling broadly, the two friends clasped hands. Then, with a sidelong glance at Rhea, Aria dared to lean over and give the High Priestess a kiss on the cheek, a greeting usually reserved for priestesses much closer to each other in rank. "Thank you, My Lady," she murmured.

"Ariadne," Eileithyia said, "I have something I would like to discuss with you."

"I had best be going," Rhea said. "We have finished our work here, and I promised my little boy I would walk with him in the herb garden. There are so many butterflies dancing through the air this time of year, and the doves in the dovecote are so pretty. He loves it when he finds a feather on the ground."

She gave Aria another quick hug, bowed her head to the High Priestess, then slipped out of the room. Eileithyia waited as Aria rearranged her face into a semblance of happiness.

"You know, my dear," the High Priestess said, "you can have another child whenever you wish. You are under no restrictions."

"Except the one." She folded her arms across her chest. "I have gone to some of the festivals and lain with men at each one. And no sign of pregnancy. Rhea thinks I need a steady lover. She keeps suggesting men, priests and artisans and merchants. But I know that would make no difference. I am barren." She blinked back tears.

"You are no such thing." Eileithyia took hold of Aria's elbows, her thumbs stroking gently against the skin. "You simply have no room for another child."

Aria let out a sad laugh. "No room? My life is empty."

"But your womb is still full."

Aria drew away from the older woman's grip. "That is ridiculous."

"Is it?" The High Priestess caught Aria's gaze and held it. "Your womb is still full with your first child. You refuse to let him go, to make space for another."

Drawing in a sharp breath, Aria turned her back to the High Priestess and pretended to examine some of the papyruses. Eileithyia stood there, silent, for several moments. Finally she touched Aria's arm. The younger woman startled at the contact but did not turn back around.

"The sacrifice must go willing," the High Priestess said.

"I know that. When he is grown, he will choose."

"I am not talking about your son."

The younger woman stiffened. "I was willing. I agreed to the rite in the pillar crypt."

"You must also agree to let him go, Ariadne. You have made the greatest sacrifice anyone can make without giving up their own life to the gods."

Aria wrapped her arms around herself as tears streamed down her cheeks. The High Priestess waited as Aria's shoulders shook with silent sobs. Aria did not turn around, did not speak, but let the tears pour in silence. Finally, she wiped her face with the back of her hand.

"My dear," Eileithyia said when the storm had passed, "I know you are interested in responsibilities other than just stacking the donations in the storerooms. I do have plans for you, I promise."

Aria shifted so she could look at the High Priestess sidelong. "Real priestessing?"

"I want you to sit as a scribe in the audience chamber on Offering Days."

"But that is still just… administration."

"It is administration that allows this temple to continue to function," she said. "We cannot eat visions. Rituals will not pay our debts."

"Yes, My Lady. I did not mean..."

"Of course you did. But you must learn that the stuff of this world—barley and olive oil, bronze and lapis and wool—has its own worth, its own place in the order of things. Though we must be careful not to value those things simply for the purpose of collecting them up, they are not lesser simply because they are physical."

Aria turned to her High Priestess, her head bowed. "I apologize. I still have much to learn."

"Now, those are wise words," Eileithyia said with a touch of a smile.

Taking the younger priestess by the hand, Eileithyia led Aria out of the room and down the corridor. The High Priestess pushed a door open, and they stepped out into the sunlight. Then she led Aria out onto the west plaza. The two women strolled along the paved pathway toward the theatral court.

A flock of doves pecked at the ground, taking flight when the women came too close. Aria watched the birds, thinking of the goddess they represented and the beautiful light, the Star of the Sea, that was her sign in the sky.

"The doves are of this world, but they stand for something that is not," she ventured.

Eileithyia nodded. "Those donations that you chafe at recording are gifts not just from the people but also from the gods. The crops, the stones and metals, the livestock, all of it. If you remember where it all comes from, you will have an easier time valuing it properly."

"And not as the mainlanders do?"

"Anyone can make the mistake of prizing wealth for its own sake, no matter where they are from." She considered a moment. "There is a man I would like you to meet." Aria rolled her eyes. "I am not playing matchmaker. He is a merchant and can teach you much about our community. He knows everyone in Malia, many in the countryside, and some who come from abroad. You should learn to recognize them all as they come to the audience room on Offering Days." She smiled at her student. "We live in troubling times. Community is a balm and a safeguard against ill winds. We are part of a larger world and must not allow ourselves to narrow our vision too much."

"And that is… administration?"

"That is important if you are to move up in the temple."

"I want to help, to keep our people safe and well, as the Mothers do." Aria watched a dove fly up into the low branches of a nearby tree. "Does this mean I will not learn to lead rituals?"

Eileithyia shook her head. "One day you will lead so many rituals, you will grow tired of them."

"But I want more responsibility."

"I am giving it to you, a bit at a time. Do not be so eager to take on everything all at once."

"Yes, My Lady," she said with a sigh.

Chapter 13

"Our Lady sent me to you," he said, making the salute to Aria. "I am honored to meet you."

She looked up from her work table at one side of the audience room. The man was handsome. His tunic was woven of fine linen with bits of gold threaded into the decorative bands on the sleeves and hem. He was smiling at Aria as if she should know who he was and why he was there. He did look familiar, but she could not place him.

"Offerings go directly to Our Lady and the Consort," she said, keeping her voice down and motioning to the spot where Eileithyia sat on the dais with Belisseus by her side. A number of priests and priestesses flanked the sacred pair. The clergy's job was to collect the offerings, apply the donor's seal to a small round of clay for identification, and record the details on clay tablets once the High Priestess and the Consort had received and blessed the items. Every now and then, one or two of the clergy would accompany a donor back outside to verify contributions of livestock and any large items that could not reasonably be brought indoors.

The donors waited in the anteroom and were let in individually or by family group to approach the High Priestess and her Consort, so the room was rarely crowded. When the donors were finished with their turn, the clergy were supposed to usher them out a side door, not let them wander over to the scribes' table. Aria had already watched Ytanos and Yassib come in that morning to make their offerings. They had nodded to her as they came in, but like everyone else who brought offerings to the temple, they knew better than to walk over to the scribal tables and interrupt the recording of the day's transactions.

As Aria turned back to her work, transferring the offering lists from clay tablets to papyrus so the tablets could be reused, the man spoke again.

"But I am here for you. I am to teach you sums."

She looked up, and he was still smiling. Forcing herself to remain patient and polite despite the embarrassment of the interruption, she tilted her head and looked down the long table, past Lexion, Rhea, and the other clergy, to Thalamika, who was sitting at the far end. "I do not need to know sums," she said to the Chief Scrivener. "The donations are already totaled up when I receive the tablets."

Thalamika shrugged. "I did not send him to you."

Aria looked back at the man. "Then who did?"

"Our Lady," he said, motioning to Eileithyia. "As I said before."

"I am needed here," Aria insisted, embarrassed at the attention and concerned that the others would think she was shirking her share of the work or seeking the man's attention on purpose when she should be scribing. He was handsome, after all. She cast a sidelong glance at Lexion, but he appeared to be engrossed in his writing. "I cannot interrupt Our Lady to discuss this with her now."

"Very well," he said. "I shall return when the offerings are finished." He inclined his head to her and sauntered out.

Aria returned her focus to her work, refusing to respond to any of the inquiring looks or murmured comments from her fellow clergy.

Later that day, when she was happily full from the midday meal—eaten late because the offerings ran long that morning, a blessing as the times grew less abundant—Aria took a few moments to stretch her legs in the temple's herb garden. Sitting at that table in the audience room for so long always made her feel a bit stiff. And the light wells, though well placed, never quite made up for real sunshine outdoors.

"My Lady Ariadne."

She turned to see the man from that morning standing among the herbs, making the salute, a small basket tucked under his other arm. As she stood there, trying to decide what to do, he strode over to her.

"I apologize for interrupting your work this morning. Our Lady pointed you out to me after I had made my offering, and I did not realize…" He made a little bow. "I am Sageleus, son of Lilia, a merchant of Malia. Our Lady has asked me to teach you sums, if you will allow me to."

The High Priestess had sent him, so what choice did Aria have? She put on a smile. "May Ida keep you safe and well."

"Shall we sit in the fresh air?" Sageleus asked, motioning to a bench set along a sunny wall among a collection of large decorative pots spilling over with herbs.

The breeze blew through the plants, wafting scents of dittany, thyme, and rosemary through the air. Dragonflies darted above the plants, their red and blue bodies shimmering in the sunlight. The day was too beautiful to let her irritation ruin it, Aria decided. Still, she made sure Sageleus' basket ended up between the two of them as they arranged themselves on the bench. From the basket he produced several fresh clay tablets and styluses as well as two small boards, one for each of them to set a tablet on for support as they wrote.

"I assume you are proficient at writing?" he asked.

"As you saw this morning," she said with pride, then realized she had chosen her words to impress him. That sort of vanity was unbecoming. Better to be honest. "I can write all the numbers, but I do not know how to add them up, except on my fingers. And I cannot do the fractions at all."

"All right, then. Let me show you."

A while later, Aria sat back and dropped her tablet into her lap. Her hand was cramping from all the writing, and she was finding herself more than a little distracted by the amount of well-muscled arm and leg that Sageleus' short tunic revealed. She forced her thoughts back to the task at hand. "I think I understand the numbers. But what about the fractions? They are confusing."

"Yes, they are." She stared at him, taken aback, and he let out a laugh. "Did you think I came by all my learning easily? Believe me, I worked hard for it. Here, let me show you how I understand the fractions." He smoothed out his tablet and drew a large circle on it. "Here is one."

She smiled. "Unity. The One. The Greatest-Mother-of-All from which all things come." She made the sacred sign with her hand. "Ourania, Mother-of-Darkness-and-Stars."

"Yes. In order to create fractions, we must begin with the whole, the unity. And now we divide it up." He drew a horizontal line across the center of the circle. "One is divided into two. Each part is one half."

"I understand that much. The World Above and the World Below with the horizon dividing them." She looked at him sidelong and smirked. "Everyone knows about the two worlds."

He grinned back at her. "All right then, we divide it again." He drew a vertical line across the center of the circle. "One divided into four."

Her eyes widened. "The four directions. Equinox sunrise and sunset and the points halfway in between." She turned to face him, considering. "Is this your own way of thinking of the fractions, or did someone else show it to you?"

"One of the old priests in the temple. My parents paid him to teach me to write some years ago. I hope they paid him well, because I certainly gave him plenty of aggravation." He chuckled, and Aria found herself smiling back at him. "He thought it would be a good way for me to understand."

"It is," she said, feeling her cheeks redden. She cleared her throat. "I believe I can tell you what happens next."

Eyebrows raised in expectation, he held the tablet out to her. She drew two more lines, a large X dividing each quarter of the circle in half.

"One divided into eight parts. The eight winds," she said,

triumphant. She reached toward the tablet with her stylus again, then drew her hand back.

"Do you not know how to continue?" he asked.

"I do," she said, shifting uncomfortably on the bench. "Next is one divided into sixteen, then into thirty-two and finally into sixty-four, the same way as before, with more lines crossing at the center point. Each division doubles the number of lines and halves the amount that is counted with the fraction." She stopped talking, her gaze lowered.

"The old priest did not teach me about those except to show me the divisions so I could do the sums. Have no fear. I am not privy to temple secrets."

She let out a breath, casting about for a different subject. "I am told the people of the Two Lands use the eye of one of their gods to show the fractions."

"It is true. They understand numbers well, just as we do. That makes it easy to trade with them."

She leaned over and broke off a stem of thyme, rubbing the leaves between her fingers and inhaling the scent. It helped to clear the smell of damp clay out of her head. "Are there people who do not understand numbers? But how could there be? How could they trade otherwise?"

"By paying scribes or other merchants to do the calculations for them." He smoothed out his tablet and began to pack the writing implements back into the basket. "The mainlanders are like that. They do not have base commodity values…"

"Base what?"

"Standardized barter. The way a certain measure of grain is always equal to a certain weight of copper, for instance. They get into many arguments in the marketplace because of this."

She leaned back against the warm wall and considered. "But they can count, can they not? How else can they bargain?"

"Of course they can count. They have fingers and toes," he said with a wink. "But they do not understand fractions. And they cannot write, most of them. That is why they pay others to do it for them, both in the marketplace and in the temple at Knossos."

"Why on Earth do they not simply learn how, like you and I did? Then they would not have to pay. I know they are different from us, and backward in some ways, but they cannot possibly be that dim-witted."

He began to chuckle, and soon he was laughing in earnest. She stared at him, perplexed, until she realized his speech was laced with a faint accent. He was fluent, to be sure, probably raised on the island, but underneath it all, he was not a child of Ida, at least not entirely. Her face turned bright red, and she wished she could melt into the ground and disappear.

"My apologies," she managed to say. "You are so dark. And you introduced yourself by your mother's name, not your father's. I did not realize…"

She stood up, preparing to flee. But he reached out and gently took hold of her wrist.

"I was born here," he said, still chuckling in between the words, "but I have something of my father's accent. He is from the mainland." He gestured to his face and arms, the deep brown skin. "But I take after my mother in looks. She is a child of Ida. I also spend a great deal of time outdoors. Kalliste has darkened my skin even more."

"You value our ways," she said, confusion evident on her face. "I guess that is because you grew up here."

"And not at Knossos?" His eyes twinkled. "Or on the mainland?"

"Now you are making fun of me. I know it is not as simple as that." She realized he was still holding her by the wrist. She shifted, and he let go of her, but she made no move to leave. "I think I do not understand… people."

"Nor do I," he said with a smile. "But I like most of them anyway. I think that is why Our Lady asked me to come to you."

"Because I have trouble dealing with people? I say the wrong thing so often..." She scowled, both at her own embarrassing behavior and at the idea of Eileithyia sending someone to help improve her social skills.

He shrugged, though the look on his face suggested that was

exactly the High Priestess' reasoning. "I do not sail but still, I trade widely. I know many people from all over the island and foreign lands as well. Perhaps I can introduce you to them one day."

"Of course Our Lady would want you to do that," she grumbled.

He stood up and picked up the basket. "When shall we meet next to work some more on your numbers?"

After some discussion, they chose a date that suited both Aria's temple responsibilities and Sageleus' marketplace activities.

"I will practice my sums," Aria promised, doing her best not to stammer as the merchant smiled at her.

"I look forward to it."

He made the salute and strode through the garden, back toward the city. She stood there and watched him go, then shook herself and stalked back into the building. Why could Eileithyia not have chosen a homely merchant for her teacher?

Chapter 14

Pressing her hand to her mouth, Aria fought the urge to retch. The scent of hot blood and animal hide hung in the air along with pungent incense smoke and sweat as the early autumn sunshine beat down on the crowd gathered at the edge of the temple's vineyards. Eileithyia stood over the bull's steaming corpse as its blood poured from the slashed neck into a basin beneath the sacrificial table. Her upper body was bare and covered in a sheen of sweat. Her cowhide skirt, originally white with brown spots, bore the faded stains of many years' sacrifices. A few bright, fresh marks matched the glistening redness on the bronze blade in her hand.

She turned to the Consort and pressed her bloody fingertips to his bare chest, drawing the symbol of sacrifice on his skin, the emblem of Dionysus' plunge into the World Below at the time of the grape harvest. The God of the Vine, born from the body of Ida herself, traveled below on behalf of his mother's people at this, the Feast of Grapes. He carried the souls of the dead down to their abode—the men, at any rate, since Ariadne bore the women's souls to the realm of the dead. And he brought the gifts of ecstasy and healing back up, his blessing on those who honored him.

Now that the High Priestess had marked him, the Consort was the god embodied, ready to descend to the World Below for the good of all. He wavered, reaching out a hand to steady himself against the post at the end of a row of grapevines. The deep purple grapes gleamed in the sunshine, ripe to bursting. But no one could touch them yet. The first cluster could not be harvested until the ceremony was completed, one of the oldest rites of Ida's children, going back to the very first vines their ancestors tended on the island. The wine, the grapes, and the god himself—her own son— were gifts to the people from the Great Mother.

Laying her bloody knife aside, Eileithyia picked up a flagon of wine, the best of the brewings from last year's grape crop. She held the vessel aloft and spoke. "Three times I pour the libation, for the Three: the three Mothers, the three realms, the three worlds."

She poured out the contents of the pitcher in three rounds, the deep red liquid twisting and streaming onto the parched ground. The earth was so dry that, instead of absorbing into the soil, the liquid sat on the surface in a quivering puddle of translucent blood red, shimmering in the sunlight.

Then the Consort raised his arms, the sacred horns embodied, and spoke. "Three times I say the prayer, for the Three: the three Mothers, the three realms, the three worlds." He threw his head back and spoke in a voice that echoed through the air:

By land and sky and sea
Blessed be the Three
By land and sea and sky
By Them we live and die
By sky and sea and land
Beneath Their guiding hand

When the overheated air was again silent, the High Priestess handed him a cup of wine. He lifted it up toward the sky, toward the Sun-Mother and the Star-Mother, then drained it in one long draught. With a flourish he turned the cup upside down on the ground and smashed it with his foot, proof that he had drunk the whole thing. Drawing in a slow breath, he began to tremble, shivering as if he were somehow freezing beneath the fiery

Mediterranean Sun.

A slow chant began, first just the Chief Song-Priest and Chief Song-Priestess calling to the god. The rest of the priesthood joined in, then the familiar chant echoed throughout the gathered crowd: "The Undiluted One. The Undiluted One. The Undiluted One." The people repeated Dionysus' epithet over and over again, a single voice of many layers pressing out the rhythm of the words, the sound pushing past this world and into the World Below.

The Consort swayed in time with the chant, his torso coated in sweat, his head lolling back. His face was flushed, his eyes glazed, his chest heaving. Slowly he raised his arms. They moved as if they were floating up through the air. When his arms were again upraised in the sign of the sacred horns, the chant changed:

"Lord of Death, Prince of Peace. Lord of Death, Prince of Peace."

Back and forth the crowd swayed, priesthood and lay people alike, chanting together, breathing together, moving together, allowing themselves to experience a small part of the god's ecstasy.

With no warning, the Consort's body snapped up straight, rigid, and his eyes rolled back in his head. "I bid you peace," he croaked, then crumpled to the ground.

A collective wail rose up from the crowd as a cadre of priests rushed to gather up the fallen Consort, lay him on a litter, and wrap his body in soft linen, as if shrouding a corpse. A slow drumbeat began as the priests prepared the Consort for the physical portion of his journey.

Glancing sidelong at Rhea to make sure she did not notice, Aria took the opportunity to scan the crowd, hoping against hope that she might recognize her son among the boys from the temple who were attending the rite. She did this every chance she got, every ritual that allowed the older children to take part. Her mental calculations told her that her son should be ten, since Rhea's boy was now eight and was standing among the youngsters who had clustered together to one side of the crowd. But as she looked over the attendees, she could not tell whether any among them was the boy she had birthed. She would not know him if he walked up and greeted her. That thought felt like a cold stone in the pit of her stomach, or perhaps in the depths of her heart.

As her gaze swept the gathering, she saw a glowing face smiling at her and recognized Sageleus. She returned the smile, then caught herself, lowered her eyelids, and turned her focus back to the ritual.

Lexion was among the priests who were lifting the shrouded Consort onto a litter. She regarded him for a moment. He was still handsome, certainly, even as he grew older, but he had a seriousness about him, like a shadow over his face. Sageleus, in contrast, exuded a kind of joy that made him attractive in unexpected ways, though he and Lexion were a similar age. She wondered what kind of priest Sageleus might have made, had he chosen that path.

Four priests lifted the litter and bore the Consort back to the temple, led by Kaeseus and flanked by Lexion and the other men, all of them chanting Dionysus' funeral dirge. The High Priestess followed behind them in silence, touching no one, making eye contact with no one, the spattered blood slowly drying on her animal hide skirt and her skin.

The crowd broke up as most of the people moved off toward the bull ring, where the leaping would soon begin: Dionysus' funeral games. Aria had watched the bull leaping many times as a child and later as a young priestess. But now, she had other obligations. Eileithyia had insisted that Aria participate in the second half of this ritual, and Aria had no objection. She was glad to finally be allowed to take part in the more important temple rites.

The vineyard workers lined up and passed silently in front of the table as Aria, Rhea, Daipita, Thalamika, and the other priestesses blessed them with a mixture of the sacrificial blood and wine. Then they headed out into the fields to begin their work, the harvesting of the grapes: Dionysus' death embodied on a grand scale.

When they were finished with the blessings, the priestesses picked up the pitchers, still half-full of the sacred mixture, and processed up to the temple in silence with Daipita in the lead. Aria's arms trembled with the weight of the large flagon she carried. The sweat dripped down her face and her torso. The linen of her skirt clung to her sweaty thighs. As she walked, her stomach rumbled from the preparatory fast, and she knew she still had much sacred work ahead of her before she could eat. But the discomfort was worth it, for the chance to take part in such a powerful rite.

The priestesses carried the blooded wine into one of the temple's ritual chambers and set the containers on the central altar. Tomorrow, they would carry the sacred liquid back out to bless the vineyards. But right now they had a rite to complete.

In silence they waited, gathered around the edges of the room. Aria could not tell how much time had passed when the High Priestess finally appeared. She had bathed, purified herself, and changed clothes. Her fresh linen skirt and open-front bodice were tinted with the blood-red murex dye, the color of birth and death. Nodding to the others, Eileithyia took her place among the women. They all lifted the veils that had hung from their waists and draped them over themselves, head and shoulders. Eileithyia's veil was blood red to match the rest of her clothing. Then the women, all except the High Priestess, picked up sistrums from the altar and held them down against their skirts to keep them from making any noise.

With Daipita leading and Eileithyia at the end, they moved as one through the temple, a snaking line of priestesses, veiled and silent. They walked down the corridors, out into the courtyard, and into the anteroom that fronted the main ritual hall. Through the paneled doors Aria heard the priests chanting low and soft, the funeral dirge they had begun back in the vineyard. They were keeping vigil as the Consort wended his way through the World Below on behalf of his people.

Daipita lifted her hand and rapped three times on the rightmost doorpost. The chanting never faltered, but a voice called out from within, "Who seeks to enter?"

"The witnesses to the journey," she answered. "Those who represent the Great Mother herself."

"What do you await?" came the voice again.

"Death become life again."

The door swung open, and the sound of the men's chanting

grew louder. Incense smoke wafted out, and the dim light of oil lamps flickered as the air moved through the open doorway. Led by Daipita, the snaking line of priestesses processed into the room and circled around the priests. The men were kneeling in a tight cluster around the prone body of the Consort as he lay atop the litter, on the floor. The High Priestess entered the room last, dropping to her knees at the Consort's head as the priests made room for her.

She leaned over and cradled the Consort's head in her hands. Tears rolled down her cheeks as she sobbed. As she rocked back and forth on her knees, the sound of her keening cut through the men's continual chant, sharp and sorrowful. The priestesses stood in a circle, swaying gently in time with the priests' singing, but still keeping their sistrums pressed against the fabric of their skirts to silence them.

For what seemed like ages, the scene continued: the unconscious Consort laid out as a corpse on the floor, the High Priestess keening over him, the kneeling priests circling him and the standing priestesses circling them. The air swirled with incense smoke and the oil lamps guttered.

Following her training, Aria allowed herself to fall deep into trance, communing with the god and the Great Mother and the powers of the World Below, following the Great Mother's thread through life and death and back again. Like the men, the women were guarding their Consort on his dangerous journey, keeping him safe so he would return with blessings for the vineyards and the people.

Some time later—whether it was moments or days, Aria could not have said—the Consort began to moan. He shifted, his body twitching as if he were trying to wake up from a bad dream. From across the room a sistrum sounded, the cue from the Chief Song-Priestess. As one, the women threw back their veils and raised their sistrums. The hissing rattle began by keeping time with the men's chant, but then the men fell silent and the sound of the sistrums began to speed up.

The Chief Song-Priestess's voice rose through the smoke, a

soaring, joyful chant of life returning. The rest of the priestesses, including Aria, joined in, bringing their focus back to the room where the Consort lay writhing on the floor. Eileithyia was no longer crying, but she was still cradling her Consort's head. Aria knew that the High Priestess was also holding onto the Consort's spirit, the thread that attached his soul to his body, so he could return safely from his journey. Several of the priests kept a loose hold on his limbs so he would not injure himself as he twitched and twisted.

The beat continued to speed up, the sistrums hissing and the voices chanting, the Consort writhing and moaning. Suddenly his body went still, and he let out a shout. His eyes flew open, and the voices and instruments fell silent. He drew in a ragged breath. Eileithyia helped him raise himself up, propped on his elbows. Everyone held still, as if frozen in time, until the Consort nodded to them and began to get up.

The group shifted until he was sitting cross-legged on the floor in front of the altar, the High Priestess kneeling by his side, with the rest of the clergy spread out in a loose circle facing them. They waited in silence for several moments as Eileithyia laid her hands on the top of the Consort's head. When she was satisfied that he had returned fully and unharmed, she nodded and drew her hands away. He drew in a slow breath and began to speak.

"I am the son of the Great Mother, who lives and dies at her behest," he said, his words slurring a little. His eyes were glassy and unfocused. "I have traveled through her realms of darkness and light. She sends a message to her children."

Aria bit her lip, waiting for this year's proclamation, the first one she had ever heard directly from the Consort.

"I have seen sweetness and sorrow," he continued. "The love of the Mother is the greatest good in life and death. It is not death that sorrows the Great Mother, but disrespect, desecration. Hold her always above me, for I am only the son. I die and am reborn. She is eternal."

Aria saw heads nodding around the room. She knew the presiding clergy at Knossos now held Dionysus in higher regard than his mother, just as they viewed men as more valuable than women. They equated Dionysus with the mainlanders' Zeus, a comparison she considered insulting: Zeus lied, he fought, he demanded his wife remain faithful to him while he was not faithful to her—the epitome of dishonor in a man, though the mainlanders did not seem to think so. Worse yet, he did not die, did not descend to the World Below on behalf of his people. He sacrificed nothing, not even himself, even though men sacrificed much to him. But this was not news. The mainlanders had been behaving this way since before Aria was born. She shrugged mentally at the melodrama some of the older priesthood expressed about this issue. As long as Malia did not follow in Knossos' footsteps, what did it matter?

"Hold the old ways sacred," the Consort said, his voice growing stronger. "Let the Great Mother be above me, and the Three-and-One above all. Do not let go of the Three-and-One, but hold them always in your heart. Do not let others take them from you, or you from them. That way lies ruin."

His arm snaked out, and he clutched at the High Priestess. "My Lady, you must ensure..." He shuddered, struggling to speak.

Eileithyia stroked her hand down his cheek. "I am here, Beloved. I am listening. Speak to me."

"They say you must not let there be..." He drew in a labored breath, his shoulders shaking with the effort as if he were doing his best not to weep. "Do not let there be any poor among you. That is an abomination. We have the means to care for all the Great Mother's children. We must do so or risk her wrath."

His eyes rolled back in his head, and he collapsed.

Chapter 15

Aria smoothed down her skirt and stepped out into afternoon sunshine in the central courtyard. "Where shall we sit today?"

"We have spent so many days on sums and fractions," Sageleus said, inclining his head toward her. "I thought we might walk today instead... outside the temple."

"You have been speaking with Our Lady." Aria narrowed her eyes at him.

"She thought you might enjoy meeting some of the people in the city."

Aria fought the urge to say something rude. The High Priestess commenting to Aria privately about the need to expand her circle of acquaintances—and think about something other than rites and visions, at least for a while—was one thing. Eileithyia instructing Sageleus to take Aria around the town and introduce her to his friends, as if she were incapable of meeting new people herself, was embarrassing and well nigh infuriating. "Now I know why she released me from my duties for the rest of the day," she managed to say without too much rancor.

"Come," he said, holding his hand out to her. "I have many things to show you."

Ignoring the proffered hand, Aria led Sageleus through the north court and out the north entrance. They followed the Sea Road past the theatral court, passing the turnoff that led to the Sea Temple and continuing into the southern edge of the city.

"You know, I have been into Malia before," Aria said. "To visit my brothers and their families and to see what the shops have to offer. I have not spent my entire life in the temple."

"You have mentioned your brothers before, but you have told me little about them except that they are all older than you."

"I have three, all traders and sailors. But only the youngest lives here anymore. His name is Ytanos."

Sageleus cracked a smile. "If he has his own ship, I know him. He trades in the Two Lands sometimes, but mostly over the eastern sea in Byblos and Tyre and the other cities on that coast."

"Yes, that is him. My two older brothers live in Byblos now. One still runs a ship, and the other is settled as a merchant in the city there."

He nodded. "Perhaps we will see Ytanos today if we go down to the docks."

"Perhaps." She twisted her skirt cord, then dropped it when she realized what she was doing.

"Here we are."

Sageleus stopped in front of a series of shops. He proceeded to introduce Aria to the people along the row: weavers, potters, wine-sellers, stonecarvers, metalsmiths, jewelers. There were also farmers in town for the day to sell their produce in free-standing stalls, bakers selling bread, and cooks offering a variety of tasty foods, from goat stew to honey-candy. The brewers and the cheese-makers were doing a brisk business, their storefronts full of customers. These were the most successful of the city's artisans and merchants. Their location along the Sea Road said as much.

Sageleus appeared to be on a first-name basis with all of them. At first Aria felt awkward having all these wealthy people, many of whom were older than she was, make the salute to her. The robe of a priestess was unmistakable. But soon she was chatting with them and laughing at Sageleus' awful jokes, apparently his signature among the locals, if their cheerful groans were any indication.

Eventually they moved away from the shops and made their way down the Sea Road toward the docks. A gentle breeze brought the sea air into the edge of the city, and Aria breathed it in deeply, a broad smile on her face. She realized that, for the first time in ages, she was enjoying herself.

"So," she said, turning to Sageleus. "You introduced me to all those people who told me what they do. But I still do not know how you make your living."

"As I said, I am a merchant." He gave her a crooked grin.

"And that means?" she asked with a smirk, perching one fist on her hip.

"I trade on behalf of the temple, goods from the temple's fields and workshops in exchange for anything the priesthood needs. You probably saw me within the temple before we met, more than once. I go there often for business."

"Yes, you did look familiar the day you interrupted my work and embarrassed me in front of the other scribes." She put a hand on his upper arm and gave a gentle shove, and he laughed.

"My apologies," he said with a bow, though the look on his face suggested he was not particularly sorry. He straightened up and looked around. "I believe we have reached our destination."

The docks smelled of salt water and fish, and the whole area was full of people of all sorts moving to and fro in the slanting sunlight of the early evening. Toward the east end of the harbor were many small fishing boats, some of them unloading the day's catch and others leaving to lay out strings of octopus pots for the night. Nearer to where Aria and Sageleus stood were the large trading ships, some fitted with up to sixty oars and huge canvas sails with brightly-painted designs on them.

At a glance Aria could see that the vessels came from all over— her island, the mainland, the cities along the eastern sea coast, and the other islands that filled this part of the sea. She could tell the ship owners easily by their fancy garments, and the sailors by their minimal attire. Simple loincloths and bare feet make for easier work on board ship.

Sageleus walked along with a purpose, Aria following in his

wake, until he reached one of the medium-sized ships. Sweaty, loincloth-clad men were unloading baskets of copper ore onto the dock while two other men directed them.

"Ytanos son of Inia!" Sageleus called.

Aria's brother looked up from his papyrus and handed it to Yassib with a few quiet words. "Sageleus," Ytanos said, striding over. "So good to see you."

The two men embraced, then Aria stepped up beside Sageleus. Ytanos grinned.

"They let you out of the temple?" he teased, moving over to give his sister a hug.

"No, I climbed out a window when no one was looking."

"Ah, siblings," Sageleus chuckled.

"Seriously, Aria, what are you doing here?" Ytanos asked. "Do you need me for something?" He cast a glance back over his shoulder at his busy crew.

"Sageleus has spent the afternoon introducing me to the people he knows in the city."

"Sageleus knows everyone." Ytanos rubbed his chin. "Our Lady must have plans for you, then."

"I certainly hope so," she said.

"And they were all quite impressed," Sageleus said, winking at Aria, "even though you laughed at my jokes."

She gave the merchant a mock punch in the arm, turning her face away from her brother to hide the rising blush.

"Ah, I see how it is," Ytanos said with a smirk.

"And what are you loading or unloading today?" Sageleus asked. Aria silently gave thanks for his changing the subject.

"Copper ore," Ytanos said, waving his hand at a stack of baskets on the dock. "Stone for carving. Some tin." His gaze swept the ship, the busy crew, and his first mate, who was directing the activity. "We did well this time to avoid the mainland and trade only on the islands and the eastern sea coast. Byblos is always a good stop for us, of course."

Sageleus' brow furrowed. "Why would you avoid the mainland?"

"They are collecting up copper and tin, refusing to sell it at all or only at a ridiculously high price. And they are not selling blades at all, either, except among themselves."

"Why on Earth would they do that?" Aria asked.

"There are rumors that they are stockpiling weapons."

"That cannot be."

Ytanos shook his head. "I have heard that on the mainland and at Knossos, they are storing up all kinds of weapons: daggers, swords, spear points. It sounds as if they are planning to equip armies."

Aria shook her head. She had discounted those visions, the ones with ranks of spearmen marching on the west plaza at Knossos, as simple nightmares. "How can you be sure?"

"Not long ago I spoke with a trader who comes from Knossos. He said the temple there put on a huge display of armed spearmen, all marching in formation on the west plaza like some sort of perverted ritual for the Young God, with the priestesses blessing the blades before a packed crowd." Aria suppressed a shudder. It was not always pleasant to have visions come true. "It was all mainlanders, mostly the new ones who have come down from the mountains."

"I see," Sageleus said, scowling. "For some time now they have been trying to take over the trade in blades from the other cities on this island. If pure force would do it, they would have succeeded by now. But their recipe for bronze is inferior to the ones Ida has given her children, and our smiths will not share their secrets, especially since the punishment for doing so is so severe. People do not want to trade for a lesser product, so the mainlanders sell their blades mostly among their own kind."

Aria let out a breath. "Thank Ida that is all. I was afraid they might be doing something more... sinister."

"One day they might," Ytanos said, his expression darkening. "The cities in the north of the mainland have tried more than once to cross the water to the east of their homeland and take over that land. But so far, they are no match for the local people there."

"War has never yet come to this island," Sageleus said. "By the

Three, I hope it never does."

They all made the sign of propitiation.

"Tell me," Aria said to Ytanos, in haste to change the subject, "is it true that Rhea's brother has joined your crew?"

"He has," Ytanos said, turning to point him out among the deeply bronzed, loincloth-clad men who were hefting cargo and organizing the ship's rigging. "I am sorry you have lost a priest, but I am happy to say, I have gained a good sailor. He learns fast."

"Rhea told me when he asked Our Lady to let him leave the temple. I suppose the priesthood was simply not right for him after all. He did give it a number of years, though, so it was not a rash decision."

"Well, sailing suits him," Ytanos said. "We are very busy this season, and I am glad to increase my crew."

"Your success is a credit to all of Ida's children," Sageleus said, clasping Ytanos' hands. "But we are keeping you from your work, and there is only so much daylight left. May the Great Mothers keep you safe until I see you again."

Aria hugged her brother goodbye, then she and Sageleus headed back into the city. When they were halfway down the main road, Sageleus turned to her.

"May I offer you refreshment—some supper, perhaps? You have put up with me for quite a long time today."

"I think we may be too late," Aria said, looking up and down the road. Most of the shops were closed, the market stalls covered until time to open again tomorrow morning. The street was beginning to dim, the shadows blurring together into a broader darkness as the Sun began to sink below the horizon.

"My home is nearby," Sageleus said, extending his hand to her.

After a moment's hesitation, she reached out and took his hand. "That would be lovely." She fell in step beside him as they walked down a side street.

Two turns later, they were standing in front of a spacious villa, its walls freshly whitewashed and the window frames painted in lively shades of deep green and bright blue, the expensive pigments a quiet testament to Sageleus' success. He led her through the main room, stopping to speak with a servant for a moment, and then out into the courtyard. The area held a central garden surrounded by a paved walkway. Clumps of lilies nodded in the faint breeze as another servant hurried to light the oil lamps.

They took seats at a table along one side of the courtyard and shortly, the servant Sageleus had spoken with earlier brought food and drink. The meals at the temple were high quality, but the dishes Sageleus presented to Aria were exquisite. As she finished the delectable servings of herb-roasted peacock with saffron (the platter decorated with the iridescent feathers the bird was so famous for), stewed leeks, lentils with coriander and almonds, sesame-honey cakes, and resinated wine, it occurred to her that the merchant was trying to impress her.

"The food is delicious," she said, smiling at him. "Thank you for all your help with… well, everything."

"It has been my pleasure."

He reached across the table and took her hand, lifting it to his lips and kissing the knuckles one by one. His head still bowed over her hand, he looked up at her through his eyelashes.

"Mine as well," she managed to say, though suddenly her heart was pounding.

He straightened up, now cradling her hand in both of his. When his eyes met hers, his gaze was soft, warm, full of desire. "Are you free to love?"

She swallowed. "I am under no prohibitions." It was not unusual for members of the priesthood to have lovers in town, so staying late—or staying the night—would not be a problem. Aria's face grew hot when she remembered that Eileithyia had released her from her regular duties not just for the afternoon and evening, but for much of the next morning as well.

"I have a most comfortable bedchamber," Sageleus said, standing up.

She rose as well, and he held her hand as he led her through the villa and up the stairs. He brought her into a large bedroom with broad windows that looked out over the courtyard. She took in the large bed with its plump mattress and fine linens, the carved wooden trunk and the little table and the brightly colored rug. She stood looking out the window into the darkness while Sageleus lit the oil lamps around the room.

"What do you see?"

She startled as his breath whispered past her ear. He was standing close, so close, but not touching her—yet.

"Nothing. It is too dark." She turned to face him, setting her hand on his chest, toying with the fancy trim that edged the neckline of his tunic. "I do not... I have not been with men except in ritual. Festivals. This is... different."

His lips brushed her cheek. "It is not your body that worries you, but your heart."

She huffed out a quiet laugh. "You know me too well."

"I will take as much care with your heart as I do with the rest of you." He leaned down and kissed her on the mouth. "Come to bed."

"Yes."

* * *

Screams. Smoke. The stench of blood pouring and flesh burning. Malia was on fire.

Women ran through the streets, chased by men with swords who caught them and raped them in broad daylight, then slew them and tore the jewelry from their dead bodies. The men broke down doors and dragged children into the street, dragged old men and women out, beat them senseless and looted their homes. They slaughtered every animal they encountered and set fire to every building that would burn.

There were dozens of these men, maybe hundreds. They were heavily armed, with mismatched shields and clothing, and a cold, grim look that made them appear less than human. A pack of them was advancing on the temple.

"Aria! Wake up!"

She struggled against the men, fighting their grip on her, until her eyes flew open and she discovered she was tangled in the bedsheet, thrashing against its folds.

"Here, let me help you," Sageleus said as he unwound the linen from her legs. "You were having a bad dream."

"It was not a dream." Her heart was still pounding. She drew in slow, deep breaths, calming herself with the methods she had learned in the temple. "It was a vision."

He narrowed his eyes at her. "Are you prone to visions?"

"I have had them all my life." She swallowed. "They always come true."

"I understand if you cannot tell me. I am not a priest." He stroked her hair and reached an arm around her shoulders, but she continued to sit upright and stiff. "Aria, please at least let me comfort you."

Relenting, she leaned against him as he circled his strong arms around her. She peered around the room, lit with gentle sunbeams, and listened to the morning birdsong and the sounds of people beginning their day. The city was safe. There were no armed men. Yet.

Sageleus sat there holding her, not asking questions, not prying. She could feel his heartbeat, strong and steady. Then she realized he was waiting for her to speak, waiting for her to share what she had seen — or to tell him that she was not going to.

"The problem," she finally said, "is that even though my visions have always come true, I cannot tell when they will happen. Maybe this one will not happen in my lifetime. I can hope."

"The vision does not come with a calendar-priestess? Where are the Sky-Watchers when we need them?"

She let out a laugh and slumped against him, the tension finally draining out of her. "No. And this one…" She swallowed. "An army was attacking the city. Burning it down. Killing…" Her voice cracked, and she blinked back tears.

He held her tighter. "We are safe right now. And, I think, for a while yet."

She shifted to look him in the face. "You believe me."

"Why would I not?"

"Not everyone trusts visions. Some say they are madness. They are not like divination, which is done with exacting ritual."

He stroked his fingers down her cheek. "Will you tell me what they looked like, the attackers?"

When she had described them in as much detail as she could remember, he shook his head.

"That is no army. Those are mercenaries. But who hired them? Did your vision not tell you this as well?"

"No. All I ever see is a scene, like a painting, but alive and moving. And this one... I think I had better tell Our Lady."

"Of course."

He rose and helped her up. They retrieved their clothes from the floor and began dressing.

"I will not tell anyone of your vision," he said, slipping his tunic on. "But if you will agree, I would like to seek some information about where this threat might be coming from. It may have to do with the things your brother spoke of yesterday."

She nodded. "And you will let me know what you find out?"

"Yes, my sweet," he said, kissing her neck and making her shiver as she was doing her best to tie her skirt cords.

"I had better go speak to Our Lady." She twirled a lock of his hair with her finger, not looking particularly eager to leave. "It is my responsibility as a priestess to take care of our people."

"Will you at least have breakfast with me first?" he asked.

"How can I say no, when dinner last night was so delicious?"

Chapter 16

"The Grain Mother's star has appeared!" the High Priestess cried out as Orestas, the Chief Sky-Watcher, made the sacred sign toward the eastern horizon. The lay people and clergy shouted in celebration, their voices rolling across the freshly-plowed field in the dawning light. "Let us plant her seeds and grow her crops so the Daughter may return from the World Below with the first green sprouts that push up through the Earth!"

Aria cheered along with the others, shaking her sistrum as eight young men in bull masks—one for each of the winds—arrayed themselves along the edge of the field, their seed pouches at the ready. Then, as Aria and the others began a steady rhythm on sistrums and drums, the men advanced across the field in a row, scattering seeds over the rich soil.

Ten days earlier, at the first dawn rising of the Torch—young Dionysus' star—Aria and the other clergy had blessed the fields with the blood-and-wine mixture from the Summer Solstice bull sacrifice. Then the Consort as Iacchus, Dionysus' youthful face, was himself blessed with that liquid. At that time he took up a torch and held it aloft, leading the procession to the sacred cave where the ten-day-long Mysteries took place. There the people—all the people, men and women, rich and poor, clergy and laity, slave and free—received the wisdom of the Great Mother and the Daughter, the knowledge of eternal life and eternal love.

Now the Great Mother had returned from the World Below, where she had gone to seek out her daughter. The Mother's star — the Ear of Grain shining in the dawn sky just before sunrise — heralded the time of planting so the Daughter could return to the World Above with the first green sprouts of barley. And so they celebrated, the priesthood and the people together, their feet pressing against the Great Mother's body as they sang to her, the song of the rising of the grain and the greening of the fields, the song of abundance and blessing and life.

The young men in the bull masks reached the far side of the field and stopped, still in a row, holding their bags of seed that were not quite empty yet. Aria wondered if one of them was her son, but there was no way of knowing. If her counting was correct, he would be thirteen now, barely old enough to participate. Rhea's boy was only eleven, not yet eligible. One of the young men was the Consort, she knew, but with their heads completely covered by the huge horned masks, they were not easily distinguishable.

Aria shook her head, annoyed at herself for continually comparing herself to Rhea, or at least, her motherhood to her friend's. The envy had slowly died away over the years but still, she found it hard to think of her own son without Rhea's boy rising up in her thoughts at the same time. And then, inevitably, her thoughts would stray to Rhea's son growing up, growing old... when her son never would.

The bull-masked figures strode away in a line toward Daipita, who stood next to four large jars, and Aria returned her attention to the rite. Ten days earlier, those same men had dug the jars up from the corners of the field, removed their contents, and scoured them clean. Now each jar contained a layer of honey, freshly gathered from the temple hives and blessed to the ancestors, the Melissae, and the Mother-and-Daughter.

As the people watched, the men poured their remaining seeds into the jars, two men for each vessel. Daipita stirred the seeds into the honey then placed close-fitting lids on the jars. Now the singing stopped, and the drums and sistrums fell silent. Each pair of men hefted their jar and carried it to the corner of the field that corresponded to the winds they represented. There, with great reverence, they lowered each jar into the hole it had come out of and covered it over once again with soil. These seeds would not sprout, but would lie waiting in the Earth as if they were outside of time, beacons of promise from the ancestors for the reverence the people gave them.

When the men were done with their task, they returned to the edge of the field where they had begun and knelt before eight elder women who held baskets of soil from their own fields. For most of Aria's life, the women who performed this part of the ritual had been priestesses who held the stewardship of temple lands—not because this was a ceremony meant for the clergy alone, but simply because the practice had fallen out of fashion with the local people. They no longer bothered to travel from their farms for the rite, even if doing so would bring a blessing on their crops. If they had enough seed of their own, they had no reason to attend.

The leaders at Knossos had long since ceased to bless their fields to the ancestors, the Mother, and the Daughter. For them, all that remained of the ritual was the blooding of the fields in honor of the Horned One, an act they restricted to men only, and the priesthood at that. The ordinary people were not allowed to attend the rite. And Knossos no longer provided blessed seed to the local farmers, either. It should be no surprise, Eileithyia had said when she explained the situation to Aria. It had been some time since Knossos had held a public feast or shared their grain and oil stores with the poor, either. They had abandoned the old ways in favor of hoarding their wealth behind the walls of their temple, keeping themselves separate from the people.

In the time since Aria had shared her vision of the attack on Malia with Eileithyia, the High Priestess had made it her business to include the people of the city and the surrounding countryside in as many temple rites as possible. With the help of Sageleus, Ytanos, and a few other prominent townsfolk, she had ensured the continuation of the public feasts that filled the west plaza. For this rite in particular, the promise of temple-blessed seed plus a feast afterward worked to draw the people in.

So on this warm autumn morning, with the mist rising through the dawn air, Aria looked across the largest crowd this rite had seen since she was born. The elder women who stood at the edge of the field were not priestesses but lay people, farmers and landowners from the countryside all around Malia, bringing the soil from their own land to bless the temple's field and be blessed in return.

The Chief Song-Priestess and Priest began a new chant. The sistrums and drums took up a fresh rhythm as the elder women began their slow walk across the field, scattering soil from their baskets to cover the freshly-sown seed. In the crowd, many more women chanted together, singing the sacred into their own lives so they could take the blessing back to their farms and families when the rite was done.

Once the elder women had crossed the field, a line of young girls formed where the women had begun, girls who had just reached the time of their first blood. Again the song and the rhythm changed. The girls danced across the field, pressing the seeds and the newly-sprinkled soil into the Earth with their bare feet. Their skirts billowed out around them, the tiers floating in the air as they leapt and turned about, crying out their joy with the people and the land.

Next came a row of nursing mothers, breasts full and leaking, pouring out a white liquid from large flagons: goat's milk and cow's milk in which coriander seeds had been steeped. They strode across the field, adding their magic to the soil as the rest of the gathering chanted the blessings of the Three upon the land.

Finally the last group stood at the edge of the field: a row of pregnant women, their round bellies bared, their breasts heavy with the promise of nourishment for their babies, a reminder of the sustenance the Great Mother provides for all her children. As the sistrums and drums played and the people sang, the women walked out to the center of the field and stopped. There, they squatted and urinated on the soil, the blessing of the Earth Mother who is pregnant with the new crop. They continued on to the far side of the field and joined the crowd there, all chanting the song of planting-time.

Now the High Priestess stepped up to the edge of the field, flanked by the men in bull masks. She raised her arms up in the sign of the goddess, and the crowd fell silent.

"We have planted the crop," she said, her voice carrying across the field and the crowd that surrounded it. "We have given the ancestors their portion. We have blessed the seeds and the soil. Now we wait." The crowd stood silent as a crow called in the distance. "We await the return of the Daughter, who climbs up from the Land of the Dead with the green sprouts of new grain on the Day of Balance. She rises with the green growing things, birthed from Ida herself, borne upward by the ancestors on whose shoulders we stand."

A collective cry went up from the crowd. The sistrums rattled and the drums boomed. When the ruckus died down to a steady beat, the High Priestess turned and strode back along the edge of the field, followed by the men in bull masks, heading toward the temple and the feast that awaited. The crowd fell in behind them, singing the song of plenty, moving toward the meal they would share together as a community on the west plaza in honor of the ancestors and the gods.

Aria looked forward to the banquet, but more than that, she looked forward to meeting up with Sageleus afterward. When he had told her he was planning to attend the rite of love after the feast, she could not hold back her smile. Maybe this time, she would get pregnant.

Chapter 17

"Approach," the High Priestess said from her seat on the dais in the audience chamber. The Consort stood next to her, partner and protector of the Great Mother's representative on Earth.

Straightening up to her full height, Aria walked across the hall, doing her best to be graceful. She stopped a short distance from the dais. "My Lady," she said, making the salute. "My Lord."

Until this morning, Aria had always met Eileithyia in the High Priestess' workroom. That was how her day as a temple priestess began, every morning for years now. After breakfast, instead of reporting to Daipita as the other women did, or perhaps to the Chief Scrivener, the Chief Song-Priestess, or the Chief Sky-Watcher depending on a priestess' specialty, she went to Eileithyia's workroom to discuss her activities of the previous day and receive her new assignments. She wondered if perhaps the High Priestess intended to create a new position in the temple and make Aria her assistant. Surely this kind of attention meant she was destined for a special office of some sort. She had seen her own anointing in a vision, so it must be true.

As they were finishing their meeting the day before, the High Priestess had told Aria to come to the audience chamber this morning instead. So now she stood before the dais, wondering what on Earth the High Priestess could mean by this change, and by having the Consort there to witness their conversation. Was Eileithyia going to confer some special honor on her?

"Tell me," Eileithyia said, "what you have learned in your time as a priestess."

Aria's eyes widened. "So many things, My Lady. I do not know where to begin."

"Then tell me what you know how to do."

"I know how to write," Aria said, her gaze flicking to the Consort and back to the High Priestess. They were both smiling, friendly, but somehow this felt like a test. "Thalamika instructed me well and continues to praise my work at the scribal table on Offering Days. Thanks to Sageleus I can do sums, even with fractions. And I know about herbs, but not nearly as much as the Medicine-Priestess does." She thought a moment. "I know how to organize and store the offerings that people bring to the temple and how to keep the records for them."

The High Priestess and the Consort exchanged glances. "And this is what being a priestess means to you?" Eileithyia asked.

Aria swallowed, suddenly panicked. "No, My Lady. I mean, that is not all there is to being a priestess. But you asked me what I know how to do."

"Do you not also know how to take part in the temple rites from one season to the next?"

"Of course I do." She sucked in a sharp breath. "Yes, My Lady, I know how to take part in the rites the whole year round. I have learned all the rituals that I am qualified to participate in. Those are things only a priestess can do." *A real priestess*, the thought came unbidden. Was she a real priestess now? She did not feel like it yet.

"And which is more important," Eileithyia asked, "the scribing and herbs and offerings or the rituals and ceremonies?"

Aria clasped her hands together while she struggled to determine the correct answer to the question.

"Well?" the High Priestess pressed.

"They are all important," Aria blurted out. "I think they are all important."

Eileithyia scowled. "Tell me why."

"Because..." Aria squared her shoulders. If the High Priestess was going to berate her, then let it be for an honest answer. "Because we honor the gods with the rites, and only the priesthood can do that. Only we can keep the gods happy and secure our traditions to keep our people safe and prosperous. But..." She pressed her lips together. "Without the offerings, and the scribes to keep track of them, and the people to store and organize them, the temple could not function. And without the herbs, the priesthood could not stay healthy to do their jobs. It is all important."

"It seems you have learned something in your time here," the High Priestess said. Aria let out a breath. "But you still have much more to discover."

Eileithyia nodded to the Consort, who smiled at Aria. "Today we will visit the temple workshops," he said.

"We?" Aria asked, looking back and forth between the two on the dais.

"You and I," the Consort said. "Our Lady has pressing business this morning."

"But..."

Eileithyia stood up. "Belisseus is my partner. He is my voice when I am not present. And he knows almost as much about this temple as I do."

Aria was startled to see the High Priestess wink at her Consort. He responded with a wry smile, taking her hand and gently kissing it, looking up at her through his eyelashes.

"Close your mouth, Ariadne," Eileithyia said with a smirk. "We are human, too. Now go and learn."

She waved them away. The Consort stepped down off the dais, heading for the doorway, and gestured for Aria to join him. Halfway across the room, Aria looked back over her shoulder to see the High Priestess seated again, bent over a leaf of papyrus, studying it intently while a young priest ushered several of Eileithyia's lay advisors into the audience chamber.

Aria and the Consort exited the room and crossed the north court. They stopped in front of the row of rooms that housed the indoor workshops.

"Our Lady tells me that you have met many of the artisans in the city."

"I have," Aria said. "Sageleus knows them all, and he has introduced me to them."

"Now you will meet the skilled folk who make things for the temple." He gestured at an open doorway through which bundles of drying herbs were visible. "I assume you are already acquainted with the medicine room?"

"Of course," Aria said. No one survived beyond infancy without the help of the Medicine-Priestess or one of her lay counterparts in the city.

"Then let us discover some new wonders."

He led her through the workrooms one at a time, beginning with the weavers and spinners, introducing her to each of the artisans in turn. Each specialty had its own chief, usually a lay person who was a master of the craft. Then from the priesthood were chosen two Overseers of the Workshops, a man and a woman. These Aria already knew, but the artisans were new acquaintances for her.

The warp-weighted looms leaned against the walls, taller than the weaving-women's heads. They worked fine linen and wool into beautiful fabric of many different colors, some of it plain but some with special designs woven in. It was the fashion among Ida's children to decorate their clothing with paint or embroidery, and these could indeed be magical when done correctly: lilies for the Great Mother's blessing, spirals for prosperity, stars with a certain number of points to call on Kalliste, or Ourania, or the Star of the Sea. But nothing matched a woven-in design for the pure power of its magic, built right into the material itself. And some designs, only the priestesses were allowed to weave, though many of the workers here were lay women.

Of course, Aria knew that the colors mattered as well. Some of the fabric was dyed after being woven, but for the intricate bands that decorated so much of their clothing, the yarn was dyed before the weaving was done. Every color had its own meaning, as did every shape and pattern. A red rosette did not have the same meaning as a blue rosette or a red spiral. The weavers' fingers flew across the looms, lifting threads one at a time to create complex designs or sliding a shuttle across a whole row for a plain weave, then beating the threads in place with carved wooden combs.

Once the fabric was woven, the sewing-women would cut and stitch it to make the ritual garments and daily wear for the temple clergy. All the linen and wool cloth that the temple needed for clothing, furnishings, ritual use, and decoration was woven in this workshop. In good years, there was fabric to spare that could be sold in the local market and sometimes, from there, traded across the sea.

Aria watched in amazement as several women spun linen thread so fine it looked almost like strands of hair, their drop spindles twirling beneath agile hands. She peered through the open doorway in the outer wall to see the dyers' vats in the yard beyond, simmering over hot coals and full to the brim with deeply colored liquids. As Aria watched, one dye-spattered woman heaved a length of sopping wet, pale green wool fabric out of a large vat, pressed the excess liquid out, and hung it up to dry.

"Come," the Consort said, "we will visit the outdoor areas shortly. First let us see all the workrooms."

Aria followed him to a room full of men and women carving small vessels from stone: alabaster, steatite, serpentine, even quartz. Shards of stone and bits of stone powder gritted beneath her feet as she moved closer to watch one man grind the center out of a chunk of greenish serpentine that would soon become a small bowl. The Consort introduced Aria to each of the artisans in turn. She began to grow tired of having so many people stop their work and make the salute to her. But then she realized this was an easy way to remember which ones were priesthood and which were lay people, since the clergy did not always wear distinctive garments.

Beyond the stonecarvers' room lay the workshop of the jewelry-makers. Here they carved and polished tiny bits of garnet, lapis, jasper, and amethyst into beads of all shapes and sizes, then strung them onto necklaces along with beautiful molded gold beads and pendants. Just outside the workshop, through the open doorway, lay the precious metalsmiths' work area. Here, hot coals allowed the smiths to melt gold and silver and pour it into tiny stone molds to make beads and the occasional commission of a gold seal ring.

Even more amazing to Aria was the workshop of the seal-stone carvers. Here, they worked with tiny hand drills while peering through small quartz lenses that made the thumbnail-sized stones look larger so they could see to carve the designs. As with so many rooms in the temple, sunlight streamed in from the openings high in the walls, giving the artisans a brightly-lit work space. Still, Aria marveled that they could create such small works of art.

"Please," she said as they stepped out of the seal-stone carvers' workshop, "may I have a moment? That is too many names to learn so fast."

"You do not need to know all their names," Belisseus said. "What is important is that they know you. Come, let us see the outdoor workshops."

Puzzled, Aria followed him out the side entrance and into the work-yard. She looked down the length of the temple wall and saw the goldsmiths working, then the dyers, and beyond them, the herb garden. The Consort drew her attention in the other direction, though. Along the wall, open-sided sheds housed potters and bronze-smiths plying their trades. By sacred tradition, the potters were all women and the smiths were all men, like the Hekaterides and the Daktyls: two different ways of using fire to transform the Great Mother's body into something beautiful and useful.

Waves of heat wafted toward Aria as she passed kilns and smithing-fires, greeting each artisan as Belisseus introduced her to them. Finally they stopped, looking out toward the city.

"There is more than just these workers," Aria said. "We make wine and oil, do we not? And we grow produce and grain." She peered around, seeing nothing else along this side of the temple. "I know we store grain, wine, and oil in the temple, but where do they come from? Where are they produced?"

The Consort nodded, smiling. "My Lady was right. You think deeply about everything."

"Is that bad?"

"No, not at all. And you are right. Our people make many things we do not see here." He gestured toward the south, to the far end of the temple that faced the fields and vineyards and farmland that rolled up toward the hills. "They brew the wine in those buildings at the edge of the vineyard. That way they do not have to carry the grapes too far."

"Do they press the oil by the olive grove?"

"Indeed, and they preserve the olives there as well. Much is done outside the temple walls, but it is still a part of our works. And some of it, you would not want to be near."

"Oh?" Aria looked across the yard, wondering what could be so bad that she would not want to see it, to meet the people who worked so hard in the name of the temple.

"The tannery," Belisseus said. He pinched his nose shut and screwed up his face. "Trust me, you do not want to know what that smells like."

The Consort laughed, and Aria laughed with him. She felt her shoulders relax down, when she had not even realized she was tense.

"Thank you," she said. "This has been most pleasant."

"You sound surprised."

Aria looked away, hoping the hot feeling in her cheeks did not mean she was blushing. "I did not know what to expect. I do not know you very well."

"You thought I would be... harsh? Unkind?"

She shrugged. "I thought Our Lady made you do this because she did not want to. Because she is tired of dealing with me. And I thought perhaps you would not want to put up with me either."

"Why on Earth would you think such a thing?"

"Is that not why she sent me out to spend time with Sageleus? To get rid of me for a while?"

Belisseus shook his head.

"Then why?" Aria asked. "It is bad enough that she does not allow me to be a normal priestess. I am beginning to feel that her interest in me is not to instruct me, but to punish me. But I do not understand what I have done to deserve such punishment." She folded her arms and stared out across the city, toward the sea.

"Does she want me to meet all these merchants and artisans because she thinks I should take up a trade and not be a priestess?"

"Did she ever say that?"

"Before my initiation, Daipita asked me whether I wanted to move in with my brother, take up a trade... maybe Our Lady thought that is what I should do. Maybe she still thinks so."

"Trust me," the Consort said. "Our Lady thinks very highly of you. That is why she instructs you herself. You are special and she knows it."

She blew out a breath. "I wish it felt that way to me."

Chapter 18

The line of priestesses shifted, and Aria moved forward across the courtyard, quietly chanting to the Three Mothers. Shortly, the doors to the hypostyle hall opened, and the women filed in, lining up along the wall, still chanting. The doors closed, and they were left in a dim, smoky room that smelled of lamp oil and incense, the sound of their chanting muffled in the depths of the hall.

In the middle of the room stood an altar between two columns, and behind the altar stood Rhea, her figure haloed by the light of two oil lamps. She was wearing the simple tunic of the new initiate, with no jewelry and no decorations in her hair. Her plain clothing contrasted with the fancy tiered skirts and jewelry that all the other women were wearing, including the High Priestess, who stood next to her.

A gong chimed and the women around the edge of the room fell silent, all making the salute. Aria drew in a deep breath, inhaling the incense smoke that hung thick in the air. She hoped it would allow her to relax enough to look like she meant Rhea well. Participating in this rite was her duty, and she had no intention of shirking her obligations or letting anyone think she was less than worthy as a priestess, regardless of the circumstances.

When Aria's attention finally returned to the ritual hall, the High Priestess was pouring a libation to the Three: milk, honey, and wine, decanted slowly into a triple-bowl libation table on the altar. When she was done, she set the last pitcher down and raised her arms up in the gesture that invites the goddesses to join their children.

"Great Mothers," she said, "your daughters have need of a new Head of the College of Priestesses. We have called one from among ourselves to take on that role. We ask your blessing on her and her work."

The High Priestess turned to Rhea, still speaking so the whole room could hear her. "The anointing is the outward sign of the blessing the Great Mothers give, which cannot be removed once it has been accepted. I ask you now, Rhea, daughter of Divia, do you accept this office? Do you choose it above all other paths in your life, giving yourself to it fully and freely?"

Rhea drew in a slow breath. "I do." Her words were loud enough to hear clearly, but her voice shook as she spoke.

The High Priestess moved behind Rhea, holding her hands over the younger priestess' head, palms down. "Bless her, Great Ladies, Mistresses of the Three Realms. Let her work be yours."

Rhea shivered, her trembling visible even in the dim, smoky room. Slowly her arms rose up into the goddess pose as her breathing grew labored and raspy. Eileithyia pressed her palms down on the top of Rhea's head, and the younger woman's eyes rolled back in her head. She wobbled for a moment, then steadied, finally opening her eyes and drawing in a shaky breath. The High Priestess lifted her hands from Rhea's head and reached for a small alabastron that sat on the altar.

"The Three have blessed you," Eileithyia said. "Witness now the ancient rite of anointing. This woman, Rhea, daughter of Divia, receives the blessing of the temple, which is the blessing of the gods themselves. She accepts the office which is offered to her. She goes willingly."

She dipped her fingers into the jar and smeared the anointing oil on Rhea's forehead, her lips, and the spot between her breasts, making the sign of the Three in each place. "We seal that blessing within you, that you may do their work in this world. May you be blessed, Rhea. May you walk in the grace and the love of the gods every day of your life. May your life and your work be a blessing to your people." The High Priestess took a step back, smiled softly, and made the salute to Rhea, acknowledging her accession to the office.

A sistrum began a rattling rhythm, and the Chief Song-Priestess started up the chant to the Three. The others joined in, the chant swelling as the voices combined.

By land and sky and sea
Blessed be the Three
By land and sea and sky
By Them we live and die
By sky and sea and land
Beneath Their guiding hand

Finally the chant ended, the last sounds muffled in the smoky room.

"Behold," Eileithyia cried out, "the anointed one! I give you Rhea, daughter of Divia, Head of the College of Priestesses in the temple of Malia."

One by one, each of the priestesses stepped up to the new Head of the College, saluted her, then moved back to her place along the wall. When it came time for Aria's turn, she forced a faint smile, though she could feel her chin trembling, tears threatening to spill. She made the salute without making eye contact with either Rhea or the High Priestess, then crossed back to her spot along the wall as fast as she could, thanking the gods that this rite took place in a dimly-lit room.

When all the priestesses had acknowledged the new Head of their College, the doors swung open, and the men entered: all the male clergy plus Kaeseus, the Head of the College of Priests. They arranged themselves in a ring around the room, in front of the priestesses, and Kaeseus stepped up to salute his new counterpart. One by one the priests acknowledged her, honoring her new position in the temple. When the last one was stepping toward the altar, Aria realized that she had not even noticed when Lexion took his turn.

Once they had all finished and moved back to their places, a gong chimed again. Eileithyia wrapped one arm around Rhea's shoulders and raised the other in an expansive gesture toward the clergy. "The Great Mothers have sanctified our new Head of the College of Priestesses. Let us celebrate this blessing together!"

The sistrum rattled, the gong chimed over and over, and all the clergy cheered their new leader. Then the High Priestess and Rhea led the procession out of the ritual hall and into the courtyard, where a celebratory feast awaited them.

* * *

"Come eat," Thalamika said, motioning to one of the tables as she walked past Aria to find a place at a table.

"I thought I might visit Daipita," Aria replied from her spot beneath the portico, where she still hovered near the doorway she had just come out of. The elderly priestess Aria had just named lay in a bed in the Medicine-Priestess' herbarium, slowly dying, while her new replacement sat at the head table in the courtyard.

Aria glanced over to where Rhea sat, basking in the sunshine, surrounded by her sister priestesses and brother priests, all enjoying the feast that followed the rite of installation. Since Rhea was now the Head of the College of Priestesses, there were plenty who wanted to curry favor with her. Aria was not among them. Having to participate in the ritual was bad enough, but she refused to shirk her duty as a priestess. The feast afterward, however, was optional.

The Head of each College was always elected by secret ballot. That was their way. But Aria was certain Eileithyia had engineered Rhea's succession. The High Priestess had great influence in the temple, much more than she let on, Aria had discovered.

Aria recalled a conversation with Eileithyia and some of the other priestesses, around the time Daipita fell ill and it became obvious she would not recover. When the topic of the next Head of the College had arisen, Eileithyia had slipped her arm around Aria's shoulders and said, "Our Ariadne is destined for great things." She had given the others a meaningful look, and then they had begun offering possible names for the next Head, with Rhea as the main contender. The list had not included Aria, when she had thought this was the office the High Priestess was preparing her for. Why else would she set her aside for personal instruction?

A hand touched Aria's arm, and she snapped out of her brooding thoughts. "Mama."

"Come join us," Inia said. "I'm sure Rhea would appreciate your congratulations. I suspect she is feeling a bit overwhelmed at the prospect of this new position."

"As well she should," Aria snapped. "She was not the best choice."

Inia gasped. "You cannot mean that. We chose her because she is dedicated and hard working and practical. She never shirks, and she is kind to everyone. Our Lady agrees, we are lucky to have her as our Head."

Just then Eileithyia looked over and caught Aria's eye. The High Priestess raised her eyebrows, a look that questioned the younger priestess' behavior, standing separate from the feast instead of joining her friend in celebration. Aria's eyes narrowed and her brow furrowed.

"You are right, Mama. I have no reason to be upset with Rhea. None at all."

Aria gave her mother a kiss on the cheek then strode over to the head table.

"May I offer my little sister congratulations?" she said, a bit too loudly.

Rhea stood up, beaming. She and Aria hugged, holding tight to each other for several long moments.

"Thank you so much!" Rhea said when they separated. "Please sit with me. I am afraid I have no idea what I am doing just yet. I could use a little encouragement."

The other priestesses shifted down the bench to make room for Aria. She served herself some stewed mutton, roasted onions, and barley bread, and ate heartily. Though she couldn't bring herself to smile much, she listened intently to the conversation around her and refilled Rhea's wine cup when it ran empty. She was careful to avoid Eileithyia's gaze, which was not difficult since the High Priestess was seated some distance down the same side of the table, next to Thalamika.

"So," Rhea said as she picked over a platter of dried fruit, "how is Sageleus?"

Aria tried not to grin but failed completely. "He is well."

"How well?" Rhea's gaze dipped down to Aria's belly.

Aria shook her head.

"Well, you must keep trying," Rhea said softly. "I am sure he does not mind." She gave her friend a sly sideways look, and Aria could not help but laugh.

"No, he does not." She drew in a slow breath, realizing how much she enjoyed having the man in her life. He was a delicious lover, of course. And much to Aria's surprise, very soon after they had begun spending the night together whenever Aria's sacred obligations allowed, Sageleus had declared his intent to lie with no one but her. It had taken her a few moments to realize the import of his announcement, but once she did, she returned the declaration. Though she could not oath herself to him the way some people did with their partners—her vows to the temple superseded any others—she was more than willing to dedicate herself privately to him alone.

In addition to the time they spent together in private, he had introduced her to practically the whole population of Malia, slowly and steadily, a few at a time. She was grateful to him for helping her learn how to deal equably with all kinds of people, from the poorest fishermen to the wealthiest merchants and artisans. He always knew what to say to put people at ease, and she was an avid student of his methods. For the first time in her life, she could expect to feel comfortable in casual conversations and social situations regardless of who she was with or what they were talking about.

But more than that, she appreciated that Sageleus treated her simply as a woman, not a priestess. It felt marvelous to be on equal footing with him and not up on a pedestal like she was with the rest of the local people. When she had chosen to become a priestess, she had not realized the extent to which the position would separate her from the lay people. Some days, she felt that if no one ever saluted her again, she would not mind.

Though Rhea laughed at her own comment about Sageleus, Aria could see the shadow of loneliness in her friend's eyes. With sudden resolve, Aria scanned the length of the table. She waited until he turned his head in her direction, then caught Lexion's gaze and motioned to Rhea with a slight tilt of her head and a sidelong glance. He looked the question at her, and she nodded toward Rhea again. A few moments later, he was standing beside the two of them, chatting with them and apologizing for not offering his congratulations to the new Head of the College of Priestesses earlier. For her part, the new Head was spending a lot of time stammering and fidgeting with a barley loaf.

"If you will excuse me," Aria said, standing up, "I am overtired from the day's events. I should go rest so I can perform my duties properly tomorrow."

She leaned down and gave Rhea a brief hug and a kiss on the cheek. Then she motioned Lexion into her seat and walked toward the hypostyle hall. When she reached the doorway, she looked back to see the two of them laughing, his hand atop hers on the table.

Chapter 19

They strode along the Dikte Road heading south, a handful of the Malia clergy laden with bags and baskets. The afternoon sunlight slanted down on them, the weather still warm two days after the Autumn Equinox. Aria found herself breathing harder as the road angled up toward the mountains.

"You have Our Lady's seal?" Lexion asked, falling in step beside her.

"I do." She patted the bag that was slung over her shoulder. It held a wool cloak, the seal in its small box, her ankle bells, and a skin of well-diluted wine. She also carried a basket full of small jars, offerings to be made at the rites.

Of the four clergy members in the group, Aria was the youngest. The High Priestess had only convinced her to go by insisting that she carry the temple's traveling seal that would officially identify them to the priesthood when they arrived at their destination: the cave shrine on Mt. Dikte. Of course, Inia, Lexion, and Orestas had made the trip before, so they were known to the clergy who were resident at the cave shrine. But the group would still make the proper gestures. That was their way. And Eileithyia had insisted that it was important for Aria to meet the priesthood at the cave.

Aria hoped the High Priestess was not simply trying to get rid of her so Rhea and Kaeseus could organize the temple's celebration of the new year without her. Apparently Eileithyia was not happy with the way Rhea leaned on Aria so often for support. The High Priestess insisted that the Head of the College of Priestesses should be able to do her job alone, and this was as good a time as any to give her that opportunity. Aria wished Lexion had chosen to stay back at the temple to give Rhea confidence, but she guessed that Eileithyia had pushed him to make the trip as well. The High Priestess was adamant about the clergy of her temple "growing their own wings," as she so often said.

Aria squinted toward the mountain in the distance, their destination. The new year rites at the cave shrine would be different from the ones at the temple, though it was the same festival. Eileithyia had explained this just before the group set out, insisting that the trip was part of Aria's education as a priestess. Back at the temple, they would perform a mystery play on the west plaza, followed by a feast with music and dancing. These were public events, open to anyone who cared to attend—and the plaza would be packed this year, thanks to the High Priestess' efforts with the local population.

Of course, the clergy, including Aria, had already undertaken the private ceremonies within the temple, open only to the priesthood and a few select lay people, on the day of the Autumn Equinox itself. But the larger celebration would occur at the exact moment of the new year: the first appearance of Diktynna's bow after the equinox, its gleaming edge touching the horizon as the Sun sets.

The shrine on Mt. Dikte was much smaller than Malia's temple, just one main building next to the cave itself, fronted by a small plaza with a central altar. Aria had no idea what the rite would look like, but she knew that few would attend. The trek up the mountain was arduous. The events at the temples and sacred houses were easier to access for all but the most rural farmers and shepherds.

The group slowed as they passed the narrow, jutting peak of Karphi. The road sloped up even more steeply between stands of fir trees. A rabbit scampered out of the way as the travelers came around a curve, and a hawk cried out from above, raising goosebumps on Aria's arms. She stopped for a moment and looked up to see the bird wheeling through the blue sky, sailing between the mountain peaks.

Smiling, she drew in a breath and continued up the sloping road. With his long legs, Lexion easily outpaced her, moving ahead of her as she drew the wine skin from her bag and took a drink. She watched him walk, his calves flexing above the leather ties that held his boots up. A faint, sad longing pricked at her heart. She had wanted him once, badly. But now, she could not identify what she felt for him, if anything at all. All she knew was that there was an emptiness inside her. Sageleus distracted her from it, and perhaps he had filled it to some extent. But there was still something missing. Whether the emptiness was in the shape of a man, a woman, or a child, or something else entirely, she could not say.

As the edge of the Sun touched the horizon, Aria and the others climbed the final segment of the path and came out on the plaza at the cave shrine, breathing hard and wiping the sweat from their faces. The area was half-full of people, perhaps thirty or so, with a few more still making their way up the mountainside. Colorful banners hung along the front of the shrine building and long tables loaded with food lined one edge of the plaza. On the other side, a huge bonfire was stacked, ready to be lit. The cave itself beckoned, its entrance dark like the night, framed above and to the sides with abundant swags of greenery. It looked to Aria as if the Mountain Mother herself was presenting her vulva to the people, the blessing of ever-renewing life.

"Come," Inia said. "We must make ourselves known."

She led the group around the edge of the plaza toward the shrine building. Anyone who cared to make the journey was welcome to attend public rituals at the cave, so there were lay people milling around the plaza. But clergy often traveled to other temples and shrines for the sacred festivals, as well as visiting in between times. They were expected to announce themselves to the resident priesthood on arrival so they could be treated appropriately.

A woman came out of the building carrying an armload of greenery, branches of the evergreen holm oak—a reminder of the blessings of life in death, the peace of the ancestors and the World Below.

"Inia!" she cried. "How good to see you!"

Inia waited for the woman to put down the greens, then she greeted the Head Priestess of the shrine with a hug and a kiss. While Inia introduced the other members of their group, Aria fumbled in her bag, trying to dig out the box with the seal in it. But it had become entangled in the bands for her ankle bells.

She finally managed to pull the box out, but not before dumping the bells onto the ground, where they chimed and clanged as they rolled around. Mortified, she snatched the bells back up and stuffed them into the bag, then held out the seal to the Head Priestess.

"Our Lady sends her greetings and blessings," she said, making the salute as her cheeks burned.

"You are all welcome," the priestess said with a smile. "The blessings of the Mothers be upon you. We must keep our ways alive in spite of those who would replace the sacred with the profane."

"Or the purely profitable," Inia said.

"Indeed. We value the gifts from the gods who have been so generous with us, and we share them with others so all may be blessed."

"Our Lady offers her hospitality whenever you and your brother and sister clergy care to visit," Inia said. "We look forward to celebrating the turn of the year with you."

The Head Priestess gathered up her greens once more. "Please find a place with the other visiting clergy. If you will excuse me, I still have some tasks to attend to."

Aria followed the others around the edge of the plaza until they found a good spot from which to view the rites. Visiting priests and priestesses were clustered along the side of the plaza nearest the altar, with the lay people spread out behind them. Aria's group set down their bags and baskets in a pile to one side and turned to the stacks of greenery that dotted the plaza.

The shrine clergy had spent several days cutting more than enough leafy branches for the number of visitors they expected. Aria and her companions clustered around a pile of greenery, nodding their greetings to several lay travelers who were already selecting their choices. Aria recognized slim stems of laurel, holm oak, and cypress as well as several others she could not place. She picked up two long, supple stems and began to twist them into a curve. She added more greenery as she went, winding the pieces together until she had a thick, leafy crown that fit her head just right. By the time she had finished hers, the others were done as well. This was one skill all of Ida's children possessed, clergy and laity alike, for they began making leaf and flower crowns, and flower necklaces, practically as soon as they were able to walk.

Stroking her creation with approval, Inia moved back over to the group's collection of belongings and perched her crown atop her bag. Then she dragged two large baskets away from the rest of the pile and began sorting through the contents. Nodding her satisfaction, she turned to the others.

"I am going to deliver our first offerings to the shrine. I will return here again in time for the rite. Would one of you please help me with the baskets?"

"My Lady," Orestas said, "may I join you? I visited here years ago, before I trained as a Sky-Watcher. I would like to speak with the Sky-Watcher here, if I may."

Inia smiled. "I should have expected you would want to talk shop. Very well, come on."

They hefted the baskets and moved away through the small crowd. Aria turned back to Lexion, wondering what she was supposed to do now. The people on the plaza had collected themselves into small groups, some of them sitting on their bags and bundles along the edge of the paved area, some standing, but all positioned well back from the side of the plaza where the bonfire lay stacked and ready.

"You have been here before," she said to Lexion.

"But not for the rite of the new year," he replied. "I am looking forward to it."

"I hear it is different from our rites back home."

"Not as much as you might think," he said. "We all celebrate the same things, all over our Mother's island, just in different ways.

Though of course our temple does not have a real cave, only the adyton." He narrowed his eyes at her. "You wish you had not come."

"The equinoxes are our most sacred times: the new year and the harvest. I do not like to be away from home for them." She clasped her hands together to keep herself from folding her arms over her chest like a petulant child.

Lexion covered a smile with his hand. "She will be fine, Aria."

"I never said…"

"If there is any problem at all, Our Lady will take care of her. I promise."

Together they watched as the last glowing edge of the Sun slid below the horizon and the sky shifted from pale blue to darker blue and then to a soft indigo. The scent of incense drifted through the air. Then Inia and Orestas reappeared through the crowd. They retrieved their leafy crowns, put them on, and took their places as torches burst into flame around the edge of the plaza. Aria fitted her crown over her hair, pulling it down tightly so it would not fly off when she moved.

Bells jingled and sistrums rattled deep within the cave, the sound echoing outward across the plaza. Goosebumps rose on Aria's arms, and a hush fell over the gathered crowd. The Head Priestess emerged from the cave, followed by the shrine's Sky-Watcher priestess. Together they strode to the edge of the plaza and sighted across the mountaintops. Long moments crept by as the Sky-Watcher peered intently at the silver crescent in the darkening sky. Then its shining edge touched the top of the sacred mountain. She nodded to the Head Priestess, who raised her arms to the sky. A triton trumpet rang out, three long blasts that echoed through the mountains.

The Head Priestess held a torch to the edge of the bonfire and it roared to life, flames cascading up the huge pile of dry wood. She tossed the torch into the fire, turning to the people gathered on the plaza.

"The new year has begun!" she cried out. "Sun and Moon of one accord! Praise to all the gods and goddesses!"

Drums pulsed, sistrums rattled, and the people began to dance. Aria recognized the rhythm. Each different beat had its own meaning, drawing the dancers to different places, connecting them with different gods and goddesses. On this night, the drums sang out the new year, the Sun and Moon dancing together, the Fire-Mother and her Silver Brother turning and turning against the Mother-of-All's field of stars.

Aria stepped to one side and drew her ritual bells out of her bag. Inia did likewise. Inia was already up and dancing by the time Aria had untangled the bands on her set of bells. The small bronze bells were sewn along a piece of narrow woven linen, much like the decorative bands the women wore along the edges of their bodices. But this one had no colorful design, just the plain texture of the linen itself. A color would have designated the bells for a particular use or a specific festival. With a plain band, the bells could be used any time. Aria wrapped the bells around her ankles, crossing the bands up her calves and tying them off securely. Then she stepped out into the plaza to join the others.

Skirts swirled and feet stomped as flutes and lyres joined in the music. Like Aria, many of the priestesses wore ankle bells. Some of them, along with the visiting lay women, also played small bronze or ivory finger cymbals, chiming in time with the beat. The men slapped their hands on their thighs and played wooden clackers and rattles. The sound rose and expanded as the bonfire burned, crackling and blazing, sending sparks flying up into the deep night sky. One by one the people danced their way past the fire, pulling the leafy crowns from their heads and tossing them into the flames.

The people danced and danced, moving together and apart, driven on by the beat into ecstasy and beyond as the stars turned slowly through the sky. The bonfire collapsed down bit by bit as it consumed itself, growing in reverse, until it was no more than a smoldering pile of glowing coals. As the bonfire subsided, the dancers reduced their pace, weaving back and forth in time with the ever-slowing drums and sistrums, forcing themselves to keep going as long as the music still played. When the last red-hot lump burned itself out and nothing was left but ash, the instruments stopped and the dancers fell still. Some of them stood, wavering in place, while others collapsed to the ground and sat or lay there, waiting to come back to themselves.

In silence, the people moved back to their piles of belongings around the edge of the plaza. Now that she was no longer dancing and the bonfire was dead, Aria felt the chill of the night air, her sweaty skin growing clammy. She took off her bells and tucked them into her bag, careful not to let them sound. Then she drew out her woolen cloak and wrapped herself in it, lying down alongside Inia and the others in her party who had already done the same. Her body buzzed from the excitement of the dance, but she knew the sensation would not last long. When it faded, it would be followed quickly by the kind of deep sleep she only experienced after ecstatic rites.

All around the plaza, people lay wrapped in cloaks and blankets, resting, sleeping. A few crickets chirped. The torches crackled. Straining to keep her eyes open, Aria marveled at the blackness of the sky this high up, away from the lamps and fires and torches of the city and the reflection of the Moon and stars on the sea. Here, the stars pierced Ourania's veil and spread their sparkling light over her like a celestial robe, blessing her with the beauty and peace of the Mother-of-All.

"May I?" Orestas spoke quietly, posing his arm over Aria as if to embrace her. "Simply for warmth and comfort, nothing more."

"Of course," she replied. He slid his arm around her waist and snuggled up behind her. With a sigh, she leaned back against him and allowed herself to drift off.

Sometime during the night, Aria woke to the sound of shouts and scuffling on the far side of the plaza. Orestas was snoring lightly, his arm still draped around her. She raised up on one elbow, squinting into the darkness as torches bobbed and dark figures moved against the background of the starry sky. She heard the Head Priestess' voice, then one man speaking and another yelling, and a woman crying. More movement in the dark, and people heading across the plaza toward the path down the mountain. A few moments later, all was quiet again. Exhaustion being more powerful than curiosity, Aria lay back down and let sleep overtake her.

Chapter 20

Three blasts from the triton trumpet announced the first sunrise of the new year the next morning, startling the people on the plaza from their sleep. Aria sat up, brushing the frost from her cloak, and shifted it to her shoulders so it could serve as a garment rather than a blanket. Yawning, the other members of their party roused themselves and prepared for the second portion of the new year's rites at the sacred cave. Aria washed the taste of sleep from her mouth with a few swallows from her wineskin, but food would have to wait until later. She heard voices from the head of the mountain path, but the argument did not carry in the damp morning air, and the people involved were soon gone down the mountainside.

As the first cold rays of dawn snaked across the plaza, the crowd gathered at the cave entrance with the priesthood at the fore. The cave was more than large enough to accommodate all the travelers who had come for the occasion, but it was important that they not crowd in all at once. One of the resident priestesses directed them in a few at a time, giving each group several moments at the first stop before sending the next party in.

Aria and her fellow clergy were the second group to enter, each of them touching the evergreen swags that framed the opening as they went in, for the Mother's blessing. They carried with them small offerings for the sacred places within the cave. Upon their arrival, Inia and Orestas had presented the temple's main offerings to the Head Priestess. One basket contained large quantities of grain, wine, and oil (for the sustenance of the resident priesthood) along with several gilt-handled bronze blades and a box of semiprecious stones. That was a gift from the temple to the shrine, to ensure the shrine's continued existence. The other basket contained their group's contribution to the feast: wheat and barley bread, dried fish, dried fruit, fresh cheese seasoned with herbs and wrapped in grape leaves, and several flagons of good wine. Again, this was a gift from the temple to the shrine, one institution to another. Now, the travelers from Malia would make individual offerings as they took part in the cave rite.

As the first group moved farther back into the depths of the cave, Aria and her companions stepped into the torchlit space. She tilted her head back, peering up at the soaring roof that bristled with stalactites, the chamber as broad as her temple's courtyard. Stalagmites jutted up from the floor all over, some of them meeting the stalactites to form natural pillars and columns. The flickering torchlight made it look like they were moving, shifting, alive. Aria knew that Ida's children had visited this cave since they first came to the island, more generations ago than anyone could count. The cave was sacred beyond memory, beyond time.

When she looked down again, Aria saw that the rest of the group had moved on ahead of her. She hurried to catch up with them, joining them at a large rectangular altar where the Head Priestess stood. On the altar rested an array of gold, silver, and bronze figurines and vessels: the shrine's sacred wealth, meant not to enrich the people but to honor the gods. At one end of the altar sat a terracotta bowl, ready to receive the offerings of the faithful: a vessel of clay for offerings to the Earth Mother.

Drawing out the small jars from her basket, Aria prepared to make her offerings. Lexion finished his and shifted out of the way, gesturing for her to move up to the altar.

She stepped in front of the huge stone table, and a chill shook her. Though it had been years, the last time she had made an offering at a cave shrine, the rite had ended with a vision of her son's death—the son who had not even been born yet when she had the vision, and who was now as lost to her as if he had never existed. She shook her head and forced her eyes to focus on the altar that stood in front of her now.

Swallowing past a lump in her throat, she untied the beeswax-infused cloth from the top of the jar and poured the honey into the offering bowl. To it she added wine, olive oil, and grains of barley, her hands shaking all the while. A sidelong glance showed her that Inia was watching her with concern. Forcing herself to draw in a slow breath, she calmed her body and then her mind. She drew herself upright and smiled at the Head Priestess.

"May the blessings of the Great Mother be upon you and yours until the end of time." Her voice did not shake as she spoke, and her feet did not waver as she moved around the altar and beyond, deeper into the cave.

The group from Malia walked through a narrow area and into another chamber, this one smaller than the first but still spacious. While they waited for the first party to finish, Aria looked around. To her left was a small chamber with a cloth hung over its entrance. She knew that this was Therasia's secret lair where she hid for three days at Winter Solstice before rebirthing herself and emerging from the cave. It was also the chamber where Ida gave birth to Dionysus at Midwinter. The mainlanders thought this was a more important event than Therasia's self-rebirth, and they esteemed Dionysus more than his mother. Aria wrinkled her nose at the idea, glad that no one trekked up the mountain at Winter Solstice, when there was too much snow and ice to make the trip safely.

She drew in a deep breath, inhaling the damp, earthy scent of the cave, the Mountain Mother herself. Though the new year rites were important, this was just an ordinary year. It was not a Minos Year. Aria did not understand the details of the sacred calendar—she had not yet received that training—but she knew that at the end of every eighth year, Minos emerged from the Mother's cave, journeying from the World Below to the land of the living once again. And on those occasions, there was a huge festival at the cave shrine, and other rites at her temple as well, rites she would rather not think about.

When the group that had entered the cave earlier left, Aria followed the other members of her party toward the back of the chamber. While she was waiting at a distance, she had thought there were a great many torches burning in this section of the cave. But as she approached, she discovered that the reality was even more entrancing. The torchlight was reflected from the mirror-like surface of a lake deep within the mountain: the Water of Life within the body of the Mother. Here the three realms met: land, sea, and sky in the form of the cave, its sacred pool, and the torches.

Aria knelt alongside her fellow clergy, dipping her fingers into the water and touching them to her brow, her lips, her breast: the Blessing of the Waters. Only certain waters conferred the blessing of the Great Mother. Shivers ran down Aria's body as the damp spots on her skin went from cold to hot to cold again.

She slipped a hand into the pouch at her waist and brought out a small figurine: a terracotta likeness of a woman, as close to her own image as she could find in Malia's market stalls. She cupped the little statue in her hands.

"Great Lady," she murmured, "I do not know what to ask of you, what blessings I should desire. I only want my heart to be full again the way it was when I was young. Fill me with your love, Great Mother. Fill me with your love."

In a single smooth motion, she threw the figurine as far as she could out into the lake. The water splashed as the terracotta broke the surface, then ripples played out in the torchlight, dancing to the edge and back, until once again the water was still.

Aria could not hear what her colleagues said as they tossed their offerings into the water, more gently than she had done with hers. Once they were all finished, they rose and touched a series of stalagmites and stalactites, from the huge one by the water down to a tiny one near the entrance to the chamber: the Mother and her children.

"We are all your children," they murmured together in the well-known formula. "May Ida's children live forever."

Staying to the side, they made their way out of the cave in silence as more pilgrims came in to make their offerings. Along with the others in her group, Aria stopped just outside the cave entrance, blinking as her eyes adjusted to the daylight. After a few moments, they returned to their spot along the edge of the plaza. They watched as the resident priesthood slaughtered several goats in ritual fashion, collecting their blood in bowls to offer to the Mountain Mother. They skinned and gutted the carcasses, cut them up, and set them to roast. Then they all went to change out of their blood-spattered hide skirts. Aria's stomach rumbled, but she knew it would still be a while before they could eat.

Eventually the last of the pilgrims emerged from the cave. The people moved back to their places around the plaza, and the Head Priestess emerged from the shrine building wearing a fresh robe. She stood before the feast tables with a gold cup in her hands. As she raised the cup above her head, the sunlight glinted on the metal, then shimmered through the blood-red liquid that flowed from the vessel as she made the libation. As the last drop fell, she lowered the cup and addressed the crowd.

"All who come in love are welcome at the Mother's table. She nourishes every one of us, body and soul. May the blessings of her bounty fill your stomach and your heart. May you carry those blessings with you every day of your life."

As one, the crowd responded with the words they had all spoken since childhood: "May the Great Mother protect us. May she grant us bounty and peace. May she hold us in her love forever."

Lexion rummaged in a basket and drew out dishes for himself and his colleagues: wooden bowls and bronze cups, less likely to break in transit than ceramic vessels. Taking her cup and bowl, Aria joined the other clergy in line at the tables. The feast was as extensive and varied as the banquets in the temple dining hall ever were. The pilgrims, both clergy and laity, had gone to great effort to share the very best they had for this meal. Only their finest produce and recipes would bring the greatest blessings from the Great Mother. She shared all she had with her children, so it was only right that they should share with each other. To do any less would be shameful.

By this time the Sun was riding high in the sky, warming the air and the stones that paved the plaza. So Aria took off her cloak, folded it, and used it as a cushion to sit on while she ate. Orestas followed suit, while Inia and Lexion preferred to stand. The food was delicious. Aria enjoyed not only the dishes her group had brought, but also lentils stewed with coriander, marinated onions and mushrooms, several different kinds of olives, sweetmeats made of dried fruit and spices, and almonds that had been roasted with spices and salt. Of course, it took multiple trips to the feast tables to sample everything. She was almost too full to try the goat meat when it was finally ready, but she managed to make room.

Eventually Inia and Lexion wandered off to chat, but Aria had a full stomach and a late afternoon sunbeam had found her, so she sat on her cloak and leaned her head back, enjoying the warmth. She sighed with contentment.

"I take it you have enjoyed the journey so far?" Orestas asked, smiling.

"I have," she admitted. "I expected to miss the rites at home, but instead I have been blessed with the ceremonies here. The Great Mother reaches us wherever we are, I suppose."

Orestas nodded, a knowing look on his face. "If you think this was moving, you should come back for a Minos Year celebration."

"That comes every eighth year, the same as our..." She broke off.

"So it does."

She took a swallow of wine. "But it is about the Moon as well as the Sun. And the Moon does not count time in Sun-years."

"Ah, but his cycles match hers: ninety-nine of the Moon for every eight of the Sun. And that is not all, either. The Star of the Sea dances this cycle as well."

"Can you teach me?" Aria asked.

"You wish to become a Sky-Watcher?"

"I do not know." She toyed with her cup. "Most of the others just want to be told when to do the rites, but I want to understand the why and how of it all. Maybe I should become a Sky-Watcher.

Then I would be doing something useful."

"But you are already doing many useful things. You are a scribe. You take part in the rites. And you are good at them. Our Lady instructs you herself. That is a high honor indeed."

Aria shrugged, staring at the dregs of her wine.

"But Our Lady did not make you the Head of the College, did she?"

"I cannot grudge Rhea the position," Aria said. "She worked very hard to become competent at all the responsibilities of a priestess. Most of the time, she works harder than I do."

"Because she has to." Orestas set his hand on Aria's. "Our Lady has told me she expects great things of you. She has not forgotten you, I promise."

"She will not tell me what she plans for me," she sighed.

"Trust her." He patted Aria's hand. "She knows your value and will not waste such a talented priestess on trifles."

Aria mumbled her disagreement.

"And if Our Lady agrees," Orestas continued, "I will instruct you."

At that, Aria smiled and poured herself another cup of wine. By the time she had finished her drink, Inia and Lexion had returned.

"I hope you two have not been arguing," Orestas said when they got close enough for him to see the expressions on their faces.

"No, not us," Lexion replied, giving Inia a sidelong glance.

"We must tell them," Inia said. Lexion nodded and Inia turned to the others. "There was an incident last night, after the bonfire rite."

"I heard something in the middle of the night," Aria said. "Over there." She gestured across the plaza to the area where the lay visitors had been sleeping.

Inia pressed her lips together. "One of the pilgrims accosted a young woman."

"What?" Orestas heaved himself to his feet. "And on sacred ground, no less?"

"One of the mainlanders," Lexion spat, "not the decent ones, but the kind from the mountains. These new ones are giving all the mainlanders a bad name."

"In the dark," Inia continued, "he thought he could have his way with her. But we are not like their women. We do not submit when we do not wish to. So he struck her."

Aria scrambled to her feet, peering around with concern. "Which one is he?"

"They have ejected him," Lexion said.

"Yes," came the voice of the Head Priestess as she strode over to them. "One of my priests removed him last night and kept guard over him until daylight. At first light, he escorted the man back down the mountain and has only just returned."

"Was he not punished?" Aria asked.

"Not formally, no. Though the thrashing my priest gave him when he tried to grab the girl again is something he will not soon forget."

"Only just the one?" Orestas asked, skeptical.

"Just the one," the Head Priestess confirmed. "He had come alone. Apparently rumors of some of our rites have been... exaggerated among a certain type of mainlander. They think all our women are free for the taking every time we celebrate a holy day."

"We are not property," Aria said, setting her jaw.

"But some believe we are," the Head Priestess replied, "because that is how they treat their own women. I have to deal with this at every festival now, and sometimes in between as well."

"At least you have some well-muscled priests to help you," Inia said.

"I do," said the Head Priestess. "I have been forced to recruit a few of the burlier ones myself since some of our visitors will not respect a priestess, or even a priest if he is smaller than they are." She met the gaze of each one of Aria's party in turn. "I hope you will not take this unfortunate incident as reason to avoid visiting again."

"Of course not," Inia said, clasping the Head Priestess' hand. "We would not think of it. Our Lady supports you and your work. We will stand fast, and those people will go back where they came from when they see that we will not change our ways."

"I hope you are right." With a sad smile, the Head Priestess excused herself and moved on to the next group of clergy to make another set of apologies and explanations.

As the Sun began to set, Aria and the others wandered back over to the feast table to pick at the food and pour themselves a little more wine. The resident clergy lit torches around the plaza, and the visitors settled into small groups, chatting quietly. Soon they would all be asleep, exhausted from the rites and sated with food, resting before the journey home the next morning.

Aria wrapped herself in her cloak and lay back, looking up at the sky as the first stars began to appear. Perhaps she would become a Sky-Watcher after all. Then maybe she would understand how the world worked and why people did the things they did.

Chapter 21

The breeze blew and Aria tilted her head back, relishing the sensation as the cool air dried the sweat on her skin.

"Enjoy it now," Orestas said. "It is not so pleasant up here in the wintertime."

The two of them stood on the temple rooftop, looking up at the stars and watching the points of light as they slowly rose and set between the giant sacred horns that adorned the roof edges.

"Surely you do not spend so many hours up here in the winter," Aria said.

"The season does not matter. We watch the sky all day and all night, every day and every night. Though we do stay indoors when it is pouring rain," he chuckled. "We cannot see the stars through the clouds."

Aria peered between a pair of horns where the Star of the Sea had set shortly after the Sun had gone down. "But why must we watch the sky anymore? The calendars tell us when everything happens."

"Because calendars can lose their rhythm with the world, so we must always watch, always make sure."

"That is a lot of work."

"It is indeed. And why do we go to so much trouble?"

She thought a moment. "We would not want to hold a rite on

the wrong day. Especially not the sacrifices. Bad things could happen."

"Exactly. No Consort must die before his time. No High Priestess either, for that matter."

Aria shook her head as visions of her son, with blood pouring from his neck, crowded into her mind along with the sudden, new image of Eileithyia floating beneath the waves, cold and dead, eyes unseeing. She swallowed and squared her shoulders. "Then I will learn, and I will watch the stars."

"Tell me what you have already learned. Which stars do we watch and when?"

"We watch for when the stars rise just before the Sun in the morning, or when they rise in the east as the Sun sets in the west."

Orestas nodded, waiting for her to answer the rest of his question.

"The stars..." Aria had learned them well in the Sky-Watchers' chamber below, but somehow their names were harder to remember now that she was standing on the rooftop in the growing darkness. "We watch for the first sunrise appearance of the star of young Dionysus and the star we call the Ear of Grain. These mark the beginning and the ending of the Mysteries."

"What else?"

"The Swallow. After its rising, there follows a Moon cycle of cold north winds, and then the worst of winter is over, and the swallows begin to return from their sojourn to the south. That is the time of Spring Equinox and harvest."

"So you have been paying attention," Orestas said.

Aria could just make out his smile. She was glad she had pleased him.

"And what sequence are we watching tonight?" he asked.

She did not have to stop and think before she spoke the answer. "The one that gives us the Minos Year. Eight times the Sun goes round to make Kalliste's year, five times the Star of the Sea completes her progression, and ninety-nine times the Moon dies and grows and dies again in Minos' cycle. When these all come together, the Consort must die. Every eighth Sun-year." She suppressed a shudder.

"Very good. What other cycle do we count by the Sun and the Moon?"

"Just the Sun and the Moon with no stars?" She shook her head, puzzled.

"You know this one, Ariadne."

She stiffened at the use of her full name. She was certain Orestas did it on purpose, since everyone else except the High Priestess called her Aria. But she could not determine the reason. The Chief Sky-Watcher was always friendly. She did not think he would choose to irritate her on purpose.

"Are you certain I have learned this one?" she asked, and then she remembered. "Oh, the peak sanctuaries! Nineteen Sun-years match up to 235 Moons. The Moon rises at his farthest points north and south along the horizon according to this cycle."

"Indeed." He swept his hand in front of him to indicate the swath of the horizon where the Moon rose. "A variation of that cycle can be used to predict the times the Sun is eaten by the darkness."

Aria shivered. She did not like those times. No one did. She was grateful they happened so rarely.

"But that is very complicated," Orestas said. "You do not need to know it unless you become a Sky-Watcher yourself. Now," he said, pointing toward the silvery crescent that shone in the dark sky, "we watched the Star of the Sea set and you can see that the waning Moon has risen."

Aria tilted her head to center the silver crescent above the sacred horns. She looked down at the temple rooftop to see the oil lamp sitting next to the mark Orestas had made once the whole of the crescent was visible within the curve of the horns. He had to be sure to stand in the correct spot in order for his marks to be accurate. There was a flat, circular stone set into the roof for the clergy to stand on for this purpose. Nearby sat the wide bronze cauldron where the Sky-Watchers lit the signaling fire, the light from the temple roof alerting the townspeople to the sacred days.

"You made that mark tonight," she said, pointing to the spot on the rooftop, "and I can see a few others that the other Sky-Watchers have made. Does the rain not wash them away?"

"It does," he said. "But you have seen the stone counters we use, and the clay ones as well."

She nodded. "So when you go back downstairs, you will move the marker into the next hole in one of the counters."

"Indeed." Aria could hear the smile in his voice. She wondered how long it had been since he had an eager student. Only two other clergy within the temple, one priest and one priestess, had the training to keep the calendars and watch the stars. And neither of them was young, though they were younger than Orestas.

He pointed to the labrys-shaped constellation in the sky, with its two angled blades and three closely-spaced stars that ran at an angle through the center. Then he drew his finger down to another star, a much brighter one. "You see this one?"

"The Jewel? Of course. Everyone knows the Great Labrys has a jewel on the end of its handle."

"Yes, but did you know the people of the Two Lands call our Jewel a dog and say it barks to herald the flood of their great river every year?"

"How odd."

He shrugged. "That is their way. Their Dog Star belongs to their Lady of the Heavens, who tells them when their year begins."

Aria narrowed her eyes at her favorite constellation, trying to picture the Jewel as a yapping dog. "So people in different lands see different pictures in the sky?"

"Indeed they do. I am sure your brothers can tell you about that. I often seek the traders out to hear their tales of the skies in other lands."

Aria strode over to the rooftop's central stone and stepped onto it. Then she gazed out at the lower edge of the sky through the sacred horns, turning slowly so the horns—and the sky—revolved around her, stars appearing and disappearing as the dark silhouettes of the horns shifted sideways through her vision.

"Does it matter how people name the stars as long as they watch them well and count the time accurately?" she asked.

"Probably not, as long as their gods are pleased." He scanned the horizon, his gaze sweeping the row of sacred horns that adorned the edge of the rooftop. "You know, the stars are sacred to Ida's children."

"Yes. We follow their movements and positions to know the days of the sacred calendar, the beginning and ending of the sailing season, the right time for certain rituals." She sighed. "It is a lot to know, a lot to keep track of."

"Indeed." He moved over to join her next to the central stone. "But though it is hard work, it is necessary."

"Of course," she said. "I promise, I am doing the work. I would never shirk."

"I did not think you would," he said with a laugh. "But there are those who think it is too much trouble to keep track of the risings and settings of so many stars." She tilted her head, puzzled. "I am speaking of the mainlanders."

"But we have mainlanders here, among our clergy."

"Indeed we do. But the ones at Knossos are different. They only want to know when to sail and when to dock their boats. For everything else, they count by the Sun or the Moon, not the stars. They say our ways are too complicated and old-fashioned."

She perched her fists on her hips. "Then they are just lazy."

"No, no," he said, waving a hand at her. "They are neither lazy nor stupid, and it behooves us all to remember that. They simply have different ideas than we do."

"Well, I do not understand their ideas. I want to learn more about our ways. I want to follow the stars."

He tilted his face up toward the Moon. "You have spent much time in the Sky-Watchers' chamber below but have only just joined me on the roof for the first time tonight. Tell me what you have learned about the days and the skies, and then we will observe."

"There are the Moons." She gestured to the thick silver-white crescent that hung above the horns. "We count from the first thin crescent after Moon-Dark to the next one. And we have the First Crescent Moon Rite to begin each new cycle."

"Very good. What else?"

"When we count by the stars, we have 366 days in a year." She tapped a finger on her chin, willing herself to remember the details. "That is how long it takes for the Sun to come back to the Flock-of-Doves, where it started out a year before."

"And why do we call those stars by that name?"

"The doves belong to Posidaeja and the Star of the Sea. We count the year by the stars, beginning when the Flock-of-Doves appears just before sunrise in the springtime, after harvest. That is when we have the Blessing of the Ships, when sailing season begins."

Orestas nodded. "And what else do we call that cluster of stars?"

"The Bee-Swarm. That is its oldest name. We call it that because its rising with the Sun in the spring marks the beginning of the time the bees go out to collect nectar and make honey. When it rises at sunset in the autumn, that is when the bees go to bed for the winter. It is also the end of sailing season, when they bring the ships in to keep them safe from the winter storms."

Aria stopped talking and drew in a slow breath, eyeing Orestas. She could see his smile in the moonlight, the corners of his eyes crinkling. She had pleased him, and she was glad of that. Though the things he taught were difficult, she always knew when she had done well, unlike with the High Priestess, whose ways often confused her.

"Tell me," Orestas said, "why do we keep the different calendars? Why not just one?"

Aria tilted her head up, watching the Moon rise higher against the sea of stars and considering the question. "Because they are different, but we need each one to keep track of certain rites and practices in the temple." She turned to Orestas, her brow furrowed as she struggled to remember the details he had taught her. "Counting by the stars does not exactly match the Sun's risings from one Spring Equinox to the next over the course of time. So the Sky-Watchers keep a special count of 123 days alongside the Sun's year from equinox to equinox and the year-by-stars. After we count 123 days four times, we take a day away from the year-by-stars to make the calendar match the Sun as she rises on the equinoxes."

Orestas was silent.

"Did I say it wrong?"

"No, my dear, you have it all correct. But... it takes most people a good bit longer to understand."

She let out a breath. "Finally, something I am good at. It took me forever to learn to write, and scribing is still hard for me, even though I do it at every Offering Day. I suspect that is why Our Lady will not allow me to declare as a Scribe, even though Thalamika said she would support me in that desire. Maybe I am meant to be a Sky-Watcher after all."

"I am not sure what Our Lady would think of that," Orestas said. "She is pleased for me to teach you these things, all you like. I will share all the calendars with you. Everything the Sky-Watchers know."

"But?" Aria's jaw clenched.

"Our Lady has asked me not to let you declare as a Sky-Watcher, though I may teach you all you wish to know."

"What?" She stepped off the central stone and paced over to the oil lamp, then back. "What can she be thinking? I am no child. I have passed more than thirty winters, yet she will not let me declare a specialty. Am I to be a general priestess forever?"

Orestas raised his hands toward her in a placating motion. "There is no shame in that. Your mother is such a one." Aria drew in a sharp breath but said nothing. "Our Lady has told me that she has plans for you. I will not go against her, not for a priestess with your name."

"Plans," she spat. "That is what she told the other priestesses so they would not vote for me to become Head of the College."

"Perhaps, before you allow this anger to eat you up, you should speak with Our Lady."

Aria turned away from him, blinking back tears, thankful for the darkness. "I have done so," she said. "She says the time is not yet right to explain herself to me. She always mentions the auguries at my birth but will not tell me the details. Neither will my mother, because Our Lady has told her not to speak of them. I do not know what to think."

"Think this: that you are beloved of all the priesthood here. That whatever fate the Three have set down for you will be revealed in its proper time." He tilted his head to look at the Great Labrys.

"The proper time," Aria grumbled. "The gods have no sense of time. If they did, they would understand my impatience."

"Come," Orestas said, taking Aria's elbow. "Let us learn about another kind of calendar. If you are serious about sky-watching, you must study for more than a Sun-year to see all the cycles."

Chapter 22

Though the Summer Solstice was most of a Moon cycle away, the weather was already warm enough for Aria to feel the sweat beading on her forehead as she stood in the central court. She looked up to see Rhea and Kaeseus on the top step leading up to the loggia. As the Heads of the Colleges, they were ready to bear witness to the rite that was about to take place, even if Aria was not.

Just below the Heads of the Colleges, the temple priesthood were gathered on the courtyard floor, novice and initiate alike, crowding too close for Aria's comfort given the growing heat of the day. They were joined by the chief lay officials from the temple: the overseers of the livestock herds, vineyards, orchards, olive groves, and fields. The crowd also included high-ranking townspeople. Aria guessed that Sageleus was present, but she refused to allow herself to look around for him. The rite was liable to be difficult enough without worrying what he thought of it. She had shared more with him than with any other except perhaps Rhea. He could well guess how uncomfortable she was. She forced herself to stand still, her head held high as befitted a priestess of the temple.

The loggia was the usual location for semi-public rites, those witnessed by both the priesthood and a select group of lay people. This chamber had its face open to the courtyard so the entire room was visible to onlookers. Four broad steps, the full width of the room, led up from the courtyard into the main portion of the loggia, with a small stone altar as its centerpiece. Behind the altar, three narrow steps rose up between a pair of columns, leading to a narrow platform at the back of the room. From this platform a curtained doorway led to a hidden room just behind. Aria knew that the High Priestess and her Consort were behind that doorway, along with the Chief Song-Priestess and Priest, who were ready to provide the sounds of their instruments at the appropriate moments during the rite. Who else waited behind that curtain, Aria did her best not to think about.

Three blasts from a triton trumpet rang out across the courtyard, and the High Priestess drew back the curtain, stepping onto the platform at the back of the loggia. She raised her arms in the gesture that calls to the Great Mother. Along with the rest of the crowd in the courtyard, Aria responded with the salute. Then Eileithyia lowered her arms, descended the steps, and moved over to the altar.

"Three times I say the prayer, for the Three: the three Mothers, the three realms, the three worlds."

She drew in a breath and began the chant, repeating the whole thing three times.

By land and sky and sea
Blessed be the Three
By land and sea and sky
By Them we live and die
By sky and sea and land
Beneath Their guiding hand

All around her, Aria could hear the people, clergy and laity alike, repeating the chant under their breath: the words every one of Ida's children knew by heart, the words used to bless every meal, every festival, every ship launch, every birth. They all knew that as long as Ida's children were loyal to the Three, no ill could befall them. That was the way of things, the reason they kept on with the rites and the prayers and libations in the old way as the world changed around them. They were in a reciprocal relationship with the gods, and they dared not shirk their side of it.

"Three times I pour the libation," the High Priestess continued when the chant was done, "for the Three: the three Mothers, the three realms, the three worlds."

The liquids chosen for libations to the Three depended on the purpose of the rite. This was a special ritual, performed only once every eighth year, on the Full Moon before the Summer Solstice. The High Priestess lifted the first flagon and poured its contents into the wide bowl that sat on the floor next to the altar. The cow's milk left a thin residue of cream along the sides of the bowl as it splashed down. With some effort Aria turned her thoughts away from the reason this rite called for that kind of bowl instead of the small stone libation tables that sat on the altar.

Next the High Priestess lifted a second flagon and poured another white liquid into the bowl. This one was goat's milk from the temple's herds. The stream of liquid twisted and curled as it poured down into the pool of cow's milk, splashing and mixing. When that vessel was empty, Eileithyia picked up the final flagon and added a libation of sheep's milk to the bowl, filling it nearly to the brim.

She set the empty container back on the altar. "The Great Mothers give to us generously. They nourish and nurture us, who are their children. We must give back to them just as generously in turn."

The hissing of sistrums snaked out from the room behind the loggia, and the curtain parted. Through the opening, two young men stepped out: the Consort and another, his junior by exactly eight years. They were both bare from the waist up, both wearing the colorful tasseled kilt that was the mark of the Consort. Aria's heart skipped a beat as the younger of the two came down the steps, the sunlight gleaming on his black hair and deep brown shoulders.

He smiled gently, his features relaxed and serene. That was the face Aria had seen in the vision in Eileithyia's cave, the face that would lie lifeless in the Sea Temple the next time a Minos Year came round.

He was her son. This she knew. But try as she might, she felt nothing for him. He was as much a stranger to her as if he had only just arrived from across the sea. He was barely grown, just the right age for the new Consort. All of a sudden she felt very old, though she was only midway between thirty and forty.

Then she went cold all over despite the heat of the day. This was what it meant to be "only a vessel." A vessel is empty inside. Empty is how she felt as she watched the Consort escort her son, whose name she did not even know, down the steps. She gazed into the loggia, numb all over, as the Consort and her son knelt together in front of the altar, facing each other, holding hands. To Aria, the two young men looked relaxed, even happy, and she wondered at that when she knew they had not drunk any drugged wine before the ritual. How could they face the responsibilities of their office without terror?

She glanced up at Rhea, who was scanning the crowd for her own son. Rhea's boy was two years younger than Aria's, two years away from coming of age. When he reached the age Aria's son was now, he would choose the direction of his adult life: become a priest or take up a trade. There was only one path he could not take, because he was born at the wrong time. Silently Aria gave thanks that at least one of their children was ordinary, not set apart from the others by the gods.

Rhea spotted her son, now a strapping youth, and smiled at him. Then she turned her attention back to the rite in the loggia. With a sigh, Aria did likewise.

The High Priestess stood behind the two young men, her hands extended, palms down, over their heads. "The Consort is the face of the god in this world," she said, "just as the High Priestess is the face of the goddess. Every Consort was anointed to his task, one before the other, for generations and generations, leading back to the time of the gods themselves."

She turned and picked up an alabastron from the altar, lifting it up above the Consort and his successor. "The anointing is the outward sign of the blessing the Great Mothers give, the blessing the Mother-of-All gives, which cannot be removed once it has been accepted. The sacrifice must go willing." She paused. "I ask you now, Kailo, beloved of gods and mortals, do you take this step willingly? Do you choose it above all other paths in your life?"

Kailo. They had dedicated him to the Young God, the Lion of Rhea, the Son of the Mothers, via his name. What choice did he have now, son of none but the gods?

The younger man looked the Consort in the eye, drew in a slow breath, and said, "I do." His voice was clear and steady, his choice firm.

"Do you choose this office for the rest of your life, according to our sacred calendar, giving yourself to it fully and freely?"

"I do."

"Do you offer your whole self up for the gods' work, your very life for the Three-and-One, forsaking all other intimacies except those allowed within the office?"

Aria saw his gaze flick to the courtyard and back, and she wondered who he would be giving up in exchange for the High Priestess' bed. She shuddered at the thought. But this was the way of Ida's children, her people's safeguard against chaos for generation upon generation. And he was of age now, able to make his own decisions.

"I do," Kailo said, squeezing the Consort's hands, the corners of his mouth lifting up into a peaceful smile.

The High Priestess spread her arms wide, a gesture that encompassed not just the two young men but also the witnesses in the courtyard and the temple itself.

"Witness now the ancient rite of anointing," she said. "Kailo, beloved of gods and mortals, receives the blessing of the temple, which is the blessing of the gods themselves. He accepts the office which is offered to him. He goes willingly."

Eileithyia turned and picked up an alabastron from the altar. She dipped two fingers into the sacred oil and, leaning down, drew the sign of blessing on the Consort's forehead. He tilted his head up, and she kissed him on the mouth. Then she straightened up and turned to Kailo, who was still holding hands with the Consort. She drew the sign of blessing on his forehead as well, then slipped her fingers beneath his chin and lifted his face up so she could look him in the eye. They gazed at each other for several long moments. Finally, she appeared to be satisfied.

With a flourish, she lifted the alabastron over the young man's head and slowly poured its contents out over him. The anointing oil, rich with resins and spices, flowed down his head and neck, down his shoulders and chest and back. Its pungent fragrance carried across the courtyard, and Aria found herself inhaling it deeply, relishing the scent. The High Priestess held the alabastron tilted over Kailo's head until the last drop had fallen. Then she set the empty vessel on the altar and placed her hands, palms down, on the young man's head.

"May you be blessed, Kailo. May you walk in the grace and the love of the gods every day of your life. May your life and your death be a blessing to your people."

The two men rose, and the Consort let go of Kailo's hands, stepping off to one side. The younger man, his bronze skin gleaming with the scented oil, stood up straight, his arms at his sides, his posture proud but relaxed. His gaze swept the crowd and landed on Aria, but she refused to meet his eyes. He was not her son. She would not give in to that grief, not again.

The High Priestess moved next to Kailo and raised her arms up in a gesture of acclaim. "Behold," she cried out, "the anointed one! I give you Kailo, son of the gods, who will be the next Consort of this temple when this Minos cycle draws to a close one Moon from now."

The hissing rattle of sistrums snaked out of the loggia, its echoes slithering around the courtyard. The crowd shouted and cheered, but Aria could not bring herself to join in.

"He is about to lose his name, and I have only just learned it." She thought back to the time before she was Ariadne, to what it felt like to lose your name and be reborn with a new one. Then she remembered that he was going to lose far more than just his name.

Chapter 23

"I am here, My Lady," Aria said as she stepped out into the herb garden. The morning air was fresh and cool. She breathed it in deeply, enjoying the sensation, a small pleasure during the heat of summer.

"Very good," the High Priestess said, her skirts brushing a mound of myrtle as she came down the path to meet her student. "I wanted to discuss some things with you this morning."

"And we could not do it in your workroom?"

"The herb garden has a better view," Eileithyia said, gesturing toward the outdoor workshops nearby where the potters and bronze-smiths were setting up for the day.

Aria huffed out a breath. The High Priestess was not yet so old that her memory should be failing. "My Lord introduced me to the artisans some years ago. Do you not remember?"

"Of course I do, my dear. And you have been suitably friendly toward all of them in the time since then. You are a good priestess and an asset to the temple. But that is not what I wish to discuss today."

A good priestess. Eileithyia had said so, yet Aria could not help but feel that her life was still missing something. She sighed. Perhaps Rhea was right and what she really needed was another child. At least that would distract her from the constant sense that she was somehow not a real priestess. In her visions, she had felt so complete, so *right* as a priestess. Except for the time she was pregnant with Kailo, she had not felt that way in real life. Was that all there was, just those nine months, and then a lifetime of emptiness?

The High Priestess walked down the path to the end of the garden, not bothering to look back to see whether Aria was following. Annoyed, Aria stalked behind her superior, then stopped next to her on the broad walkway that separated the herb garden from the workshops.

"These people," Eileithyia said, gesturing to the artisans working in the open-air shelters and scurrying between them, carrying supplies. "These people work for the temple, but they do not live here. They are not clergy."

Aria nodded. "They go home at night, like some of the priesthood. Not everyone has a room upstairs."

"Every interaction we have with these people is an interaction with the city. When they go back to their homes in the evening, they talk to their families and friends about what they experienced here."

"Oh." Aria smiled, not wanting to admit that she had never thought about the situation that way before.

"So we must always do our best to treat them well and make sure the overseers do their jobs fairly." She put her hand on Aria's arm. "If any of them ever make a complaint to you, please bring it directly to me, and I will see that it is taken care of."

"Yes, My Lady." Aria's brow furrowed. "Have there been problems that I should have told you about?"

"No, my dear. But the world is changing, and we need to be sure to keep our portion of it peaceful and stable. That includes seeing to the well-being of the people who ply their trades on our grounds. They are all Ida's children."

Again the High Priestess began walking, this time striding down a pathway through the workshop area. Aria hastened to draw even with her as they passed the smiths' forges and the potters' kilns. The heat from them pressed against her skin in the cool morning air.

"My Lady," Aria ventured, "we are keeping Ida's children peaceful and safe. We follow our ancestors' ways. We keep the sacred calendars and the rites and the agreements we have with the gods. We have changed nothing."

"Indeed," Eileithyia said. "But there is more to the world than just rituals and traditions. And though our ways have not changed, the world most certainly has."

They came out on the Sea Road, and the High Priestess began walking down it, away from the temple and toward the city. Puzzled, Aria followed, but Eileithyia stopped as soon as they passed the theatral court. She turned and gestured out across the ruins of the old city, never rebuilt after the Great Darkness. It was a fearful place that even the local stray dogs avoided, though every generation had its crazy old man or woman who wandered the ruins, spouting dire prophecies between unintelligible ravings. Some of them claimed they had visions of the new city of Malia, indeed all the island's cities, as ruins like these. Aria scanned the area, breathing a sigh of relief that she could see no one else among the stones on that particular morning.

"Our people kept the rituals generations ago," Eileithyia said. "They honored the gods. Did that save them from Kalliste's wrath?"

"But..."

"Did it?"

"No, My Lady."

"Why do you think that is?"

Aria squinted at the ruins. The old city was little more than knee-high rubble. What the Earth-shaking and the fires had not destroyed, Posidaeja had wiped out with a single gargantuan wave. The stories people told about that time were still enough to send shivers down the spine.

Aria fingered her skirt cord. "My Lady, people say the Great Darkness was Kalliste's doing."

"Indeed."

"But I think all three of the Great Mothers had a part in it."

"How do you mean?"

"Kalliste destroyed her own sacred island, but Ida shook the ground, and Posidaeja slung her waters upon us. They all did it together, the three realms attacking us at once." Aria felt her pulse pounding as she imagined what that time must have looked like, felt like, sounded like. "I prefer to think that it was not punishment for anything our people did. That is not the Mothers' way. But the very horror of it makes me wonder sometimes. At the very least, it was a warning, though of what, I am unsure."

The High Priestess stepped off the Sea Road and into the ruins.

"My Lady?" Aria called, not moving from her place on the pavement.

Without answering, Eileithyia continued walking along the rock-strewn pathway that was once a broad street in the old city. Aria shifted from one foot to the other, hovering at the edge of the pavement. Still the older woman did not turn around or acknowledge her.

Finally, Aria gathered up the courage to follow the High Priestess. She stepped off the pavement and picked her way between rocks and bits of broken walls, moving slowly through the dusty ruins, being careful not to touch anything. The people said the dead city was haunted, not just by the spirits of Ida's children who had been killed in the disaster, but also by the wrath of the goddess whose work the cataclysm was.

Aria came up next to the High Priestess and stopped, waiting. Finally Eileithyia spoke.

"Look around you, Ariadne."

Aria's gaze swept the rubble, the low remains of walls with tangled drifts of dirt, rocks, and broken seashells pressed up against them. Even the weeds had not seen fit to grow among the ruins. She shuddered.

"It must have been horrible," she whispered.

"Indeed. Why do you think this happened?" Eileithyia asked, sweeping her arm around to encompass the whole ruined city.

"Everyone says we made Kalliste angry."

"I did not ask you what everyone else says. I asked what you think."

Slowing her breathing, Aria softened her gaze and looked out over the rubble, opening herself to whatever the gods might care to show her to help her understand. All of a sudden she felt a lump in her throat and tears stinging her eyes, as if some great sorrow were washing over her. The ruined city in front of her wavered, and she saw it fresh and new, the whitewashed walls two and three stories tall, the people busy and happy. She saw the wealthy merchants, their ears, arms, and necks dripping with jewelry, the men's waists adorned with shining bronze daggers, the fancy tunics and bodices and skirts trimmed with blood-red bands, the color of the murex dye that had brought such riches to them. Kalliste's color, her sacred dye, even more valuable than saffron.

The merchants wandered among bolts of woolen cloth, delicately carved stone vases, and brightly painted ceramic pots. Aria saw them counting stacks of shining bronze daggers, spearheads, and swords, weapons they would sell in neighboring lands. Some of them would be used for hunting. But most of them ended up in weapons stockpiles in lands where Ida's children did not discourage war because doing so would mean a smaller market for their blades.

Then Aria saw the poor people down by the docks in the old city. They eked out a living as best they could, being paid little to carry back-breaking loads on and off the trading ships. Their children scrounged in the trash heaps along the harbor, searching for bits of food to take back to their tumbledown shacks that lined the unpaved roads along the edge of the city. She could smell the rotting fish, the moldering trash, the stagnant water that pooled along the land behind the gleaming docks where the big ships tied up.

And she could feel the despair. She could feel Ida's children calling out to the Great Mothers to help them. It was as if an entire generation of people cried out to her, their collective wail slicing through her heart like a knife.

When Aria came back to herself, she was sitting on the corner of a broken-down wall. Eileithyia was seated next to her, fanning the younger priestess's face.

"Ah, I see you have returned," the High Priestess said. "Will you share your vision with me?"

Aria swiped at a tear that had run down her cheek. "When..." She swallowed, then drew in a calming breath. "When the Consort journeys, at the Feast of Grapes and the Summer Dawn-Fire Rite and the other times, one of the messages is always the same." Eileithyia raised her eyebrows. "They always say we must feed the poor and care for them so they will be poor no longer. They say the fact that we have poor people in our cities..." She trailed off, overcome with the desire to weep.

The High Priestess nodded. "Yes. It shames us before the gods, when we have such wealth that should be shared." She brushed a lock of hair back from Aria's face. "Why do you think we give out grain and oil every season? Why do you think I send you, and others in my charge, into the city to see how the people are doing? Every one of Ida's children is precious. We must take care of them all. That is what the Mothers teach us."

Aria stared out across the rubble of what had been a thriving city not too many generations earlier. "We grew rich. We did not take care of our own. And when we would not listen, the Great Mothers smacked us down, like a lioness with her cubs."

"Is that all?"

Aria shifted on the edge of the ruined wall. "We do not fight. We have no armies. We are a peaceful people," she said, sounding as if she did not believe her own words.

The High Priestess narrowed her eyes at her student. "What have you seen?"

"Blades. Weapons." She swallowed. "We do not fight, but we sell weapons to those who do. We encourage them."

"The more they war, the more blades we can sell."

"Yes." Aria's voice was a frightened whisper. She stared down at her hands.

Eileithyia touched Aria's arm, and the young woman looked over at her superior. "If we stopped selling our blades," the High Priestess said, "would they stop making war?"

"No. But..." She shook her head, willing the thoughts to arrange themselves in a meaningful order. "But we do not have to take part in it. We could be rich enough with all the other things we trade, the fabric and the dyes and the carved stone vases and the pots and jewelry. But the blades make us richer still."

"What has the vision shown you, Ariadne? Tell me what it means."

The High Priestess sounded like she already knew the answer. Aria felt herself growing angry. If Eileithyia knew the meaning, why must she press her for it?

Aria twisted around to look toward the living city, turning her back on her teacher. She saw the smooth paved streets, the freshly whitewashed buildings with their bright trim, the happy and prosperous people going about their business in the morning sunshine. But she knew that if she walked a few streets over, away from the main road and toward the edges of the harbor, she would find shacks like the ones she had just seen in her vision. Maybe not as many of them as there had been before the Great Darkness, but they were there, a testament to the work that still needed doing. Her anger drained away as her heart ached for the people of her island.

"It means," she said at last, "that we must not be blinded by greed. Wealth by itself is not a bad thing. But we must not allow our desire for riches to cloud our judgment about what is right and what is wrong. Most of all," she said, drawing in a slow breath as she realized the truth of what she was saying, "we must never stop sharing and taking care of the people. The most sacred thing we can do is take care of each other."

"So it is. And so we give from the temple stores, and we travel to other cities to encourage their temples to do the same."

Aria's brow furrowed. "Do they not all do likewise?"

"Most of them, yes, though of course Knossos..." The High Priestess pressed her lips together. "They have their own values, this new breed of mainlander. Whether or not I consider them ethical is another matter entirely."

Aria stood up and looked around, back at the ruins and then

down the Sea Road again. "Why are you showing me all this? I already know we are supposed to help the poor and share the temple stores. Everyone knows that."

"Why do you think I insisted you go to the New Year rites at Mt. Dikte a few years ago?"

"I thought," Aria said, looking away, "I thought you were making sure Rhea could do her job without my help. Or Lexion's."

"That was part of it. But I also wanted you to meet the clergy there so they would know you. We must keep up relations with the other temples and shrines, and encourage them to hold to the proper values. We make generous donations where we can and support those who cling to the old ways. We help each other."

"That is..." Aria scowled, thinking. "That is politics."

"You made the same face many years ago regarding administration," Eileithyia said with a smirk.

"But we are priestesses, not merchants or chieftains."

The High Priestess rose, linked arms with Aria, and led her back onto the Sea Road. They strolled back toward the temple as the Sun rose higher and the day warmed. When they were once again standing at the edge of the outdoor workshops, they stopped.

"Ariadne, do you think that these kinds of dealings—keeping an eye on the townspeople, maintaining relationships with the clergy of other temples—are beneath you?"

"No, My Lady," Aria answered quickly. "Of course not."

"Will you concede that diplomacy is a useful skill regardless of one's circumstances in life?"

Aria blew out a breath. "Yes. I have learned a lot from you and from Sageleus. Even within the temple, I am better at getting along with others and making sure the work gets done without anyone getting upset." Aria slipped her arm out of Eileithyia's and looked at her sidelong. "Are you dissatisfied with my work?"

The High Priestess turned and set her hands on Aria's shoulders, looking her in the eye. "I have never been dissatisfied with you, my dear, as a child or as a grown woman and a priestess. I simply want you to have all the skills you need for whatever duties the temple may see fit to bless you with."

"Duties?"

"Your responsibilities always increase. That is the way of the priesthood. There are still rituals you do not know and skills you have not learned." The High Priestess turned toward the north entrance to the temple. "And I have my responsibilities as well. Please go to Rhea and help her with the novices today. I believe they are learning about the First Crescent Moon rite. It is time you shared your knowledge with the young women who will follow in your footsteps."

The High Priestess stepped through the gateway and into the shadows of the temple, leaving Aria standing on the pavement, wondering what the older woman's words meant.

Chapter 24

Filling the Sea Road from side to side and for some distance down its length, the procession moved toward the Sea Temple at midday. The previous night, the first Full Moon following the Summer Solstice had ridden across the sky. Now the High Priestess and her Consort led the priests and priestesses, novice and initiate alike, their steps keeping slow time with the beat of a drum. They were organized according to rank, with Rhea and Kaeseus first, then Orestas, followed by Thalamika, the Chief Song-Priestess, and the Chief Song-Priest. Behind them walked the Keeper of the Bees, the Overseer of the Storehouses, the Ward of the Grain, the Ward of the Wine, and the Ward of the Oil, then the Overseers of the Workshops. The rest of the priesthood followed in no particular order. Aria found herself in the middle of a cluster of younger priestesses who all appeared nervous. She tried not to think about how she must have looked at that age. This was her third time to the Sea Temple for this purpose, and she still found it difficult to bear. Though the years wore on, some of the rites always cut straight to her heart.

Behind the Malian clergy walked a cluster of priests and priestesses who were visiting from other temples and shrines. Though the island's cities were independent of each other in terms of governance and administration, they were all still Ida's children, sharing a common reverence for the Great Mothers and their divine children. Malia had especially close ties with the cave shrine at Mt. Dikte to the south, the sacred house at Nirou Khani to the west, and the temple of Gournia to the east. But several other temples, including Knossos, had also sent clergy to represent them and to acknowledge the change of the Consort. Following the visiting clergy, a large group of laypeople brought up the rear of the procession. In accordance with the island's most ancient traditions, the Summer Solstice sacrifice was always public, to be witnessed by any of Ida's children who wished to attend.

As the procession turned off the Sea Road and down the path that led to the Sea Temple, Aria noticed a pair of local men—not priests, but burly laymen—standing at the turnoff. Guards. Half a Moon earlier, the priestesses had held a rite at the Sea Temple that was interrupted by drunken mainlanders looking for women to pleasure them and ritual ware to steal. This sort of problem was becoming more and more common at the temples and shrines, in any location that was accessible to the public, especially the outdoor rituals. It had taken a great deal of effort to remove the intruders. In the end, the priestesses had abandoned the rite and returned to the temple, some of them in tears, and one with a black eye and a torn dress from her efforts to protect the others.

So Eileithyia was taking no chances, it appeared. As the procession neared the Sea Temple, Aria spotted two more guards standing just inland of the temple, positioned to stop anyone who attempted to reach the area across the small open field that flanked the ritual site. These two guards, Aria noted, were also laymen, hired by the temple for this purpose. Of course the High Priestess would not have asked any of the priests to stand guard. Her clergy would all want to witness the sacrifice. This was a Minos Year.

While the drum continued its steady beat, the High Priestess and her Consort stepped barefoot into the little temple, she wearing the hide skirt of the sacrificial priesthood and he the colorful kilt of the Young God. The rest of the procession arrayed themselves around the outside of the small building. The midsummer sunlight beat down on the assemblage. The dry grass and weeds crackled beneath their sandals as the people shifted and milled around. Grateful for the faint breeze off the sea, Aria wiped the sweat from her forehead.

When everyone was in place, the drum sounded a loud double beat then fell silent. A triton trumpet blared three times, its echo carrying over the sound of the lapping waves along the shore just a few steps away. The ritual was timed with the tide: the Consort's body would be returned to Grandmother Ocean, the receding tide carrying it away into her bosom. This was the reason the sacrifices were held at the Sea Temple and not at the tombs, where the bones of the dead were seasonally cleaned and re-interred in pithoi and sarcophagi. While plants are born from the Earth, people are born from water, the tiny ocean within the mother's womb. So certain sacred people were returned to the water, their bodies subsumed as if they had not died at all, but simply floated away into the Sea-Mother's waiting arms, like the deities whose names they bore.

The last echo of the trumpet died away, and only the sound of the waves and the sea birds remained. When Aria looked up at the High Priestess and her Consort, she saw that their eyes were glassy, their features oddly serious and euphoric at the same time. She knew they had drunk drugged wine before leaving the main temple, and she could see that it had begun to take effect.

The Sea Temple was already prepared for the rite. Eileithyia and the Consort had taken care of that task earlier in the day before returning to the main building to prepare themselves. The small table that stood off to one side within the little temple held a full censer as well as a cup, a bowl, some folded fabric, and several figurines. Now incense smoke wafted through the pillars, shifting with the breeze. Next to the censer, Aria could see a gleaming bronze blade lying on the table. She shuddered and looked away.

Now the High Priestess and the Consort stood in the temple, their arms upraised, calling to the gods to witness the rite. The Consort's voice rang out as he invoked the Great Mothers:

By land and sky and sea
Blessed be the Three
By land and sea and sky
By Them we live and die
By sky and sea and land
Beneath Their guiding hand

Then Eileithyia spoke, more quietly but still with a voice that carried across the crowd.

By the Sun
By the Moon
By the Star of the Sea
Our Fates are woven
Our lives are set
Our time ends when it must
We give ourselves to the gods

She picked up a cup from the table, offering it to Belisseus. As she held the cup for him, he drank until it was empty. Then she turned it upside down on the table like a tiny tomb, the shape of the beehive and the Great Mother's womb.

The two stood facing each other, holding hands, as they recited the declarations of the Goddess and her Consort to each other. But the crowd did not hear this speech. Their voices were too low. The High Priestess teaches the sacred words to the Consort when the time comes for the sacrifice. They are passed down from one High Priestess to the next but never spoken otherwise and, like all the sacred rites, never written down. Fixing them to any material substance would profane them.

All too quickly the speech was done. Eileithyia and Belisseus embraced, kissing slowly and deeply, taking their time, touching and holding each other. The drum started up again, a slow heartbeat this time, steady, relentless. The two stepped back from each other. He unfastened his kilt and let it fall to the floor. Then he moved over to the large table in the center of the temple, beneath the opening in the roof. The table was the same design as the one in the pillar crypt, the same as the one the priests carried into the vineyard every year: heavy wood with decorative legs in the shape of the Horned Ones' heads, sturdy and large enough to hold a young bull—or a man.

In one graceful motion, Belisseus hefted himself up and stretched out on the table in a pool of sunlight. He lay on his back, his arms relaxed at his sides, and let his eyes close. Eileithyia stepped up beside him, a series of conflicting emotions playing across her face. She touched his forehead, his eyelids, and his lips. Then she swallowed hard, drew in a deep breath, and raised her arms, the polished bronze blade glinting in the sunlight as she gripped its hilt. The drum pounded, its heartbeat rhythm pulsing through the hot air.

"Naked we are born into the world," she said, her voice carrying easily across the crowd, though it wavered a tiny bit.

Belisseus opened his eyes. "And naked do I willingly leave it to return to the Mother's arms," he said, gazing up at his High Priestess, his speech slurred from the drugged wine.

She held the blade over his neck, poised and waiting. His lips moved, speaking to her too quietly for anyone else to hear. He looked at her and their gazes locked. His eyes never closed. Then she drew the blade across his neck. The blood spurted and his body trembled, then he stopped moving. The drum fell silent.

Eileithyia stroked her fingertips across his face to close his eyelids. With some effort, she tipped his body sideways so his blood would drain into the large bowl beneath the table. Later on, she would prepare his blood with wine, seawater, and herbs, to be used to bless the temple's fields and vineyards and certain rooms within the building. Though all the sacrificial priests and priestesses—the Hide-Bearers—could handle the blood of animals, only the High Priestess could touch the blood of a Consort. It was death to anyone else.

Aria realized that she, along with everyone else, had been staring, mesmerized, at the blood as it poured from the edge of the table into the bowl. She did not know how much time had passed, but now the blood had stopped dripping from Belisseus' neck. Gently Eileithyia turned his body onto its back once more.

Now four of the priests approached the little temple carrying a large white cloth. Two of them held the cloth level with the tabletop and the other two drew Belisseus' body off the table and onto the waiting sling, careful not to touch the blood. Each priest grasped a corner of the cloth, and together they carried him out of the temple. Eileithyia removed her hide skirt, lay it on the sacrificial table, and followed them, naked like Belisseus, across the sand and out into the water.

They moved out until they were in the water up to their shoulders, Belisseus' body floating between the priests as they held the fabric up. Then Eileithyia gave the signal, and the priests released the cloth. Belisseus' body dipped, the linen swirling around it as the receding tide pulled him under and out to sea, back to the womb of the Mother. They waited, watching, until they were sure Posidaeja had claimed him, the depths of the sea being a sure route to the World Below.

The five then waded back out of the water. Eileithyia returned to the temple, but the priests stood to one side on the sand, away from the crowd. They would touch no one, speak to no one, make eye contact with no one until they had been properly purified. A dead body in and of itself was of no consequence, a natural part of the cycle of life and death. But what they had touched was not just a human body: this was the Consort, the god made flesh to serve and love the Great Mother and her children.

Eileithyia crossed to the small table at the edge of the temple. She lifted the bowl from the tabletop and held it up for all to see, then she slowly poured the herb-steeped water over herself. It flowed from her head and shoulders, streaming down her body to run in rivulets across the temple floor, spilling off the edges onto the sandy ground. Now she and the temple were purified, ready for the next portion of the rite.

From within the crowd a young man emerged, dressed in the kilt of the Young God, his glossy black hair gleaming in the sunlight. Aria bit back a gasp. He stood before her, yet she felt no connection to him, this young man who was her son. She looked on in a daze as he embraced the High Priestess and kissed her, holding her naked body against himself.

Aria watched as the new Consort lifted a fine linen tunic from the table and dressed the High Priestess in it, wrapping a tiered skirt around her hips and tying it at the waist. He had just watched his predecessor die—had, in fact, watched the previous two die as well, a requirement as part of his training. He knew exactly what lay in store for him in just a few years' time. Yet still he did it willingly, all for the love of the Great Mother.

He could have said no, she thought. The boys who were chosen and trained as Consorts for each calendar cycle could refuse the honor and elect instead to serve as priests in the temple with no shame. It was their decision. They could not, however, leave the priesthood, but they did not have to sacrifice themselves against their will. Then Aria remembered: there had been no other boys, no other choices. Her son was the only one the right age, the only one of the temple babies who had been born during the right time, from the Consort-Bearer rite or even from ordinary lovemaking.

He had no choice. She shuddered.

Of course, the augurers had done divinations at every turn: when Aria had accepted her role in the process, the night of the rite in the pillar crypt, at his birth, and every year since then.

It is his right to give himself this way, she reminded herself. All of a sudden she felt terribly empty, as if she had been sacrificed and drained and only the shell of herself remained. She shook her head in an attempt to dispel the dark spiral of thoughts.

She returned her attention to the rite as Eileithyia and her new Consort moved to the entrance to the Sea Temple. The Consort knelt before his High Priestess, and she placed her hands on his shoulders.

"The Young God dies yet he lives again," she said, her voice carrying over the gathered crowd.

"All who die live again in the Great Mother," he responded.

The crowd shouted with joy. Sistrums hissed and rattled, and drums took up a celebratory beat. But Aria just stood there, staring blankly, waiting for any of it to make sense.

The new Belisseus rose and embraced Eileithyia. Then, holding hands, they descended the temple steps and strode down the path, leading the people back home.

Chapter 25

"Where are you going, all dressed up like that?" Aria called. She was holding a stack of fresh clay tablets wrapped in linen, an assignment Eileithyia had tasked her with in the city. She had come back to the temple along the Sea Road, but had decided she needed a few moments of solitude before meeting again with the High Priestess. Those few moments had stretched longer and longer as she wandered through the gardens along the east side of the temple, basking in the late afternoon sunshine. Finally she had forced herself to walk past the dovecote and turn toward the temple's south entrance. She had seen Lexion and his companions as she rounded the corner to the south face of the building and had stopped, calling out to him.

Lexion paused by the corner of the building, motioning his fellow priests to continue on. "You are teasing me," he said, smoothing down his tunic. It was made of coarse linen, not the fine fabric he usually wore, and had no ornament. He wore sturdy, rough boots, and his forearms were wrapped in leather bracers. He shifted the bundle of spears to his other hand and pushed his pack farther back on his shoulder to give her the salute.

"Now you are teasing me," she laughed. "But my question was serious. Is there a hunt?"

"The Ibex Brotherhood," he said, sweeping his hand in the

direction of the men who were now halfway across the field, heading purposefully toward the foothills. "We hunt to initiate a new member. We will be gone two or three days."

She squinted at the handful of men in the distance. Most of them were as old as Lexion, or older, but one appeared to be just barely of age: the new member. "There are not very many of you now," she said, recalling slightly greater numbers during her childhood, and greater still in the stories people told of the times before she was born.

"We will not let the Brotherhood die," Lexion declared.

"I would like to believe you. But Kalliste's sacred Horned One is less and less fashionable these days. Even the stag and the goat are losing ground to the bull."

"We can add the bull without taking away the others," he insisted.

"The mainlanders do not think so. I wish they would all jump into the sea and swim back where they came from." She shook her head. "Our Lady says the ones from the highlands in the north of the mainland are the worst. They do not revere our mountains as the body of the Mother, only as lumps of dirt where they can hunt and cut down trees to build more boats. I suppose they see their own mountains, where they come from, in the same way. And they say we are the backward ones."

A pained look flashed across Lexion's face. "I wish Our Lady would be more prudent in her relations with Knossos."

"But they are trying to take over the island!"

"Perhaps. And perhaps they simply do not understand how we do things here. Maybe they could learn, if we were patient enough. Dialogue is always better than argument, do you not agree?" He narrowed his eyes, waiting for her to nod before he continued. "The mainlanders are human, too. Surely we can find a way to live in peace with our neighbors. The last thing I want is to see our beautiful island full of fighting."

Aria toyed with the edge of the linen that wrapped her clay tablets. "How is Rhea? We have both been so busy, I have not seen her since the First Crescent Moon Rite, except for fleeting glimpses in the corridors."

"She is well, but like you, I rarely see her. She is so busy. More than once she has pushed me toward my fellow priests when she was too tired for me in the evening." Aria's eyebrows raised. "I do not wish to lie with any other woman, but she does not want me to go without," he explained. "You should take some time to chat with her, perhaps tempt her out into the fresh air. She works too hard. A bit of leisure would do her good."

"I will do that."

"And Sageleus? He is well?"

Aria looked down and cleared her throat. Today's assignment had taken her into the city. Sageleus had been instrumental in helping her make an accounting of all the merchants, artisans, and traders who worked independent of the temple. When they had finished the rounds, he had brought her back to his house for some wine and a bite to eat. Neither of them had time for a leisurely encounter today, but they had made judicious use of a few stolen moments. Aria had left his house with high color in her cheeks and a spring in her step.

"He is well," she managed to say, doing her best to suppress a grin, and Lexion gave her a knowing look. Then he kissed her cheek and bade her farewell, taking off at a run to catch up with the others.

Squaring her shoulders, Aria turned toward the south entrance and made her way into the temple building. She found the High Priestess in her workroom, dust motes floating in the light that streamed in through the high windows.

"You finished in just one day," Eileithyia said with a smile, motioning Aria to a bench.

"I had help," Aria replied, hiding a grin behind her hand.

The older woman held out her hand, and Aria gave her the wrapped stack of clay tablets.

"I saw Lexion on the way back in. The Ibex Brotherhood is initiating a new member."

Eileithyia nodded. "We may add the bull to our divine family, but the original three Horned Ones still stand: ibex, goat, and deer."

Aria shifted closer to the work table as Eileithyia drew the tablets out of the fabric. "I hear that at Knossos, they say the bull is the third Horned One," Aria said. "They are trying to blot out the ibex as if they never existed."

"There was a time, generations ago, when there were no cattle on the island. Things change, and cattle are important now. But they cannot make the ibex go away, have no fear." She laid the tablets out on her work table, rearranging them until she was satisfied with the organization. "The problem is not the addition of the bull."

"I do not understand."

"My friends at Knossos tell me the mainlanders now call the male Horned Ones the Three, and they do not include the ibex in that saying."

"As if they were equal with the Great Mothers." Aria's eyes widened.

"They take oaths on those three as well. No good will come of it, I tell you. We must remain vigilant and as unmoving as the Great Mothers." Her gaze dropped to the clay tablets. "That is why I asked you to collect this information for me today."

"I have divided them up for you," Aria said, motioning to different tablets as she spoke. "The merchants and traders are here, and the artisans are here. I have noted their specialties as well. And Sageleus helped me rank them according to wealth."

"Very good."

"As you asked, I have also noted whether they mostly stay here or travel, and whether they are native or mainlander. Why you needed that, I do not know, but at least now we can give to the people from the temple stores according to their needs and make sure no one goes hungry."

Eileithyia squinted at a tablet, running her fingertip along a line of writing. "That is not the main reason I wanted this information, though it will also help with the fair distribution of the grain, wine, and oil."

Aria tensed. "Why have I asked the people all these questions, My Lady?"

"So we may know who is likely to stand with us against Knossos and who is likely to go astray and need... persuading." She set her hand on Aria's arm, and the younger woman flinched.

"You are spying on our people."

"No, my dear. You went in broad daylight and asked questions which they were not required to answer. But answer they did, since they know you and like you, and now we can see who we have in our city."

Aria narrowed her eyes at the tablets. "We have the records from the Offering Days."

"The wealthy come often; the poor rarely, if at all. This is a more accurate representation." Eileithyia stroked her finger down the side of one tablet, perusing the names of the wealthy traders.

"I wish you had told me before I went out."

"Could you have kept it a secret?"

Aria huffed out a breath. Even though she was closer to forty years old than thirty, keeping a blank face was not her strong suit, even when she believed whole-heartedly in what she was doing.

"Very well," Eileithyia said. "This information is valuable. It will help us make plans and safeguard our temple and our people for the future. That is our sacred task."

Aria tilted her head, scanning the lists she had written. "But some mainlanders respect our ways," she said. "And some of the native people like the mainlanders quite well. Too well." She cringed a little, hoping she had not spoken out of turn.

"I know about Thalamika's leanings," the High Priestess said, patting Aria's hand. "She ogles the mainlanders' wealth, but she is devoted to our ways. The desire for gold and silver is a weakness, not a crime." Aria looked away, not convinced. If the temple were not well off, would Thalamika still be loyal? "The fact that you do not like someone does not automatically make them an enemy. You need to learn some patience, my dear."

Aria drew in a sharp breath, stung by the comment, and suddenly she was angry. "Patience? I have been so patient for so long. You send me out on errands without telling me what I am really doing, as if I were a child. You let me study any subject I wish,a but forbid me to declare a specialty, as if I were only initiated yesterday. You ask me to teach the novices, then treat me as if I were still among them." She clenched her jaw, gritting her teeth. "You take my son as your Consort as if he were nothing to me, while I watch Rhea's son come of age and leave the temple for my brother's ship. I am not made of stone, My Lady."

"I promise, there is sound reasoning behind all my decisions, Ariadne."

"You talk about my place in the temple," Aria said, pushing herself up from the bench. "But I have no place. I am your errand-runner, your little priestess you send into the city with pointless tasks just to keep me busy. You are glad when Sageleus distracts me from my duties now that Rhea is too busy for my company."

"I am glad you have friends," Eileithyia said.

"I work hard, My Lady. I have done my best never to disappoint you. Yet I may do anything except rise in the temple hierarchy. What are you trying to do, turn me into a merchant? Or perhaps you wish me to become the next Overseer of the Workshops?"

"Those are both perfectly respectable jobs."

"But they are not priestly work," she spat. "They are not what I have trained for all these years, what I have had visions of. I deserve to be a real priestess." She folded her arms across her chest. "What is so awful about my priestessing that you will not even tell me?"

"Nothing," the High Priestess said, reaching out for Aria's hand. The younger woman backed away. "Everything I have done is to prepare us both for the future. Our times are uncertain, Ariadne. You know that."

Aria backed up toward the door. "Then let me rise! Let me be a proper priestess! Let me hold the offices I have seen in my visions!"

"You *are* a proper priestess." Eileithyia pressed her lips together. "What offices, exactly, are you expecting?"

"I..." Aria drew in a slow breath. "You made sure Rhea was elected as Head of the College, even though you were training me for the office. I have not seen her untimely death, thank the Mothers, so I do not know why you will not let me claim a specialty and let me work to be... perhaps the Chief Scrivener or the Chief

Sky-Watcher. Be anointed to one of those offices. My visions always come true. I have seen my anointing!"

Eileithyia reached a hand out toward Aria, then drew it back. "At the right time, I will make it all official. We cannot change fate. The goddess weaves the web as she desires. We must prepare ourselves as best we can to deal with whatever she gives us."

"She gives me nothing," Aria seethed. "Or perhaps you refuse to let her." She turned and stalked from the room.

Chapter 26

For the better part of two Moons, Aria avoided her High Priestess. She did her work diligently and was quietly helpful to her fellow clergy, never complaining or making negative comments about her superior. But she did her best to avoid Eileithyia. Of course, she had no choice but to report to the High Priestess for her assignments. But she kept her answers to the older woman's questions as short as possible and excused herself the moment their business was concluded. She made sure to sit as far away as possible from Eileithyia in the dining hall and stopped volunteering to take part in the temple rites, participating only when assigned to do so.

"What is troubling you?" Rhea asked one day as they were walking in the herb garden, Aria keeping her promise to Lexion about getting their friend outdoors more often.

"Nothing and everything."

Rhea gave her a concerned look and took her hand. "You can tell me."

Aria blew out a breath. "I am going nowhere in the temple. All Our Lady does is stall and evade. After all these years, she still insists on giving me tasks herself instead of letting me be a part of the regular work with you and the rest of the College. Is it wrong to want to do the same things the other priestesses my age are doing?"

"Of course not." Rhea's brow furrowed. "Are you certain you understand Our Lady's aims for you?"

"I have seen my anointing!" she exclaimed.

Rhea stopped walking, and Aria paused as well, turning to face her friend.

"Oh Rhea," Aria said. "I am happy for you to be the Head of the College."

"But you wish Our Lady had chosen you."

Aria looked away. "Maybe. I do not know what I wish, to be honest. I just know that I am unhappy with my life as it is. None of it feels like the visions I have had, and they always come true. I do not know what is wrong."

"Perhaps..."

"What?"

"Perhaps if you had a child. Then you would have someone to help fill your time so you would not have to be so impatient with Our Lady."

Aria drew her hand out of Rhea's grasp. "I am barren now. All the seasonal rites. All this time with Sageleus, and nothing. My womb has done all it will." She sighed, but no tears came. She had already cried all the tears this subject had.

"So you want to make up for that emptiness by some position in the temple, regardless of Our Lady's plans for you?"

"No. Yes. I feel... there is something I am meant to do, yet I cannot see what it is. No new visions come, no quiet voice in meditation, nothing."

Rhea offered her hand again, and Aria took it this time. "Perhaps you are trying too hard."

Aria shook her head. "Or not hard enough."

Aria left her friend in a workroom, instructing a handful of young priestesses how to clean, store, and organize the temple's ritual vessels. At least Rhea did not question her purpose or her usefulness in the temple, and neither did those young women.

Wandering aimlessly through the corridors, Aria came to one of the smaller ritual rooms. Struck by a sudden idea, she stepped through the doorway and slipped her sandals off. Barefoot, she approached the altar, stopping on the rug just in front of it. The low wooden table was topped by a strip of saffron-dyed linen embroidered with rows of blood-red lilies along the edges. On top of the fabric sat a collection of ritual objects. A footed terracotta offering stand, currently empty, and a small stone libation table, also vacant, stood to one side.

In the middle of the table sat a pair of terracotta sacred horns with a gilded wooden labrys rising up from the center. An oil lamp stood ready to be lit when the room grew dark, and a tall, narrow stand held several seal stones all piled together. Someone had laid a bunch of fresh lilies in front of the horns. Their deep red blooms were beginning to wilt and brown around the edges, though their sweet fragrance lingered.

Standing before the goddess' altar, Aria made the salute, then dropped to her knees. The thin rug was little relief over the cold stone floor, but the discomfort only intensified her resolve. If the High Priestess would not help her, then she had no choice but to appeal to a higher power.

Since this was a spur-of-the-moment decision, Aria had not brought the usual offerings with her: goat's milk, honey, almonds. She cast about for ideas. It was unthinkable to ask the goddess for help without first providing her a gift. The relationship with the gods went both ways.

A thought flickered through her mind, and her hand went to the necklace that lay heavy against her skin. The large central carnelian bead was flanked by smaller ones of deep blue lapis and crystal-clear quartz. Then the design continued on with the quartz, punctuated every few beads with a small fluted ring of gold. It was her favorite piece of jewelry, one she wore almost every day. Inia had gifted it to her the day Aria became a priestess, all those years ago. Valuable as it was in market terms, sacred terms, and emotional ones, would it be enough to gain the goddess' favor? Enough to finally get some answers, find a direction? Aria could not remember the last time she had experienced a vision. It was as if the gods had stopped speaking to her, and the more she despaired, the more silent and distant they became. No price was too high.

With shaking hands she lifted the necklace over her head, then she laid it on the offering stand. "Please," she whispered. Clutching fistfuls of her skirt, her curled hands pressing hard against her thighs as she knelt on the hard stone, she began the invocations.

Mother of the Dark Earth,
Mother of the Waves,
Mother of the Sky.
Daughter-Bearer,
Spirit-Keeper,
World-Mover,
Hear your child.

She drew in a trembling breath. Calling to the Three was one thing. Everyone did that all the time, at home and in the temple. Addressing the Greatest Mother via her Daughter was another thing altogether, one she generally avoided except during formal ritual. Even though she was the goddess' namesake, Aria feared the Daughter more than the Great Mothers. For the Daughter reflects the mirror of the Sun, the wave of the sea, and the shadow of the Earth into the world as she weaves the fates of Ida's children together, the web of threads spun by the Great Starry Mother from the beginning of time until its very end. The Daughter may be born into this world via the Mother of the Dark Earth, but ultimately, she comes from the stars.

"Daughter of the Star-Mother," Aria began, her voice cracking. She cleared her throat and began again. "Daughter of the Three-and-One, I call to you. Please..."

And suddenly she did not know what to ask. How could she fill the emptiness inside her? Not even a goddess could do that. No title, no riches would give her a sense of purpose. She was no longer even sure she wanted a child. Another child.

"Great Lady," she whispered, "please help me. I am... I am aimless. Please show me which way to go. Give me a vision, a hint. Something, anything to tell me how to move forward." She drew in a slow breath and blinked back tears. "I do not know what to do. If you have a path in mind for me, please share it. I feel so alone."

As she stared at the altar, willing her gaze to soften so the visions might come, she heard a faint click. A small stone had fallen off the tall stand. It dropped onto the offering stand below, where Aria had set her necklace, bounced gently on the altar's tabletop, and then fell to the floor. It rolled across the thin rug, stopping a hand's breadth in front of Aria.

Her heart pounded in her chest as she reached out, her hand wavering over the tiny stone. It was a bead seal carved of green serpentine, no bigger around than her fingertip. It belonged to the High Priestess, who used it to mark certain offerings that were given to ask for the Daughter's aid as a conductor of souls. Though the regular priestesses were not forbidden to touch such things, they usually avoided doing so anyway. Great power resided in objects like this one. To touch them was to tap that power, and if the one who touched it could not control what they connected with...

After a moment's hesitation, Aria grasped the seal stone with her fingertips and lifted it up, examining it. She could not fathom what kind of message it might embody. Was she supposed to assist with the offerings instead of simply recording them at the scribal table? Should she ask to be trained as a conductor of souls? Did she need to dedicate herself to Ariadne? Of course, she had the goddess' name, whether or not she wanted it, so any dedication would be almost pointless. Surely this meant that she was special in some way, even if Eileithyia did not see it in her. At least, she hoped that was the case. It was a good sign, regardless, she decided.

Curling her hand around the seal stone, she twisted her head to see if anyone was near the doorway into the shrine room. Seeing no one, she tucked the stone into a fold of her bodice.

"Thank you, Great Lady," she whispered, then rose, smoothing out the wrinkles where she had clutched her skirt so tightly. "I will do my best to understand your gift, even if no one else believes I am worthy."

Her heart was still pounding as she stepped off the rug and

slipped her sandals back on. She took a few deep breaths, allowing the weight of what she had just experienced to sink in. The goddess had heard her and had answered, though what that answer meant, Aria still had to determine. But her prayer had been heard, and that was enough for the moment. Her head held high, she stepped out of the room and nearly collided with the High Priestess.

"My Lady!" Aria exclaimed, grasping her bodice to ensure that the seal stone did not fall out.

"I was just coming to find you," Eileithyia said, eyeing the folds of Aria's bodice where she had enclosed the stone. Aria dropped her hand away from the garment. "May we go somewhere private to talk?"

"If we must," Aria said, avoiding the High Priestess' gaze and fighting the urge to touch her clothing again to be sure the seal stone was still secure in the folds of fabric.

"Please, Ariadne," Eileithyia said.

Taken aback at the older woman's gentle, beseeching tone, Aria nodded and let the High Priestess lead her to a nearby workroom. As they stood among the tables and storage shelves, Eileithyia reached out and took Aria's hand. Aria let her, though she made no move to close the space between them.

"I must apologize," the High Priestess said. "You have been upset with me, and with good reason." Aria stared at her, puzzled. "I should have handled the situation differently. I have gone about it all wrong."

"Gone about... what?" Aria managed to say.

"I have known you since your birth, my dear."

"You were my mother's midwife. I already knew that."

The High Priestess let out a slow breath. "That means I have known you as an infant and a child. Perhaps I have been unwilling to see that you are not just an adult now, and have been for some time, but also a supremely competent and devoted priestess."

Aria took a step back, bumping into the shelves behind her as she pulled her hand out of Eileithyia's grasp. "Why are you suddenly being nice to me?"

"My dear," the older woman said, allowing Aria her space,

"there are things I should have told you long before now, things you are beyond ready to hear. I should have explained my plans to you some time past. But I was unable to see you for who you are now and not who you were so many years ago."

"I am listening." Aria's brow furrowed.

"You are angry that I have insisted on giving you assignments myself instead of allowing the Head of the College of Priestesses to do so, as is our custom for ordinary priestesses." Aria nodded. "But did it not occur to you that working directly under the High Priestess is an honor?"

"At first, yes. But then it seemed more like a punishment." Aria blinked, confused. "I thought..."

"I know." Eileithyia took a tentative step toward Aria. When the younger woman stayed in place, the High Priestess reached out and offered her hands. Aria looked away, then back, and finally clasped the older woman's hands in her own.

"You were not just keeping me busy?" Aria asked. "Or keeping me away from the other priestesses because I am not good enough, not sincere or dedicated enough?"

"Oh, my dear," Eileithyia sighed. "*Not good enough* has never been among your attributes." Aria stared at her, perplexed. "Your name gives you no hint as to what I have planned for you? What the gods themselves have set out for you?"

"What does my name have to do with anything?"

The High Priestess pressed her lips together, scowling. "This is where I have failed you. It is an old tale, and I suppose people these days do not set much store by it anymore. The clergy no longer whisper about it in the corridors, so only the older ones are aware..." She drew in a breath. "You know each priestess' name is chosen by divination, by sacred auguries." Aria nodded. "My dear, the initiate who bears the Daughter's name is always the next High Priestess. You are our Ariadne."

Aria's mouth fell open. She stared at her High Priestess, gripping the older woman's hands for support as she felt her knees begin to buckle.

"Breathe, Ariadne."

Feeling dizzy, Aria leaned back against the shelves and took slow, deep breaths. After a few moments, her heart stopped pounding, and she was able to speak again.

"Your name is not..."

"No," Eileithyia said. "There was no one of my generation chosen from birth. Sometimes that is the case. Often, in fact."

"The divination," she said. "You have always said the divination at my birth prophesied something, but you would not tell me what."

"I should have told you sooner," Eileithyia said. "I swore your mother to silence as well. You should know that the College of Priestesses has approved you in a secret vote, just this morning."

"But... you tried to talk me out of being a priestess."

"I had to be certain you were sincere. I could never forgive myself if I thought I had convinced you to do something you did not wish to."

"Not wish to? How can you even think that?"

Eileithyia smiled. "Then I take it you accept."

Remembering herself, Aria dropped to her knees, though she wobbled a bit. Once she was steady, she bowed her head, clasping her hands together to keep them from shaking. "I am honored, My Lady. Yes, I accept." She was relieved that she managed to keep her voice steady.

"Very well." Eileithyia touched Aria's shoulders then made the sign of blessing over the younger woman's head. "I will make plans for the ceremony to announce you as my successor at the Summer Solstice rites."

Gripping the shelves for support, Aria struggled to her feet. "How can I ever thank you?"

"Believe me, my dear, when I tell you that this is not a gift. When the gods mark us out for their work, it is rarely for the easy tasks."

She held out her arms, and Aria accepted the embrace, angling her body at the last moment so the High Priestess would not press against her side where the bead seal was hidden. Eileithyia stepped back, examining Aria's face. "It is a shock, I know," the High Priestess said. "But you will soon grow used to the idea." She gave

Aria a kiss on the cheek, then went out of the storeroom, leaving the younger woman standing there, leaning against the shelves, staring blankly.

She expected to cry. This was a momentous occasion, after all. The goddess had heard her plea and answered right away. This was her vision coming true. She would be anointed to the highest office of all. Yet Aria felt nothing. Perhaps Eileithyia was right, and she was still reeling from the shock of it. Being the High Priestess of a temple was no small task, even if Malia was not as large as Knossos.

Summer Solstice was only a few Moons away. Among the usual rites—the divinations, the dancing, the lovemaking, the bull sacrifice since this was not a Minos Year—Eileithyia would include another ceremony, one Aria had never seen before: the anointing of the High Priestess' successor. Then Aria would begin her year of training for that office.

She made a sound as if someone had punched her in the stomach. Her head rocked back against the storage shelves, and she grasped the edge of one to steady herself. This was not a Minos Year, but it was the seventh of the series. In just over a year's time, Eileithyia would sacrifice herself along with the Consort. The High Priestess had barely more than a year left to live, as did Aria's son.

She clutched the seal stone within the folds of her bodice. Yes, the goddess had answered her prayer, but her reply was as much a curse as a blessing. Perhaps this was her punishment for stealing the stone.

Carefully she retrieved the stone from the folds of fabric and gripped it in her fist. Setting her jaw, she stepped out into the corridor and stalked back down to the shrine room, aiming to return the stone to the altar. She drew up short as she neared the doorway. There were voices coming from within the room. As she peered around the doorpost, she saw Lexion and two other priests making offerings and singing the goddess' song, their sandals piled haphazardly next to the door.

Her heart pounding again, she drew away from the room and pressed her back against the wall, clutching the stone. Seeing Lexion had made her think of Sageleus, and that reminded her of the rules. Of course, the High Priestess could only be intimate with her Consort. Everyone knew that. It was the way of Ida's children. But the priestess who was anointed, the one who was marked out to undergo a year of training before becoming the next High Priestess—she could touch no one at all.

Chapter 27

"We will still see each other," Sageleus said, trailing his fingertips down Aria's arm as they lay together in his bed in the afterglow of gentle lovemaking.

The starlight shimmered in the open window, and Aria remembered that the Daughter delivers Ourania's messages of tangle-woven fate to mankind. Never had she felt more tangled than now, hung up in the threads like a fly struggling in a spider's web.

"I think that will make it harder, not easier," she said. She lay back against his chest and drew the bedlinens up to cover herself, even though it was a warm night. "To have to see you on temple business and not be able to touch you."

He wrapped his arms around her, warm and strong. "I have always known that your position comes before everything else, including personal relationships. That is the way of the priesthood." His lips traced the shell of her ear. "I am grateful for the time we have had together."

"By Ida, why must you be so understanding?" she snarled, fisting a wad of the bedlinen.

He laughed, and she punched him in the arm, but not hard. "Are you certain it is the dove goddess you serve," he said, "and not the goddess of those large wild cats up in the mountains of the mainland?"

She tried to laugh at his joke but instead, against her will, tears came. He held her as she cried, great heaving sobs of sorrow at all she would be leaving behind, rocking in his arms as the waves of pain overtook her. It was like losing her baby to the temple all over again, but this time she felt as if she was losing herself, the very core of her being ripped out and torn away.

When her sobs finally died down to ragged breaths and the occasional hiccup, Sageleus drew up a corner of the bedlinen and dabbed the tears off her face. He smoothed her hair down and kissed the top of her head.

"I love you," he reminded her. It was not something they said to each other often.

"And I you," she managed, her voice rough from crying. "That will not change."

"I know. And you are strong."

She let out a bitter laugh. "That is why I am crying now, because I am strong."

"It is true," he said, cradling her face in his hands and shifting to meet her gaze. "Our Lady knows you through and through. She would not have let the Colleges choose you unless you could do the job." He kissed her cheek. "The gods would not have chosen you if you were not worthy."

Aria considered the idea. Eileithyia had clearly been scrutinizing her for some time now, no, for her entire life, ever since the auguries at her birth. The High Priestess had repeatedly pushed Aria to learn new skills, even if—or perhaps especially if—those activities made her uncomfortable. And not once had Eileithyia behaved like she thought Aria would be unable to meet the challenge.

It occurred to her that the High Priestess had probably had auguries done regarding Aria at regular intervals throughout her lifetime, just as was always done for the young men destined to become Consorts. She toyed with the corner of the bedsheet, avoiding Sageleus' gaze.

"You know I am right," he said softly.

"Perhaps you are," she admitted. "But that does not mean I am not frightened."

"No sane woman walks into a job like that without a healthy dose of fear," he said. "Courage does not mean you feel no fear. It means you do what is necessary anyway."

"You are wise," she said, a faint smile curling the corners of her mouth.

"I am also very good in bed," he said, rolling over on top of her. "Can you stay until daybreak?"

"Only if you feed me breakfast before I go. Our Lady will have me busy again from the moment I set foot back on the temple grounds. Summer Solstice is only a few days away."

Chapter 28

The afternoon sunlight slanted across the central court as the crowd gathered in front of the loggia. Rhea and Kaeseus had already purified the area with herb-water and incense smoke, and all those who were to participate in the rite had taken water-baths and smoke-baths. Now Aria waited out of sight in the curtained area behind the loggia along with the High Priestess and the Consort. The Chief Song-Priest and Priestess took their places in this room as well, where they had gathered their sistrums and a triton shell trumpet on a small table.

Hot air wavered in the court. The people shifted, trying not to stand too close to each other. The courtyard was packed full, not just with the clergy but also with the temple's lay overseers and workers as well as many prominent townspeople and a few visitors from Nirou Khani, Gournia, and the cave shrine at Mt. Dikte. They would all witness the anointing, all acknowledge the High Priestess' successor. Rhea and Kaeseus stood at the top of the steps that led up to the loggia, their usual place as Heads of the Colleges.

The Summer Solstice dawn rites were long past and the sunset ceremonies were yet to come. The bull sacrifice would not take place until the Full Moon, several days hence. But now, the people stood in the heat and listened as three blasts from the triton trumpet signaled the beginning of the Rite of Anointing. Eileithyia pushed the curtain aside and stepped onto the platform at the rear of the loggia. The Consort followed, standing next to her. Then she moved down the narrow steps between the columns, stopping behind the altar. Belisseus came down the steps behind her and crossed to one side of the altar.

From the room behind the loggia, sistrums sounded, a rattling hiss that reverberated for a few moments after the instruments had stopped playing. The High Priestess strode to the front of the loggia, raised her arms, and spoke the preliminary invocation.

"Three times I say the prayer, for the Three: the three Mothers, the three realms, the three worlds."

Then her words rang out across the courtyard as she intoned the whole invocation three times:

By land and sky and sea
Blessed be the Three
By land and sea and sky
By Them we live and die
By sky and sea and land
Beneath Their guiding hand

She lowered her arms and moved over to the altar. "Three times I pour the libation, for the Three: the three Mothers, the three realms, the three worlds."

Aiming carefully for the wide bowl that sat on the floor next to the altar, she lifted the flagon of wine, a special vintage reserved for the most sacred of rites. She poured it out slowly so it did not splash beyond the borders of the bowl. The blood-red liquid twisted and gleamed as it streamed down. When that pitcher was empty, she returned it to the altar and picked up the one full of olive oil, the temple's best from the previous year. Again she held up the flagon and poured its contents into the bowl, allowing the golden-green stream to flow slowly so it entered the bowl without disturbing the wine. She returned that container, now empty, to the altar and picked up the final offering vessel, full of honey from the temple's many hives. The day was hot enough that the honey poured almost as easily as water, pooling in the center of the bowl, surrounded by the wine as the oil floated to the top.

When the final flagon was empty and Eileithyia had returned it to its place on the altar, she nodded to the Consort. From the altar he retrieved an alabastron full of oil scented with resins and spices. Then he knelt in front of the High Priestess, lifting the small vessel up in front of himself. Eileithyia held her hands over the container and made the sign of the Three-and-One, blessing the oil to its special purpose in this rite. Then Belisseus stood up, set the alabastron back on the altar, and moved toward the back of the loggia.

He ascended the steps between the columns and strode over to the doorway at the back. Making the sacred salute, he stood to one side of the doorway and waited. A hissing rattle issued from the room behind the loggia, continuing on without stopping, as if a great serpent were slithering through the courtyard.

Swallowing hard, Aria took a deep breath. She drew the curtain aside and moved through the doorway, pausing between the columns at the top of the steps. When she stopped, the sistrums fell silent. From her vantage point she could see the whole crowd: her fellow priests and priestesses, the temple's lay workers, the townspeople. Her heart pounded as Sageleus' face resolved itself in her vision. He was smiling, but she could see the sadness in his eyes. How could she do this to him? To herself? The gods do not tell us how to fulfill their commands, only that we must.

Her attention snapped back to her fellow clergy in the loggia. They were waiting for her to move. She descended the steps and stopped behind the altar, forcing herself to breathe slowly, steadily. It helped to keep her gaze lowered so she did not have to see all the eyes that were focused on her. She had taken part in many rites, but this one was different. This one mattered more than all the others. Infinitely more.

Eileithyia gestured with her hand, and Aria crossed to stand in front of the altar, facing out into the courtyard. Slowly she lowered herself to her knees. She had to grip her hands onto her thighs to keep her legs from shaking. When she had found her balance again, she lifted her head and looked out over the crowd, choosing to rest her gaze on a spot along the roofline on the far side of the courtyard. That way she would not have to see anyone's face until it was all over. She was not sure she could maintain her composure if she caught Sageleus' gaze, or Lexion's, or Rhea's. Fortunately, she would not have to look the High Priestess or the Consort in the eye until the rite was completed.

Eileithyia and Belisseus moved to either side of Aria, facing each other over her kneeling form. The Consort was holding the alabastron from the altar. He stretched his arms out and cradled the jar in his hands over Aria's head as the High Priestess spoke. It dawned on Aria that she had not thought of him as her son for quite some time. He was simply Belisseus, the Consort, and nothing more. Her heart kicked in her chest, and she fought to keep her focus on the ritual.

"The High Priestess is the face of the goddess in this world," Eileithyia said, "as the Consort is the face of the god. Each High Priestess has been anointed to her task, one before the other, for generations and generations, leading back to the time of the gods themselves." She reached out and held her hands, palms down, over the alabastron. "The anointing is the outward sign of the blessing the Great Mothers give, the blessing the Mother-of-All gives, which cannot be removed once it has been accepted. As the sacrifice must go willing, so must the High Priestess step into her role freely, of her own choosing." She paused. "I ask you now, Ariadne daughter of Inia, do you take this step willingly? Do you choose it above all other paths in your life?"

"I do," Aria said, her voice shaking.

"Do you choose this office for the rest of your life, giving yourself to it fully and freely?"

"I do."

"Do you offer your whole self up for the gods' work, for the Three-and-One, forsaking all other intimacies except those allowed within the office?"

Unbidden, Aria's gaze dipped down into the crowd, where Sageleus was watching her, his brow furrowed. She swallowed. "I do," she said, her voice barely louder than a whisper. Sageleus' face relaxed into a gentle sadness, and Aria felt a cold weight in the pit of her stomach.

Eileithyia turned her head toward the assembled crowd. "Witness now the ancient rite of anointing. This woman, Ariadne daughter of Inia, receives the blessing of the temple, which is the blessing of the gods themselves. She accepts the office which is offered to her."

With gentle motions she grasped the alabastron, her hands wrapped around the Consort's hands. Together they tilted the small vessel sideways until the sacred oil poured slowly out onto Aria's head. It felt cool against the heat of the day as it drizzled onto her scalp, slithering down through her hair, dripping onto her shoulders and running in rivulets down her chest and back. As the oil warmed against her skin, the scent surrounded her like an invisible cloud: labdanum and myrrh and sweet spices, pungent and almost overwhelming in the heat.

The High Priestess and the Consort tilted the alabastron over further until it ran empty. Then Eileithyia let go of it, removing her hands from atop the Consort's. He set the empty vessel on the altar and returned to his place at Aria's side.

When Eileithyia placed her hands, palms down, on Aria's head, the younger woman wobbled where she was kneeling, her vision going black around the edges. She gripped the fronts of her thighs, steadying herself, and drew in slow, deliberate breaths. She refused to be the first woman ever to faint during an anointing.

"May you be blessed, Ariadne," said the High Priestess. "May you walk in the grace and love of the gods every day of your life. May your path be true and your heart pure."

Eileithyia lifted her hands from Aria's head and gestured to her. Aria knew this was the point in the ritual when she was supposed to stand up again, but her legs simply refused to work. She tried to blame her dizziness on the heat and the fumes from the anointing oil, but she was a seasoned priestess and she knew better than to lie to herself like that, even in her thoughts.

"Oh no," she muttered, shifting to try to get up. She glanced up at Eileithyia and shot her a look of panic. The High Priestess turned to her Consort and made a silent signal that Aria did not recognize.

Before Aria understood what was happening, the Consort and the High Priestess had slipped their hands beneath her arms and were helping her stand up. They each kept a hand behind her back, steadying her, as they turned toward the gathered crowd.

"Behold," Eileithyia's voice rang out across the courtyard, "the anointed one. I give you Ariadne, daughter of the gods, who will be the next High Priestess of this temple when this Minos cycle draws to a close."

Behind Aria, sistrums hissed and rattled. In front of her, the crowd shouted and cheered. She looked down to see Sageleus forcing a smile, nodding at her in approval. Despite the warm sunlight on her skin, she shivered.

Chapter 29

"Very good," Eileithyia said. "I am pleased with how fast you are learning. Next I will teach you the words for the Consort sacrifices."

Aria stood looking out at the sea, one hand pressed against one of the Sea Temple's columns. "I think my head will burst if I have to memorize any more words." She tried, and failed, to convince herself that her resistance to learning this next rite was simply due to the volume of work she had already done.

Leaning into the sea breeze, she gave silent thanks for the way it gentled the late summer heat. It had barely been two Moon cycles since she was anointed, and it felt like she had learned more rituals in that short time than in her entire career as a priestess before then.

The two women had spent most days and many evenings together, any time Eileithyia was not required by her position to lead a rite, sit in the audience chamber, or take care of administration. And Aria knew they would continue to do so until the following Summer Solstice. A year of training. A year of learning more than she had in her whole lifetime before that fateful midsummer day.

"Come," Eileithyia said, patting the cushion next to her. "I know it is a lot, but you must know all these things well and fully. When I am gone, you will have no one to ask if you forget."

Aria crossed the temple and positioned the cushion on the floor next to Eileithyia, in the slim shadow cast by the narrow roof ring. Then she dropped down with a sigh.

"I wish you would not constantly remind me that you will soon be dead."

Eileithyia reached out and touched Aria's hair, smoothing a loose strand back into place. "I will always be with you, Ariadne. Love never dies."

Blinking back tears, Aria smiled. "I love you, too," she managed to whisper, realizing the truth of the words as she said them for the first time.

Eileithyia offered a soft smile, then she drew in a breath and returned to the practical. "Now, there is still much to learn. I know you tire of repeating the same things to me over and over, but it is important that you get the words exactly right. There is power in these rites, ancient magic. If you speak the words incorrectly, the spirit of the working will be lessened. You might even do damage if you get some of it wrong."

"Of course." Aria sighed. "How much easier it would be if we could write these things down."

"You know better than that."

"Ever since Thalamika taught me to write, you have constantly reminded me that everything we do is sacred, including scribing. Even administration is the gods' work, the work of the Great Mothers."

"That is so," the High Priestess said. "And writing is a great help for offerings and donations and those sorts of things. Everything we do is sacred, but not every act is as sacred as every other. Ritual is special."

Aria's brow furrowed. "But some people use writing for sacred acts. What about the inscriptions I have seen on vessels and libation tables? Why is that not forbidden?"

"That is a special situation," Eiliethyia said, shaking her head. "Writing—or more specifically, inscribing words onto ritual objects—can be used for certain purposes. But we avoid it most of the time. It creates problems." Aria looked the question at her. "It makes the people think that writing itself is magic, and not simply a tool like all others. People who do not know how to write will instead imitate writing to make their own coarse magic..." She trailed off, scowling.

"For inappropriate purposes."

"Indeed. To try to gain wealth without work or to overtake a rival or to seek revenge on an enemy. Or an imagined enemy. I have seen traders try to use writing magic to sink their competitors' ships."

"Oh." Aria ducked her head. "I keep forgetting that not everyone wishes their fellow human beings well."

Eileithyia set her hand on top of Aria's. "You are a good woman. I know it is hard for you to understand the darkness in some people's hearts. But it is there, all the same, and you would do well to remember that." She gave Aria's hand a squeeze. "Let us return to our work, shall we?"

Aria forced a smile. She did not like being reminded how awful people could be if they were given free rein with their baser desires. That was why it was so important to teach people the Mothers' ways and refuse to let those traditions change. She nodded to Eileithyia to continue.

The older woman spoke the private words for the Rite of Sacrifice—not the ordinary rite involving an animal, but the greatest one, the one in which the Consort is reunited with the gods. Dutifully Aria repeated the words, doing her best to memorize them without thinking about what they meant, that she would one day draw a knife across the throat of a beautiful young man.

She stood up and paced, repeating the words until she knew them by heart. Then she recited them back to Eileithyia.

"Very good. We will review all the rites every few days to be certain you have them properly memorized. Once you are High Priestess, you should review them yourself every so often, just to keep them fresh." She drew in a slow breath and let it out, renewing her focus. "Now I will teach you the sayings you will need for next summer, when you receive the new Consort. You will speak these words with each new Consort as he enters the temple and becomes yours."

Aria blinked. "How many..." She broke off, thinking better of asking such a question.

"The current Consort is my fourth."

"And last."

"Yes." The High Priestess eyed her apprentice. "There are no rules as to how long a High Priestess may hold her office. The only requirement is that she must go in a Minos Year, at the Summer Solstice Full Moon rite."

"So she may not die of old age."

"No." She held out a hand and Aria took it, resuming her position on the cushion next to Eileithyia. "You will know when it is time. The gods will tell you. Though it is usually the case that the High Priestess stays until past the ability to bear children." She narrowed her eyes at her protege. "You know you may not get children while you hold this office."

Aria nodded. "I know how to prevent pregnancy. I was taught well, just like every other girl in the temple. I will consult with the Medicine-Priestess to ensure that I have what I need."

"Good." Eileithyia smiled, then her brow furrowed at the look on Aria's face. "Is there something else you wish to know?"

"What if..." Aria began, then cleared her throat. "What if the woman who is chosen as High Priestess does not like men?"

"Ariadne, what are you telling me?"

"Oh, no, My Lady, I like men. You know that." She sighed as Sageleus' face popped into her mind. "But what if the next one does not? Or what if the Consort does not like women?"

Eileithyia thought a moment. "It has never happened, as far as I know. The gods choose the one who best suits the office. All we do is mark the one the gods have already set apart. But I suppose," she said, tapping a finger on her chin, "if it were to happen, the High Priestess and the Consort are only required to lie together at Summer Solstice. Whether they do so at any other time is their own choice."

"I see." Aria toyed with her skirt cord, avoiding the High Priestess' gaze.

"You may ask me anything, Ariadne. Now is not the time to be shy."

"I was just thinking..." She kept her gaze directed down as she spoke. "So many people died during the Great Darkness. The temple was destroyed. Surely..."

"Go on."

"Surely some of the secret rites were lost."

"Ariadne." Eileithyia touched Aria's arm, and the younger woman looked over, meeting her gaze. "I am not making up any of these things that I am teaching you."

"I did not mean..."

Eileithyia rose and walked over to the edge of the temple. After a moment, Aria followed. They stood there side by side, looking out over the rolling waves with the sunlight glinting on the water, the place where the great killing wave had rolled onto the shore and destroyed the old city and temple, destroyed the original Sea Temple. Finally the older woman spoke.

"It is true," she said reluctantly. "Much was lost, and not just people and buildings."

"But we still have the rites," Aria said, puzzled. "Did someone write them down? I thought we were not allowed to write such things."

"No, my dear. We retrieved them."

"I do not understand."

Eileithyia turned and took Aria's hands in hers. "Everything that ever has been still exists, in one way or another. I do not know how to explain it in words. Once you have experienced the Key-Bearer rite, you will understand better."

"Key-Bearer? That is one of the Young God's names. The Lion of Rhea."

"Indeed it is. And he is vital to that rite." Eileithyia thought a moment. "Everything is connected. You know that."

"Of course."

"All of time is connected: past, present, future. All the worlds are connected, for those who know the paths between them."

Aria looked up at the Sun, then out across the sea, then to the dry land behind the little temple. The three sacred realms: sky, sea, and land. "The Key-Bearer knows the way. He is the son of all the Mothers, so he has access to all the worlds."

"Yes," Eileithyia said. "After the Great Darkness, when the people were rebuilding the temple and the city, the clergy who survived worked hard to rebuild the sacred rites. They journeyed through the realms to find the rites and bring them back, word by word, gesture by gesture."

"Will I learn how to do that? Will you teach me the Key-Bearer rite?"

"Of course. Belisseus and I together will teach you, since he carries the Lion of Rhea within him, along with the other aspects of the Young God."

Aria tilted her face up to the Sun, feeling the warmth on her skin, tasting the salt spray on her tongue, and feeling how small she was against the broad tapestry of the sea and the sky.

"What if..." she finally said, looking away from the High Priestess, who remained silent, waiting for her to continue. "What if I am not good enough? What if I do not do the job as well as you have?"

"I will tell you a secret, Ariadne, and you will tell it to the woman you train to be High Priestess after you."

Aria turned to gaze at Eileithyia.

"Every woman who holds this office," the High Priestess said, "doubts her ability to do so."

"But..."

"Every one of us is chosen by the gods, by the Great Mothers. Every one of us is elected unanimously by both Colleges. And every one of us worries that she is not the right choice."

Aria stared at her High Priestess, eyes wide. "That cannot be."

"That is the way of mortals," Eileithyia said, smiling. "We doubt ourselves. But we must not doubt the gods. Now let us get on with the memorization. You still have much to learn."

They returned to their seats in the curving sliver of shade, and Eileithyia began reciting again. But Aria had a hard time focusing. Though she trusted the older woman not to lie to her, she worried that the clergy back in the time of the Great Darkness might have failed to be exact in their work. What if the rites they had now were not the same as the ones from before the cataclysm? What if they were saying the wrong words, performing the wrong gestures, performing the rituals incorrectly? If that were the case, then they might not have the same protection they used to. They might not be honoring the gods properly. And that might put them at risk. After all, were they not already battling an influx of foreigners who were slowly chipping away at the island's way of life? What if the gods were no longer protecting Ida's children because they were not honoring the sacred the way they should?

Chapter 30

"Now add the incense to the coals," Eileithyia said.

Aria sprinkled the powder onto the hot coals in a bronze brazier beside the altar. The incense was a special blend, only used for certain rites. The earthy-sweet smell wafted up and goosebumps rose on Aria's arms as she remembered her own initiation into the priesthood in this very room.

But today she did not stand in a dark chamber full of veiled figures and drifting smoke. This time the room was well lit, with sunshine streaming in through an open door and lamps glowing in the corners. Over the years, Aria had taken part in many initiations and other rites in the small room. To her it had become a beloved part of the temple, a doorway through which a person could enter the priesthood or travel the unseen paths of the many worlds.

The three of them—Aria, Eileithyia, and Belisseus—stood in front of the altar, their arms upraised in the pose of invocation and reverence. The High Priestess and the Consort sported their usual ritual garb: a fancy tunic and tiered wrap skirt for Eileithyia and a colorful kilt for Belisseus. But Aria wore only a simple linen tunic. For this rite she was just a child of Ida, nothing more.

Silently they called to the Three and to the Young God, the Son of the Mothers. Aria drew in a heady breath of incense smoke and felt the Mothers descend around her, blessing and protecting the rite. The Son would come later, in his proper time.

The invocations complete, they stepped back from the altar. Aria looked over at Belisseus. "Will you be making this journey with me?"

"This one is for the priestess alone," he said. "But I will help you, as Our Lady helps me when I journey." He held up a sistrum, indicating that he would be playing it for her.

"Come," Eileithyia said, holding out her hand. Aria took it, and together they went down into the adyton at the back of the room. Belisseus closed the door to the ritual room then followed behind them. The cool stone steps pressed against Aria's bare feet, a familiar sensation, a reminder that a journey was about to take place. She had witnessed many rites in the adyton, but today she would be the traveler.

Though the upper part of the room was well lit, the adyton was dark and shadowy, a cave-like chamber below floor level. In the dim light, Aria could see that a blanket lay on the stone floor, the place where she had died and been reborn so many years earlier. She hesitated, her breathing purposely shallow to avoid inhaling too much of the drugged incense.

"This is not an initiation," Eileithyia reminded her. "It is simply a journey. Today you will meet the Lion of Rhea in the realm beyond ours, and he will show you the doorways. He is the Key-Bearer, the one you must call on when you need to travel to the World Below."

Aria nodded, allowing herself to relax and draw in a deep breath. She knelt, then stretched out on her back on the blanket, the hard stone beneath it pressing against her hips and shoulders. "Is this how the people found the rituals again after the Great Darkness?"

"It is. Now breathe deeply. Belisseus and I will guide you from here, and the Key-Bearer will guide you from the other side. Once you know the way, you will be able to make the journey with your own Consort."

Moving silently, Eileithyia knelt down and positioned herself at Aria's head, her hands resting lightly on Aria's shoulders. Belisseus knelt at her feet and began a slow rhythm on the sistrum, the double-beat of the heart, though the hiss of the instrument made Aria think it was a serpent and not a human being whose heartbeat reached her ears.

Though her own heart was pounding, Aria closed her eyes as she drew in a deep breath of the incense smoke. The room was silent except for the beating of her heart and the slow hissing rhythm of the sistrum. Following her training, Aria focused on the sound of the instrument, drawing in deliberate, deep breaths, doing her best to trust in her teachers and the gods.

After a few moments, her heartbeat slowed to match the rhythm of the sistrum. Her breathing eased until she was no longer thinking about it, no longer thinking about anything at all except the Key-Bearer, the one she sought in the World Below.

She found herself standing in a cave: not the adyton but an earthen cave, one she did not recognize. Her mind suggested that it should be chilly—were not all caves cool? But her skin felt comfortably warm, her bare feet at ease on the soft ground. As she looked around, her eyes became accustomed to the dim light, and she saw a figure silhouetted in the cave entrance.

The Key-Bearer.

With some effort she picked up her feet, one after the other, and began walking toward him. Her body did not want to obey her commands as she struggled to move. Then the quiet voice in the back of her mind reminded her that her body was still lying on the floor of the adyton. All of a sudden she was standing at the cave entrance, so close to the Key-Bearer that she could touch him if she lifted her hand. He was beautiful and strong, a radiant young man much like the Consorts who bore his name and carried his power in ritual. A sense of awe overcame her, and she stared at him, transfixed. A moment later, panicking at her proximity to the divine, she stepped back and made the salute, waiting for him to give her permission to speak.

"Come, Little Sister," he said, motioning for her to stop saluting him. "You have called me for a reason."

"Little Sister?" she said, confused. "I have not lain with you."

Then she cringed at her impertinence, praying she had not offended the god.

He smiled, his face lighting up with a joy that radiated through her, warming her to her toes. "But you will soon be the High Priestess. So in times to come, you shall indeed lie with me. All time is one to me." He tilted his head, waiting for her to speak.

"I..." she began, then stopped, flustered. She took a slow breath and gathered her thoughts. "I seek the Key-Bearer to show me the doorways."

"Of course," he said, smiling again, but more softly this time. "Come. I will show you what you need to know."

He held his hand out, and she hesitated before taking it. The moment her hand touched his, the cave wavered. Suddenly the two of them were standing in a long corridor lined with closed doors.

"It looks like the temple," she gasped.

The Key-Bearer smiled. "Your own thoughts give this place form. This is where you will come when you seek knowledge or healing for yourself and others. Here, you see," he said, waving his hand, and suddenly the air was full of threads, some running from Aria and the Young God to the doorways, some running from one doorway to another, and some running off down the corridor, their ends disappearing into the far distance. One thread ran between her and the Key-Bearer, connecting them heart to heart.

Amazed, she lifted her hand up and gently touched the thread. It turned a vivid shade of gold and began to vibrate. "Everything is connected," she said in awe. The Key-Bearer nodded. "I did not think my teachers meant that so precisely."

He led Aria down the corridor. "I am the Key-Bearer because I am the son of all the Mothers," he said, placing his palm flat on the first door. An iridescent gleam swirled on the surface of the door in response to his touch. "Here is the doorway to the Earth-Mother, whom you call Rhea or Ida."

They continued down the corridor, stopping at each door, the Key-Bearer naming each one. There were doors to all the Great Mothers, to the Daughter, to Dionysus and Minos and all the other gods and goddesses. There were also doors to the blessed dead and to the spirits of the sacred mountains, springs, and rivers of Ida's island.

When they reached the last doorway, Aria turned around and gazed down the corridor, a look of confusion growing on her face. "I cannot remember which one belongs to which god or spirit!"

"Fear not," he said. "I will give you the keys." He reached out and laid his palm flat on Aria's chest, between her breasts. She felt a warmth flowing into her body, suffusing her from head to toe.

She held her hands out, palms up, looking down at herself. Her whole body was glowing a subtle gold, like the first glimmer of dawn. "But..." She gazed at her empty hands. "I have no keys."

"You are the key," he said. "Which doorway would you like to open?"

She shook her head. "I do not know one from another."

"You misunderstand me. Tell me whose doorway you would like to open."

"Oh." She drew in a slow breath, thinking. After a moment she said, "The Daughter."

He gave her a quizzical look. "You fear her more than all the Mothers, yet you would open the door to her realm? You would seek her directly?"

Aria looked down, avoiding his gaze. "She is the reason I am here with you, the reason I will soon be High Priestess. Perhaps I should face her and accept the consequences for the things I have done."

"Very well. Call to her."

Fighting a growing anxiety, Aria lifted her head and forced herself to stand tall, as a priestess should. "I call to the Daughter," she said, her voice shaking. "I wish to open your doorway."

A few paces down the corridor, one of the doors began to glow.

"There, you see," the Young God said, "this is how it works." He motioned her toward the glowing doorway.

Fear suddenly boiled up in her throat, and her feet dragged as she edged down the corridor. After what seemed an interminable time, she found herself standing before the glowing doorway.

"What must I do now?" she whispered.

The Young God gestured, and she imitated him, pressing her palm to the door. Instantly she was standing on the other side, in a field of blooming lilies, a warm breeze ruffling her hair even though she knew the year was approaching wintertime. She turned around slowly, seeking the goddess, but found herself alone.

"I have failed," she sighed.

"No, my child, you have not," came a voice that raised goosebumps all over Aria's body. The hair stood up on the back of her neck, and she felt a strong presence, a sense of great power close by. She jerked around, looking every which way but finding no one.

"You are used to seeing me in the guise of a priestess in your rites," the voice continued. Aria could not tell whether it was speaking from somewhere nearby or from inside her head. "Though I may ride a priestess in ritual, I also have my own being, separate from that of humans."

Aria made the salute, still unsure which direction she should be facing. She felt her heart pounding and struggled to keep her breathing steady. The last thing she needed was to offend the goddess whose altar she had stolen from.

"You have no need to fear me," the voice said. "I do not judge your actions, though you must live with their consequences."

Aria dropped her hand from her forehead and stood there, confused and conflicting notions careening through her mind. "I thought..."

"I know," said the voice, flowing gently, soothing Aria's very being. "But you have hard work ahead of you. Even had you not taken the seal from the altar, you would still be the next High Priestess."

Aria drew in a sharp breath.

"We chose you," the voice said, "because you can do the work. You are strong. No matter what happens, we will always be with you."

The wind picked up and swept around Aria, strong gusts bending the lilies sideways. Then she was standing in the corridor again, her hand still pressed to the door.

She drew her hand back and clasped it with the other, feeling disoriented. Then she lifted her head to see the Young God still standing a few steps away, watching her.

"You have done well," he said. "You will remember the way for the next time."

Aria drew in a ragged breath and found herself standing in the cave once again, her bare feet soft against the warm ground. She drew in another breath and felt the hard stone floor pressing against her hips and shoulders. Odd groaning sounds came out of her mouth, though she felt as if someone else were making them.

"Shh," came Eileithyia's voice. "Do not try to speak just yet. Open your eyes first."

Aria felt Eileithyia blowing gently on the top of her head and in her face, ensuring that she came all the way back to her body. With some effort she raised her eyelids. Dim lamplight flickered in the distance, growing brighter. Then Belisseus was there, holding a lamp, bending over her.

"I will sit with you until you are ready to stand," he said, settling on the floor by her side.

"Breathe slowly and deeply," Eileithyia said. Then she was moving, getting up. "I will be in my private quarters should you wish to discuss your experiences."

Then she was gone, and Aria was alone with Belisseus. She lay there, afraid to move, for some time. Finally her bladder made its needs known, and she realized she was going to have to get up.

Raising up on her elbows, she looked sidelong at him. "I am sorry," she said.

He held out a hand and helped her up to standing. "You have nothing to be sorry for." When the look on her face made it clear she disagreed, he spoke again, very softly. "I am the son of none but the gods."

She gasped, feeling as if he had stabbed her in the chest.

"You have not failed me in any way," he continued. "I made this choice before I was born. I am happy to walk this path."

She blew out a breath of relief, then felt a sudden pang of guilt. "You feel no loss for having no human parents?"

"I am a child of the gods. What more could I want?" he said, his smile gentle and understanding.

Together they stepped up out of the adyton, crossing the ritual room to the doorway.

"Here I will leave you," he said. "I must clean up from the rite."

He drew the door open, and she stepped through, out into the light.

* * *

After emptying her bladder, Aria found herself wandering the temple corridors, wondering how the Otherworld could possibly look just like her own world. After a short while, she found herself heading up the stairs to the residential area, her feet moving of their own accord. And then she was standing before the doorway to the High Priestess' private quarters. She was not sure how long she had been there when a voice spoke from within.

"Come in, Ariadne. Conversation will be much easier if we are in the same room."

Aria drew the door open and stepped through to find Eileithyia sitting on a stool at a small table, eating some barley bread and herbed cheese and drinking a cup of wine.

"Come, join me," she said, gesturing to the other stool.

Aria took a seat, doing her best to avoid gazing around the room.

"You may look," Eileithyia said with a laugh. "It is not that much different from yours."

Then Aria did look, taking in the wide bed, the colorful painted trim along the ceiling and around the window, the large trunk that surely held Eileithyia's clothing and jewelry. She noticed a door in the side wall and realized that it led to the Consort's private quarters next door: they could meet each other privately, without going out into the corridor the way everyone else had to do. Not that anyone cared whose bed anyone else lay in. Still, privacy was a lovely luxury.

Though the High Priestess' room was bigger than Aria's, and the wall paintings more intricate, the furnishings were no finer. Then she realized that all the furniture and household goods in the temple were high quality, the best the local artisans could produce.

They easily matched the furnishings in Sageleus' house—a house she realized she would likely never enter again. Perhaps the temple was wealthier than she had thought, at least in some ways.

"Ariadne," Eileithyia said, snapping the younger woman out of her reverie. Then she sat back and eyed her successor. "You do not like it when I call you by your full name."

Aria shrugged, unsure how to answer. Still watching the younger woman, Eileithyia poured a cup of wine and set it in front of her.

"Drink some," the older woman said, "and have something to eat." She slid the plate of bread and cheese across the table. "You will feel better when you have come all the way back to yourself."

Aria took a sip of wine. "I am not entirely certain who *myself* is anymore." Flickering memories of this same feeling after her initiation into the priesthood flashed through her mind. If the training for the office was this disorienting, how much more so would the act of becoming High Priestess be?

Eileithyia urged the food on her again. This time Aria took a small barley loaf and ate a portion of it. The High Priestess sat in silence while Aria finished the bread and drank some more wine. Then, when it was clear the younger woman was not going to speak, Eileithyia reached across the table and took her hand. Aria looked up, and Eileithyia met her gaze.

"You are well worthy of this position, Ariadne."

The younger woman drew in a shaky breath. "I have done things..."

"As have we all. The Mothers do not judge us," she said. "You know that."

Aria nodded, wondering whether she really believed it. Her own conscience might beg to differ. "When I..." She swallowed. "In the journey..."

"Yes?"

Aria drew her hand back, wrapping her arms around herself. "I met the Lion of Rhea. He showed me the doorways."

"Excellent." Eileithyia beamed.

"And I met the Daughter."

"Did you?"

Aria rose from her seat and moved to the window, her arms still wrapped around her middle. She gazed out the window, unseeing. "I asked to go to her."

Eileithyia rose and joined her protege by the window. "And what happened?"

"She said they chose me. She said... I am destined to be the High Priestess." Her words came out almost as a question.

"And so you are." Eileithyia took Aria's hands, unwrapping the younger woman's arms from around herself. "When we did the divination for your priestess name at your first blood-time, we did it three times. Three different priestesses."

"What?"

"We had to be certain."

Aria leaned back, narrowing her eyes at Eileithyia. "And all three..."

"All three divinations said the same thing. You are our next High Priestess, my dear. The gods have chosen you every bit as much as they have chosen me or the Consort."

Eileithyia slid her arms around Aria, embracing her, as the younger woman began to cry. They stood there together, holding each other, until Aria's sobs finally wore themselves out.

"I am sorry," the younger woman said, doing her best to wipe her face on her sleeve.

Eileithyia reached for a linen cloth from the table and dabbed at Aria's face. "There is nothing to apologize for. You are not the first woman to find this office overwhelming. I would even say you ware wise to be intimidated."

When Aria's face was dry, Eileithyia leaned in and kissed her on the cheek. Aria returned the kiss, the traditional greeting and blessing from one member of the clergy to another. Then the younger woman tilted her head and kissed the High Priestess on the mouth.

Gasping, shocked at her own actions, she retreated out of Eileithyia's embrace. "I am sorry, My Lady. I was not... I do not..."

Eileithyia reached out and drew Aria back to her. Then she

smoothed the younger woman's hair off her forehead. "There is no need to apologize, my dear. I feel the same way about you."

"But..." Aria's brow furrowed. "I thought you were not allowed to have lovers. Except the Consort, of course. And I am forbidden as well, am I not?"

"There are some conditions of the office that are known only to the High Priestess and the Consort. One of those is that, should they so desire, the High Priestess and her named successor may lie together during the year of training."

Aria stared at her, eyes wide.

"Of course," Eileithyia continued, "there are other private things you must know as well, and I will share them with you soon. But this..." She stroked her thumb across Aria's lower lip. "Do you wish to lie with me?"

"Yes," came Aria's answer as she drew in a breath, shocked to admit it to herself for the first time.

Then she dared to kiss Eileithyia again. This time the older woman returned the kiss, slow and gentle. Then she drew Aria over to the bed, reaching to untie Aria's skirt.

"Do you fear me?" Eileithyia asked when Aria just stood there, stiff, letting the other woman undress her.

"Of course not."

"Good."

"You are certain this is allowed?"

"I swear by the Three," Eileithyia said, moving Aria's hands over to untie her skirt.

Her heart pounding, Aria unwrapped Eileithyia's skirt from around her hips and slipped her tunic off her shoulders. Then she slid her palms down the other woman's arms. "My Lady," she whispered into her ear as she stepped in close, pressing their bodies together.

"Elli," the older woman said. "In private, please call me Elli."

"Elli," Aria sighed as the two of them lay down on the bed and slid beneath the covers.

Chapter 31

The late morning sunbeams slanted in through the light well at the corner of the audience chamber. Eileithyia sat on the dais, with the Consort standing in his usual place at her right. Aria stood on the High Priestess' left side, wishing she could have a chair. She had stood there since shortly after dawn as Eileithyia's advisors—a dozen priests, priestesses, and lay people, Sageleus among them—had entered the hall for their regular meeting with the High Priestess.

Eileithyia had insisted that Aria meet them all a Moon earlier. Now the High Priestess-in-training took part in the meetings every time, listening to the advice and opinions the men and women offered. Though the High Priestess was the de facto authority in the temple and the city, she did not rule by might, but by consensus. It was her job to maintain order, to make sure no one went hungry, and to resolve disputes among the people. Eileithyia leaned heavily on Belisseus and the Heads of the Colleges, of course, but her cadre of advisors provided a variety of viewpoints that kept her decisions level-headed and fair.

"Of course, Ariadne," Eileithyia said once her advisors had left the room, "you may choose different people once you have taken the chair. Just be sure to pick some whose opinions differ from yours." Aria raised her eyebrows. "There is always more than one way to look at any situation. Take care you do not forget that."

"Yes, My Lady." Aria smiled, glad that there was only one more order of business left before she could step off the dais. Her legs were beginning to ache from standing in one place for so long. This was not a rite, so she could not ignore the discomfort by dropping into trance. Instead, she drew in a slow breath and prepared to meet their next visitor.

The doors swung open and two priests, one of the older clergy and one strapping young man, entered the hall. The two men moved to stand before the High Priestess, making the salute. She acknowledged them, then directed them off to one side.

They waited for some time, everyone in their proper places. Finally Aria leaned over to the High Priestess and whispered, "He cannot have gotten lost. Our temple is not that big."

Elli's lips pressed together in a thin line. "He is showing his power by making us wait."

After another long interval, the door to the audience chamber swung open, and a man strode in. The gold and silver threads on his tunic and the jewelry on his arms and hands glinted as he moved across the room, head held high and shoulders thrown back, the expression on his face suggesting that he thought he was the one who belonged in the sacred seat. He stopped closer to the dais than was customary and made the briefest of salutes.

"Hedamos," the High Priestess said. "Welcome."

He gave a curt nod then turned to the Consort. "Belisseus," he said with a thick mainland accent, "I trust you are well. I hope this season's donations are in keeping with your temple's level of prosperity." He swung his gaze around the room, peering pointedly at the fresh whitewash and the trim painted in costly Egyptian blue.

The Consort glanced sidelong at the High Priestess, shaking his head almost imperceptibly before speaking. "Hedamos," he said, "you know very well that Our Lady speaks for the temple. You slight her by addressing me in her stead, and in doing so, you slight the Great Mothers as well."

The envoy from Knossos rolled his eyes and turned back to the

High Priestess. "My deepest apologies," he said, his voice oozing insincerity. "Your ways are so foreign to me, it is difficult for me to remember that the men are not in charge here. Your old goddesses are so... quaint."

"I trust our hospitality is to your liking," the High Priestess said, her face impassive. "I hope you do not find the old laws of hospitality too quaint, since they are what feeds and houses you when you come here."

"I have finally become used to the way your people cook, so the dinner last night was edible. And of course, the accommodations are always adequate. Your temple is like a smaller, simpler version of Knossos." He smiled, all teeth. "Now, shall we get to the business for which I have traveled here? Yours is not the only little temple I must visit on my rounds."

Her face still showing no sign of emotion, the High Priestess held her hand out. The older priest, who had been waiting off to the side, strode over and presented her with a sheet of papyrus.

She scanned the list. "The donations are prepared," she said, "and all in good order. My two priests here will accompany the wagon and the herdsmen to Knossos and witness your temple's acknowledgment that the goods have been received." She held out the papyrus, offering it to Hedamos.

"You know very well that I cannot read," he snarled.

"Very well. I shall read it to you," she said. "We are sending one bull from our prize breeding stock, ten of our best brood cows, twenty head of sheep, one full pithos of wheat, one of barley, one of olive oil, and one of wine. In addition, the wagon carries two large baskets of dates, a basket of dried fish, a casket of fine stone necklaces and gold bracelets, and a box of Egyptian blue powder."

Again she held the papyrus out, and this time he took it. "This is insufficient," he said, his uncomprehending gaze raking the page. "You have made your calculations incorrectly. We are to receive a certain portion of the donations you take in every season, and these amounts are far too low. There is no honey, either, and we expect honey from your many hives. I suggest you correct the amounts. I will wait."

Aria drew in a sharp breath, glancing sidelong at Eileithyia. Hedamos held out the papyrus, but neither the High Priestess nor anyone else made a move to take it from him.

The High Priestess's face went as hard as stone. "These amounts are correct. If our relations with your temple are to remain cordial, I suggest you accept them. It has been our people's tradition for generations to share from one temple to the next so we all have plenty. That is what the Mothers have taught us: share and share alike so none of her children are in want. We have always honored Knossos as the foremost of the temples on our island. " She narrowed her eyes at him. "But your people have misunderstood our tradition and taken it to mean they can demand goods from the other temples, especially those you helped during the Great Darkness, even if we repaid our debt to you long ago. That is not our way. If you expect to continue to receive a portion of our bounty, I suggest you work to understand our values." She nodded toward the papyrus in his hand. "Now set your seal where it belongs. I have other matters to attend to today, and surely you do as well."

The older priest stepped over to the envoy and proffered a lump of clay on a small tray. His expression sour, Hedamos mashed his seal into the clay. Then, tossing the papyrus at the priest, he turned and stalked out of the room. Eileithyia directed her priests to wait a few moments, allowing Hedamos some distance. Then she sent them out to accompany the offerings to Knossos.

As soon as the doors were shut behind them, Aria turned and gripped the arm of Eileithyia's chair. "How can you bear such a horrid man? I would have thrown him out."

Eileithyia sighed, slumping back in her chair. She reached out, and both Aria and the Consort took her hands. Then she kissed their hands, first Belisseus' and then Aria's.

"If I could get away with turning him out," Eileithyia grumbled, "I would do so. But we must maintain cordial relations with Knossos."

"If they do not follow the old ways," Aria said, "then must we still share with them? The people at Knossos are certainly not honorable, from what I have heard, at least not anymore. Perhaps they once were."

"But they are powerful," Belisseus said. "If they cannot get their way through diplomacy, the mainlanders have a tendency to turn to arms, especially these new people from the mountains. We cannot risk such an outcome."

Aria stared at him. "They would attack us? Another city on their own island?"

"Up on the mainland, the cities attack each other all the time, each vying to take over the others. It is their way."

"What a horrid way to live!" Aria cried.

Eileithyia patted her hand. "You see, my dear, why I wanted you here this morning. I will deal with him the next time or two that he comes, but after that, he will be your problem."

"I am not certain I can handle him as well as you do. I find myself wishing to push him off a cliff."

Eileithyia let out a soft laugh. "As do I. But listen, you must know these things." Aria nodded. "You must never say anything to him that would reflect badly on us if he were to repeat it to his superiors at Knossos. You must not let him rattle you."

"I understand."

"He is not a priest, but a layman, and a devious one at that. You must always chose strong, reliable priests who will not anger if they are treated badly when they deliver the donation."

Belisseus shook his head. "The mainlanders do not treat our priests badly, only our priestesses. To our priests, they say how sorry they are that the men must be subservient to the women. To the High Priestess." He leaned over and kissed Eileithyia's cheek.

Aria tilted her head and gave him a quizzical expression. "But you are superior to all the priests here. They are beneath both you and Our Lady."

"The mainlanders do not see it that way. They only see that we take women to be equal to men, and they think that means we put women above their natural place."

"That is..." Aria folded her arms over her chest. "We cannot allow them to behave this way. It is horribly disrespectful!"

Eileithyia narrowed her eyes at her successor. "Do not poke a stick in a hornet's nest. They are attempting to consolidate power, as they have done on the mainland."

Aria gave her a dubious look.

Eileithyia stood and straightened her skirt. "You have known this all along, Ariadne. You know what they are about, whether or not you care to admit it. Previous generations at Knossos have behaved better than these new mainlanders, but they have all had the same goals. The fact that you are kind and generous does not mean the rest of the world is. Do not allow your soft heart to make your head soft as well."

"Yes, My Lady."

"Now go attend to your daily tasks. Belisseus and I have work we must do today."

Aria offered them both the salute before crossing the room and exiting into the north court. Her thoughts abuzz with contradictions and unpleasantness, she wandered through the workshops and out into the herb garden.

Though the early autumn sunlight shone warm on her skin, she barely felt it. She stumbled down a path and dropped onto a bench that stood against the temple wall. A butterfly floated past her, bees buzzed from plant to plant, the doves cooed in their dovecote, and the familiar scent of myrtle wafted up, calming her.

Of course Eileithyia was right. Aria had long known what kind of people the Knossos mainlanders were, what they valued—or failed to value. She had simply chosen not to think about those things, hoping the mainlanders would tire of their travels and go back home.

But instead, they had made Ida's island their second home. They had come here after the Great Darkness, supposedly to help Aria's people rebuild. But now that the darkness was gone, they were refusing to leave. And if Eileithyia was correct, they desired to take over all the cities. They brought a darkness of their own, one that cast a shadow across the whole island.

She shuddered. Surely the Great Mothers would protect their people from such a horror. But what if they did not? Everyone knew that the Great Darkness was a warning from Kalliste herself. But the darkness had ended. The Sun had come back out, and the crops had begun to grow again. Surely this meant the Fire-Mother was no longer angry.

Aria gazed around the garden, with its clumps of fragrant oregano, rosemary, dittany, and myrtle, the shining blooms and the buzzing insects and the sunbeams. She felt so happy right here, so warm and safe. But she had not felt at all safe in the audience chamber, even though it lay within her own temple.

What if the Sun-Mother was still angry? What if she and the other Great Mothers were no longer protecting their children? That would explain why the mainlanders were able to stay and grow in numbers, disrespecting women and dishonoring the island. Perhaps the rites the priesthood had recollected after the Great Darkness were not the correct ones. Or perhaps it was time for new rites, ones that could protect Ida's children and drive the intruders back to their mainland homes. Aria had no idea how long it had been since anyone had introduced new rites in the temples. Probably no one living could remember. She certainly did not feel qualified to create such rituals herself.

She looked down at her hands, at the bracelet that held the stones denoting her positions in the temple. What if rites alone were not enough? Eileithyia was certain that simply being firm and sticking to the traditions would keep the Knossians from overstepping their bounds. Aria was not so sure.

If the mainlanders were willing to commit dishonorable acts, how would it be possible for Ida's children to overcome them without also committing acts that were repellent to the Great Mothers? If Aria was to serve as High Priestess of the temple, she was going to have to solve that problem, because she was certain the mainlanders were not going away.

Chapter 32

The cold wind whipped across the bare land, whistling between the tombs. Wrapped up against the late winter storm in leather boots and woolen cloaks, the clergy made their slow way down the path toward the cemetery. Two priests and two priestesses bore Inia's shrouded body on a litter. Eileithyia and Belisseus led the procession, with Aria walking beside her mother's corpse and the rest of the priesthood—with a few of the townspeople who had known Inia—following behind.

It had not been a bad winter, all things considered. The gentle rains had been plentiful and the storms had been few. Still, a fever had begun down by the port in the autumn at the end of the sailing season, imported from some foreign land by traders, or so the sailors said. It had spread slowly, piecemeal, and had not been nearly as virulent as some of the plagues people told stories of, deadly diseases that killed half the people they touched.

But Inia was old. Aria was the last of her children, gotten when Inia was almost past childbearing, and Aria herself was now nearing forty. So when the fever came around, it hit Inia hard, putting her to bed for many days, and then it went to her chest. The Medicine-Priestess' best efforts only slowed the inevitable end. Aria felt sure she would remember the sound of her mother's death rattle for the rest of her life.

Now they were trudging slowly down the path, leaning into the wind, bearing the corpse of a priestess to the tombs. Eileithyia had insisted that Aria lead the funeral ceremony. Normally, the High Priestess performed the funeral rites for members of the clergy. But not this time, not with a successor-priestess training for the office.

Their footsteps crunched on the gravel as the procession came to a halt in front of the tomb. As the sea-wind whipped around her, Aria tasted salt, then she stepped closer to the gaping black doorway and into the shelter of the tomb wall. The tomb building, shaped like a giant stone beehive, rose up from the bare ground, blocking the wind. The doorway was flanked by a pair of walls that ran outward from the tomb at widening angles, like the Great Mother's legs opening to allow the deceased to return to her ancient womb.

The corpse-bearers brought the litter up near the doorway and set it on the ground. When they had moved off to the side, Rhea and Kaeseus came forward bearing the offerings. Several of the younger clergy followed with a small altar table and the other ritual gear. While they set up, Aria drew in a few slow breaths, preparing herself. She had cried all the tears she had while her mother was still alive, in those last few days when it had become obvious the elderly woman would not survive the illness. Now Aria had a job to do, the sacred task of opening the way for her mother's spirit to descend to the World Below.

She scanned the gathered crowd as they huddled together around the tomb entrance. Inia was well beloved. The whole priesthood had come to bid her farewell, along with some of her friends and family from the city. Aria noted Orestas, Thalamika, and Lexion near the front. Nearby stood Ytanos and Yassib, who were home for the winter, along with Rhea's brother and son, members of Ytanos' crew. Then Sageleus' face came into focus, toward the back of the group. He had barely known Inia, but he had come nonetheless, to pay his respects without intruding.

Aria's heart kicked in her chest. Then she looked over at Elli, standing next to the altar with Belisseus, confident in Aria's ability to perform this rite. Though Aria missed Sageleus from time to time, she realized she no longer felt that old emptiness inside. With a sudden certainty, she knew it was not a man or a woman who had filled that space within her, but a sacred office.

She looked down at her mother's body, wrapped in plain, soft linen. Had Inia died during the warm part of the year, her shroud might have been strewn with fresh flowers. But few were available now. And even had they made use of the blooms that grew in sheltered areas this time of year, the wind would have swept them off the litter on the stormy walk to the tombs. As the mourners looked on in silence, Elli moved over to Inia's body and sprinkled the linen with dried myrtle, hyssop, and juniper, sacred herbs that would purify the corpse and make her spirit ready to move on.

While Elli blessed Inia's remains with the herbs, Belisseus took the lid off a container of hot coals and sprinkled incense over them. The smoke swirled in the sheltered area in front of the tomb. Aria inhaled it, allowing the myrrh to rest on the back of her tongue, the taste of death and the World Below.

Steeling herself to her task, she moved over to the altar, which was now flanked by Elli and Belisseus on one side and Rhea and Kaeseus on the other. Her gaze swept the small table, with its ceramic censer and terracotta figurines. No metal was allowed in funeral rites. Young men even left their fancy bronze daggers at home. Metal would anger the spirits of the dead and keep them from accepting the soul of the newly-deceased.

When Aria gave her the signal, Rhea lifted a flagon of wine from the altar and presented it to her. With a nod, Aria took it and stepped over to the doorway that led into the dark tomb.

Raising the pitcher up, she said, "Three times I say the invocation. Three times I pour the libation. Three times, for the Three Mothers, the three realms. May they open the doorway." She drew in a slow breath, willing her heartbeat to remain steady. "I call to the Daughter, Blessed One, and to the Melissae who serve her. May the spirit of Inia, daughter of Lilia, go in peace to the Cave of the Dead."

Then she offered blessings to the powers she had invoked:

By land and sky and sea
Blessed be the Three
By land and sea and sky
By Them we live and die
By sky and sea and land
Beneath Their guiding hand

Daughter of all the Mothers
Blessed One, Queen of the Dead
Melissae, Buzzing Ones
Guardians of the ancestors
May blessings rain down upon you
May your powers never wane
May you always and forever
Keep and guard the spirits of the dead
In peace and safety
In the World Below

She poured the blood-red wine on the ground in front of the doorway in a slow stream, then she stepped back so the gathered crowd could see. At first the liquid pooled, but then it began to soak into the sandy soil. After a few moments, there was nothing left but a dark stain.

She handed the empty pitcher to Kaeseus and received the second full one from Rhea. Drawing in a slow breath, she lifted it up and repeated the invocation. This time, when Aria tilted the flagon, the liquid that poured out was a pale, creamy color: milk and honey, heated together in the temple kitchen until the honey melted and infused throughout the milk, though the liquid was now only barely warm after the long walk to the tombs in the winter wind. The mixture streamed onto the ground, pooling over the dark spot where the wine had been, blotting out darkness with light.

Again Aria moved back, and they all waited for the liquid to soak into the soil, to pass into the World Below. The cold air thickened the mixture so it stood in quivering puddles on the ground. They all waited as the wind whistled between the tombs and the sea birds wheeled above, crying out as they circled inland and back out to the sea. After a time, the puddles of the milk-and-honey mixture thinned then disappeared into the ground: offering received and accepted.

Letting out a small breath of relief, Aria turned to hand the empty container to Kaeseus and accept the final full one from Rhea. Raising the flagon up, she spoke again, calling out the invocation. Then she tipped the pitcher over and slowly poured the water out onto the ground, taking care not to let it splash. Where first there had been dark wine, and then creamy-white milk and honey, now the water from one of the island's sacred springs cleared away all traces of the first two offerings, washing them down into the ground, down to the World Below.

Again Aria stepped out of the way and waited as the saturated soil slowly accepted the liquid, drawing it down to the realm of the dead, clearing the way for Inia's spirit to descend to its place of respite. To Aria, it felt like ages passed as the pool of water gradually subsided. She kept her gaze focused on the ground, willing the offering into the hands of the Melissae, the guardians of the spirits of the dead.

When the last bit of water had soaked in and all that remained was a faint damp spot on the ground, Aria drew in a slow breath. She lifted her head to meet Elli's eyes and gave a nod. The rite was successful. The offering was accepted. The way was open. Elli gave a small smile and slid her gaze sideways toward the tomb building, indicating the next act in the rite.

Though Aria had attended many funerals over the years, she had never performed one herself. Now it was her job to ensure that her mother's spirit descended to the realm of the dead. If she failed, her mother would not rest, but would disturb the living and bring misfortune on those who knew her.

Still holding the empty pitcher from the final offering, Aria crossed to the tomb entrance. The open doorway gaped black against the pale stone of the building, the doorway that was a gateway for the spirit as well as the flesh.

Aria raised the pitcher above her head and the wind picked up, howling around them. "The offering is made. The offering is accepted. The pitchers are empty," she said, raising her voice to be heard over the wind. "Make open the way to the World Below for the spirit of Inia, daughter of Lilia!" she cried, bringing the empty pitcher down against the doorpost of the tomb and smashing it to bits. The shattered pieces fell to the ground, scattering over the damp spot where the offerings had made their way to the world of the dead.

The corpse-bearers once again lifted Inia's body. This time they carried her into the dark tomb, head first, and set her on an empty shelf, the light from the doorway barely sufficient for their task. They drew the litter out from beneath the corpse and retreated back out into the grim daylight, staying clear of the others and keeping their gazes lowered. They would return to the temple separately from the rest, burn the litter, and purify themselves with water and smoke before returning to their usual responsibilities. The body itself was simply a corpse. They cleansed themselves to ensure that no remnant of the deceased's spirit clung to them.

Once the corpse-bearers were clear of the tomb, Aria picked up a small terracotta pot from the altar. Rhea had already filled it with the appropriate amount of water. Now Aria raised it up, balancing it on her palm. She used the other hand to tap on it with a small wooden rod: a slow single-beat rhythm that rang out like a bell, cutting through the sound of the howling wind, driving through the air and the Earth, urging Inia's spirit on to the World Below. She continued to beat on the bowl as several strong priests moved a stone slab back into place, sealing the tomb's doorway shut. It would not be opened again until harvest time in the spring, when the priesthood would perform the ceremony of secondary burial for any corpses that had decomposed to the point that only their bones remained. Then the people could be assured that the deceased's spirit had no remaining ties with the world of the living and was happily resting in the care of the Melissae and the Daughter.

The priests moved back out of the way, and Aria stopped her

rhythm with the earthenware water-drum. When she set the bowl down, the sound continued to echo among the tombs for several moments. Then all was silent. Even the wind ceased its noise.

Giving a quick sidelong glance to see that Elli approved of her actions, Aria raised her arms and called out to the gathered crowd, "The body of Inia, daughter of Lilia has been laid to rest in the tomb. The spirit of Inia, daughter of Lilia has come to rest in the World Below. Let us thank the powers of land, sea, and sky and the powers of the World Below for her safe journey. Let us celebrate her life and mourn her death as befits the children of Ida."

Though some of the townspeople continued the ancient tradition of holding the funeral feast with its toasts to the dead at the tombs, the clergy had long since developed the practice of feasting back at the temple instead. Aria silently thanked the gods for that custom, drawing her cloak tighter around her shoulders. As Kaeseus and Rhea collected up the parts of the small altar into baskets, the rest of the clergy lifted up wooden and ivory clackers and began an assortment of unmatched rhythms with them. Still making a ruckus with their instruments, the crowd parted, allowing Aria, Elli, and Belisseus through, followed by Rhea and Kaeseus with their laden baskets.

As Aria passed through the back of the crowd, Sageleus caught her eye and offered her a gentle smile, a look that combined sympathy, pride, and fondness in a way that struck her hard in the gut. She managed to smile at him just a little, then turned quickly back to the pathway. The crowd followed, clackers still clamoring—a precaution to keep the spirits of the dead from following the living back home. The noise did not cease until the group reached the main road and turned toward the temple.

Chapter 33

Though Elli lightened Aria's workload for a short while after Inia's death, the press of time meant that her training had to resume as soon as possible. Adding to the tension were the sudden changes at Knossos that had spurred gossip about who was really in charge at Malia's neighbor city to the west. After several years of worrying shifts in the larger temple's activities, this was distressing indeed.

Now Aria sat at one of the scribal tables behind the High Priestess' dais in the audience hall, the flickering flames of the oil lamps offering little respite from the late night gloom. Though the season was well into spring, Aria felt a chill as she shifted in her seat. The room was quiet and empty except for their small group, all the doors shut tight. Along with Belisseus and a handful of other clergy, Aria listened to Elli explain the details of a journey most of them would begin the next morning.

"The Spring Equinox has passed," Elli said, "harvest is over, and now we have a little time in which we can travel. The events at Knossos are..." She shook her head. "I do not know what to make of them. But we must ensure that these new people know me and my successor." She gave Aria a pointed look.

"Perhaps," Belisseus said, "we will understand what has happened once we are there."

"I certainly hope so," Lexion replied, a sour look on his face.

"There is much that is suspicious. Ida grant that honest communication will help allay our fears. I do not want conflict."

"As Chief Scrivener, I oversee all the messages that come from Knossos as well as those we send there." Thalamika paused, nodding toward Elli. "Except those sent directly by Our Lady, of course. But I have heard nothing untoward. These are only rumors. We have no reason to make this journey."

"Will someone please explain the situation to me?" said Presfa, one of the younger priestesses at the table. She reminded Aria of herself and Rhea so many years earlier, eager and serious and dedicated. "I have heard many stories that contradict each other."

"We do not know all the details," Elli said, "but I will tell you what I know that is certain. Zephyra, the High Priestess at Knossos, has died."

"Died?" Aria said, a feeling of foreboding settling over her.

"Yes. She has not gone in sacrifice, as is our way, but has died in office."

"We do not know how," said Belisseus in response to the shocked looks around the table, "though there are many wild tales that claim to explain the situation. Whether her death was the working of the gods or of mortals, it was out of time."

"A new High Priestess has already been installed," Elli said. "She is called Melena."

"And we are going to visit and acknowledge her?" Presfa asked.

"Yes," Elli said. "It has long been our way to send a contingent to recognize every new High Priestess at our sister temples."

"I thought..." Presfa began, throwing nervous glances around the table. When Elli gave her an encouraging nod, she continued, "Will I be allowed to go to Knossos? Is that why you have asked me to join this discussion?"

"Yes it is. I want many eyes in Knossos," Elli explained. "You are young, so you may see things differently from the older clergy." She gazed down the table at the small group of men and women gathered there, old and young, meeting each one's eyes and offering a look of gratitude for their presence. "We have... concerns regarding the people who are now in charge at Knossos. They do not respect the ways of Ida's children. They do not believe in sharing their bounty or honoring women as the living embodiment of the goddess. They honor only men and gods, or so I am told, and so I have heard from their emissaries. So it is important that they see women as well as men representing our temple." Her gaze swept the table again. "It is also important that you all pay careful attention while we are there. Listen much and speak little. Do not antagonize them or argue with them, but let them speak as they wish. Once we have returned, we will meet again to discuss the journey. Perhaps then we can understand how these events have come to pass."

"They still have a High Priestess and a College of Priestesses," Lexion said, "so perhaps they have not made such great alterations as we think."

"This change of office has happened out of turn," Aria said, scowling. "Summer Solstice is more than two Moons away, and this happened some time ago. Do you not find that troubling... or suspicious?"

"What makes the situation worse," said Belisseus, "is that we did not hear about Zephyra's death and Melena's installation until it was over and done with."

Lexion leaned back, crossing his arms over his chest. "No announcements beforehand? No messengers to the other temples? That is troubling."

Thalamika harrumphed but said nothing.

"Because of this odd turn of events," Elli said, standing up from the table, "we leave for Knossos at first light to discover what has really happened." She set her hand on the Consort's shoulder. "Belisseus will remain here to oversee the temple and to receive— privately—any messengers we send while we are away."

"Is that really necessary?" Thalamika asked. "I could appoint one of my scribes to receive messages in my place while we are gone."

"I believe it is necessary," Elli said. "May I remind you what the diviners have seen, that we are in a time of change and upheaval? We must act with care to keep our own temple and city stable and independent."

"And so," Belisseus said, rising to stand beside Elli, "Our Lady will lead the group that travels in the morning."

Aria saw surprise on the others' faces, then realized that her own mouth was hanging open. No wonder. The High Priestess was the heart of the temple. For her to leave for more than a simple day trip to a nearby shrine was rare, almost unthinkable. Aria realized the situation was more serious than she had thought.

"Has this... has a High Priestess ever died in office before?" she asked.

"Not that I know of," Elli said. "No one can remember a time when a High Priestess died except by her own hand, in accordance with the sacred calendar. So I feel I must go myself to find the truth of the matter."

Belisseus leaned over, his hands resting on the edge of the table. "There is more. Once this new High Priestess took office, she sacrificed the Consort—also out of turn, since it is not yet Summer Solstice—and appointed a new one."

"We are told," Elli said quietly, "that the new Consort was not raised from birth for the office, but was chosen by the mainlanders who are now in power at Knossos. We are not even certain that he was a priest at all before he was appointed to this office."

Aria heard gasps around the table. She peered at Belisseus in the low light and could see that he was distressed, lines of worry creasing his face, white-knuckled hands gripping the edge of the table. No wonder: the gods alone knew what kind of disaster the people at Knossos were courting by flouting the old ways so brazenly. What horrible fate might the Mothers be contemplating for people who undertook such sacrilegious acts? And how might that punishment affect those near enough to Knossos to be in the shadow of its consequences?

"He has refused..." Belisseus began, a pained look on his face. He drew in a slow breath, then let it out. "They call their Consort Minos, as I am called Belisseus. But this new man has refused to take that name. Instead, he insists on being called by his birth name, Glymenos."

"Perhaps they simply want to start a new tradition," Thalamika offered. "They seem to be doing quite well in terms of the offerings they receive and the size of their herds."

"A new tradition that dishonors the people who have lived on this island since the very beginning?" Aria snapped.

"Our Lady said these are times of change," Thalamika continued, waving a hand toward the High Priestess. "Could they simply be keeping in step with that change? They still have sacred rites. They have not forsaken the gods."

Elli slapped her hand down on the table, and the rest of them jumped. "They have forsaken the people!"

Belisseus set his hand on hers. "There is power in our rites, the strength of generations of wisdom, maintaining the balance, keeping time with the cycles of the three realms and the ways of the Great Mothers." He squeezed Elli's hand then let go, drawing himself up to his full height. "They have broken the cycle. Damaged something invisible but powerful. No good can come of this."

"Perhaps," Aria dared to say, "perhaps they will destroy themselves in so doing. Then we will be rid of them."

Elli turned to her. "The diviners have said they may do exactly that." Aria nodded, satisfied. "But the diviners have also said they may take the rest of the island down with them."

Chapter 34

They set out at first light in two wagons, eight clergy plus a generous offering to the Knossos temple in honor of the new High Priestess and Consort, as had always been their custom. Aria sat with Elli, Lexion, and Thalamika in one wagon while Presfa rode in the other, along with one more priestess and three priests. There was barely room for the people and their small bags. The gifts to Knossos filled the wagons almost to overflowing. Elli had said this was no time to be stingy, and she must have meant it, Aria thought as she contemplated the heavy load that pressed against her back.

The wagons creaked as the oxen plodded westward along the Coast Road. Aria remembered making this same journey when she was pregnant with the man who was now running the temple in Elli's absence. The scent of wild herbs on the breeze and the sight of so many flowers blooming along the roadside made her yearn for a time when the world seemed simpler, when she understood less about the worries and troubles of temples and priesthood. Songbirds called in the distance, reminding her that it is only humans who make life so complicated. Ah, to be a wild bird on the wing!

It was midday by the time the two wagons passed the road that led off toward Eileithyia's cave. A short while later, they rolled through the busy port at Amnisos. Aria's gaze swept across the broad harbor, not that much bigger than Malia's but far busier. The docks were packed with people and goods being loaded and unloaded.

"Those are mostly mainlander ships," Lexion explained when he saw Aria's puzzled expression.

"They do not look quite like ours," she said, her brow furrowed.

"That is one thing we have in common with them," he said. "We all sail. We all ride Grandmother Ocean's waves."

She narrowed her eyes at the collection of sailing vessels along the docks. "These new mainlanders do not honor her or the other Great Mothers."

"I am simply trying to find common ground," he said, a note of apology in his voice. "Is it not good to try to understand others? Then we can live in peace together. The people along the coast at the eastern end of the sea, where your brothers live, are different from us as well. Yet we still trade with them."

"But they honor goddesses... and women. They are respectful even if they are different."

"No mainlander has ever been disrespectful to me."

"Of course they have not," Aria said. "You are a man."

The Sun was beginning to tip toward the west as they approached the island's largest city. Houses and shops sprawled out in all directions, with the enormous temple complex itself gleaming in white, blood red, and deep blue at the top of the hill. Aria lost sight of it as they wound their way through the city, their wagon hemmed in by market stalls and presses of people and animals. The scents of sweaty people, springtime flowers, animal dung, and fresh-baked bread swirled around her, the layered smell that had always meant city to her. Though no individual street looked that different from the ones in Malia, it seemed the buildings never ended as they rolled past one shop after another, one house after another, turning corner after corner and making their slow way toward their destination.

Several times as they moved through the city, dirty children in ragged clothing approached their wagons, begging for food. Aria saw that her fellow travelers were just as horrified at the sight as she was. To leave anyone in the community in need was an offense against the Mothers, but hungry children? The very idea was unspeakable.

Aria and her companions had already eaten their midday meal on the way. All they had left was a few small skins of wine and the large pithoi of grain, wine, and oil that were the traditional gifts upon the accession of a new High Priestess. When Elli asked the children why they did not get food from the temple if they were hungry, they responded with confusion.

"The temple does not sell food," one of the older children said. "And even if it did, we have nothing to trade."

"And your parents do not feed you?" she asked.

"We have no parents," came the bitter response.

Elli stared at the child, appalled. In Malia and the other cities around the island, though there certainly were poor people as well as wealthy ones, orphaned children with no other family or friends to help them were always taken in by the temple. No child was ever left to fend for themselves. The Great Mothers took care of their children, and so must humans do as well. It had been the same at Knossos for many generations, but apparently the mainlanders had abandoned the practice—along with the children.

Before Elli could continue the conversation with the children, a man came out of a nearby shop and chased them away, cuffing the slower ones in the head and shouting at them as they fled. Though Aria did not understand much of the mainlanders' language, she could tell the man was using profanity as he yelled at the children. Then she realized that most of the voices she had heard as they moved through the city were foreign, not Ida's children. Sageleus had taught her a few words of the mainlanders' speech, and she heard it everywhere now as they rolled down the cobbled road. She almost felt as if she was in a foreign land.

After the second group of hungry children approached the travelers a couple of streets farther on, with Elli's approval one of the priests climbed down from the slow-moving wagon and bought several large baskets of bread from a nearby stall. He divided the baskets between the wagons and the travelers began giving out bread, one small loaf per child, as they made their way through the city. As the children clustered around the wagons, Aria noticed that many of them had the pale skin and light hair of the mainlanders, or the coloring of mixed parentage. Word must have spread quickly, because every time they turned a corner, another group of children appeared, dirty hands reaching out, begging, snatching the bread and scampering away before the shopkeepers could come out and beat them.

"Are we certain they are not trying to trick us to get free food?" Thalamika asked, leaning away from the grasping fingers while her fellow clergy handed out bread. "There cannot be this many hungry children, even in a city this large."

"I have been watching carefully," Elli said. "I have not seen the same face twice." She narrowed her eyes at Thalamika. "Have you forgotten our sacred vow to feed the hungry and care for the children?"

"Of course not."

"Do not forget that the purpose of wealth is not to hoard it, but to share it with those in need."

Thalamika looked away, and the wagon rolled on.

Just when Aria thought they were lost and would spend the rest of their lives bumping down strange streets full of hungry children and foreign-speaking peddlers and bleating goats and over-laden carts, suddenly they were rolling up the temple's broad hill past Rhea's sacred grove of cypress trees. The sunlight warmed the road as it curved up the slope, past smaller buildings that also belonged to the temple.

Every temple on the island was a sacred house named after the goddess who presided over it, though all of them honored the Three together as well as the Daughter, the Young God, and their other divine children. Malia belonged to Kalliste, the Lady of the Date Palm, Lady of the Bees. The temple at Knossos was the House of Rhea, with her sacred cypress trees. But this was no ordinary sacred house. As the travelers moved up the hill, the enormous complex rose higher and higher, looming above them. Aria counted three stories across most of the sprawling building, four in some places, with pairs of sacred horns jutting up from the roof's edges at all levels. Much of the expansion, both upward and outward, had occurred during Aria's lifetime or that of her parents and grandparents, that much she knew. More than once, she had listened to Inia and Elli rant about the way the Knossians poured their wealth into their fancy temple rather than sharing it with the people.

Though Aria knew better, she felt as if the Knossos temple complex was as big as the whole city of Malia. It certainly was imposing. Perhaps it was meant to be that way, she thought. The Mothers always welcomed their children, but she had heard that the mainlanders' gods were more interested in intimidating people than anything else. She hoped she had heard wrong. Those were not the sorts of gods she cared to meet.

Finally the travelers arrived at the temple itself. The wagon drivers tended to the oxen while a servant took Elli's message inside. Aria and her companions had each brought a bag with a change of clothing. It would not do to wear dusty traveling garb to an audience with the new High Priestess and her Consort. They all retrieved their bags from the wagons, then Elli read off the list of gifts from a small sheet of papyrus as Aria and Lexion checked to be sure everything was still there: large jars full of wine and oil, heavy sacks of grain, plus generous quantities of jewelry, carved stone vases, and rare resins for incense.

Just when Aria was beginning to think her group had been forgotten, a servant with a large scar running across his cheek appeared and offered to lead them to their guest quarters. Leaving the drivers to safeguard the wagons and their contents, the travelers followed the servant into the building. They went along corridors, up stairs, around corners, up more stairs, and along more corridors before finally stopping.

The servant opened two adjacent doors. "One room for the men and one for the women," he said, his speech heavy with an accent Aria could not place. "You have time to wash and change. My Lord will send for you when he is ready for an audience."

They all stared after the servant as he retreated down the hall and disappeared around a corner.

"He is not one of us or a mainlander," Aria said.

"The mainlanders trade in slaves the way we trade in bronze, but with far less care for their merchandise," Elli said. "He could be from anywhere."

"Are we required to separate according to sex?" Lexion said, peering into one of the rooms.

"I think we had best follow their customs while we are here," Elli said, stepping through the other doorway and motioning for her fellow priestesses to follow. "We will show them that we respect them, and perhaps they will respect us."

As the other women began rummaging in their bags for fresh clothing, Aria looked around. The whitewashed room was painted with complex borders around the windows and ceiling, with a small fresco of an outdoor scene centered on one wall. Several brightly colored rugs covered the floor, and fine linen curtains fluttered in the warm breeze.

The furnishings were finer than she was used to, the wood carved with fancy patterns and buffed to a shine with beeswax and oil. There were three wide beds with thick mattresses, plenty of space for the five women who would occupy the room. A basin of fresh water and a stack of towels stood on the sideboard, and in the middle of the room a table with wine and bread awaited the travelers.

They took turns washing off the road-dust and sweat, then changed their clothes.

"Are you certain we need to be this fancy?" Presfa said as she adjusted the sleeves of her best tunic, making sure all the beads and tassels hung down straight and untangled. Her tiered skirt, lavished with beads and fringe, would be the next layer she donned.

"If I have been informed correctly," Elli replied, "even our best clothing may leave us looking like country bumpkins compared to the Knossos clergy. They spend much on finery and do not take seriously anyone who appears less wealthy than they are."

Upon hearing that, Aria set to work arranging her hair, applying makeup, and donning every piece of jewelry she had brought. The others did likewise, helping each other as they could. Only Elli had thought to bring a mirror, and their hosts had not supplied one in the room.

Aria wondered if they had failed to supply that item due to a concern about theft. When Aria was a child, no traveler would have dared take anything from a temple. That kind of sacrilege tempted the wrath of the Mothers, who had bidden their children to be generous and honest with each other. But these days, she regularly heard rumors that items large and small went missing from the sacred houses, the shrines, and even the temples, taken by traveling mainlanders or some of Ida's children who had picked up the mainlanders' questionable habits. She swallowed hard, remembering the seal stone hidden at the bottom of her small box of jewelry. She hoped against hope that the Mothers understood that act, driven by a kind of sacred desperation and not greed. Turning back to her preparations, Aria forced her mind toward less disturbing thoughts.

Finally the women finished getting ready and sat down to have a little wine and some bread. But hardly had they begun when a knock sounded at the door. Aria rose to open it, finding the scarred servant from earlier waiting in the corridor.

"My Lord will see you now."

"Very well," Elli said. She stepped over to knock on the other door.

A moment later, they were all standing in the corridor, the men wearing almost as much makeup and jewelry as the women, their hair glossy with scented oil and their finest tunics and sandals on display.

"The servant's announcement does not bode well," Elli said quietly to her companions. Aria wanted to ask what that meant, but the servant was already heading down the corridor, and they all had to hurry to keep up.

Some time later, after a nearly interminable number of staircases and turns and corridors, they reached a wide landing. The servant knocked on a door and it opened. "You will wait in here," he said, turning to walk away before they had even stepped over the threshold.

With a sigh, Elli led the others into the room. It turned out to be fairly spacious, though not very well lit, and empty of any benches or chairs on which they might rest while they waited. There were no light wells to let in the afternoon sunshine, and the two lamps that guttered in opposite corners did little to dispel the gloom.

Aria contented herself with examining the large spiral designs on the borders that ran around the room, though it was hard to make out the details in the flickering lamplight. The group mostly remained silent, though Thalamika dared to whisper to Elli once or twice as they stood there waiting. After what seemed like quite a long time, one of the doors in the far wall swung open, and a priest beckoned to them.

"Your leader will go in first," he said, motioning to Lexion, "and the rest will follow."

Elli stepped up in front of the priest, whose eyebrows rose. The others gathered behind her, waiting. Given the look on the priest's face, Aria expected him to comment. But after a moment, he moved through the doorway and off to one side. Elli went through with Aria directly behind her, the others following close on their heels.

Aria and the others arranged themselves behind Elli in the middle of the audience chamber. The room was larger than the one where Elli presided, and much more heavily decorated. The walls were paneled in polished stone up to waist height, then covered with more spiral designs like the ones in the anteroom. Lamps ringed the room, throwing circles of light onto the colorful paintings. At the center of the far wall, in the High Priestess' chair, sat a man.

Aria saw Elli's fists clench and unclench as they waited in silence. It was disrespectful to address the High Priestess in audience until she had first addressed you. But now some man, a mainlander from the look of him, sat in the high seat while a woman stood to one side, in the place where the Consort belonged. Aria looked the woman up and down. She could have been one of Ida's children, or perhaps of mixed parentage: her skin was light golden, but her hair was black. She was dressed in fine clothing and a great deal of jewelry, with beads and gold rings in her hair. She did not look happy, but she did not appear interested in fighting for her rightful place in her own audience hall, either. Her shoulders were bowed, and after an initial look at the travelers, she kept her gaze lowered.

The man raised a hand in greeting. "Clergy of Malia, I welcome you."

Elli made the salute, but the look on her face was sour.

"I am Glymenos," the man said, "and I preside over this temple. This is Melena," he waved a hand dismissively at the woman beside him, "the High Priestess."

"I am Eileithyia, High Priestess of the House of Kalliste at Malia," Elli said, her voice strong and confident, her gaze taking in both Glymenos and Melena. "My Lady and Honored Minos, I bring you greetings, blessings, and gifts on behalf of our temple and our city."

"You will call me Glymenos," the Consort said, his jaw clenched. Then he smiled, showing all his teeth. "They have told me about your well-filled wagons. We are pleased with your generosity." He squinted at the group standing behind Elli. "Now tell me, which one of you is the Consort for your temple? I would speak with him."

"He has not come with us today, My Lord," Elli said. "I speak for our people."

Glymenos sat back, folding his arms across his chest. "I see. And what do you say to me, on behalf of your people?"

Elli motioned to Aria, who stepped up beside her High Priestess, her heart pounding. She did her best to disguise her shock at the situation, but she was not sure she succeeded. It took some effort to keep from squirming as Glymenos looked her up and down. His gaze made her feel like a prize heifer at the livestock market, but she forced herself to keep her posture tall and her head held high.

"Just as you have recently had a change in office," Elli said, "so we are planning one for this Summer Solstice, the *traditional* time for such events. This is Ariadne, who will be High Priestess after me. I have brought her so you and Our Lady will know her once she takes the high seat in our temple."

Unsure how to behave in such an unusual situation, Aria opted for tradition, making the salute.

"And who will be the next Consort?" Glymenos asked. "Would that be you?" He motioned to Lexion, whose eyes widened. He was far too old to be a Consort. But then, Aria realized, so was Glymenos.

"Our next Consort is in training in the temple, according to our tradition," Elli said, her lips pressed together in a thin line.

Glymenos let out a loud laugh and slapped his thigh. "You native women are indeed stubborn," he said, throwing Melena a pointed look. "Very well. I have heard your greetings, and I accept your gift. The servants will make sure you can find your way to dinner."

He waved a hand, dismissing them without a blessing and without a word from his High Priestess. As the group retreated, Aria glanced back over her shoulder to see Melena wincing as Glymenos gripped her hard by the wrist, speaking to her in a low voice.

Chapter 35

Once they were back in the guest quarters and the servant who guided them there had left, the travelers all gathered in the women's room, sitting on the edges of the beds and on the stools that surrounded the table.

"This is indeed troubling," Elli said. "The rumors are more than true." She set her hand on Aria's knee. "I am sorry to be leaving you with this mess."

Aria shook her head. "You have taught me well, My Lady. The mainlanders need not follow our ways, but they should not insist that we follow theirs. This is our island, our home."

"They have come here as if they wish to own the island," Lexion said.

"But even we do not own it," Elli said. "If anything, we belong to the Mother. We are her children."

Aria squared her shoulders. "We will keep to our own ways, like the rest of Ida's children. The people at Knossos may do as they wish. To each their own."

"It may not be that simple," Elli said, looking around her small group. "We have a relationship with these people, whether we like it or not, and they are not that far from our doorstep."

Lexion shook his head. "We trade with so many different people from so many different lands, and we manage to be on good terms with all of them. I think we just need to work harder at being diplomatic."

"I agree, up to a point," Elli said. "As long as the House of Rhea is willing to treat with us as equals, we will be on good terms with them. But they have already begun to make threats..."

"They are greedy," Aria snarled.

"They are wealthy," Thalamika countered, "and powerful. Perhaps we could learn from them. Look at this!" She swept her hand around, encompassing not just the room with its fine furnishings but the whole temple, with its elaborate frescoes and gilded columns and enormous footprint that took up the whole top of the hill, rising to four stories tall. "We could build our own temple up like this, attract more people and goods, more silver and gold and precious stones. Do you not wish to glorify our gods the way they glorify theirs?"

Elli looked over at Thalamika. "We glorify the Mothers by sharing and giving, not by holding tight to what we have."

"But that does not mean we cannot have things to begin with," said Thalamika. "Perhaps the mainlanders would respect us more if we were wealthier." She toyed with her necklace, stroking a gold bead. "We are clergy. We should have nice things. We are not ordinary people."

"It seems to me," Aria said, working the ideas over in her mind, "that Glymenos and his people are not glorifying the gods so much as themselves. I think they are doing this on purpose, to show how wealthy and powerful they are, not how holy they are."

"But look at the temple!" Thalamika exclaimed. "It is beautiful. People admire it."

"I agree, it is impressive," Aria said, "but it feels contrived. They are not celebrating the gods, but challenging Ida's children, trying to provoke us. That is not beautiful. That is ugly."

Just as Thalamika was drawing breath for a reply, a quiet knock sounded at the door. Lexion rose and opened it, finding a young woman standing in the corridor, her head bowed.

"Hello there," he said.

"I have come to take you to dinner," she said, her voice quiet and meek.

"That is good news, since we are hungry," he said with a smile. "I am Lexion. What is your name?"

Still keeping her head bowed and remaining silent, she motioned for the group to follow her. With a shrug, Lexion turned back to his fellow travelers.

"I guess we had better go," he said.

As they followed behind the young woman, Aria noted that her garments, though clean, were rough and of poor quality. They did not fit her well, either, as if they were someone else's castoffs. Once, when the servant's tunic slipped off her shoulder, a portion of her back was bared, and Aria saw a cluster of scars. Her stomach lurched as she realized that the pattern of stripes on the woman's skin was the kind that came from a severe whipping.

After another long walk along corridors and down staircases, the group arrived at a wide doorway. The young woman who had guided them there motioned them into the room, then walked away. The room turned out to be a dining hall, with rows of long tables and benches full of people already enjoying a lavish dinner. Aria wondered if the servant had been sent to fetch them late on purpose.

Though Aria could clearly see Glymenos seated at a table on the far side of the room, with Melena right next to him, no one acknowledged the group from Malia or offered them a seat. As she looked around, Aria spotted Hedamos, the emissary who had been so rude to Elli back in the autumn. He was seated near Glymenos. Aria nudged Elli and nodded toward Hedamos. The High Priestess' eyes narrowed, and she turned so her back was to him.

"I do not expect we will get a warm welcome from anyone here tonight," Elli said. "So let us have some dinner and go quietly to our beds. We will leave for home as soon as daylight comes. I have seen enough to know what we are dealing with."

With a sigh, Elli led her people to a nearby table that had some room at one end. They took their places on the benches, introducing themselves to the men and women at the table, who all turned out to be low-ranking priests and priestesses. Aria shifted in her seat, adjusting the fringe on her skirt, when she realized that these junior clergy were all wearing garments finer than hers.

The people at the table were kind and friendly toward Aria and her companions, sharing the dishes of food down the table. Aria wondered whether the temple had put on such a fancy meal to impress them, or whether this was the way they ate all the time. In addition to the roast goat, lamb, and beef, there were lentils and chickpeas, onions, leeks, olives, wild greens, a variety of cheeses, several different kinds of bread, dried fruit, sweetmeats, and an abundance of wine. Servants moved among the tables, refilling wine jugs and replacing empty platters and bowls with full ones.

As the Knossians chatted with the visitors at their table, Aria listened to their speech. While many of them looked like Ida's children, they all spoke with the accent that told her their native language was that of the mainlanders. Perhaps that was now the language of Knossos, she mused, a foreign tongue taking over the House of Rhea and the city that surrounded it. It was one thing to hear any number of different languages in Malia's port and the parts of the city where the foreign traders stayed when they visited. But to have an entire city become foreign? A chill ran down Aria's spine. This boded far worse than just a difference in speech, she was certain.

As they tasted the various dishes, the sound of music rose from the front of the room. Aria looked up to see a man playing a lyre and another playing a double flute. In front of Glymenos, two nearly naked women danced and played small finger cymbals. Glymenos leered at them while Melena looked away. Aria found herself wishing to leap up and scream at the Knossos Consort. But she knew better, so she directed her anger toward her meal, ripping the bread apart and tearing the roast meat into small pieces before chewing them viciously.

"We were terribly sorry to hear about Zephyra," Elli was saying when Aria finally brought her attention back to the conversation.

"It was a fever," explained a young priestess who had introduced herself as Medea. "They said we were lucky it did not spread through the temple. Only Our Lady and her two closest servants succumbed."

"I hope her death was not an omen," Presfa commented. Elli shot her a warning look, and the young priestess fell silent.

"An omen of what?" Medea asked.

"Like the time of Great Darkness," Aria dared to say, ignoring the way Elli suddenly gripped her knee under the table, tightly enough to hurt. "Kalliste sent that as a warning that we must keep to the old ways and honor the Mothers."

"Oh, that," Medea said, dismissing the idea with a wave of her hand. "Glymenos tells us not to worry about such things. They are mere superstitions. We are meant to leave behind those backward ways and replace them with something better. We are not losing anything of value."

The Knossian priest seated next to Medea, who had introduced himself as Dolios, leaned forward so he could see all the visitors. "You native people do not understand power or wealth. You give away all you have instead of building it up. We can show you what it means to be real men, to take what is yours the way our gods do." He threw pointed looks at Lexion and the other Malian priests.

Aria and her companions stared in shock as Medea nodded her agreement. "You have mistaken your gods for children," she said, "the little sons of great mothers. But we women are weak. We must have men to rule over us, just as Zeus rules over the goddesses."

"And where is your Zeus now?" Elli said, visibly working to maintain her composure.

"You call him Dionysus," Dolios said, "but he is the same as our Zeus, and he is no child. He rules over the goddesses, not the other way around."

"Our people have worshiped the Great Mothers for generations," Elli said, the muscles in her jaw flexing as she gritted her teeth.

"Only because you do not know any better," Dolios replied. "Your people are backward, primitive. We will teach you a more modern, more civilized way, just as we have done with the temple at Phaistos and the sacred houses at Hagia Triada and Kommos."

Elli drew in a sharp breath and fell silent. None of the others dared to comment. Aria found herself picking at the food, her appetite gone, her thoughts so chaotic that she no longer heard the conversation at the tables around her. Soon after, the music stopped, and Glymenos rose from his seat. He said something Aria could not hear, then he bundled the two dancers and his High Priestess out of the room ahead of him, two burly guards helping to ensure that the women went where Glymenos directed.

As soon as he was gone, the rest of the people began getting up and leaving the dining hall. Aria and her fellow travelers rose from their places and stood together at the end of the table. Elli spoke in a low voice to Lexion, who stepped away from the group. A few moments later he returned with a servant who could guide them to their rooms.

"Will you not join us for some entertainment?" Dolios asked. "We always have music, and sometimes dancing as well, after dinner." He motioned toward the doorway, presumably to some other room in the temple. "You need not go to bed right away."

"I do not think your Consort cares to see too much of us," Elli said.

"Glymenos will not be there," Dolios assured her. "He takes his own... entertainment in his private quarters."

"I had best turn in," Elli said. "But the rest of you are free to do as you like."

After some discussion, Presfa and two of the priests decided to join Dolios. The others moved toward the servant who was to guide them back to their rooms.

"If you do not mind," Aria said, "I need some fresh air. Surely they have an herb garden I can walk in. There is a moon tonight, so it will be light enough."

"I can take you there," Medea said. "Our Medicine-Priestess taught me many things when I was just a novice. I still walk in the gardens from time to time."

"Very well," Elli said to Aria. Then, to the whole group, "Do your best not to wake us if you come back late."

The group split up, Dolios leading his guests toward the evening's entertainment and the servant showing Elli and the others the way back to their rooms. That left Aria and Medea standing at the end of the table as the hall emptied.

"Come," Medea said, linking her arm in Aria's. "I will show you the garden."

Medea led Aria out of the dining hall, down several corridors, through the expansive workshops—silent and empty at this hour of the evening—and out a side door. As they stepped out into the cool night air, Aria realized that the Knossos temple was built on the same plan as the one at Malia, even though it was so much bigger. She might get lost among the many rooms and corridors, but all the main sections of the two temples were in the same places.

The two women strolled through the moonlit herb garden side by side. Occasionally, Medea would stop to identify a plant and comment on what she had learned about it. Aria made sure to compliment the other woman on her knowledge, even though most of it was fairly basic. She was happy to have a friendly companion to chat with in a place that felt like it might become a battlefield at any moment.

The night was not warm enough for the scents of the herbs to float up through the air. So instead, Aria picked a small stem of myrtle and crushed its leaves, inhaling the familiar aroma, the plant that had been sacred to the Mothers for as long as anyone could remember. She mentioned that fact to Medea, who responded with the plant's medicinal uses, not its sacred ones.

After they had been walking for a while, Aria heard footsteps behind them and turned to see Hedamos striding down the path between two large rosemary bushes. He came right up to the two women, stopping closer than Aria was comfortable with. Without thinking, she took a step back and looked up to see him grinning at her.

"Are you two ladies having a moonlit stroll?" he asked, sliding between them and taking them each by the arm. "Such a lovely night for it," he said as he gave a push. They began walking awkwardly down the path that was not quite wide enough for three abreast.

As they passed the next large herb bed, Medea's skirt became entangled in the low branches of a dittany plant. When she finally managed to pull it free, Hedamos said to her, "It is late, and I am sure you have matters to attend to in the temple. I will be happy to see Ariadne back to her room."

Medea stared at him, nonplussed, but the look on his face brooked no argument. "Y-yes," she stammered. "There are things I must do." She turned to Aria. "I enjoyed our walk. Blessings of the Great God be upon you." Then she went back down the path and disappeared into the building.

When Aria realized Hedamos was still holding her by the arm, she slipped out of his grip and took a step back. "You must forgive me, but it is late and I am tired. Traveling wears me out. I should go back to my room."

"Of course," Hedamos said. "I will show you the way." His leering smile sent a chill down her spine.

Once again he took hold of Aria's arm, leading her back into the building. As they moved down corridors and up stairs, she kept an eye out for any servant she might ask to direct her back to her room. Then she could bid Hedamos good night and be rid of him. But it was late, the corridors were empty, and Hedamos kept a firm grip on her arm.

After a few more turns and yet another staircase, Aria realized they were higher up in the building than the level her group's guest rooms were on. Though the temple was large and complicated, its levels were clear: the rooms Aria's people were staying in were on the third floor, and Hedamos had led her to the fourth floor.

"I think we are in the wrong place," she said, attempting to pull free from his grip. "Perhaps there is more than one set of guest rooms. Ours are on the floor below this one, I am certain."

"We are very much in the right place," Hedamos said, steering her around a corner and through a doorway. "This is exactly where I want you."

The room was dark except for a beam of moonlight that slanted in through the window. In the faint light, Aria could see that this was a small storeroom of some sort. The shelves along one wall were full of folded lengths of fabric. There was no other furniture.

As she was trying to determine whether the cloth was material meant for sewing or banners for decorating the temple, Hedamos pushed her back against the wall.

"You are hurting me," she said, straining against him as he gripped both of her wrists and pushed them up above her head.

"It will hurt less if you cooperate," he said, his voice like coldest silk.

Then he grasped both of her wrists in one of his hands, moving the other hand down to grab her skirt cord and tug it loose.

"No!" she cried out.

His hand flew to her mouth, and he leaned close to her, his nose nearly touching hers. "I suggest you keep quiet," he said. "The linen on these shelves is dyed with the murex. It is terribly valuable. I would hate to have to tell Glymenos that I caught you trying to steal it to carry back to Malia in your little wagons. I am sure the punishment for such a crime is quite severe."

"You would not dare," she hissed.

He drove his shoulder against her, hard, and she gasped with the pain. "I would dare that and more, little native girl. You will learn your place, like all the other dark little women of this island. And that place is beneath a man."

With that, he tore her skirt away and pressed himself between her legs. He still held her wrists above her head in a painful grip, his other hand grasping her thigh, hard fingers digging into soft flesh. Then he shoved into her, the full weight of his body crashing against her with every stroke.

Her whole body shook with fear and rage. She bit her tongue to keep from crying out, casting about desperately for any way to escape. He was pressed so close against her, she had to turn her head to the side to see the window, the open window—four stories in the air, too high for a getaway.

"Do not think you will escape me, you little whore," he growled between thrusts, his wine-soaked breath washing over her face. "You will never escape me. I will keep coming to your pitiful little city long after your precious High Priestess is dead. I will demand tribute, and you will pay it. And every time you see me, you will remember this."

When he had finished, he let go and stepped back from her all in one motion. She crumpled to the floor, her clothing in disarray, sobbing and shaking.

"Go home now," he spat as he tugged his tunic back in place. "But remember, our business is not finished."

The next time Aria looked up, she was alone in the room. She could not tell whether she had passed out, or fallen asleep, or simply gone blank for a time. The Moon had moved across the sky, and the room was now much darker. Groping about in what little light remained, Aria found her skirt. She used a corner of the fabric to wipe the tears off her face. She could feel that her makeup had smudged, but there was nothing she could do about it without a mirror.

Though she was still trembling, she managed to stand. Then she realized the evidence of Hedamos' wickedness was smeared along the insides of her thighs. She patted at it with the corner of her skirt, trying to clean herself, but some of it had dried already. With shaking hands she wrapped the skirt around her body, fumbling to make it stay in place. Hedamos had torn one end of the cord loose.

Holding her skirt together at the waist with one hand, she stepped through the doorway and out into the dark corridor. Her mind did not want to function. All she wanted was to slip into the black oblivion of sleep. But she needed to get back to the guest rooms for that. She must not sleep on the bare floor, only to be found by the servants the next morning in such disarray.

Forcing herself to focus, she moved slowly along the unlit corridor, her free hand on the wall, aiming for the pale light at the far end. When she reached it, she realized it was moonlight coming in through a light well, illuminating a staircase.

Down. She needed to go down. She was too high up. There was just enough moonlight that she could see where to step, so she managed to make her way to the bottom of the staircase without incident. But from there, where? The guest rooms were on the third floor, of that she was sure. But the third floor was huge, and she feared that, like the fourth floor, some parts of it were separate from the others, only accessible by going down one more floor and then back up again farther on.

She did not know how much time elapsed as she walked slowly down dark corridors, moving from one pale sliver of moonlight to the next, examining each doorway she came to. How could she possibly know which was the right one? Perhaps her mind was playing tricks on her. She could swear she had passed some of the doors more than once, sobbing, stumbling, and bumping into the walls as she went.

Finally, exhausted, she rounded a corner and crumpled down onto the floor, staring at her fingers as they twisted the remains of her skirt cord. It was her best skirt, and now it was ruined. Would Elli be angry?

Then her mind took a different turn. She was lost, irretrievably lost. No one was awake this time of night. She would simply have to wait for daylight and hope someone found her, someone who would be kinder to her than Hedamos had been. What if another man like him came upon her in the night? She felt like she wanted to cry again, but no more tears would come. She slumped down, her chin on her chest, unable even to pray to the Mothers. All she could do was wait for morning.

A sound echoed from down the corridor, and she lifted her head to see a light hovering a short distance away. In the glow of that light Aria could see a face, the features slowly resolving until she recognized...

"Elli!" she croaked, her voice hoarse from crying.

A moment later, Elli was crouching over Aria, holding the lamp up, examining the younger woman.

"What in the Mothers' name has happened?" Elli cried. Her hands smoothed down Aria's ragged hair and stroked the sleeves on her rumpled bodice. "My dear, are you hurt?"

Aria saw the worry in Elli's face and knew she could do nothing to allay it. "He..." She tried to speak, but the word ended in a sob.

"Come, let us get you back to the room," Elli said, helping Aria to her feet and supporting her as they made their way down to the guest room.

The other women were awake but quiet, watching as Elli walked Aria over to the bed, helped her sit down on the edge and hold a cup of wine. As Aria drank, Elli wrapped an arm around her shoulders, a comforting presence. By the time Aria had finished the wine, her hands had stopped shaking. Elli tenderly swept a lock of hair off Aria's forehead and took her hand.

"Can you tell me what happened?" Elli asked.

"He..." she began, drawing a shuddering breath.

"Who?" Elli said. "I left you with Medea. You were going to the herb gardens."

"We went," Aria managed to say. "But then..." She wrung her hands.

"Did someone try to rob you?" Elli said, her gaze taking in Aria's jewelry, disheveled but still intact, and her makeup, now smeared in dark smudges around her eyes.

Aria shook her head. "Hedamos." His name came out in a hoarse whisper.

Elli drew in a sharp breath. "What has he..." Her gaze shifted to Aria's trembling hands, which drew aside the edge of her skirt to show the substance clinging to her thighs.

"By all the gods!" Elli cried out, leaping up from the bed. "That son of a dung heap has violated a priestess!" Her hands clenched into fists.

By now Thalamika, Presfa, and the other young priestess were sitting up, watching. Elli began pacing back and forth, practically shouting as she vented her anger at Hedamos and all the other men who thought such behavior was anything other than pure blasphemy worthy of the worst punishment possible. Shortly, Lexion appeared in the doorway.

"My Lady," he said, making shushing motions with his hands, "you will wake the whole corridor. Is there some trouble?" Then he looked over at Aria, who angled her head down to avoid meeting his gaze. In two strides he was kneeling before her, a horrified look on his face. "Who has done this to you?"

"The piece of mainland trash they call Hedamos," Elli spat.

Lexion rose. "Then we will make him pay. At daylight, we will bring him before the High Priestess."

"We will go now," Elli hissed.

"Then I will come with you."

With a fuming Elli in the lead, the three of them made their way through corridors and down stairways, their path lit by Elli's small lamp. Aria stumbled along the way, exhausted and frightened, so Lexion took hold of one of her arms to support her. She was glad he did not wrap an arm around her waist or press up against her. She did not care to have any more contact with men than necessary just at the moment, not even a man she liked.

Finally they reached the first floor, though Aria could not tell which part of the temple they were in. Unable to find the audience hall, Elli began calling out until a servant appeared at the end of the corridor.

"We must see the High Priestess!" she demanded. "Wake Melena!"

The servant scurried down the corridor and poked his head through a doorway, then returned a few moments later with a guard.

"You must take us to the High Priestess," Elli said to the guard. "I am the High Priestess of the temple in Malia, visiting here with my people as your temple's guests. One of our group has been attacked." She waved a hand toward Aria.

"That is a matter for Glymenos," the man said, his gaze raking over Aria in a way that suggested he might do the same thing to her, given the opportunity.

"Melena is the ruler of this temple," Elli said. "You must go wake her."

"You misunderstand, old lady," the guard said, his lip curling up in a sneer. "Melena rules nothing, not even her own bedchamber. Glymenos is in charge here, and it is him I answer to. I will not wake him just because one of your women decided to play hard to get."

Lexion let go of Aria's arm and took a step forward, his hands balling into fists, but Elli raised a hand to stop him. He stood in place, his nostrils flaring, his eyes narrowed at the guard.

"Are you telling me," Elli said through gritted teeth, "that this temple does not consider the rape of a priestess to be a crime?"

The guard shrugged. "If she did not want it, she should not have led him on. It does not matter who he was."

Elli stepped up close to the guard, who towered more than a head above her, and pointed a finger in his face. "I do not know who raised you, but she did not teach you right from wrong. Now heed the word of a High Priestess and go wake Melena, before the Great Mothers teach you a lesson the hard way."

Laughing, the guard drew his sword and pressed its point beneath her chin. "You are the one who needs to learn a lesson," he hissed. "Perhaps you and your little whore should entertain me this evening..."

Lexion took a step forward, and the guard shifted his sword, pressing the tip against Lexion's chest.

"I will slice your belly open if you take one more step toward me," the guard growled.

"Come, My Lady," Lexion said, taking Elli's arm and drawing her back from the guard. "We will find another way to deal with this problem."

"We do not know our way back to our rooms," Elli said, a little too loudly. "I am sure you do not want us wandering the corridors, waking up others and telling them of our troubles."

Muttering under his breath, the guard stomped down the corridor and said a few words into the room he had just come out of. A woman appeared, her hair in disarray, drawing her clothing around herself in haste. She followed the guard back to their group, and when the light from Elli's lamp touched her, Aria recognized her as the servant who had shown them through the temple earlier that evening.

"You will take them to their rooms," the guard instructed her. "Then you will come back here. We are not done with you yet." He ran a hand down her chest, squeezing a breast, and she stiffened, a frightened look on her face. Then he shoved her toward Elli.

"We are on the third floor, among the guest quarters," Elli said, her voice gentle and kind.

Nodding, the woman scurried around their group and continued on down the corridor, hunched over as if she were trying to hide in the middle of an open hallway. They had no choice but to follow her, or end up lost in the enormous temple. It was all Aria could do to keep up with her, even with Lexion helping her along. When they finally reached their rooms, pushing the doors open to confirm that they were in the right place, the servant woman nodded to them and rushed away.

Chapter 36

Once Aria had washed and changed into clean clothes, Elli allowed her to sleep until dawn. Aria woke to find herself huddled in Elli's embrace, clutching the older woman's arm, with Elli gently stroking her hair.

"I am sorry," Aria said, sitting up. "I have caused so much trouble."

"You have nothing to be sorry for," Elli said. "You have done nothing wrong. I fear we must leave here quickly or have Glymenos angry at us for making trouble. Who knows what he might do, with his guards and their swords. But there is something we must take care of, and quickly."

Elli's gaze went to Aria's belly, and the younger woman sucked in a breath. "How?"

"The Medicine-Priestess, of course," Elli said.

It took a few moments to find a servant who could direct them—few people were up yet—but soon, they found themselves standing in the front room of one of the temple workshops. Bundles of dried herbs hung from the ceiling and from pegs along the wall. Bowls, baskets, and jars full of all kinds of concoctions lined the shelves. A large mortar and pestle stood at one end of a long table next to a container of dried seed pods. A man was breaking open the seed pods and shaking their contents into the mortar. Aria wondered if he was an apprentice, though he looked too old for it. The only healers she had ever known were women. The man looked up when Aria and Elli stepped into the room.

"How can I help you?" he said.

"We are having... female problems," Elli said. She gave him a bashful look, something Aria was sure was an act. She had never known Elli to be bashful about her body, or anyone else's, for that matter.

"Oh, er..." the man stammered. "Perhaps Teledike can help you."

He waved them on through a doorway into another room, where an elderly woman was binding bunches of rosemary branches with twine, humming to herself as she hung them up in the corner to dry.

"Excuse me," Elli said, "we are looking for Teledike."

"I am Teledike," the woman said, smiling broadly. "You must need something for female complaints. Cramps, perhaps? He..." She tilted her head toward the front room. "...always sends the women to me."

Elli ushered Aria toward the back of the room and beckoned Teledike to join them.

"We are in need of certain remedies," Elli said quietly. "My priestess was..." Elli stopped, searching for the words.

"One of the men here attacked me," Aria hissed at the herbalist as the anger flared in her. "He took me against my will."

Teledike's smile disappeared, and she pressed her lips together. "This happens a lot these days," she said in a low voice as she shot a sidelong glance toward the doorway. "All I can do is offer my sympathies and a remedy afterward, and the advice not to speak of it to anyone. The men who rule this place believe the woman should be punished if she protests when a man does this to her. I have seen priestesses slain, or worse, for demanding justice." She crossed the room and lifted the lid from a large jar. "The situation is bad enough that I must keep this on hand all the time these days."

She ladled a small amount of a dark liquid into a cup and handed it to Aria. "Drink this now. I will give you enough for another dose tonight and two tomorrow, one in the morning and one in the evening. Do not take it all at once thinking it will work better that way. Do as I say, in four doses, or it will only make you bleed miserably." She waited while Aria downed the bitter liquid and handed the cup back. Then she filled a small jar with more of the liquid, tying a piece of beeswax-soaked cloth across the top to seal it. She handed the jar to Aria and eyed both the visitors.

"You are not from Knossos, I see. I will tell you, I meant what I said earlier. You must not speak of this to anyone," Teledike said, clutching at Aria and Elli's hands. "These new people, these men..." She swallowed, glancing again toward the doorway that led to the front room. "No one will believe you. They will only believe what the men say. And they will punish you instead."

"We had already determined as much," Elli said, bitter. "We only wish to go home."

"I am sorry," Teledike said. "Knossos is not what it was when I was a girl."

Aria clutched the jar of herbal remedy as Teledike directed them toward a doorway in the back of the room. When Aria pushed the door open, she saw that it led out to the herb garden.

"You can ask any of the servants out there to take you back to your rooms," Teledike explained. "This way, you do not have to pass the Medicine-Priest again, in case he might ask questions."

The two priestesses stepped through the doorway and nearly collided with a middle-aged woman who was coming down the garden path.

"My Lady!" the woman exclaimed, taking a step back and making the salute.

"You know us?" Aria asked, perplexed.

"She knows me," Elli said, reaching to embrace the other woman. "This is Vanadia, a priestess here. Come, let us walk in the gardens for a few moments. I think we have that much time before we must go. I suspect Glymenos does not rise early."

The three women strolled down the path with Elli in the lead, Aria clutching her jar of herbal liquid and wondering what was going on. The gardens were still empty, and the outdoor workshops were only just beginning to show signs of activity so early in the morning. When they reached the far corner of the gardens, some distance from both the temple building and the outdoor workshops, Elli stopped, and the other two women did likewise.

"I had not thought to introduce you," Elli said, "but divine providence has brought us together. Aria, Vanadia is a friend to us at Malia. I am sure you have wondered how I know so well what is happening here." She set her hand on Vanadia's arm. "You have been a blessing to us, with your messages and visits."

"I do my best," Vanadia said, glancing around nervously. "I do not like the changes that are happening here. They go against the vows I took when I became a priestess. But I can no longer visit Malia. They do not like women to travel. These days, only the priests are allowed to journey to other temples."

"I understand." Elli nodded and let out a sigh. "If we cannot stop these changes, at least we can keep abreast of them with honest information rather than wild rumors. As long as you have a trusted servant who can send messages, I hope you will still write to me." Vanadia nodded confirmation. Elli reached out, slipping an arm around Aria's shoulders. "Vanadia, this is Ariadne. She will be the next High Priestess after me at Summer Solstice this year."

Vanadia's eyebrows shot up. "You are..." She swallowed. "I am honored to have known you, My Lady." She made the salute. "By all the Mothers, I swear to you that I will send my messages to Ariadne after you."

"Thank you," Elli said, and brushed a kiss across Vanadia's cheek. "You have no idea how helpful you are to me. To us."

"I do what I can."

"Ariadne," Elli said, "you may believe what Vanadia tells you in her messages. And you must never reveal her identity."

"Not to anyone?"

"You may trust your Consort," Elli said, "but no one else."

"Not even our own people?"

"Not anymore," Elli said with a sigh. "And of course, trust no one in Knossos except Vanadia."

"I did not realize you were coming to visit," Vanadia said. "Things are bad here. I would have told you to stay away."

Elli shot a sidelong glance at Aria, who stood with her arms wrapped around herself, the small jar clutched in her fist.

"I knew some of it, thanks to your messages," the High Priestess said, "but the way they treat women now." She shook her head, her face full of anger. "And those children! In the city, we encountered hungry children everywhere. Orphans."

Tears welled up in Vanadia's eyes. She turned her head, blinking them away. "The mainlanders have brought slaves here, women they keep for their pleasure, both in the temple and in the city. Many of these women do not know how to prevent pregnancy, and the men refuse to let them learn. In the temple, when the women fall pregnant, their children are kept as slaves or sold in the market."

Aria gasped, and Elli set a hand on her arm.

"But in the city," Vanadia continued, the pain clear in her voice, "the wealthy merchants also keep such slaves. When the women fall pregnant, the men turn them out into the street. These women survive as best they can down in the port, offering their bodies to traders and sailors, but once the children are old enough to walk and talk, the women often abandon them."

"How could a mother do such a thing?" Aria gasped, feeling a pang of grief as her own son's face flashed through her mind.

"These women cannot feed themselves, much less their children. The temple no longer shares its grain with the people." She drew in a sharp breath, steeling herself to continue. "Sometimes the women are sold again, but often they are not attractive enough, starving and filthy. And their children... the girls who survive to womanhood will suffer the same fate as their mothers." She hid her face in her hands, her chest heaving as she attempted to suppress the sobs.

Elli reached out to squeeze Vanadia's shoulder. "These are difficult times. May the Mothers give us the strength to survive them." Elli nodded toward the handful of people who were beginning to move out into the gardens. "We had better go."

They bid their quick goodbyes to Vanadia, then Elli led Aria around the edge of the outdoor workshops, toward one of the smaller side entrances to the temple.

"We will find a servant to take us back to our rooms," Elli said as they walked, "and then we will pack up and leave."

As they reached the doorway, Aria stopped and turned to Elli. "Is there nothing we can do about Hedamos?"

"I have kept the cloth I used to clean you with," Elli said in a low voice. "There is magic that can be done with his fluids."

Aria's eyes widened. "What will that do?"

"It depends on the individual. Some of them fall ill. Some succumb to accidents. It may take time, but I promise you, he will pay for what he has done to you. I can only hope it happens quickly enough that I am still here to see it."

"I..." Aria picked at the cloth that served as a lid on the jar of herbal remedy. "Will I still be the next High Priestess?"

"Of course. Why would you ask such a thing?"

"He... I am not supposed to lie with a man during my year of training."

Elli's face screwed up with anger. "You did not lie with a man. You were attacked! You are not to blame, and you have most certainly not violated your vows. He is the filthy one, not you." Elli took Aria by the elbow and directed her into the building. "Now we will leave, and gods willing, we will never return to this cursed place."

Chapter 37

"Thank the Mothers for familiar ground," Aria said as she climbed down off the wagon and gazed up at the walls of her home temple.

Elli handed Aria her bag then stepped down to stand next to her. The High Priestess looked back and forth at both wagons, now empty except for her people, who were stretching out the aches of the journey and exiting the vehicles.

"I would like to speak with each of you," Elli said to the group, "to tell me anything you may remember about your time at Knossos. As soon as you are able, please come to my workroom where we may speak privately."

They all voiced their assent as they gathered their bags.

"Oh, Presfa," Lexion said, "it looks like your blood-time has begun." He motioned to the stain on the back of her skirt as she stepped down off the wagon. "At least you are home and can change into clean clothing."

She twisted around and pulled at the back of her skirt, making a face. Then she murmured her thanks to Lexion and lifted her bag, hunching over as if in pain.

"Oh dear," Elli said, patting Presfa's shoulder. "The bumpy ride has given you cramps. You should go to the Medicine-Priestess for a remedy."

Presfa nodded, avoiding the High Priestess' gaze.

A short time later, the travelers had dispersed, and Aria was walking through the temple corridors with Elli when they came upon Presfa again. She was leaning against the wall, still holding her traveling bag. Her face was pale and sweaty.

"My dear," Elli said, "I believe you are ill. Let us get you up to your room, and I will call for the Medicine-Priestess."

"I will be fine," Presfa said, pushing off from the wall and turning to move in the opposite direction.

Aria and Elli both gasped when they saw the large patch of bright red blood that streaked the back of her skirt. They each took one of her arms, supporting her as they helped her down the corridor toward the herb room.

"Yvata," Eileithyia called to the Medicine-Priestess as she and Aria helped Presfa into the herb room, "are you here? We need your help."

Yvata helped them remove Presfa's stained clothing and get her to lie down on a small bed in the corner.

"It is just a bad blood-time," Presfa insisted as Yvata pressed a folded cloth between her legs to staunch the flow.

"You have bled a lot," Yvata said, scrutinizing Presfa's pale skin and her hunched position, curled around herself on the bed.

The Medicine-Priestess held up the skirt and examined the bright red stain. To Aria, it looked more like the blood from a fresh cut than from a blood-time. Yvata drew a blanket up over the young priestess on the cot, then motioned Elli over to them. Elli took Aria's hand and brought her along as well.

"This is no blood-time," Yvata said. "It looks like a miscarriage to me."

"No," Presfa insisted, groaning.

Elli leaned over her. "These things happen," she said, patting Presfa's hand. "Yvata will take care of you and give you something to make it finish quickly. You can try again for a baby later on."

"No," Presfa said, shaking her head. "No more herbs. No more men."

Yvata cast a questioning look at Elli, who shrugged. Then Aria sucked in a sharp breath as the realization dawned on her.

"You went to the Medicine-Priestess at Knossos," Aria said to Presfa. "She gave you a draught, and you took it all at once instead of in several different doses."

Presfa curled up tighter, groaning. "I did not want to carry the jar around and have anyone ask what it contained."

Elli gave the young priestess a puzzled look. "You know how to avoid pregnancy. You were taught when you first began your blood-time. All our girls know these things."

"I had nothing with me."

"You could not ask a servant for a wad of wool and a flagon of vinegar?"

Presfa shifted, pressing her face into the bed. Just then, Yvata bustled back over with a cup of warm herbal tea.

"Drink this," she said. "It will slow the bleeding and stop the cramps." Presfa took the cup in trembling hands and began to sip. "The next time a Medicine-Priestess gives you directions, you had best follow them," Yvata chided before crossing the room to work on another herbal preparation at the table.

Presfa held the empty cup out, and Elli took it, setting it on the table. Then she turned back to the young priestess, her brow furrowed.

"Who was it you lay with?" she asked. "A man, obviously. One of our priests or one of theirs?"

When Presfa looked anywhere but at Elli, Aria's hands curled into fists. "You did not lie with anyone willingly, did you?"

Presfa's eyes filled with tears, and she began to cry. When Aria shot Elli a pointed look, the two women knelt next to the bed and held the young priestess. Aria was thankful that Elli did not try to soothe Presfa with words. She knew no words would help, but a kind embrace might. After a time, the sobs slowed until finally, Presfa spoke.

"He was... Dolios was so nice. The others were going to bed, and he invited me back to his room. But then he met a friend, another priest, in the corridor and invited him in as well. When I said no..." She began sobbing again.

When no more tears would come, Elli brushed Presfa's hair back off her face. "Why did you not come to me?"

"I was ashamed."

Elli reared back, a look of horror on her face. "You have nothing to be ashamed of! It is those men who have committed the crime!"

"They said..." She hiccupped. "They said it was my fault they had to do it like that, because I would not say yes. They said..." She squeezed her eyes shut. "They said it is the woman's job to always say yes."

Elli reached her arms out and held tight to both Presfa and Aria. "It is your job to know what you want or do not want. It is the other person's job to honor your wishes. Always. Especially if you say no."

Exhausted from the physical and emotional trauma, Presfa soon fell asleep. Yvata promised to keep an eye on her, so Elli and Aria stepped out into the corridor.

"Let us go back to my workroom," Elli said, "and talk about what has happened."

"What can we do?" Aria shook her head. "The men at Knossos are more powerful than we are. They listen to no one but themselves. And apparently they kill those who protest too loudly, if what we heard in their temple is true."

"At the very least, we will no longer send any women to Knossos."

Aria coughed out a bitter laugh. "That is what Glymenos wants."

"It is the only way to protect ourselves unless we take an armed guard with us." Elli paused, thinking. "We have not asked any of the others if they were forced against their will. If Presfa is any indication, they might not come forward unless we ask."

"Do you think they would do that to our men as well as our women?"

"I do not know what to think. They seem to want dominance more than anything, and I suspect that includes dominance over everyone, regardless of their sex."

"Everyone who went on the journey is already planning to come speak with you in private."

"I will speak with the women, but I will have Belisseus speak to the men about this," Elli said. "If any of them were forced, then I will talk with them myself."

Aria blinked back tears. "I hope everyone else is all right."

"I fear that if these mainlanders have their way, none of us will ever be all right again."

Chapter 38

"I cannot do this."

Aria was standing in the doorway to Elli's private quarters, her arms folded across her chest. Elli looked up from the table where she was sorting her jewelry.

"Cannot do what?"

"This!" Aria said, rushing across the threshold and flinging her arms around, her wild gesture encompassing nothing and everything.

Elli narrowed her eyes at Aria, then set her own cup of water aside and picked up a pitcher. "Have some wine."

She poured a cup full and pushed it across the table. Aria snatched it up and downed the contents in a single draught. When she set the cup back down, she was breathing hard.

"I have some things to give you," Elli said, her voice level and calm. She began picking through a collection of necklaces, lifting each one up and examining it, then setting it back down in one or another pile on the table.

Aria perched her fists on her hips. "How can you just sit there playing with your jewelry?"

"I am not playing. I am sorting. Some of these will go to you, some to Rhea, some to other women, and a few to certain men. I will have no tomb, so all my possessions must pass on to others."

"No."

Elli looked up at Aria, a necklace dangling in mid-air from one of her hands. She caught the younger woman's gaze and held it but did not speak.

"Elli, I cannot do this. I cannot watch you die and then take your place in the temple, sleep in your bed..." She gazed at Elli's bed, its linens tucked neatly in place. "I cannot watch my own son die then take to bed some other young man who shares his name, a young man I do not even know," she said, her voice cracking.

Elli reached her hand out to Aria, but the younger woman ignored it.

"The Consort is not a normal man, but the son of the gods," Elli said. "He has no human mother or father. You know that."

Drawing in a slow breath, Aria crossed the room to the window. She set her hands on the windowsill and looked out into the dark night.

"You expect me to accept this new young man who is like my son but unlike him." She clutched the windowsill, her knuckles turning white. "Then I must sacrifice him and take another one whom I also do not know." She shook her head. "I am not strong enough for this. You must choose someone else."

Elli rose from her seat and joined Aria at the window. "You will know the Consort the same way you knew the Mothers the first time you met each of them in ritual, the same way you have known every Consort I have had since you were born." Aria continued to stare out the window, her gaze fixed on the dark sky with its spattering of stars. "They are all vessels, just as a good priest or priestess is during the sacred rites. But the Consort lives it all the time, from the day of his installation until the day of his sacrifice." Elli turned to face Aria. "You already know all this."

"I am not sure I believe it."

"Must you believe in the date palm tree in order for the Fire-Mother to call it hers?"

Aria gave her a puzzled look.

"This is not about what you believe. These things simply are. The Consort is the vessel for the Young God as he walks on Earth, just as you are the vessel for the Daughter when you step into the ritual chamber."

"I am not a worthy vessel."

Elli took Aria's hand. "None of us are. Yet the gods still accept us, flaws and all."

Aria moved back to the table and poured herself another cup of wine. She stood there silently, sipping the blood-red liquid, as Elli lowered herself back onto her seat and continued sorting her jewelry. After a few moments, the older woman spoke.

"I need you to promise me you will do some things."

"What things?"

Elli stroked the central bead on a necklace of lapis and gold. "We know now that the people at Knossos cannot be trusted. Promise me you will keep them away from our most sacred rites."

"But we have always invited the clergy from other temples to the rituals. It is our way."

"Yes, and they have always honored our ways. Until now." She motioned for Aria to take a seat, but Aria shook her head. "You can be sure the people from Knossos will come here again and again. They want to control us, to take over our temple and our city, to change our ways."

Aria shuddered as the image of Hedamos groaning on top of her boiled up her mind. "I wish the Mothers would crack all their skulls open. Or perhaps they should all fall into the sea and drown."

"But they will not." Elli set the necklace down. "So you must provide the Knossians with entertainment, keep them occupied. Allow them to attend the sacrifices and any other ceremonies where the public is invited. But keep them away from any rites that are restricted to clergy."

"I suppose I can do that."

"I have already arranged for them to be occupied in the temple during the Dawn-Fire Rite the day after tomorrow, so you need not worry about that one. But after that, the job of keeping them at bay falls to you."

Aria dropped onto a seat and leaned her elbows on the table, pressing her palms to her temples. "This is all so complicated. Why can we not simply worship the gods and live our lives?"

Elli reached out and took Aria's hand. "I am not sure there ever was a time that simple. We must do our best with what we are given."

Rocking her head back, Aria swallowed the last of the wine from her cup. "And if we do not like what we are given?"

Elli pushed a pile of jewelry across the table. "I hope you like these."

Aria recoiled, leaning back and drawing her hands away from the table.

"Remember me when you wear them," Elli said, rising from her seat. "I will always remember you."

Choking back a sob, Aria rose and embraced her High Priestess, holding her tight.

"I love you," she whispered.

"And I love you," Elli said, kissing her softly. Then she leaned back, cupping Aria's face in her hands. "The Mothers love you as well, no matter what you think or do or believe. Never forget that."

Aria gave a jerky nod, wiping a stray tear from her cheek with the back of her hand. Elli scooped the pile of jewelry off the table and pressed it into Aria's hands.

"Will you please tell Rhea that I wish to see her now?" Aria nodded, flashing Elli a tight smile. "I will see you in the morning to prepare for the rite."

Forcing herself to maintain control, Aria made her way to Rhea's room, conveyed Elli's message, then stumbled down the corridor to her own quarters. She managed to light a lamp then slumped down on her bed, Elli's jewelry tumbling into her lap and spilling off onto the bed linens and the floor.

She picked up the necklace of lapis and gold, the one Elli had saved especially for her. "It makes me think of Ourania," Elli had once said, "Mother-of-Darkness-and-Stars." Aria's hand trembled as she held up the string of stones, the golden flecks sparkling against the dark blue in the light of the Full Moon that shone through her window—the first Full Moon after Summer Solstice.

A sudden calm descended on her as she realized that she really was going to go through with the rite the next day, the eighth year in the cycle of eight. Just as she and Elli had arranged, just as she had agreed to.

"Have I chosen this path?" she said, speaking to the Great Mother whose stars shone in the necklace she clutched in her hands. "Or are the gods simply moving me around like one of those dolls on strings that the entertainers make to dance for people's amusement?"

Then she realized she did not know which was worse, for the gods to play with humans like toys or for the gods to abandon the people altogether. Then it struck her: what was truly worst of all was for the people to abandon the gods. That she would not do. She would go to the Sea Temple tomorrow and undertake the most sacred rite her people knew. She would honor their ways and become their new High Priestess, even if she was the last woman ever to do so.

Then she blew out a breath, clutched Elli's necklace to her breast, and cried.

Chapter 39

The midday sun shone down through the open center of the Sea Temple, illuminating Elli and Belisseus in a circle of brightest white as they stood there, naked, holding hands. Aria had stayed off to one side from the beginning of the rite, occasionally glancing at the large crowd of clergy and lay people who were gathered around the temple. She did her best to ignore the guards who were now a regular fixture at the temple's outdoor events. Though it took an extraordinary amount of self-control, she also refused to allow herself to examine the crowd in search of Sageleus' face. Instead, she kept her focus on the rite as much as she could. It occurred to her that Elli and Belisseus were doing a remarkable job of speaking clearly and remembering all the details of the ritual, considering that they had both fasted for three days and then drunk large quantities of drugged wine that morning—mixed this time with far more potent and dangerous substances than just opium. Timed carefully, the dosage ensured that their end would be certain and quick.

A soft breeze rolled in off the sea, ruffling Aria's hair and caressing her skin as the waves roared in and broke along the shore. She breathed in the salt air, the reminder that Grandmother Ocean always embraced the island that Ida's children called home.

Then a white butterfly appeared, fluttering into the temple and circling Elli's head, spiraling up and out through the temple's roof ring, toward the Sun as it hovered at its highest point in the sky. Aria steeled herself, choking down the sob that threatened to rise in her throat as she turned her attention back to the rite that was now ending.

"Naked we were born, and naked we return to the Mothers' loving arms," Elli said. She turned her head to catch Aria's gaze, a blissful smile on her lips. Then she and Belisseus, still hand in hand, walked to the front of the temple and came down the steps.

The crowd turned to watch as the living embodiments of the Great Mother and her Son walked through the dry grass, across the sand, and into the waves. Aria found herself staring, unable to look away as they moved farther out, the water rising first to their knees, then their hips, then their shoulders. Finally even the tops of their heads disappeared.

Aria continued to stare at the waves, her mind refusing to process what had just happened, her eyes squinting at the sparkling brilliance as she strained to see any vestige of the two people who had stood right in front of her just a few moments earlier. Startled from her trance by the sensation of a hand on her shoulder, she whipped her head around to see a beautiful young man standing before her, wearing the colorful kilt of the Consort. He smiled at her and gestured toward the steps that led up to the temple. All of a sudden she felt awkward, wrong, as if she were some pretender wearing the High Priestess' sacred garments, the same clothing Elli had put on just a few days earlier. She should be mourning her loss, not celebrating a new position in the temple. But she had a job to do, and she had made a promise to the High Priestess—and to the Great Mothers.

Drawing in a shaky breath, Aria nodded and took hold of the hand the young man held out to her. Together they went up the steps and into the temple, stopping in the center, in the circle of light where Elli and her Consort had stood moments earlier. Aria went through the words and motions of the rite as if someone else were moving her, speaking through her, as if she were standing off to the side somewhere, watching. Briefly she wondered if she might be dreaming, if perhaps the rite had not yet taken place and Elli might still be alive, waiting in the temple somewhere.

Then, as the ritual neared completion, the new Consort squeezed her hand and dropped to his knees in front of her, and she knew, as surely as if someone had plunged a dagger into her heart, that Elli and the baby she had borne so many years ago were dead, gone, subsumed beneath the waves.

Holding the new Consort's hands as tightly as she dared in order to steady herself, Aria drew in a slow breath. Then she let go and set her hands on his shoulders, a blessing and acknowledgment at the same time. She forced herself to speak the words Elli had taught her, the words she would one day teach to another priestess, gods willing.

"The Young God dies yet he lives again."

He looked up at her, his dark eyes soft, their corners crinkled with a smile. "All who die live again in the Great Mother."

A prickling sensation crept up her spine as she felt the goddess rise in her, take her over. For once, she did not fight it, but let it fill the great emptiness within her, the void where Elli and her Consort had been. She drew herself up to her full height and spread her arms, lifting them up in the ancient gesture that called to the Mother herself, to all the Mothers who were, ultimately, One.

"Who am I?" she said, her voice ringing out across the crowd.

"You are Kalliste," the Consort said, still kneeling, his head rocking back and his eyes going wide.

"I am," she said, breathing in the effect the goddess' power was having on the young man. "And you are Belisseus."

She held out her hands, and he took hold of them, rising to stand facing her. Taking a step forward, she leaned up toward him and tilted her head back. He bowed his head to meet her, and they kissed. But it was not a woman and a man kissing. It was the goddess and the god, moving through the bodies of two people who loved them enough to give their very lives to their service.

They parted and stood side by side, still holding hands, facing the crowd. A pair of voices rang out in unison: Rhea and Kaeseus, who stood at the front of the assembly, just a step away from the little temple. Rhea had her arm around Kaeseus to support him. The elderly priest was growing frail, and the long walk from the temple had worn him out. But he refused to turn over his duties to one of the younger priests as long as he was able to perform them himself.

"Hail Kalliste!" the two Heads of the Colleges cried out. "Hail Belisseus!"

The crowd responded in kind, shouting the acclamations over and over. Aria felt the waves of it wash over her, the goddess pulsing warm within her. Then as the words rang on, she became herself again, a mortal woman, a priestess standing in the temple with her Consort.

Finally the people fell silent. With a sidelong glance at Belisseus, Aria moved to the front of the temple. From somewhere off to the side, a triton shell sounded three blasts. Then, together, the new High Priestess and her Consort descended the steps, the crowd parting in front of them as they strode toward the path that led back to the temple.

The drums picked up a slow walking beat as the sacred pair reached the far side of the crowd. Moving silently, the people shifted into a smooth column, with the local clergy once again closest to the front. As the crowd moved around, Aria recognized faces: her own people, some of the clergy she had seen during her recent visit to Knossos, and then Sageleus. She forced herself to face forward and keep moving.

The procession moved steadily along the Sea Temple pathway. Then, when they reached the Sea Road, they turned toward the main temple, the drums maintaining a steady beat as the people paced along. A short while later, Aria found herself seated at a table on a dais along the temple wall, the focal point of the Summer Solstice celebration on the west plaza. Her Consort sat next to her as the servants brought out the dishes for the feast. He would not eat, though, only sip some well-diluted wine. He had fasted for two days already and had to continue fasting in preparation for the next morning's rites. But Aria had to eat, had to bring herself back down to Earth since she would be his anchor when dawn came.

As she ate, Aria looked out over the gathering, rows and rows of tables filling the plaza, people eating and chatting, lay folk and clergy together. There were more people feasting than had attended the rite. Not everyone wished to witness the sacrifices, but all were welcome to the celebration afterward. The Mothers bid their children share their bounty and their joy with each other, and so the people of Malia would continue to do, as long as Aria had anything to say about the matter.

At one of the tables near the dais, several of the local clergy had taken seats with some of the visiting priests and priestesses. It was always pleasing to hear news from other temples and sacred houses. Aria enjoyed that kind of conversation herself. Then she noticed that Rhea and Lexion were seated next to each other, leaning in close.

She let out a shaky breath. Of course, the two of them had every right to love. Aria had done her part to bring them together. She had not desired Lexion in a long time, though she did miss Rhea sometimes. Seeing the two of them together, however, reminded her that for the rest of her life, her loving was restricted to a single man, or more accurately, a series of them.

"Will you share your thoughts with me?" Belisseus said, taking Aria's hand.

She made herself smile at him, though she was not sure the effort was convincing. "I am looking at my people. Our people. Ida's children."

"We are blessed," he said, squeezing her hand.

He offered her a sip of wine from his cup. She accepted, and as he tipped the cup up to her lips, for the first time she really looked at him. He was beautiful, and not just his body. He was, indeed, the Young God incarnate. She could see it in his eyes. He had let the divine fill him up, and it shone out from him like a light. She swallowed the wine then offered him a sip from her cup. He smiled, wrapping his hand around hers as she guided the drink to his mouth. Whether it was the wine or his presence, or both, she was not sure, but suddenly she felt very warm and very loved.

The feasting continued for the rest of the day, with the servants bringing out more food and wine as the dishes and jugs ran empty. Soon the musicians began to play, and the people rose to dance, celebrating the turning of the seasons and the years, the turning of life and death and love. Aria did not dance, though, and neither did her Consort. Their place was on the dais, the still center of the swirling, spiraling celebration.

Chapter 40

When the edge of the Sun touched the horizon, the dancing slowed and then stopped. Though the musicians continued to play, their tune was more leisurely now, quieter as the long day drew to a close. The servants began cleaning up, clearing the cups and dishes from the tables. The lay people gathered up their belongings, said their thanks to the gods and the temple, and began to make their way back to the city and the nearby countryside. The clergy moved out of the way as the servants began to haul the benches and tables back into the storage rooms.

Once the crowd had dispersed, Aria rose from the table and turned toward the door that led into the temple.

"I had best get to bed."

"Yes," Belisseus said, joining her as she stepped through the doorway. "We must be up before the Sun in the morning."

They made their way through the temple and up the stairs to the residential quarters. But when Aria made to turn down the corridor, Belisseus caught her by the arm.

"Where are you going?"

"To my room," she said, pulling away from him. Then she reeled back, dizzy with the realization: that was no longer her room.

"Come," Belisseus said, gesturing in the correct direction.

Aria went reluctantly, shifting awkwardly in the corridor when he kept moving back beside her, unwilling to walk ahead of his superior. When they reached the door to the High Priestess' private quarters, she froze, unable to move.

"This is your room now," he said, pushing the door open. "Mine is right next to it. But you already know that."

He crossed the threshold and turned to her, waiting. After a moment, she managed to force her feet to move. He closed the door behind them and went to light the lamps. Once the room was filled with flickering light, Aria saw that all of Elli's belongings were gone and her own possessions had been moved in. The bed was made up with clean linen. Her trunk sat at the foot of the bed, with her jewelry box on top of it. Then she saw that the small table in the center of the room held dishes of food and a small jug of wine.

"I thought you might like some bread, at least," he said. "You did not eat much at the feast."

With a sigh she dropped onto one of the stools and began nibbling at a small barley loaf. He drew another stool over and sat down next to her.

"Here," he said, pouring a cup of wine and handing it to her. "You are the High Priestess now. All this is yours."

She shook her head. "None of it is mine. It all belongs to the Mothers, just as you and I do."

She lifted the cup and took a sip. She wrinkled her nose. The flavor told her the wine was laced with a small quantity of opium.

"I am not trying to drug you," he said, "just help you relax. I know this is difficult for you. But it is what I have trained for my whole life. Please, let me help you."

She took another sip of the wine. "It is not..." He smiled, waiting for her to speak again. "I have lain with a man before, obviously. I had a baby, after all." The brittle laugh that finished the sentence fell flat in the dim room. She had spent her son's whole life mourning for him. Now that he was truly gone, her heart did not know how to go on. He was gone. Elli was gone. She was left alone with a stranger, expected to pick up the threads of Elli's priestessing and move forward as if there was no distinction between herself and Elli, or between her son and this young man.

She took a long drink of the wine and choked on it. Coughing, she wiped her mouth and set the cup back down. When she glanced up again, he was still sitting there, a look of patience and acceptance on his face. At the very least, she owed him an explanation for why she was not tumbling straight into bed with him to complete the private portion of the day's rites.

"Before, when I have been with men, it was either in ritual or with a longtime lover. I suppose, at the seasonal rites, we were caught up in the moment, the joy of it, so it did not matter so much how well I knew him. But now..." She drew in a shaky breath and caught herself before it could become a sob. "Now I am sitting with a beautiful young man I do not even know."

"It is our way, My Lady." She shuddered at the term of address, the profound reverence in his voice. "You must not know the Consort as a man, but only as the god when he appears to you in the rite."

She tapped a fingernail on the wine cup. "I feel nothing right now. Not just for you. Nothing at all." She stopped, feeling lost, staring into the cup. "They are dead. I have not even had time to understand what has happened. And one day soon you will die and that does not even bother you." She lifted the cup and downed the last of the wine.

"Come," he said, rising and crossing to the bed. "I will comfort you."

He drew the covers aside then unwrapped his kilt, draping it over the corner of Aria's trunk. Aria looked him up and down. He was beautiful and brown, lithe and vibrant. Her mind told her that much, but her heart was silent, as if it, too, had been sacrificed that day.

Her fingers fumbled as she worked to untie her skirt cords. In the end, he helped her undress, reverently removing the layers of clothing and jewelry one at a time, until finally she was just herself and nothing more. When he slid into bed, she followed, curling up in his embrace as if she were a newborn babe—or a corpse in a funeral vase.

Gently he stroked her hair, humming a melody she had not

heard in years, a tune the country folk sang to celebrate the joy of lovers uniting. As soon as she began to remember some of the words, a knot tightened in her chest. She tried to hum along with him, but her throat constricted. And then the tears came.

He held her as she cried, great heaving sobs scraping her insides raw for aching ages until there was nothing left but the rough, panting breath of exhaustion.

"I am here," he said as she struggled to breathe normally, his arms still wrapped around her. "I am here."

She stroked a hand down the muscles of his arm. "So you are." She huffed out a quiet laugh. "Look at me, crying for what I have lost and not appreciating what I have. Some High Priestess I make."

He kissed her hair. "I am honored to have you as my High Priestess."

She snuggled against him. He was real, present, alive. He smelled of incense and perfumed oil and man. His skin was warm against hers, his arms strong around her body. His voice was soft and deep, the sound of the Young God incarnate.

"Tell me what you want," he said, stroking her hair.

She knew what he was asking, but she was not ready to think about that yet. She was silent for a few moments, deciding how honest she should be. She was going to have to spend years in an intimate relationship with this man, both in and out of ritual. She might as well begin by being truthful, even if that truth might hurt him.

"I want to talk to Elli." She let out a long sigh and silently thanked the gods that she was too tired to cry anymore.

"Oh, but you can. You know that."

She shifted to look him in the eye. "She is dead, Belisseus. Gone back to the Mothers. You saw her go."

"Exactly." He brushed a strand of hair off her forehead. "She is a spirit, along with everyone else who has ever lived and died. Guided by the Melissae, guarded and succored by the Daughter."

She stared at him, her mind refusing to work properly. "You are a priestess. You know how to reach the spirits of the dead, how to converse with them. They are not gone from us, not entirely."

The shadow of a smile crept onto her face, and suddenly she felt that she had not lost quite so much. Though her heart still held sadness, now it was a bittersweet feeling rather than a hopeless darkness.

"Yes," she said, cupping his face, "you are right. Of course you are right. I knew that. I had just forgotten. It has been... a difficult day."

She leaned in and kissed him, his mouth soft and full beneath hers. Then his hands were on her, slow and gentle, and he was asking her questions and obeying her answers. His touch was a comfort and a welcome distraction, the pleasure a blessing in the midst of pain.

Chapter 41

Aria's gaze swept the area between the Sea Temple and the water as the next day dawned. This time the rite centered on the beach, not the small building. A bonfire lay stacked on the damp sand just seaward from the open field. A large, dark patch between the bonfire and the little temple betrayed a necessary precaution: long before dawn, the novice priests and priestesses had come down to prepare the area. By the light of the Moon they had carried buckets of seawater up from the tideline, wetting the weedy ground all around so the bonfire could blaze without setting the field aflame. Now the faint pre-dawn light showed Aria that they had done their job with diligence. Fire was not to be trifled with, especially not for this rite.

Turning toward the gathered crowd, she breathed a sigh of relief that she could see only her own people and a few trusted clergy from some of the other temples and sacred houses. This rite was attended by invitation only, and for good reason. Besides Kaeseus and Rhea, both of whom were required to take part in the ritual, she noted Lexion, Thalamika, and Orestas among the people Elli had approved to attend. She saw that Psoreia had come from Eileithyia's cave, and Nestia from Nirou Khani as well. Elli had probably invited them. Aria had spotted them in the crowd at the Sea Temple the previous day. She also knew that there was a breakfast feast being held in the main temple for the visitors from Knossos, complete with musical entertainment. Elli had done as had she said she would and assured privacy for the Dawn-Fire Rite.

As the crowd settled into place and the Consort stepped up between Aria and the unlit bonfire, the sound of shouting down by the road carried up to the Sea Temple. Heads turned as Aria spotted a handful of people in the distance, five or six men arguing with the armed guards who were stationed along the path that led to the little temple. Squinting, she could see that the people raising their voices were clergy visiting from Knossos. They were supposed to be attending the feast back at the main temple. The guards, three burly laymen Elli had hired for the occasion, stood their ground, refusing to let the people through. After a few more rounds of shouting, the visitors gave up and turned back the way they had come. Aria watched them go, making a mental note to put the guards on the temple's regular payroll if they were willing. If armed guards were what it took for her people to be able to celebrate the rites in peace, so be it.

Problem averted, Aria directed her full attention to the ritual. The gods used humans as they saw fit, after all, and not always in a loving manner. It was only through carefully constructed ritual, safeguarded down the generations, that the people maintained a relationship with the gods that was pleasing on both sides. This was one such rite.

As the sky lightened and the first edge of the Sun's burning disk slid up in the east, she relaxed her grip on the cup she had been clutching and handed it to Belisseus. He drank the drugged wine, tilting his head back to empty the cup. She watched his throat work as he swallowed, remembering what it had felt like to have her mouth on that skin the night before. Blinking, she shook herself as he handed the cup back.

He turned and received a torch from Kaeseus, who was seated on a small stool. His health was bad enough that he could no longer stand for such a long rite, not after having walked all the way to the Sea Temple. But he insisted on doing his job regardless.

With a nod of thanks to the elderly priest, Belisseus thrust the lit torch up into the air, its flames streaming landward in the sea breeze. Then he drew in a breath and called out the invocation, his voice ringing through the dawn:

Fire of Heaven,
First and Last,
Kalliste the most beautiful,
Come to us now!
Rise up from the World Below
Where you have spent the long, dark night
And bring us your light; birth the day.
Birth yourself from the Earth
As she has birthed us all
From her womb.
Heat our blood,
Inflame our visions,
And share yourself with us,
Your adoring children.

He had invoked the goddess, Mother-of-Sun-and-Fire, and now it was Aria's job to allow that divinity to come into her. He was counting on her. Everyone present was counting on her. If Elli could do it, so could she. But then the thought of Elli twisted her heart, the sadness aching like a bruise inside her chest, and suddenly she could not breathe. Panic began to rise in her, constricting her throat. What if she was unable to fulfill the duties of the High Priestess? What if Elli and the College of Priestesses had made the wrong choice?

A quiet cough sounded beside her, and she turned her head, locking eyes with Belisseus, who still held the flaming torch aloft, calm, confident, waiting for her. She could see in his eyes that he believed in her. To him, she was the High Priestess. There was no doubt.

Elli was gone, and it was up to Aria to ensure that the rites proceeded as they must. She drew in a breath, tilted her head back, and opened up her soul. Her arms rose into the air of their own accord, and the goddess slipped down onto her like the softest, most delicate garment she had ever donned. And then she felt herself step back, watching herself as the goddess guided her motions and spoke through her mouth, a voice both hers and not hers, older than time, resounding like a bell.

My children, I am here.
Revel in my heat!
Seek my light always,
Here and in the depths of the World Below.
For I am ever with you,
Even in the darkest night.

She did not need to remember the words Elli had taught her, for the goddess knew them already. The movements and the speech flowed from her like a river, pouring forth to bless the assembled crowd.

She reached up to caress Belisseus' face, cupping his cheek, her thumb stroking the line of his jaw. "This is my beloved son," she said to her people while still gazing at the Consort, "given to you for a time. Treat him with care and reverence. Listen as he speaks, for his wisdom is mine, though he be but mortal. Let him go down and rise up again, to show he is the One. Only the Lion knows the way down and back."

She dropped her hand away from his face. With a quick nod to his High Priestess, he leaned over to the stacked bonfire, pressing the flaming torch into the pile of wood until it caught, then tipping the torch wholly into the flames. The sea breeze whipped the fire up quickly. In moments the flames were licking out the top of the woodpile, flicking up toward the brightening sky.

His hands now empty, the Consort bowed his head to the High Priestess. She set her hands on the top of his head, and again their gazes met.

"Who am I?" she said.

"Kalliste," he answered, his gaze unwavering.

"Yes," she said. "And you are my Belisseus."

She felt him quake beneath her hand, then his knees buckled, and he dropped to the ground. When he tilted his head back to look up at her, his eyes were glassy, his gaze unfocused. He was not looking at her, but through her. She reached out and touched his cheek, nodding for him to continue with the rite. He drew in a breath, and suddenly the Young God was there, his eyes locked with hers, piercing her.

"I am the Fire, and you are the Light."

A drum boomed and sistrums rattled, and the dancing began. The drums rocked out their echoing rhythm, the sistrums hissed, and the priestesses drew the fabric covers off their skirts, their belled aprons jingling with every step. Unable to think, guided by the goddess, Aria shifted behind Belisseus and set her hands on his shoulders. Stepping in time with the rhythm, the priestesses arrayed themselves in a broad arc in front of the Consort and the High Priestess, the bonfire making up the back of the circle.

Aria gripped Belisseus' shoulders as the priests moved in, circling tightly around the central pair. The two rings of clergy, men surrounded by women, danced and chanted as the drumming drove them onward. Still kneeling, Belisseus began to sway beneath Aria's hands, leaning back and forth in time with the beat. Then, faster than Aria could understand what was happening, his eyes rolled back, his head tipped forward, and he crumpled to the ground.

Just before his body hit the sand, two priests dove in and caught him, lowering him the last short distance with reverence and care. Aria knelt by his head, her fingers tangling in his hair. His eyes were closed, and the look on his face was serene. The priests draped a soft cloth over his face. The whole group continued their dance as Aria knelt by his shoulder, her head bowed, waiting, guarding him during his perilous journey.

She had taken part in enough of these rites to know that the journey could take the whole morning. Time did not pass in the Otherworld the way it did in this one. Magically, the bonfire always took the same amount of time to burn down as the Consort took for his journey, no matter how long or short it happened to be.

She settled down, her knees shifting in the sand, preparing to remain in that position as long as it took. Her fingers twined in the glossy locks that splayed out around his head. She would be his anchor, his mooring, so he could return safely from his first journey as the Consort.

As the drumming and dancing beat on around her, Aria allowed herself to fall into a light trance. She was still aware of her surroundings, still aware of the young man whose head she cradled in her hands. But she also floated on the rhythm, riding its waves, allowing the goddess to weave in and out of her as she desired.

Then suddenly she was back in her body, as present as if someone had slapped her in the face. Belisseus' head was jerking in her hands. He began to moan, his arms and legs flailing, his whole body quaking. Aria tried to hold him still, to no avail. His movements became more erratic and frenzied. The priests who had helped him lie down stepped over, unsure how to proceed. Aria nodded toward the Consort's head, and they lifted the cloth they had draped him with earlier. His face was contorted as if he were in agony, his head thrashing back and forth. A seagull gave a shriek above them, and Belisseus flung himself up to sitting, letting out a horrific cry, a look of terror on his face.

The drums fell , and the dancers froze in place. Aria glanced around. The bonfire was not even half consumed. The Sun was nowhere near the high point in the sky. The people were confused, and her Consort was terrified, half-slumped in the sand, shaking and disoriented, blinking hard as he tried to focus on her.

Not knowing what else to do, Aria continued with the rite as if the Consort's return had happened in the usual way. She rose and stood over Belisseus, leaning over to cradle his face in her hands. Then she blew onto the top of his head and into his face, ensuring that his entire soul returned intact from the Otherworld.

"Speak, Son-of-Earth-and-Fire," she said.

"I have journeyed..." he began, his voice shaking as he groped for the words that always began the Consort's message at the Dawn-Fire Rite. His eyes still held a sort of terror as he gazed at her. Breaking with the forms of the rite, she knelt beside him and took his hands. They trembled in her grip, and she knew this had been no ordinary journey. This young man had trained for years. He knew what he was doing. For this experience to shake him so profoundly...

"Speak," she said softly, meeting his gaze and doing her best to show him her confidence in his ability.

He drew in a shuddering breath then began again. "I have journeyed from the Fire Below through the Earth to reach for the Fire Above." His voice cracked as he spoke the traditional words of the Consort returning from the journey. "I have news for the people." Aria let go of his hands and moved back, giving him space, letting him speak to the small crowd. "I have traveled the red road. Now I sit in the space where the three realms meet. The Three-and-One, the Great Mothers and the Mother-of-All, they worry about us. All is not well in our world."

Gasps sounded from within the crowd. With a start, Aria realized she had done likewise.

"We have done well for a very long time," he continued, his voice wobbling. "I have journeyed in the required manner. I have offered our thanks and goodwill to the Great Mothers and to all their children. And I have asked their protection and goodwill in return."

A wave crashed along the shore, and Aria felt the cool spray sprinkle her skin. On a hot summer day like this, the sensation would normally have been pleasant. But instead she felt a dread chill, the sudden coldness that comes with an omen from the Underworld.

The Consort swallowed, a dry clicking sound in his throat, and lifted his head up with some effort to look around at his people. "The Mothers spoke to me. They said there are dark forces pressing against this place, against our beloved island, forces that have been moving this way for some time."

The priests and priestesses surrounding the Consort made the sign of propitiation, though Aria had the feeling it would do little good.

"They said..." he continued, wincing as if speaking of his

experience pained him. "They said they cannot protect us forever. Not even if we continue the rites and uphold the traditions. They will do their best. But no matter how well we keep our ways, they can no longer promise our safety. Times change. Their power wanes."

Bells jingled and sistrums clinked as the people shifted in place, murmuring to themselves and each other. Aria looked around for someone to tell her what to do, how to handle the situation. Then she remembered that she was in charge. Her thinking was cloudy, fuzzy. The goddess was still upon her. Drawing in a breath, silently she asked Kalliste for help and direction.

A comforting warmth suffused her, and she found herself motioning to the drummers to take up the slow beat that signaled the end of the rite. As the gentle rhythm began, she drew the two priests back over to the Consort. They helped him to his feet and wrapped him in a blanket as Aria gave him fresh water to drink. After a short while, he shrugged out of the blanket and gave Aria a look that said he was ready to continue with the rite.

Holding hands, they moved toward the bonfire, their steps matching the unhurried drumbeat. Three times they circled the fire, keeping their distance so its still-burning flames did not singe them or catch their clothing on fire. When they completed the third circuit, they stopped between the bonfire and the water, facing the sea. Belisseus gave Aria's hand a squeeze. With a sidelong glance to see that he was all right, she led him down to the water's edge.

There, in keeping with the ancient rites, they knelt down and set their palms on the water. In them, at that moment, the three realms met: land, sea, and sky. The cosmos balanced itself around its center. Coated in sand and heated by the bonfire at their backs and the Sun above their heads, Aria and Belisseus lifted their damp fingers to their foreheads: the god and goddess in communion with all the realms.

Before they rose, Belisseus put his hand on Aria's arm. He leaned over, his head close to hers, and spoke in a low voice. "After the Mothers gave me their message..." He swallowed. "Before I could finish, before I had begun to journey back, a huge bull rose up and charged me."

"Our Horned One?" she whispered, confused that one of their gods would harm one of his own people.

"This was no god I had ever met before. It chased me away from the sweet field where I had met the Great Ones. It was all I could do to return at all, much less safely."

They exchanged worried glances before rising and moving back to the center of the circles of clergy, their steps still matching the slow drumbeat. Belisseus made to begin the procession back to the main temple, but Aria held him back. With a few brief comments, she instructed three of the priests to remain with the bonfire until it burned down completely. When it was nothing more than smoldering ashes, they were to shift the remains down to the water in the usual way so the tide would wash it out to sea.

Aria thought to head back to the main temple, but she found the goddess guiding her to speak instead. She raised her hands, and everyone's attention turned to her.

"The Great Mothers have sent us a message today, one we must heed, and one we must learn to understand. To that end, the Consort and I will go to the pillar crypt in the temple basement in order to perform divinations. I would have some of you go with us." She pointed to Rhea, Kaeseus, Lexion, Orestas, Thalamika, and Psoreia—people she trusted. "The rest of you will take the midday meal in the dining hall, as we always do on this day. You will not speak of what has happened here. It is one of our most sacred rites. You will not profane it." Her voice rang out with authority.

Taking Belisseus' hand, she stepped forward. Together they moved through the circle of priests, then the circle of priestesses. The clergy gathered behind them as they began the procession back to the temple, the women's skirt-bells jingling in time with the drumbeat. As they passed the guards, it occurred to Aria that no matter how big and strong they were, those men had been unable to protect her Consort in the Otherworld.

Chapter 42

As they reached the temple entrance, Aria realized that Belisseus' hand was still trembling in hers. She peered at his face. He did not appear unduly distraught, considering what he had just been through. Then she remembered that he had been fasting for three days. If he was going to be any help with the divination, he needed food.

She sent the others on ahead to the ritual chamber to purify it and prepare for a standard rite of divination. Then she led Belisseus to the kitchens where she collected some cheese, bread, and barley beer.

"Why did you not simply send a servant for whatever you wanted?" he asked as they sat on a bench in the north court. "Or we could have eaten in the dining hall with everyone else, or even in our private quarters."

"This is faster," she said. "We need to go directly to the ritual chamber before your memory of the journey fades. This situation..." She shook her head. "Elli knew bad things were happening, but she did not realize that the trouble extended into the Otherworld. I only hope this is not an omen for my time as High Priestess."

Once she was satisfied that he had eaten enough, she handed off their dishes to a servant and led him down the stairs. They walked side by side along the narrow, dark corridor, brushing shoulders as they went. She had been down to the ritual chamber just a handful of times in the years since the rite that had made her pregnant. Every time, she still felt like a young girl stumbling into a situation far larger and deeper than she had bargained for. This time was no exception, only now, she was in charge.

They stepped into the room to find the others already gathered there, the lamps lit and the incense burning. Aria could smell the hyssop and rue from the herb-water they had used to asperge the room. But she was taken aback to see a small goat lying on the table, trussed for sacrifice.

"What is this?" she said, waving her hand at the animal. "I said a normal rite of divination. The goddess was clear in her message to me: we are to spill no blood today."

"We thought..." Thalamika began. "This is a serious situation. It requires serious rites." She lifted her chin in defiance.

"We thought? Or you thought?" She looked at the others, whose faces told her Thalamika had done this on her own. "If I cannot trust you to follow simple directions, I certainly cannot trust you to assist with the divination," she snapped. "Go, and take that animal with you."

Thalamika stared at Aria, her mouth hanging open. Then she shook herself. "You would send me away, a senior priestess of this temple, but let her, from a cave shrine a day's journey away, stay?" She jabbed a finger at Psoreia.

"You heard me," Aria said. "And do no harm to the goat. I will check with the herdsman to be sure you have returned it safely."

Scowling and muttering to herself, Thalamika hefted the goat from the table and stomped out of the room. Once she was gone, Aria turned to the others.

"Yes?" she sighed in response to Lexion's pointed look.

He shook his head. "You were right to send her out. She challenged your authority on your very first day. But the way you did it..." He rubbed the back of his neck.

"It has been a difficult day," she said, wondering how much damage she had done in her impatience and insecurity. She had a bad feeling about the incident, but other matters were more pressing. She could only douse one fire at a time. "Shall we begin the divination?"

They gathered around the altar: Aria, Belisseus, Rhea, Psoreia, Kaeseus, Lexion, and Orestas. Noting how unsteady the elderly Kaeseus was on his feet, she directed him to a bench next to the altar. "There is no rule against sitting," she declared when he insisted that he should remain standing with the others. The day had already included two long processions and a demanding, upsetting rite. It was a wonder any of them were still upright. More than that, she did not have the time or energy to worry about Kaeseus at the moment, though she knew his advanced age and ill health would bring his life to a close soon, and she would miss him terribly when that time came. Pushing those thoughts aside, she turned her attention back to the current difficulty.

"We will each do the divination," she said, "silently. Then when we have finished, we will share what we have seen. It is my hope that the gods will give us direction and understanding."

Each of them took a cup of drugged wine and drank it down. Aria was thankful they had all fasted that morning for the Dawn-Fire Rite. The wine would take effect quickly thanks to empty stomachs. And she expected that the small amount of food Belisseus had just eaten would moderate the effects, since he was already well dosed from his part in the Dawn-Fire Rite.

As the lamps flickered, each of the clergy picked up a shallow bowl filled with undiluted wine and held it in front of them with both hands. Aria focused on her breathing, as she had been trained to do. Her heart insisted on pounding, though, making it difficult to relax into the trance state she was used to using for scrying. Finally her breathing slowed, and she sank into the gentle floating sensation that told her she was ready to look.

As the wavering lamplight reflected on the surface of the wine, she let her vision go soft. The dark red wine rippled, and then she was looking at a pool of blood, glistening against a pale stone floor. She shifted her gaze along the edge of the blood until she saw the body it had poured from: a young man sprawled on the floor, his side slit open. His long, gleaming locks spilled out around his head, but his face was turned away from her. Try though she might, she could not change the angle from which she viewed the scene, nor did she recognize the room, though it looked like a typical ritual room in any of the temples on the island.

She continued to gaze at the bowl in her hands, but no more impressions came. After a time, she lifted her head and drew in a slow breath, coming back to herself. The others had already finished. She set her bowl back on the altar, and her fellow clergy did likewise.

"Tell me what you saw," she said, looking first to Belisseus.

"I saw a sack full of altarware—copper, bronze, and silver pitchers and bowls."

"A sack?" Rhea said, her brow furrowed.

"Yes, rough cloth like a farmer might use. But everything in it was exquisite and skillfully made."

Doing her best to ignore the feeling that she had made a dreadful mistake somewhere along the line, Aria asked the others to share. Their visions made no more sense than Belisseus': heavily laden ships full of people and goods sailing from the harbor; a broken bowl on the floor in a small, dark passageway; a woman holding a crying baby and knocking at the temple door; a group of ragged, burly men hiking up the trail to Mt. Dikte; a young priestess crying; a merchant's house on fire. Finally, she shared her own vision of the young man dead on the floor.

"What can the gods possibly be telling us?" Psoreia asked.

"These visions make no sense," Lexion said. "What do any of them have to do with this morning's rite?"

"There is a story in all of this," Kaeseus said, his voice thin and quavering, "if only we could piece it together."

"It portends something terrible," Aria said quietly. "Just like this morning's rite does. You all know it."

They spent the next little while discussing the visions, doing their best to find any connection among them. None of the impressions made sense by themselves, though each of the participants was certain they had seen a true vision. They were all experienced clergy, so Aria did not doubt them. But she could not make sense of the collection of images beyond the vague impression that they all belonged together and boded ill.

The only thing the group could agree on was that whatever evil the divination foretold must have something to do with Glymenos and his people. There was no question that the mainlanders' ambitions would continue to press upon Ida's children and do them damage. But no matter how Aria and her fellow diviners turned the visions over in their minds, they could not determine what, exactly, the threat was, what they should do about it, or whether the danger could be avoided or mitigated in some way. Eventually the discussion deteriorated into argument. When Lexion and Orestas began shouting at each other, Aria stepped between them.

"Enough. We are all tired." The two men moved back, looking sheepish. "Let us leave this for now. Perhaps one of us will dream the answer. Whatever the problem is, it will still be there tomorrow," she said with a sigh.

She went around the room, embracing each of her people and thanking them for their help. "We may try again later. In the meantime, if anything comes to you that might help us understand these visions, please let me know right away."

They all agreed, then everyone except Aria and her Consort began making their way back up into the main part of the temple. Blinking back tears, Aria poured the wine from the bowls into the moats around the pillars.

"To the ancestors and the gods of the Underworld," she murmured. "Thank you for your help, even if we do not understand the visions just yet."

When she was done, she stood in front of the altar, staring blankly at the empty bowls. They were all experienced clergy, Aria and Belisseus and the others who had just left. They had done the divination correctly, but the visions appeared to be arbitrary and meaningless. At least, they had no context for interpreting them, which rendered them meaningless until a context could be determined.

They had also performed the Dawn-Fire Rite properly, as well as the sacrifice the day before. She knew Belisseus had prepared faithfully according to tradition. Yet the journey he had taken made no more sense than the scrying the small group of clergy had just done.

She started when he touched her arm, then reluctantly walked out of the room with him. All she could think was that she had done something wrong somewhere along the line without realizing it. Or perhaps the gods were testing her somehow, testing her people. Though why they would do such a thing, she could not fathom. Until now, she had happily believed what she had always been taught: that the Mothers required only that we do our best. Now she wondered if there were other conditions she was unaware of.

As she and Belisseus went up the stairs, he took her hand, drawing her out of her downward spiral of dark thoughts.

"You do not doubt me," he said, his voice full of wonder.

"Why would I doubt you?"

"After what happened this morning... I must not have performed the rite properly."

She stopped one step up from him, her eyes level with his. "You did everything correctly. Sometimes the gods decide to do things their own way, and we simply have to take that as it comes."

"Yes, My Lady."

Chapter 43

"The emissary from Knossos is here to see you," the priest said, glancing back at the audience room doors.

Aria's eyebrows shot up. It was less than a Moon past the Summer Solstice rites. Hedamos was not due to visit again for some time, and Aria was struggling to keep up with her duties as it was. She had borne a heavy load since her installation. In addition to the disastrous Dawn-Fire Rite and the divination afterward—and Thalamika's icy coldness to her since then—Aria had watched Kaeseus grow pale, collapse, and die right before her in this very room.

Though the Medicine-Priestess had warned him that his heart was weak and he should rest, he had refused to give up any of his duties to the younger priests. "I will die doing my job," he had joked, but it had been a prophecy. So Aria had presided at his funeral and staunched her tears in order to oversee the election and installation of the next Head of the College of Priests: Lexion. That was only a few days past, and now Hedamos had come to harass her.

She drew in a breath and steadied herself. She was the High Priestess. She had spent the morning solving disputes among the local people, who had all gone away happy with her judgments, the last of them just moments earlier. She could handle Glymenos' emissary.

"Send him in."

A few moments later, he was standing in front of the dais, making the salute. "Greetings, My Lady. I am here to welcome you and the new Consort and offer blessings from Knossos."

"I thank you, Hedamos, but your journey was unnecessary. The clergy who visited for the rites have already delivered greetings from your temple."

"I am sure they made the usual official pleasantries, but I wanted to come and deliver the message to you in person," he said, his leering smile sending a chill down her spine.

"I appreciate your effort, but this is not the usual way these things are done here." She focused on her breathing, willing her heartbeat to remain steady as images of him shoving her against a storeroom wall flashed through her mind.

"These are new times, My Lady, so we are doing new things."

His gaze flickered to the spot on Aria's right where the Consort usually stood. Belisseus was not with her just then, having a previous commitment to a men's ritual. Even though there were four of her own clergy—two priestesses and two priests—flanking the audience room doors, all of a sudden she felt exposed, endangered. When Hedamos squared his shoulders and drew himself up to his full height with a little swagger, she felt sure he could tell exactly how badly he was discomfiting her.

"Knossos is happy to help you in any way you might need," he continued. "We can send clergy and scribes to assist you, help you learn how to run a temple. Our people are experienced. I know this is a difficult job, especially for a woman."

"I have all that I need right here, thank you," she said through gritted teeth. "Now if you will excuse me, I have many tasks to attend to today."

"My Lady, I was hoping to speak to your Consort—Belisseus, I believe you call him?" He peered pointedly at the empty spot to her right.

"My apologies," she replied, her voice cold, "but he has sacred obligations today that cannot be interrupted."

"Perhaps when he is finished?"

She drew in a slow breath. Knossos was not going away, so she would do her best to maintain cordial relations with them, no matter how much they angered her. But she would not let them change the relationship between the two temples. "We will be happy to offer you accommodation tonight, if you would like to speak with him tomorrow. You can meet him right here, in my presence, in the morning."

Hedamos' smile dissolved. "I am afraid my responsibilities do not allow me that much time," he said. "I must return to Knossos immediately." He made a cursory salute then turned and stalked out of the room.

The moment the doors shut behind him, Aria slumped down in her chair, her heart pounding, her breathing ragged. She wiped a hand across her face. Unable to calm herself with the usual breathing techniques, she sent a servant on an errand, heaved herself up from the chair, and made her way to her workroom. When the servant appeared with the wine she had requested, she poured a full cup and downed it in one draught.

When Belisseus came some time later, he found her leaning over her work table, her forehead resting on her arm, the other hand clutching an empty wine cup.

"Here, let me help you," he said, his voice soft, his hand settling lightly on her shoulder.

She sat up and rubbed her temples, worry creasing her brow. "I am sorry," she said. "It is just too much." She choked back a sob.

"What is?" He slid onto the bench and slipped an arm around her.

"Everything I have had to do in recent days. And now this." He looked the question at her. "Hedamos came to the audience room today while you were in the rite."

"Hedamos? The emissary from Knossos?" He squinted at her tear-streaked face, her red-rimmed eyes. "By all the Mothers, what has he done to upset you so?"

She tapped the wine cup with her fingernail. "There are things you do not know."

"Tell me."

And so she did, gripping his hand the whole time, tears trickling down her cheeks as she forced out the words of what he had said to her, done to her, at Knossos and then in her audience room that morning. By the time she was finished, she felt a bit better, but Belisseus was fuming, shaking with rage.

"Is there nothing that can be done about such an abomination? What kind of man does that to a woman? And without reprisal! He should be executed, the monster!" He leapt up from the bench and began pacing around the room, muttering under his breath. "We have no authority over Knossos," he growled. "Every temple is independent. And they do not respect our ways."

She shook her head. "We are powerless against them. Elli did her best, but still he harasses me." Sniffing back another round of tears, she poured more wine and offered him the cup. "Now I understand what Elli was talking about. The men at Knossos—and mind you, I mean the men, for the women have no say—the men are changing the way things are done in that temple. And now they want to change the other temples as well."

"We must stand our ground," he said, taking a swallow of the wine and scowling. "They want to do far more than just change the way we run the temples and the rites, or so I have heard."

She looked up at him, feeling a cold dread at his words. "I try not to think about it."

"But we must think about it," he said, coming to stand at her side. "They want the whole island for themselves, or so the rumors say. They want our wealth, our prized recipe for bronze. That way they can make all the high-quality blades they desire and not have to pay us for them." He took a breath. "They want those blades not to trade, but to rule any land they can conquer."

"Do you believe the rumors?"

"I fear they are true."

She reached for the box that held the temple's seals. Lifting the lid, she drew out the one that represented her: the High Priestess, the ultimate authority in the temple. She was also the de facto authority in the city and the surrounding countryside, but only because the people accepted her as such.

The temple gave out food, performed public and private rites, and worked to maintain the blessing of the gods on the people. In return, the people supported the temple with goods and services and the acceptance of its authority. It was a relationship of sharing and cooperation, not one of domination. Every temple and sacred house on the island had a similar connection with the local people. It had always been that way, for as long as there had been temples.

Then the mainlanders had come, with their horses and chariots and armor, their powerful gods who ruled over every goddess, their dreams of war and conquest rather than peace and plenty. They did not honor the Great Mothers or even their own human mothers. Ida's children had needed their help to rebuild after the time of Great Darkness, or so it was said. Perhaps, instead, the mainlanders had seen a weakness and exploited it, had taken advantage of the island's injuries to do even more damage. Why the Mothers did not protect their children from this incursion, or at least warn them so they could protect themselves, Aria did not know.

She turned the seal over in her fingers. "I cannot fathom how people can think as the mainlanders do, viewing women and men as anything other than equal, wealth as something to be hoarded rather than shared." She looked up at Belisseus, his beautiful dark eyes that held only love and respect for her. "Ida's children do not understand such ideas. And that lack of understanding, I fear, will keep us from seeing what they are plotting until it is too late."

Chapter 44

The servant left, closing the door behind her.

"Go ahead," Belisseus said. "I will clean up from breakfast."

"I have not even finished eating," Aria grumbled, stuffing the last of a barley loaf in her mouth and washing it down with a swig of beer. "But he would not come asking for me like this if it were not important."

She leaned over to press a kiss to his cheek, then rose and straightened her clothing. "I will be in my workroom if you need me."

As she made her way through the corridors and down the stairs, she wondered what on earth Ytanos could want that was so urgent it could not wait until a more reasonable hour. The Sun was barely up, the pale morning light casting soft shadows below the high windows as she passed through the doorway into her workroom. Then she realized with a jolt that she truly did consider it to be her workroom, and not Elli's, even though she had only held her new office for a handful of days.

She had just had time to sit down and begin tidying up her work table when the servant showed Ytanos in. He crossed the room to stand in front of the table, blinking, eyebrows raised. Then he cracked a broad smile and made the salute, drawing himself up fully into the proper arched posture.

"Oh, by all the Mothers, Ytanos, stop that and sit down."

"Yes, My Lady." He was still grinning, but there was no trace of sarcasm in his voice as he took a seat on the bench across the table from her.

"Can it be that you are actually proud of your little sister?" she said, feigning shock.

"I have always been proud of you," he answered, sincere. "But now I am worried as well."

"Is that why you have come so early?" She glanced around, wishing for a jug of wine so she could offer him some. But his appearance had been too hurried for her to think of such things, and she did not wish to call a servant now and interrupt their privacy.

He shifted in his seat. "I was not here for your installation. I am sorry to have missed it." She waved away his concern. "It is the sailing season, and I only just returned to port yesterday."

"I can see that you are well. How are Rhea's brother and son faring?"

He smiled. "They are among my best sailors, strong and smart and dedicated to the Sea-Mother. I am grateful the temple loosened its grip on them." Then his smile faded.

"You have less pleasant news for me now, I suppose?"

"Last night I took my dinner at one of the public houses near the harbor so I could catch up on the news, and I heard things that concern you."

"In that case," she said, squaring her shoulders, "you had better tell me."

"There are rumors..." He hesitated. When she gave him a nod, he continued. "The bonfire ceremony that is held the morning after the sacrifice..."

"The Dawn-Fire Rite. Everyone knows about it. It is no secret, though only a select few are permitted to attend."

"They are saying that something went wrong with it this year, that your Consort was unable to perform the rite properly, and that perhaps you also failed to complete it." The look on his face said he did not believe the gossip but wanted to hear confirmation from his sister.

She let out a long sigh. "It did not go as we expected," she admitted, "but it was completed in good order."

"Not as you expected?" He drummed his fingers on his thighs, a mannerism that Aria knew meant he was unsettled.

"Of course, I cannot tell you the details. But I promise you, Belisseus and I were properly prepared. There was no break with tradition. We performed the full rite as we always have. It was only the gods' message that was... odd."

He narrowed his eyes at her. "An omen." It was not a question.

She leaned her elbows on the table. "Probably. But I cannot understand how there could be rumors about it. I know the Sea Temple is visible along the beach from a distance, but there was no one nearby, so no one could have heard what went on. We even posted guards. And you know we only allow a small group of carefully selected clergy to attend."

"Then one of them must have said something."

She rocked back as if someone had struck her.

"Aria, that is the only way anyone could know the details I heard."

A cold dread settled over her. "Tell me."

"They said the Consort did not complete the journey but instead went mad, shouting that the gods have deserted us. Some of them even said the bonfire did not burn down but went out on its own, half-finished."

"That is too close to the truth, though I can assure you, neither of those things actually happened." She suppressed a shiver. "And these false tales, everyone is sharing them, all over the city and down at the harbor?"

"Sageleus is the one who told me all the collected rumors, the wild stories. He said the tales had already gone to Knossos and back by the time he heard them."

"That explains Hedamos' visit yesterday," she muttered, scowling.

"It is a shame Sageleus only likes women, now that he is available again," he said, winking at her.

"How can you joke about this?" She leapt up, her bench scraping on the stone floor.

"Please," he said, rising and reaching a hand out to her. "I was only trying to make you smile."

"I am sorry," she said, realizing that his comment about Sageleus had hurt as much as the information about the rumors had. Would her heart never give her any peace?

"I will be happy to help you any way I can. I can see how hard this is for you."

"Do you think I cannot do my job?" she snapped.

"I have never thought that, I swear by all the Mothers, no matter how much I might have teased you when you were younger."

She looked him in the eye and saw the truth of his words. "I suppose I had better accept your offer. My predecessors only had to concern themselves with maintaining good relations with our sister temples and shrines. Now, it seems, I must placate the new leaders at Knossos so they will leave us alone."

He slid back onto his bench and let out a breath. "I do not think they will ever leave you alone, Aria. I have heard a great deal in my travels."

She paced the room, her arms folded across her chest, as he told her tales of the mainlanders and their ways, some things she had already heard in scraps of rumors but never thought could be true, and other things she could not even have imagined. The mainlanders traded in slaves, she knew that. It was a common practice among many different peoples around the sea coast and in lands farther from the water. But she did not know until she heard Ytanos say it, that the mainlanders roamed the islands and coastlines to the east and north, capturing women and children as slaves wherever they could, even priestesses and royal women, killing any men who tried to protect them. The mainlanders counted women and children among their possessions, along with their cattle and sheep, and always craved more in order to increase their wealth.

Aria shuddered in revulsion. How could the people allow such an outrage? For that matter, how could the Mothers allow it? Did the Mothers not speak to the mainlanders, or did the mainlanders simply not listen to goddesses, just as they chose not to listen to human women?

According to Ytanos, their way appeared to boil down to simply taking whatever they wanted. They stole people and livestock and land. They fought among themselves as badly as they fought against outsiders. And they had no concept of sharing, no thought of helping those less fortunate than themselves, but only a desire to hoard whatever they could. How awful, Aria thought, to spend your life thinking there would never be enough, no matter how much you gathered in.

As far as Ytanos could tell, this was all down to the new wave of mainlanders, the ones who had come down from the mountains to the north speaking their own version of the mainlanders' language. These were the people who had slowly taken over Knossos in the last few generations and made such dreadful changes. Unlike the earlier waves of migrants from the mainland, these new men refused to respect Ida's children and their ways. And apparently, now some of Ida's children had taken sides with these barbarians against their own people.

When Ytanos finished, Aria stood staring at him, unable to form words. He rose and took her hand. "I will bring you the news as often as I can," he promised. "It is important that you keep abreast of everything that is going on."

"I appreciate your help."

They embraced, then he said his goodbyes and headed back to the port. Aria gazed at her work table, at the seals and the clay tablets and all the other items she used to make sure her people honored the Great Mothers and shared with each other so everyone had enough. One of those people had decided to break their vows and endanger the temple. Aria could not fathom why, but she knew she must discover who had done it. She hoped she could stop the problem before it went too far.

She fingered a small roll of papyrus that lay on the table. A messenger had brought it to her the previous day, a message from Vanadia. The priestess did not understand everything that was going on at Knossos—the women in the temple were no longer privy to many of the meetings Glymenos held—but she wanted Aria to know that rumors were flying about her incompetence as a High Priestess. Glymenos had apparently made noises to the effect that the Consort should run Malia's temple if Aria was unable to do so effectively.

When she had read the message, Aria had taken Glymenos' words to be so much blustering, with no substance. Now she realized that he would use every scrap of rumor and wild exaggeration against her and against the traditions she was sworn to protect. Resolved, she rose, stepped out into the corridor, and turned toward the audience hall. She would send a servant for Rhea and Lexion, and they would puzzle out a way to proceed. She would not call in her lay advisors. This problem came from deep within her own temple, and that thought chilled her to the bone.

Chapter 45

The morning sunlight slanted across the west plaza as Aria and Belisseus led a group of priests and priestesses toward the grain storage bins. The bins, tall stone cylinders each with a single column in its center, stood in two rows of four at the southwest corner of the temple. A soft breeze ruffled Aria's hair, carrying the scent of fresh blossoms with it, and birds chattered in the nearby trees. But she was too preoccupied to enjoy the signs of spring.

After several seasons of diligent effort, Rhea and Lexion had been unable to discover who had begun the damaging rumors about the Dawn-Fire Rite, despite their—and Aria's—suspicions of two or three of the clergy. Suspecting her fellow priests and priestesses of such treachery made Aria's stomach turn. Even though the Dawn-Fire Rite that began Aria's second year as High Priestess had taken place without any trouble, she continued to be concerned.

Ytanos' regular visits let her know that rumors about her temple continued to fly, some of them appearing to come directly from Knossos, each of them containing a kernel of truth that only someone inside the Malia temple could possibly know. Unfortunately, though, whoever circulated the rumors had added a great deal of falsehood on top of that seed of truth, enough to make people begin to doubt Aria's competence as High Priestess.

Hedamos had made mention of these tales during his seasonal visits, a look of superiority on his face that made Aria want to smack him. But apparently Malia was not alone. To Aria's surprise and dismay, her brother reported that similar rumors were circulating about several of the other temples. She agreed with him, that the mainlanders had probably developed clandestine connections inside the temples in order to discredit the native leadership. The idea that a priest or priestess could violate their vows in such a manner infuriated her. What kind of a person could turn their back on the Mothers and their fellow clergy like that?

Still, she was unable to determine who could be doing such a thing. She suspected several of the newer clergy, those young enough to be easily influenced by outside forces and impressed by the mainlanders' bravado and wealth. But she had not seen any evidence of suspicious behavior. It was a small temple. She knew who came and went, when and for how long.

Thalamika, Aria recalled, had always been outspoken about her admiration of the mainlanders, or at least, of their wealth. People were so easily swayed by the glint of gold, but they did not always see the blood behind it. Aria's relationship with Thalamika had thawed somewhat as time had put some distance between them and the divination after that first Dawn-Fire Rite. But Aria still had a bad feeling about the woman.

So she had watched the Chief Scrivener closely and had asked Rhea and Lexion to do likewise. But they had found nothing suspicious. Thalamika did not meet with anyone they worried about, not even mainlanders from the city of Malia. In fact, she seemed to scrupulously avoid the mainlanders. All of her lay students were Ida's children. And she performed her sacred duties with exacting care, keeping track of the messengers who came and went within the temple and reporting that information directly to Aria. Though Aria's gut told her the Chief Scrivener was not innocent, there was nothing she could do without some evidence of wrongdoing, so she remained puzzled and anxious.

Aria kicked a stone off the path as she continued along the side of the temple building with the others following behind her.

Lexion's occasional visits to Knossos were little help in the matter of the rumors. No matter who he spoke with, who he befriended, he was unable to find any hint of who had set the false tales in motion from Malia. He was concerned that Malia would not be able to maintain peace with Knossos for much longer, given Glymenos' tendency to threaten. One thing Aria knew about Lexion: he valued peace above all else. And he worried that the mainlanders valued conquest above all else.

Feeling desperate, Aria had even gone as far as telling Lexion about Vanadia and having him deliver Vanadia's messages to her himself. These days, it was much safer to have a man moving between the temples. She did not trust the roads to be secure for priestesses to travel anymore, and she was not certain of the honesty of the messengers the Knossos temple employed.

She was sure of one thing, though: the mainlanders were indeed aiming for her temple, and from there, the rest of the island. That was one thing she could not allow.

"My Lady?"

She jumped as Belisseus touched her arm.

"Sorry," she mumbled.

The group stopped in front of the grain storage bins, their arms full of rakes and brooms and ritual paraphernalia. The temple had given out the last of the previous year's grain at the Spring Equinox a few days earlier, a gift to the people of Malia, sharing as the Mothers had long commanded them to do. Of course, the temple would not go hungry. Plenty of grain was kept in the large pithoi in the east wing for use in the temple kitchens, and there would not be any more public feasts until after the new crop was brought in. The gods had already received their share as offerings, along with generous measures of wine and oil from the temple's storerooms. The liquids were mingled in the trenches in the storage areas and then drained down into the small pits at the end of each row of containers, where the grain was added and the triple offering blessed to the spirits of the dead and the Two Ladies, the Great Mother Ida and her Daughter, the force behind the continued growth of grain to sustain the people.

Once the temple's portion of the grain had filled the pithoi and the offerings had been made, the seed grain was safely stored away for the next year. But the excess, from the temple's fields and the people's offerings, was stockpiled each year in the large outdoor bins. This grain was shared among the people to ensure that no one went hungry, and it was a safeguard against disaster as well. It was the temple's job, the High Priestess' responsibility to take care of the people. Where the Great Mothers shared their bounty with their children, so must their children share with each other.

Now this year's grain crop had just been harvested. The threshing and winnowing would continue for several days on the round stone threshing floors by the fields. The people would separate the wheat and barley from the stalks and the chaff, until the individual grains were clean and ready to be stored for use over the upcoming year. When the grain was ready, the storage bins also needed to be ready, emptied and cleaned and blessed to receive the new crop.

A young priest and priestess set up a small altar table by the temple wall. Then Lexion and Rhea sprinkled incense on the hot coals in ceramic incense burners. Smoke wafted out the holes in the tops of their censers as they walked the length of the two rows of storage bins, stepping in time with the group's chanting, opening the way for the release of the old and the entrance of the new. When they returned and set the censers back on the altar, the group fell silent. Aria stepped forward, facing her people. She raised her arms in the goddess pose and spoke.

"Our Lady Ida, Grain-Mother who sustains us all, we call to you. You have blessed us with your bounty and your great love. We honor you as we prepare the way for the gifts of the season, your blessings that will fill our bins and our hearts for the year to come."

Aria would not ask the goddess to descend upon her for this rite. It was a ritual of sacred work, not ecstasy. The Chief Song-Priestess took up a rhythm on her sistrum, the cue for the clergy to begin their task. Aria joined in with the rest of them, working alongside Belisseus and their fellow priests and priestesses. With rakes and hands they gathered up the broken bits of grain as well as the leaves and other trash that had blown into the bins over the course of the year whenever they were open. Then they swept the floors, cleaning every last bit of remaining grain until the bins were bare. When had they finished, the Chief Song-Priestess set down her sistrum and the sound of bird-song once again filled the air.

Once the bins were clean, the younger clergy—four priests and four priestesses—took up bowls of herb-water and bundles of herb branches. Elli had always made sure that the younger clergy participated in the rites as soon as they were able, and Aria continued that tradition, expanding it wherever possible. She hoped it would give them a sense of pride and belonging, a buffer against the enticements of the mainlanders, especially for the men.

The eight younger priests and priestesses went around the bins, dipping the bundled herbs in the water and sprinkling it all over the insides and outsides of the bins, bottom to top. The rue and hyssop would purify the area, making it ready to receive the new grain. As soon as they were done, the Chief Song-Priestess walked down the passage between the two rows of bins, shaking her sistrum at each bin to cleanse them all with sound. When she had finished, Aria and Belisseus prepared the offering.

Into a large bowl Belisseus poured grains of wheat and barley as well as dried lentils. The hard kernels made a faint hissing sound as they landed. To this mixture Aria added a double handful of poppyseeds, harvested from the Grain-Mother's sacred poppies that grew in the fields alongside the grain. Then she poured four liquids from four separate pitchers into the bowl: olive oil, milk, wine, and honey.

Lifting the bowl from the altar, Belisseus stepped into the space between the rows of grain bins. He raised the bowl up above his head. The rest of the clergy made the salute as Aria spoke:

"Rhea Pandora, All-Giver, Grain-Mother, we make this offering to you. As your gifts from the fields sustain our bodies, so does your love sustain our souls. You pour out the bounty of the world from your infinite pithos. Grant that we may always be worthy of that which you have so generously shared with us."

Each priest and priestess in turn touched the mixture in the bowl then dabbed their damp fingers on side of the first storage bin. When they had finished, Beliseus knelt and poured the contents of the bowl into a hole in the ground next to the stone structure. Then he rose and stepped back beside Aria. She and Belisseus made the salute, and the rest of the clergy followed suit. A rattling hiss from the sistrum acknowledged that the ritual was complete.

Rhea and Lexion kept an eye on the younger clergy as they gathered up the altarware. The others picked up their rakes and brooms, then the group headed back down the plaza to get on with their day. Aria and Belisseus stayed by the bins, watching the offering-marks on the stone dry out as the day warmed. Belisseus gave Aria a sidelong glance before speaking.

"Have you spoken with Lexion recently?"

"He has not been back to Knossos for a while, if that is what you are asking." She turned to him. "Are you concerned that he might be unduly influenced by that priest whose bed he shares when he is there?"

"No, not Lexion. He is incorruptible, I think. All he wants is peace." He huffed out a laugh, then his brow furrowed. "But I am concerned about what they are doing at Knossos—or not doing."

She set her hand over the place where the offering-marks had been on the side of the grain bin. "They no longer share their grain with the people of their city. I know. They gave up that practice some time ago." She pursed her lips.

"That is not all."

She turned to him, concern on her face. "What have you heard?"

"This is not rumor, Beloved, but fact." He looked away then back at her. "The public feast they gave at Winter Solstice was their last one. They will no longer share a meal with the people on the sacred days."

"I find I am no longer shocked at their selfishness."

"They still hold the rites, of course, but those who are not clergy must pay to attend."

Her eyebrows shot up. "This I had not heard. I do know that they are now selling their excess grain stores for profit and buying up all the copper and tin they can. But to exact a fee to participate in a sacred rite? Are they not wealthy enough already? What are they playing at?"

"You know as well as I do," he said. "They want power. Conquest. They want our temple, then the other temples east of us along the coast, then the whole island."

"Well, they cannot have it, not as long as I live and breathe."

Chapter 46

"But I did not kill a man."

Belisseus gripped the back of Aria's chair as she stared at the man, her eyes wide. The dead woman's partner and her two daughters, just barely into adulthood, stood in the audience room a short distance from their mother's killer, a wealthy mainland trader. Two of Aria's temple guards stood behind him, though he made no attempt to escape. He had, in fact, swaggered into the audience hall with a smile on his face.

"You sailed into our port," Aria seethed, "took advantage of our city's hospitality, and killed one of our people. Her name was Samara."

He shrugged. "I will be happy to pay however much she would have fetched at market. She was neither young nor attractive." Samara's partner let out a sob, and one of her daughters moved to embrace the grieving woman. Her other daughter took a step toward the mainlander then stopped herself, her hands balled into fists. Samara's partner shot a look of dismay at the High Priestess.

Aria made to rise, but Belisseus' hand on her shoulder steadied her. She drew in a slow breath, banking her fire. "Samara was a respected merchant with a lifetime of experience and connections," she said. "Her loss is a profound blow to her family and to our community."

"As I said, I will be happy to pay her fair market price." He gave Belisseus a pointed look, as if he expected the Consort's support in the matter. Belisseus remained silent.

"You freely admit that you killed Samara on purpose and not by accident."

"Yes," he said with a shrug. "We were negotiating over some merchandise and she became unruly."

"Unruly?" Aria snapped. She scowled, a crease forming between her eyebrows.

"I wanted one of these..." He waved a hand at the woman's two daughters, who shrank back. "...for the evening. I offered a reasonable payment, but she refused. I slapped her to bring her back in line, and she attacked me."

Aria had already heard the tale from the woman's children as well as three bystanders who had witnessed the incident, each one speaking to her separately, out of hearing of the others. Their stories all matched. Samara's partner had not been present at the time, but had returned to find Samara dead and her daughters in hysterics, the trader still insisting he had a right to them. Though the trader had a different view of what Samara's actions meant, it was clear he was telling the truth as he saw it.

Samara had dared to grab the trader's wrist and push him away when he attempted to slap her a second time, and he took that as an attack. Apparently, up in the part of the mainland where he came from, women were not allowed to defend themselves against men, but were required to take whatever punishment was meted out. They were also expected to accept a man's offer without argument, regardless of their own feelings in the matter.

Aria narrowed her eyes at the man. "I cannot bring myself to feel anything but contempt for you. Many people come to our island from all directions, and they manage to conduct their business without killing anyone. How is it that you are unable to do so?" He stared at her, his jaw set, and did not reply. "In Malia," she continued, forcing her voice to remain level, "the punishment for murder is to pay the victim's life-price."

"As I said, I am quite willing," he said, spreading his hands and offering a smile that showed all his teeth.

"Not her price as a slave." She spat out the distasteful word. "But her value as an esteemed member of our community, a mother, a partner, and a business owner. You have killed her, hurt her family, and damaged their business. That is what you owe her family."

He drew himself up and squared his shoulders. "You expect me to pay an honor-price for a woman? I have made you my offer." Again he shot a glance at Belisseus, who refused to respond.

"This is not a negotiation," Aria hissed. "In addition to the damage you have done to Samara's family, you owe the temple for her funeral rites and the purification rites for her soul since you fouled her with violence." She named the total price, which came to a significant portion of the goods on his ship.

"I will do no such thing."

"Very well, then you may work off your debt as an indentured servant to the family. The temple will provide guards to ensure that you do not sneak away before the debt is paid and that you behave yourself while in service to the three remaining women of their household."

"Listen here, you insolent woman!" He took a step toward the dais, and the two guards seized him by the arms, holding him back. "Why will you not speak on my behalf?" he cried to Belisseus.

"Because," the Consort replied smoothly, "Our Lady is my superior. I answer to her, not the other way around."

The trader stood with his mouth hanging open for a moment, then snapped it shut. "I suppose it would do me no good to tell you how they handle this sort of thing at Knossos," he snarled.

"Tell me, then," said Aria, tapping her fingers on the arm of her chair. "I am interested to know."

He perked up a bit. "As I said, I am willing to pay the woman's market price. That is how they do it at Knossos. But of course, they also pay a fine to the temple as well, for their trouble," he said with a wink.

"Unfortunately, you are in Malia, not Knossos," Aria said. "So you may pay the amount I have specified, or you may serve Samara's family until the debt is fulfilled. Which do you choose?"

"How dare you!" he roared. The guards were barely able to hold him in check as he lunged for the dais.

"Servitude it is, then," Aria said, motioning to the guards to shackle the man.

"No, wait, I will pay! I will pay!" he shouted, trying to shake loose from the guards.

"Very well. We will send a wagon to the port for the temple's portion. You will have your sailors unload the family's portion from your ship and carry it to their shop."

Red-faced with anger, the man stood stiffly in the guards' grip while Aria made arrangements for more guards and several priests to accompany him back to the port. She wanted no chance for him to leave without paying the full amount to all concerned. When she had finished, the trader twisted his head back toward her.

"I will tell every trader I know about this insult," he snarled. "We will never come to your city again."

"I hope that is the case," Aria said.

The guards escorted the man out while Aria offered her condolences and apologies to Samara's partner and children, promising them that the temple would conduct all the appropriate rites to bring Samara's soul to a place of peace. Then they, too, left, headed for their home, where Samara's body was laid out, awaiting burial.

"I do not know what kind of world this is becoming," Aria said once the audience hall was empty. She rubbed her temples, scowling, fighting the desire to cry.

"We should hire more guards," Belisseus said, kneeling next to her and taking her hand.

"Yes. Would you please take care of that as soon as possible? I am beyond tired of interviewing people to protect us." She stroked her fingers through his hair, as much to comfort herself as him.

"You do not like this part of your job."

"Elli always said I disliked administration because it is not as exciting as ritual. But this..." Tears glittered in her eyes. "If the world is to sink into depravity and horror, why must I witness it?"

Chapter 47

"It has been so long since I have seen you," Aria said as she walked beside her guest in the herb garden. The grape harvest was past, as were the Mysteries and the New Year celebrations, but the rains had not yet begun even though the autumn was progressing. The gardeners did their best, hauling water in buckets to soak the plants in the garden. But as the two women walked down the path, their skirts brushed a clump of myrtle and brown leaves fell off, fluttering to the dry ground and crunching beneath their feet.

"I am sorry to wait so long between visits, but these days we have trouble getting away." Navila offered a rueful smile.

She and several of her fellow priests and priestesses had arrived from Gournia just past midday. Aria had met several of them years earlier, when she had accompanied Kaeseus and a group of Malian clergy on a visit to Gournia. Their sister temple was the next major stop eastward along the Coast Road, and the two temples did their best to keep in touch. Now Gournia's Head of the College of Priestesses had brought a group to visit.

When the group had arrived, the servants had shown them to the guest quarters to wash and change clothing. But Navila had foregone that comfort and asked to speak with Aria right away. Now she moved down the path in the herb garden beside Aria, the dust of the journey still clinging to her clothing.

"Would you not rather do this in your audience hall, My Lady?" Navila asked.

"Too many ears." Aria sighed. "Knossos is too interested in us these days. I find myself trusting fewer and fewer people, even in my own temple."

"We have the same problem." Navila turned her head, scanning the garden, but no one was near. "My Lady would like to hear news of Knossos and the sacred houses near to it, should you know anything about them. We find it difficult to get reliable information from the visiting traders anymore, since so many of them are beholden to Glymenos."

"She will not like what she hears."

Navila shrugged, a gesture of resignation. "There is very little news these days that any of Ida's children like to hear."

"All the temples, cities, towns, and sacred houses along the North-South Road are now under the rule of Knossos, against their will for the most part."

"What!?" Navila stopped in her tracks, turning to face Aria. "Of course we honor Knossos as the pre-eminent temple, but it has always stood alone, just as Malia and Gournia and all the others. We have all been independent for generations, for as long as Ida's children have lived on this island!"

Aria set a hand on Navila's arm. "You wanted the news, and this is what has happened. Through a combination of manipulation and threats, the men at Knossos have taken over all of them: Archanes, Vathypetro, Phaistos, Hagia Triada, and Kommos."

"They rule the port at Kommos?"

Aria turned to walk again, and Navila moved to keep in step with her. "They do, along with Amnisos. So they control a great deal of the trade that comes from both north and south."

Navila was silent for some time. Aria let her be, doing her best to enjoy the pungent scent of the Sun-hot herbs they passed along the path.

"They want to control the whole island," Navila finally said, her voice wobbling with emotion.

Aria nodded. "But we will not let them. We will stand our

ground and keep to our ways, gods willing."

"What if we are not strong enough? We are not warlike, the way they are. How can we fight them?" Navila said, looking at Aria sidelong. She swallowed. "There are things My Lady wanted me to tell you."

Aria stopped walking, and Navila paused beside her.

"You had better tell me everything," Aria said.

"There is an emissary who comes from Knossos every season. They send one to every temple to pressure us to give more and more to them." Aria nodded as Hedamos' face flashed through her mind. "Last time, he came with another man who remained at the temple when the emissary left. He said he was there to help, but we know better."

Aria's eyebrows shot up. "Your Lady allowed this?"

Navila's brow crinkled with worry. "I do not know how to say this without being disrespectful."

"The truth is never disrespectful."

"My Lady is..." She pressed her lips together. "She is kind and generous and an inspired priestess."

"But..."

"But she has trouble saying no to people," Navila said, "especially if doing so will cause a disturbance. And you know how insistent these mainlanders are, pushy and even aggressive until they get their way."

A butterfly wobbled by, and Aria wondered whether it ever had concerns like hers. Ah, to be a floating soul with no care in the world beyond finding the next flower.

"In times past," Aria said with a rueful smile, "Your Lady would not have had any trouble. No one would dare be so demanding of a High Priestess."

"These are new times, bad times," Navila said, wringing her hands. "This man is not a priest, yet he lives at our temple, sending messengers back to Knossos all the time. Our Consort has done his best to help, but now that the man is there, My Lady is unable to remove him. We fear that more will come to join him, and our temple will go the route of Knossos. And you would be caught in between."

Aria began moving down the path again, gesturing for Navila to accompany her. "They tried to do something like that to us, but I would not stand for it."

"We have heard from the temples to the east that they have tried the same thing there as well, at Palaikastro and Zakros."

"Have they succeeded?"

"Not yet."

Aria let out a breath, relieved. "Then perhaps there is hope."

"We had a great deal of trouble simply making this journey," Navila said. "Our Consort had to help My Lady stand up to the man from Knossos so we could come. He does not like us visiting the other temples."

"Of course he does not," Aria snapped. "This is our great power, that we support each other even though we are independent. They do not understand that. All they understand is conquest and submission. They do not know what the word *equal* means." She thought a moment. "This is why the mainlanders would not help us rebuild some of the peak sanctuaries."

"I do not understand."

"After the time of Great Darkness." Navila made the sign of propitiation, but Aria did not bother. She did not think a simple hand gesture, even a sacred one, would make much difference anymore. "The people of the Two Lands helped us rebuild some, but most of our aid came from the mainlanders. They helped us reconstruct all the temples and the cities, but only some of the peak sanctuaries."

"Why would they want fewer peak sanctuaries? I thought they wanted to be wealthy. The sanctuaries receive offerings, just as the temples and cave shrines do."

"I think," Aria said, "that the mainlanders want control more than anything. Many of the peak sanctuaries are remote."

"So they would be harder to control."

"Yes. They only helped us rebuild the ones closest to the cities, where they can be easily commanded." Aria tapped a finger on her chin. "The cave shrine at Mt. Dikte has managed to remain free of

Knossos' domination. I must send some of my people there for a visit again soon. The stronger our ties with each other, the weaker the mainlanders' grip remains."

They reached the far edge of the garden and stopped next to a waist-high clump of rosemary, not too far from the dovecote. Aria plucked a narrow leaf and crushed it between her fingers, inhaling the bracing fragrance. The scent sharpened her mind, and she turned to Navila.

"We will help you rid yourselves of your unwanted visitor."

A relieved smile spread across Navila's face, but then her brow furrowed. "How can you do that?"

"I will send some of my priests back with you when you return to Gournia. These mainlanders will not listen to women, I have seen as much. But a few strong-willed men should take care of your problem, at least for now. And they can teach your people how to stand up to Glymenos' men."

"Oh, thank you! My Lady will be so glad of your aid!"

She reached out and clutched Aria's hands, bending to kiss her knuckles. As she straightened back up, Rhea came out the side door of the temple, accompanied by one of the Gournian priests. The two moved quickly down the path toward Aria and Navila.

"My Lady," the priest said, "the shrine room is prepared. The rest of us are ready for the rite."

"Very well," Navila answered. She turned back to Aria. "Thank you so much for your help."

When Navila and the priest had gone, Rhea looked at Aria. "What help are we offering them?"

Scowling the whole time, Aria repeated what Navila had told her about her temple's situation. Rhea's face reflected Aria's dismay at the situation. But when Aria explained her plan to help the Gournia temple rid itself of the unwanted guest, Rhea grew angry.

"Do we not have enough troubles of our own already?" she snapped.

"We will have more if we do not help each other."

"But Knossos..." Rhea waved her hand in the direction of the city. "They will be angry when they find out what we have done. They will send that awful Hedamos again, or someone even worse. Perhaps this time they will come and stay here and not leave. You must not do this!"

Aria perched her fists on her hips. "That is exactly what they want, Rhea. They want us to fight each other, to separate from each other and stop helping our brothers and sisters. Alone we will fall. Together we are much stronger. This is what the Mothers teach us."

Rhea opened her mouth to speak, then shut it again.

"You know I am right."

"But how can we stand against them," Rhea asked, "if we are not organized like they are?"

Aria shook her head. "They do not understand cooperation, only domination. They do not help each other. They are not like a herd of Horned Ones, but like a pack of wild dogs. They help only when it suits, and otherwise they are at each other's throats."

"But when a pack of wild dogs works together, it can take down a herd."

Aria shivered. "Let us pray it does not come to that."

Chapter 48

Aria stared out over the sea as the newly-risen Sun reflected on the water, a small pitcher of opium-laced wine clutched in her hands. Belisseus adjusted the censer on the altar table as he stood beside her in the Sea Temple. Then he picked up a cup and held it out for her to fill. The pitcher wobbled in her trembling grip, but he managed to shift the cup so no liquid spilled.

"I know this is difficult for you," he said, setting the cup in its place on the altar.

They had already purified the temple with incense smoke and herb-water in preparation for the rite they would perform at midday. The purification and preparation were acts the High Priestess and her Consort performed alone. No one else accompanied them to the Sea Temple that morning, though Aria had already posted guards along the road as a precaution. The previous night's sky had borne the first Full Moon following the Summer Solstice, the eighth Summer Solstice since Aria's installation as High Priestess.

Now she and Belisseus were setting up the altar with the items necessary for the rite: the censer, the cup of drugged wine, several figurines, a bowl of herb-water, and a shiny bronze blade that Aria had sharpened herself. Belisseus had already set a wide bowl in its place on the floor beneath the edge of the large table in the center of the temple: not the altar but the other table, the one that had held a yearling bull this time last year.

Aria folded her ceremonial garb—a fine linen tunic and matching tiered skirt—and set it in its place on the altar. She did not turn or look at Belisseus when she spoke.

"The people at Knossos no longer sacrifice the Consort. They take a bull in his stead, even in Minos years. I know it is wrong, but I understand what could drive a person to do that."

He moved next to her and set a hand on top of hers where it still lay on her stack of clothing. "They have corrupted the traditions out of greed and lust for power."

"How can anyone kill someone they love?"

"It is not murder," he reminded her, "but sacrifice."

She slipped her hand out from under his and moved to the edge of the temple, folding her arms across her chest, her hands balled into fists. "Dead is dead, whether it is murder, or self-defense, or a willing sacrifice."

Belisseus stayed where he was, in the center of the temple. "I know how much you love me," he said, and Aria's body began to shake with sobs. "I love you that much as well."

"Then do not ask me to do this," she said, wiping the tears off her cheek with the back of her hand.

Then he crossed to stand next to her, reaching out to her until finally she took hold of his hands. "Please look at me." After a moment, she lifted her head and met his gaze. "I have given myself to the gods. You know what that vow means." She nodded slowly. "If you cannot do the deed, I will do it myself." She drew in a sharp breath and squeezed his hands, holding on tight. "If I live beyond sunset today, my whole life becomes meaningless. All my work is forfeit."

The truth of his words sliced through her heart like a knife.

"How did Elli do this?" she whispered.

"She had to."

She let out a shaky breath. "Too many things in life are like that." She let go of his hands and went to finish setting up the altar.

* * *

Just past midday, as the tide was turning, Aria and Belisseus led the procession, the slow drumbeat driving the large crowd of local clergy, visiting clergy, and lay people down the path to the Sea Temple. Gripping Belisseus' hand, Aria stepped into the Sea Temple alongside him, barefoot and wearing only the hide skirt of the sacrificial priestess. She clenched her free hand into a fist to stop herself from picking at the hair on the skirt.

She and Belisseus had both fasted and then drunk the traditional cup of drugged wine before leaving the main temple, but she feared it would not be enough to calm her for the task ahead. She looked her Consort up and down, from his bare feet to his colorful kilt to his deeply browned chest, so very warm and alive. When her gaze reached his face, she found him smiling gently at her, trusting her to do what she must.

The drum sounded a loud double beat and fell silent. Then the triton trumpet blared three blasts that reverberated across the beach and out over the water. Though some part in the back of Aria's mind knew that the day was hot, the bright sunlight beating down on her and her Consort through the center of the temple, she could not feel it. Her whole being was cold, as if she were the one sacrificed, already dead.

As Belisseus raised his arms, Aria did the same, but she felt as if someone else were moving her body. She could remember what she needed to do, but at the same time she felt far, far away. She listened, emotionless, as her Consort spoke the invocation:

By land and sky and sea
Blessed be the Three
By land and sea and sky
By Them we live and die
By sky and sea and land
Beneath Their guiding hand

She felt herself draw in a breath, and she heard the words come out of her mouth, the words that alerted the gods to the impending sacrifice:

By the Sun
By the Moon
By the Star of the Sea
Our Fates are woven
Our lives are set
Our time ends when it must
We give ourselves to the gods

Her hand reached for the cup on the altar. She picked it up and offered the drugged wine to Belisseus, who drank it down, watching her over the rim. When he was finished, she turned the cup upside down on the altar, a symbol of readiness for what came next, the shape of too many vessels of birth and death, both human and divine.

They had not called the goddess into her. This was not that sort of rite. But Aria knew she could not complete the ceremony alone, as a simple mortal. She was too weak, too ready to scream, to cry, to run away. So she silently called to the Daughter, her thoughts a desperate plea to keep her from failing at her sacred task.

Daughter of the Three-and-One, Lady of the Labyrinth, Spinner of Fate: yours is the thread that binds us all, that draws us along the path to our destiny. Be with me now, I pray. Steady my mind and guide my hand as I do what must be done.

As she drew in a breath, the warmth of the day finally reached her skin. She felt the goddess slip up beside her, not into her as in a rite of trance, but close by her, bearing up her namesake against the tide of emotions that threatened to overwhelm her and carry her away.

Aria found herself turning to face Belisseus and reaching out to hold his hands. The words she had memorized, words Elli had taught her and made her repeat over and over again until she thought she would scream, spilled from her lips one after another. Her speech was too quiet for the assembled crowd to hear, but loud enough to capture Belisseus in the swirling sound of her sacred speech.

"I am the hand of the Mothers, the Three-and-One," she said to him, "their tool and their face in this world. I hang by the thread of Fate, my life given to their bidding."

"I am the child of the Mothers, the Three-and-One," Belisseus said, the words painfully familiar to Aria. Elli had made her memorize Belisseus' speech along with her own, even though it was each Consort's duty to teach them to the one who would take his place. "I am their gift to this world, given for a time only."

"You were a gift at your birth," Aria continued, looking him in the eye, awed that he returned her gaze with gentle acceptance and unabashed love. "You were a gift again at your anointing. And you are a gift at your death."

He gave her hands a quick squeeze. "I welcome the next step on the journey. May the thread of Fate draw me ever onward toward the stars."

The words finished, she swallowed thickly and drew him to her. He slid his hands around her waist as she gripped his shoulders, solid and warm. She tilted her head up, and he leaned to kiss her, slowly, softly. As they breathed each other's breath, the drum began again, a slow heartbeat. Aria glided her hands across his skin, feeling his heat, knowing there was not enough time left to memorize him any more than she already had.

Finally she drew back and his hands lifted from her waist. As she watched, he stepped away from her and unfastened his kilt, letting it fall to the floor. He stood before her naked, holding himself tall and straight but relaxed. She wanted to attribute his sense of ease to the cup of drugged wine he had just downed, but she knew better. He was ready for this, and so must she be, to do right by him.

The drum beat on as he moved over to the table in the center of the temple. On this same table Elli's Consorts had died, one after another, by her hand, and the Consorts of the High Priestess before her, and the one before her. On this table Aria had sacrificed a young bull every year in place of a man, this man. Now here he was, beautiful and warm and alive, sliding onto the table and lying down, stretching out in the circle of bright sunlight, ready to meet his fate.

Aria found herself moving over to the table, leaning over Belisseus as he smiled up at her, as he closed his eyes, trusting in her. Her hand hovered over him, then she made the gesture of blessing, touching two fingers to his forehead, his eyelids, and his lips: blessing him to the Mothers, to the afterlife, to the journey onward.

Turning, she reached for the blade on the altar, the polished bronze glinting in the sunlight as she lifted it up, her arms in the pose that marked her as the goddess incarnate, her embodiment on Earth. Sweat beaded on her forehead, but she dared not move her hands to wipe it away. She drew in a breath and spoke, her voice sounding stronger and steadier than she felt.

"Naked we are born into the world."

Belisseus opened his eyes and looked up at her. "And naked do I willingly leave it to return to the Mother's arms," he said, his voice calm and deep, the sound of the Young God incarnate.

Aria held the blade over his neck, angling it the way Elli had showed her. His death would be swift and nearly painless, she knew that. As she gazed down at him, she felt her eyes fill with tears. She swallowed against the growing lump in her throat.

"My Lady," Belisseus said softly, his gaze locked with hers. "I will always love you as I love the Great Mothers. Let me go to them now. Do this for me."

And so, still gazing into his eyes, she slid the blade against his neck, bearing down as hard as she could. Her greatest fear was that she would only injure him and leave him alive and suffering, as she had heard some inexperienced butchers did to the animals they slaughtered for food. So she leaned into the cut with her full weight, and the blood spurted, its metallic tang hanging heavy in the hot air, settling on the back of her tongue. Belisseus' body quaked and then stilled, his gaze going glassy and unfocused. A cloud passed across the sun, dimming the light in the temple. And then he was gone.

The drum fell silent. Aria shook herself, feeling the Daughter pushing her to keep moving, to finish the rite, to fulfill her duties.

She forced herself to look at Belisseus as she stroked her fingertips over his face, closing the eyelids over the beautiful dark eyes that had gazed at her with so much love. Then she worked her hands beneath his shoulder and hip and shoved hard to tip his body sideways, ensuring that his blood would continue to drain into the bowl beneath the table.

In the days to come, it would fall to her to prepare that blood in the same way that the blood of the sacrificial bulls was done, mixed with wine, seawater, and sacred herbs. But while any properly trained priest or priestess could make the bull's blood mixture, only the High Priestess was allowed to touch the blood of the Consort. To anyone else, doing so meant certain death.

Aria could not tell how much time had passed when she snapped back to herself. The crowd was still silent. Even the sea birds had chosen to keep away and not disturb the scene with their cries. Now Aria could see that that Consort's blood had stopped dripping. Gently she eased his body onto its back and motioned to the four priests who stood just outside the Sea Temple.

Together they stepped up into the temple and crossed to the sacrificial table. They spread out a large white cloth, two of them holding it level with the tabletop and the other two sliding Belisseus' body off the table and onto the cloth, which acted as a sling. His head lolled about as they moved his body.

Each of the priests took a corner of the cloth and bore Belisseus' body to the edge of the temple. They waited as Aria unwrapped her hide skirt, laying it on the now empty table, and joined them. Then together they went down the steps, across the sand, and over to the edge of the water.

Keeping to one side and fighting the urge to reach out and touch Belisseus' body, Aria accompanied the priests into the sea. They continued moving through the water, urged on by the retreating tide, until Aria was neck-deep and the water reached up to the priests' shoulders. The retreating tide pulled at her legs. She dug her heels in to stay in place. Then, at her signal, the men released the cloth. Belisseus' body bobbed once, twice, as the fabric swirled around him, then the water closed over him and he was gone, drawn out to the sea, to the great water-womb of the world.

Forcing herself to move, Aria turned and fought the tide to make her way back to the shore, the priests following behind her, fanning out in an arc to protect her in case the water overcame her. For just a moment, Aria was tempted to give in and let the sea drag her down, take her life along with Belisseus'. But the moment passed. She set one foot after another, pushing against the water, until she reached the shore.

The corpse-bearers moved off to one side as Aria climbed the steps into the Sea Temple once again. They would touch no one, speak to no one, keep their gazes lowered until they had cleansed and purified themselves. Corpse-bearers always did so simply to be certain the deceased's spirit did not linger among them. The body itself was of little consequence. But these men had borne the body of the Consort, the god made flesh, whose power echoed between the worlds, so they had to be especially careful.

Forcing herself to focus on the task at hand, Aria lifted the bowl of herb-water from the altar. Her hands trembled as she raised it up and poured the liquid slowly down on her head. The cool water ran down her neck and shoulders, down her bare body, and out across the floor, taking the pall of death with it. She and the temple were purified. She set the bowl back on the altar and turned toward the people, the witnesses to this rite.

The crowd parted, and a young man stepped forward, clad in the colorful kilt of the Consort, an exact copy of the garment that lay crumpled on the temple floor near Aria's feet. He was beautiful: deep brown skin, dark eyes, glossy black hair. He moved across the ground and up the steps until he was standing in front of her, those dark eyes gleaming, waiting for her to accept him.

The midday Sun shone down on him, but he was glowing from inside as well. The Young God was on him, in him. Letting out a breath, she held her hands out to him, pleased to see that they did not tremble. He took her hands, then shifted to embrace her, tilting his head to whisper in her ear, "I am here, My Lady. I have never left you. I will never leave you."

Her eyes stung with tears as she kissed him, the final step in the

High Priestess' acceptance of the new Consort. He flashed her a smile then withdrew from her embrace, crossing to the altar table. He returned a moment later carrying her garments. Then he proceeded to dress her, slowly and reverently. First he slipped the fine linen tunic up her arms and onto her shoulders. Then he wrapped the skirt around her waist, tying its cords so the edges of the tiers overlapped in the front, falling like waves down her legs. Then he stepped back and bowed his head, obedient to her will.

"Come," she said quietly. Together they walked to the top of the steps, where he dropped to his knees before her. She set her hands on his shoulders and lifted her chin, speaking so her voice rang out through the heated air, full of every emotion: "The Young God dies yet he lives again."

Belisseus tilted his head up and met her gaze. "All who die live again in the Great Mother."

The crowd cheered and shouted as the drum began a lively beat, the sound of celebration. Sistrums and bells took up the rhythm as well. Aria gripped Belisseus' hand. He rose, and they descended the steps together. When they reached the ground, he knelt again and slipped a pair of sandals onto her feet. Then he stood and followed her, the crowd parting to make way for them. When they reached the far side of the group of onlookers, she took his hand once again and led the people back to the main temple for the feast.

Chapter 49

Aria shook her head as the Consort offered to refill her wine cup. "I have had enough," she said. "It is not helping."

Forcing a tight smile, she ate another bite of fire-roasted beef. Her stomach churned, but she knew she needed food. No matter what was going on in her mind and her heart, she was the High Priestess. She needed to function, to perform her duties. She owed the people that much. She owed the gods even more.

She thought back to the Summer Solstice feast with her first Consort, eight years earlier. Her own son had gone into the waves that day along with Elli, and Aria had taken up the mantle of High Priestess. She had been numb, dazed, going through the motions automatically but feeling nothing. In the intervening time, she had learned much about running the temple and being a priestess on a level she had never imagined. And now, sitting at the feast with her new Consort, she was no longer numb. She felt everything, and it was overwhelming.

Holding the Consort's hand, she looked out over the crowd as the feast drew to a close. The sunlight slanted across the plaza as the Sun touched the mountaintops, throwing long shadows toward the temple. Ytanos was still at sea, so he and his crew, including Rhea's brother and son, were not present. With a pang of guilt, she realized she was grateful they were gone. Though she wished

Rhea's son well, seeing him right now would be more than she could bear.

Ytanos was not the only one missing from the crowd. The tables were only half-filled with the people of Malia and the surrounding countryside: her people, the ones she served, the ones she was obligated to protect and support. She had vowed that much to the Mothers.

But she was no longer sure how well she would be able to fulfill that vow. Fewer and fewer people came to the feasts and the seasonal rites. Few even came anymore to receive grain and other food from the temple, even though she offered it the same as always. Knossos was a growing thorn in her side. But even here in Malia, the new breed of mainlanders had begun to settle and spread their backward ways among Ida's children. Greed and self-interest overtook the sense of community Aria had loved when she was younger. The people no longer wanted to serve the gods. They wanted the gods to serve them, to give them what they desired in exchange for a few trinkets. And when the island's gods would not do that for them, they turned to the mainlanders' gods instead.

No matter how carefully Aria followed her people's traditions, no matter how well her clergy performed their duties, no matter how good she became at diplomacy, it seemed the Mothers were no longer willing, or worse, no longer able, to protect their children. Knossos grew richer and more powerful while the other temples suffered, scrambling for donations and practically begging to get anyone to participate in the rites. She felt it in her bones: her people would not be safe for much longer, no matter how much the few devout people gave of themselves. Were the sacrifices no longer effective? Had she just killed that beautiful young man in vain?

"Ariadne."

She started as the Consort said her name. When she turned to meet his gaze, the look on his face told her that he could see what she had been thinking about.

"You can worry about all that tomorrow," he said. "None of it is going anywhere. Today we celebrate the turning of the year."

"Time turns, yes, but I fear we are not moving forward

anymore."

"You are just feeling overwhelmed, that is all."

She tossed the remains of a barley loaf into her bowl, staring at it where it lay in the dregs of some stew. "You dare to tell me what I am feeling," she snapped.

"I am sorry," he said quickly. "I know this day is hard for you."

She lifted her head and looked at him. "Have you ever killed a man?"

He sucked in a sharp breath. "It was a sacrifice, My Lady."

"You did not answer my question."

"No." He shook his head. "I have witnessed every Consort sacrifice since I was old enough to remember, but I have never killed anyone, in ritual or out."

"Well, I just killed a man. A man I lived with for eight years. A man I cared about. And now I am expected to behave as though the act never occurred, as though he is still sitting next to me instead of someone else." She put up her hand as he opened his mouth to comment. "I know that every Consort carries the Young God, so in a sense you are all interchangeable. But in another sense, you are not. And even if you were... it is not the same as slaughtering a bull, I promise you."

She pursed her lips, watching as the scant gathering began to disperse, people rising from the tables as the day drew to a close and the sky began to dim. Reaching for the discarded piece of bread, she saw that her hands were trembling again. She had eaten, so that was not the problem. And the day was cooling as the Sun sank down, so the heat should not be bothering her. Then she realized that her breathing had grown ragged, as if she were walking down the Sea Road as fast as she could. And now her heart beat rapidly in her chest, pounding against her breastbone so hard it almost hurt. She looked up to see the Consort gazing at her with concern.

"Come," he said, rising. "Let us get away from the crowd."

"What crowd?" Aria's gaze skimmed across the emptying courtyard, not that it had been that full to begin with.

He held the door open for her as she stepped into the cool

darkness of the temple corridors. Together they walked through the building and up the stairs to the residential quarters, shoulders brushing. When they reached Aria's room, he stepped back and let her enter first. She knew that his belongings had already been moved into the room next door, but he crossed the threshold behind her, following her into her room. As she expected, there was bread and wine waiting on the small table.

"It is customary," he said in response to her look of exasperation. "In case you did not feel like eating at the feast."

"I ate at the feast!" she snapped. "I have done everything right. I have maintained all the traditions. I have made sure my clergy performed their duties properly. I have encouraged the townspeople to share and support each other. I have given of myself..." Her voice caught. "I sacrificed a young man today, at his bidding, according to our ways. And still the world falls to pieces around us." He reached out for her, but she pushed him away. "I am tired of being comforted."

"Do you not wish to feel better?"

"Just let me be." She picked up the pitcher of wine and sniffed at it. It was just wine, with nothing added. "Belisseus always used to..." Her voice trailed off.

"I am Belisseus."

"I know." She set the wine down and let out a slow breath, staring at the table, willing her mind to work. All she could see was the bowl of blood that was left after they returned her previous Consort's body to the water. Was his death a blessing? Would the blood do any good against the encroachment of the mainlanders? It was meant to sanctify the temple, the ritual rooms, the temple's fields, the sacred spaces indoors and out. But she feared it was no longer a protection, just an empty gesture. The tide was turning, and it was going to sweep them out to sea, unwilling sacrifices all.

She dropped onto the bed, weary to her soul. "I cannot keep doing this."

The Consort moved to stand before her, then he slid down onto his knees, the motion so full of reverence, it made her heart ache. "Tell me."

"My visions always come true." He looked the question at her. "You do not want to know."

"I believe you, My Lady. But what I want does not matter. I am here for you. I will be with you for the rest of my life. I am dedicated to you and only you."

She sucked in a breath and looked at him, really looked. He was young, yes, but his eyes held a level of understanding she had not often seen even in people her own age. She knew the Consort's training was rigorous, far beyond that of the regular priesthood. He knew all about not just the running of the temple and the keeping of the traditions, but also the politics of the day. He had been trained to be her partner in every way. He was anything but innocent.

While she had allowed herself to become emotionally attached to her first Consort, there were some things she had chosen to keep from him. Perhaps that had been a mistake. Elli had emphasized that the Consort was the High Priestess' support, the one she could lean on and trust in all matters. Aria was good at delegating tasks — she had worked hard to develop that skill — but not at relying on others on a deeper level. She had kept her heart closed, and now she realized that was, more than anything, a weakness.

The Consort held his hands out, and she took hold of them, meeting his gaze. "I need someone to talk to," she said. "Someone who will not retreat if the things I say are..." She groped for the right word. "Outlandish."

"I am yours," he said, sincere. "I will not leave you until the day I die."

A cold chill ran down her spine, and she snatched one hand away from him to make the sign of propitiation. She waited, but no vision came. Perhaps she was being unreasonably fearful. But she could not shake the feeling of dread that fell over her with his words.

"Tell me," he said again.

She gazed at him for a moment, then something shifted inside her, and she patted the bed next to her. "You had better sit down. This is going to take a while."

She told him everything: her vision of the destruction of Malia, the trip to Knossos before she became High Priestess, the horrible Dawn-Fire Rite with her first Consort and the divination afterward. He lit a lamp and poured them both some wine, and she kept on talking, sharing everything she could think of that might be related, from her childhood up to the present: visions and rituals and human encounters.

The night was well dark, the broad-faced Moon riding high in the sky by the time she was finished. The wine pitcher was empty, and their half-finished cups sat disregarded on the table. Aria lay curled on the bed, feeling hollowed out and raw, as if she had been crying for hours, though she had not shed a single tear.

The Consort lay down and nestled beside her. "None of it is your fault," he said.

"But what if I could have prevented any of it? What if I could still change the course?"

He stroked her cheek. "It is not our job to change Fate, but simply to navigate what we are given."

"What if..." She swallowed. "What if this is all a message, a warning, just as the Great Darkness was?"

"And what was that warning, back then?"

She squinted at him, his face all shadows in the lamplight. "I do not know. Everyone still argues about it. Perhaps you can help me discover the real meaning."

"I will be happy to," he said, leaning in to kiss her cheek, then her mouth. "We should think on the matter and then try a journey-rite."

She tilted her head back, scrutinizing his face. "You are serious."

"Of course. You are the High Priestess, My Lady. You know things no one else does. And it is my place to help you." He looked away, a faint blush rising in his cheeks. When he looked back, she saw tears shimmering in his eyes. "Being with you is the greatest honor I can imagine. You are the love of my life."

Unbidden, a smile spread across her face even as she blinked back tears. She cupped his cheek, stroking the line of his jaw with her thumb. "You amaze me. My Beloved. My Beli."

Then she leaned in to kiss him, slow and deep, and to show him how to please her as they consummated their bond.

Chapter 50

Doing her best to ignore the sand that was creeping into the sides of her sandals as she stood in front of the Sea Temple, Aria held up the cup of opium-laced wine. The light of dawn rippled over the surface of the dark liquid. Beli slid his hands over Aria's and drank deeply until the cup was empty, watching her over the rim the whole time.

There was no cause for concern, Aria told herself. The last seven Dawn-Fire Rites, on the last seven Summer Solstices, had passed without difficulty, without trouble. But they had all taken place on the morning after a bull sacrifice, the same Consort performing the rite each time. The last time a new Consort had undertaken this rite, bad things had happened, an omen at the beginning of Aria's tenure as High Priestess. Now a new Consort stood before her, wearing the colorful kilt that denoted his office, his face open and loving. She found herself silently praying to the Great Mothers for a safe and uneventful journey, an ordinary message.

Then her thoughts turned to the visitors from Knossos, a dozen or more clergy and laymen who had come to Malia for the previous day's sacrifice. Beli had resolutely refused to speak to them at the feast afterward beyond a few words of pleasant greeting, conceding the conversation to Aria every time with a stubborn smile. Now they were busy with a breakfast feast, which would be followed by musicians and acrobats to entertain them in the central court during the time it took for the Dawn-Fire Rite to be completed. The past few years had taught Aria to maintain a guard on the visitors until the rite had ended, to ensure that none of them slipped out and headed toward the Sea Temple. Of course, there were additional guards on the Sea Road and the path to the little temple as well. These days, it paid to be careful. But that meant even more things for Aria to worry about when she should be paying attention to the ritual.

Once she forced her focus to return to the rite, she realized that Rhea was standing at the front of the small crowd, looking directly at her, her chin raised and her shoulders squared. Her friend's gaze was full of confidence, full of faith and trust in her High Priestess. The look in Rhea's eyes said that this time, the Dawn-Fire Rite would proceed without a problem. Aria let out a shuddering breath. This time, yes, all would be well.

Beli drew his hands away from the cup and reached for the lit torch that Lexion was holding out to him. He raised his arms, holding the torch aloft, its flame streaming landward in the breeze that rolled in off the water. Then he drew in a breath and called out the invocation:

Fire of Heaven,
First and Last,
Kalliste the most beautiful,
Come to us now!
Rise up from the World Below
Where you have spent the long, dark night
And bring us your light; birth the day.
Birth yourself from the Earth
As she has birthed us all
From her womb.
Heat our blood,
Inflame our visions,
And share yourself with us,
Your adoring children.

Aria spread her arms, and the goddess descended on her, a familiar garment slipping over her ordinary being. A beautiful warmth spread through her, from her head down to her toes, until she felt as if she must be radiating light like the Sun itself. She turned to the assembled crowd, her heart overflowing with love for her people. Her hands moved to make the sign of blessing as the words flowed from her mouth:

My children, I am here.
Revel in my heat!
Seek my light always,
Here and in the depths of the World Below.
For I am ever with you,
Even in the darkest night.

Then she turned toward Beli, her hands reaching to cup his face. When she looked into his eyes, it was not just a human priestess acknowledging her Consort, but the goddess herself meeting her son and lover. She felt the fire flowing between them, so strong it took her breath away. When she spoke, the words came from a place deep within her, beyond simple memorization, a kind of knowing that Elli had spoken of but that Aria had not truly understood until now.

"This is my beloved son, given to you for a time. Treat him with care and reverence. Listen as he speaks, for his wisdom is mine, though he be but mortal. Let him go down and rise up again, to show that he is the One. Only the Lion knows the way down and back."

She stepped away from him, giving him room to move. Flashing her a glowing smile, he leaned to press the flaming torch against the stacked wood of the bonfire. The dry wood caught instantly, crackling into flames that the wind quickly fanned into a roaring fire. The sudden heat crinkled Aria's skin as the Consort tipped the torch into the pile and backed away from the flames.

Together they moved several steps away from the fire. Turning to face his High Priestess, the Consort bowed his head. She lifted her hands and set them gently on top of his head, feeling the thick, glossy locks beneath her palms. Then he shifted so their gazes met, god and goddess in communion through their mortal vessels.

"Who am I?" she said.

"Kalliste," he said, the name dripping from his tongue like honey.

"Yes," she said, smiling. "And you are Belisseus."

Heat built up on the back of her neck, and suddenly there were fiery serpents twisting across her shoulders and down her arms, wreathing his head, setting her hands aflame where they touched him. He gasped, his gaze still locked with hers, fire flowing between them. Then he trembled, and his legs buckled. He collapsed down, knees digging into the sand, still looking at her, though his gaze was now soft and unfocused, as if he were looking through her to something beyond. He drew in a slow breath and spoke, his voice echoing like an otherworldly bell.

"I am the Fire, and you are the Light."

Aria's heart kicked in her chest as a drumbeat rang out through the morning air. The drums pounded, the sistrums rattled, and the priestesses flung off their wraps to add their apron-bells to the mix. Aria moved behind Beli, her hands on his shoulders to steady him as he knelt in the sand. In accordance with tradition, the priestesses arrayed themselves in a broad arc around the sacred pair. Then the priests moved into a tight circle inside the ring of priestesses, dancing and chanting to the Consort, calling him to the journey.

The voices and the instruments moved along with a relentless beat, driving the Consort away from this world and toward the one below. Aria felt him sway beneath her hands, and then he was falling, collapsing to the ground, two of the priests rushing to catch him before he landed face-first in the sand. Gently they stretched him out, his bare back and legs pressing against the body of the Mother. Aria rearranged herself so she was kneeling by his head as the priests draped a cloth over his face. Her hand reached out to touch him, her fingers weaving themselves through the night-black locks of his hair. She was his anchor, his path of return to this world. While the High Priestess journeyed only in the secret, sacred spaces of the temple, the Consort journeyed in front of an audience, the priests and priestesses witnessing the messages he brought back from the Mothers.

Now was the time to sink into a light trance, time to be a bridge between this world and the one where Beli journeyed. Aria knew that, yet she resisted. What if unwanted visitors made their way past the guards? What if the Consort needed her when she was floating away on the tides of the rite? What if things went wrong again when she could have prevented the problem?

Great Lady, be with me now, I pray. I cannot do this alone.

A gentle warmth seeped through her body, enveloping her like a blanket, a feeling of comfort and safety. A voice echoed in her mind, in her heart.

All will be well, my child. Trust in me.

Letting out a slow breath, she allowed herself to relax, to soften, to slip into that state of there-and-not-there, floating between the worlds, riding the beat of the drums and the sistrums. Her hand tangled in Beli's hair, anchoring her as much as she anchored him, while the rest of her drifted free, beyond the material world, beyond space and time, into the arms of the Mothers.

After moments or eons, she could not tell which, she found herself blinking, looking out through her own eyes once again. An instant later, the bonfire crumpled down, the last of the burned-up sticks falling into a pile of ash and glowing coals. Aria looked up. The Sun was nearing its high point in the sky. Then Beli's head shifted beneath her hands.

As he began to mumble and groan, the priests lifted the cloth from his face. His eyelids fluttered, and his eyes opened. Then every instrument fell silent, every dancer stopped, frozen in place. Tilting his head around, Beli focused his gaze on Aria and smiled.

Trembling just a little, he shifted to raise himself up on his elbows. It took Aria a moment to disentangle her fingers from his hair. She had wound them tighter among his locks while she was in trance. Then she cradled his head in her hands, blowing onto the top of his head and into his face. This way, she could be assured that he had returned fully from the World Below. She smiled at him, blinking back tears as she helped him sit up all the way.

"Speak, Son-of-Earth-and-Fire," she said, her voice rough with emotion.

"I have journeyed from the Fire Below through the Earth to reach for the Fire Above," he said, the words every Consort spoke when returning from this journey. He drew in a slow breath, his chest rising and falling with some effort. "I have traveled the red road. Now I sit in the space where the three realms meet." Aria tensed, waiting for the next words. "The Three-and-One, the Great Mothers and the Mother-of-All, watch over us. We have kept our bond with them, and they are pleased."

She let out a shaky breath as he shifted to raise his hands up in a double gesture of blessing. Perhaps everything would be all right after all.

"My people," he said, "we live in difficult times. The Mothers know this. They value our loyalty and our love for them." He looked around at the tight circle of priests and the larger ring of priestesses who surrounded him. "We must do our best in the face of darkness. This darkness is a part of the natural cycle, and the Mothers cannot stop it. No matter what others may do, we must continue to share, to support one another, to live the Mothers' love in our daily lives." He drew himself up, sitting tall, looking each one in the eye in turn. "The Mothers do not judge us. So long as we do our best, regardless of the circumstances, they will hold us in their embrace, no matter what happens in the end." He slumped back down, steadying himself with his hands pressed into the sand. "Fire of Heaven," he said, a little breathless, "First and Last, the Most Beautiful One has spoken."

A slow drumbeat began, soft and steady, as Aria and the priests helped Beli to stand. Her heart had pounded throughout his pronouncement, but now it began to slow as she held a cup of water for him to drink. He looked at her over the rim, his dark eyes gleaming, the corners crinkling with happiness. She found herself smiling back at him. The worst of it was over. He had returned, safe and sound. Something about his message prickled in the back of her mind, but she set the thought aside for the moment.

She held her hand out, and he took it, his grip warm and firm. Moving in time with the unhurried drumbeat, they circled the remains of the bonfire three times, then walked down to the edge of the water. They stood for a moment in the place where the three realms meet: land, sea, and sky, the physical embodiment of the Three, brought into being as a place for their children to enjoy life and share the Mothers' love with each other. Aria focused her attention on the world around her: the warm sand beneath her feet, the ocean spray blowing on her skin, the golden sun shining down on her face, and she silently gave thanks for them.

Still holding hands, Aria and Beli knelt at the water's edge, the sound of the lapping waves washing over them. With their free hands they reached out and touched the water, then stroked their damp fingers on their foreheads: Grandmother Ocean's blessing. Rising, they turned and moved back up the shore, stopping between the smoking bonfire coals and the Sea Temple.

As they waited, three of the priests shoveled the remnants of the bonfire farther down the shore toward the water. Soon, the rising tide would envelop the coals and quench them, then the retreating tide would draw their remains back out to sea.

Beli squeezed Aria's hand. She turned her head to look at him and found him smiling softly at her, a look of reverence on his face. She made herself smile back at him. She was not yet ready to believe that everything was all right. Then, drawing in a bracing breath, she moved forward with him at her side. The ring of clergy parted to let the pair through, falling in behind them as they stepped in time with the drumbeat, down the path toward the main temple.

Shortly, Aria found herself seated in the dining hall, her Consort at her side. The clergy who had fasted for the rite now enjoyed a bountiful midday meal, the Consort included. They had barely had time to begin eating when the visitors from Knossos entered, heading straight for Aria's table.

"Our congratulations," Hedamos said to Beli, "on a rite well performed. You have now taken your place in the temple." He gave the Consort a pointed look, waiting for his response. Without speaking, Beli reached for Aria's hand and lifted it to his lips, kissing her knuckles. "I see how it is," he spat, looking daggers at Aria. Then he turned back to Beli. "Do not let these women keep you from your rightful place in the world. The gods are mightier than any goddess, no matter what the women say."

While Hedamos was speaking, Lexion had risen from his seat. Now he stepped up beside Hedamos, setting a heavy hand on the man's shoulder. "Your wagons are ready outside," he said.

Hedamos twisted away from him, snarled a few vulgar words under his breath, and stomped out with his entourage behind him.

"I will see that they leave promptly. We will have peace in our temple and our city," Lexion said before he, too, strode out of the dining hall.

Aria picked up her cup to take a drink and discovered that it was empty.

"Here," said Rhea, sliding onto the bench on the opposite side of the High Priestess from the Consort. She held up a full pitcher of wine, fighting back a grin. When Aria nodded, Rhea filled the High Priestess' cup and then her own.

"Thank you," Aria said. She downed half the cup, then set it on the table and rubbed her forehead. "I do not know whether I am up to this."

"You are not alone," Rhea said, setting her hand on Aria's arm as she also motioned to the Consort.

"I know," Aria said, reaching her arm around Rhea's shoulders. "You are my best and oldest friend. My little sister, always."

"Even if..."

"Even if you find yourself in Lexion's bed more often than not," Aria said. "And even if my bed is reserved only for one." She reached for Beli's hand, holding tight to his warmth and strength. "But sometimes I think that even a temple full of bold and fearless clergy will not be enough to stop..." She shook her head.

"I will never desert you," Rhea said, her voice rough with emotion. "Never."

Aria shifted back and looked at her friend, really looked at her. "You mean that." She had only seen that level of devotion in one other person, or more precisely, two of them with the same name.

The power of that realization nearly knocked the breath out of her. She blinked back tears and reached for her dearest friend, enfolding her in an embrace, holding tight to one of the few things she could count on anymore.

Chapter 51

"My Lady." Sageleus made the salute. "Thank you for seeing me."

"I am always happy to speak with you," Aria said. "I value your opinions, and I look forward to every visit. May the Mothers bless you in all you do." She sat back in her chair in the empty audience hall.

He flashed her his usual dashing smile, and she realized that she no longer thought of him as anything but a friend and a trusted advisor, had not thought of him in any other way for a long time. It occurred to her that perhaps she should feel some sort of loss at that, but in the end all she could feel was gratitude for his presence in its current form.

When she had first become High Priestess, she had insisted that the Consort accompany her in the audience hall every time Sageleus came to the temple to share his news. She could not even say exactly why she needed him there. Sageleus would never have behaved improperly, would never have disrespected her office. That was not his way. Perhaps, she realized, she had been afraid she herself would behave inappropriately. Having the Consort at her side reminded her of her position, her responsibilities and obligations.

She no longer needed the Consort to attend these meetings, but still she held them in the audience hall rather than her workroom.

Since Sageleus was not family, it was more appropriate to meet with him in a public space. But since the news he brought was often sensitive, she preferred to be alone with him, dismissing the priests and priestesses who usually witnessed audiences with townspeople and visitors. She still had no idea who among her people was passing confidences on to the men at Knossos, so she did her best to be careful.

"I apologize," she said when she realized that Sageleus had been waiting patiently while she was lost in thought. "I hope the season is going well for you?"

"As well as it can these days, My Lady. I have been busy in Malia, but I also had time to visit my sister and her family in Knossos."

"Idomeneia. Yes, I recall you telling me about her. I trust she is still healthy and prosperous?"

His shoulders drew up in tension. "Things are changing. It is becoming more and more difficult for her to take part in trade. She does not have a husband to speak for her the way the mainlanders expect of a woman, so her oldest son is now running the shop while she and her daughters spin and weave in the back room. She says it is easier to avoid trouble that way."

"Oh, Sageleus, I am sorry to hear that." She shifted forward in her chair. "Are they safe?"

"So far, yes. Her son keeps the predators at bay, though many of the men in Knossos seem to think that her lack of a husband makes her fair prey. I visit her as often as I can, but I cannot talk her into leaving Knossos. She has built up a clientele over the years and does not want to lose it."

"She could move to Malia to be near you," she said, motioning toward the city that sprawled out north of the temple, "and then send her weavings back to Knossos for her son to sell. I am sure the cloth she makes is beautiful and would still fetch a good price even if she were not there to trade it herself."

He shifted from one foot to the other, avoiding her gaze.

"Sageleus, what are you not saying?"

"Trade has changed, My Lady."

"Tell me."

He pursed his lips, scowling. "The temple at Knossos has begun charging a tax on all goods that come through the ports at Amnisos and Kommos. They charge even more for any goods that go in or out of the city on the roads."

"What?" It had been a number of days since she had adjudicated any of her people's grievances, and just as long since she had spoken with her other lay advisors. She realized that the situation was changing quickly enough to warrant more frequent meetings.

"These levies are in addition to the tribute they wrest from the sacred houses and temples along the North-South Road."

"How dare they do such a thing!" Her legs twitched as she fought the urge to rise and pace the room. She was the High Priestess in audience. The seat on the dais was her proper place as the goddess' representative on Earth.

"There is more," he said. "You know the Knossos temple sends envoys to the Two Lands, to curry favor with the officials there, giving them gifts of all sorts."

"I had heard. We, too, have relations with some of the cities there. Our people trade with them, and they helped us rebuild after the Great Darkness."

They both made the sign of propitiation, though Aria realized she now did it simply from habit and not out of the belief that it might actually protect her people.

"My Lady, the Knossians have told the people of the Two Lands that they represent our whole island."

Now she did rise, leaping up from her seat, stomping down off the dais, and striding over to stand before Sageleus, her hands balling into fists. "That is a lie. A monstrous lie."

"I know that. You know that. But the officials in the Two Lands do not, and they believe the envoys."

"Must I now send my own emissaries to the Two Lands, with gifts and words of flattery to counteract these falsehoods? This is what comes of letting those people at Knossos twist their religious pre-eminence into something more political, more... sinister." She rubbed the crease between her eyebrows. "We have little to spare anymore. Trade has slowed, as I am sure you already know, and the roads are no longer safe. Many of the farmers keep to themselves and do not even come into the city anymore. Donations have declined even as Hedamos continues to demand an increasing share for his temple." Her lip curled in distaste as she pushed the emissary's name out through gritted teeth. "These men have decided they are owed what had once been given freely as a sacred gift. Now they behave as if we were their vassals rather than an independent city."

"I think it may be too late for emissaries. The damage is done." Sageleus sighed. "The people at Knossos—this new breed of mainlander—they have a thirst for war."

"Do you think they would attack us?"

"I cannot say. But I do not trust them."

"Excuse me a moment." Aria crossed to the nearest door, pushed it open, and stepped out to speak briefly with a servant. In a few moments, the servant returned bearing a tray with a pitcher of wine and two cups. Aria thanked the servant, who left, closing the door.

"It is not really that bad," Sageleus said half-heartedly as Aria set the tray down on a small table and poured wine into the cups. She handed him one and took a long drink from her own.

"I know you, Sageleus. There is more you are not telling me."

She looked him in the eye. The gaze he returned was one of respect and admiration, tempered with the gentle affection of old friends. But behind all that, there was a fear she had not seen in him before.

"Please," she said, reaching out to touch his arm. "I need to know."

He nodded, a rueful smile playing across his face. "You know the mainlanders at Knossos have that temple's recipe for bronze."

"At least they do not have ours. Malian blades are prized along every trade route."

"But they want the Malian formula. They want everything for themselves: the donations, the trade, the land, the temples. Even the secret rites."

"I already know this, Sageleus." She took another swallow of wine. "We are standing our ground as best we can."

"I will tell you what I tell every local trader I meet: Malia must look to the east now, away from Knossos. We must trade with Gournia and Palaikastro and Zakros, share with those cities and the others to the east. We must keep each other strong."

"Are you saying that all our traders should avoid Knossos entirely?"

"Yes. I think that would be wise." He swirled the wine in his cup, watching the motion of the murky liquid. "You have heard the stories of what happened after the Great Darkness."

Aria shivered, folding her arms across her chest. "Some of the people at Knossos tried to take over the island. Some of our cities had to build fortifications to protect themselves."

"We do not know whether they were Ida's children gone mad from the cataclysm, or mainlanders trying to take advantage of the chaos."

"And you think that may happen again?"

"I have not forgotten your vision, My Lady. Neither should you."

Chapter 52

"Good morning," Ytanos said, stepping into Aria's workroom and making the salute. His usual grin was dulled, and he moved gingerly as he crossed the room.

"I heard you were back in town." She pushed a plate of fruit and cheese across the table and poured him a cup of beer, thankful for the interruption. She never enjoyed tallying the goods her temple was forced to send to Knossos in order to keep the peace. "You look like you celebrated your arrival pretty thoroughly last night. I hope the rest of your crew is in better condition than you are." The images of Rhea's son and brother reared up in her mind. She gave quiet thanks that they were free to sail away from the power struggle that now beset their home island. Better a hangover than an argument with an emissary from Knossos.

Ytanos sat down and raked a hand through his hair, squinting at the morning light that poured in from the high window. Though his eyes were bloodshot, his face was still full of delight at seeing his sister again.

"Sailing season is over for the year," he said. "The Flock-of-Doves has set. It is a time of celebration."

"So your summer went well?"

He took a sip of the beer, eyeing the plate of food in a way that suggested his stomach had yet to recover from the previous night's festivities. "My summer went much better after I heeded your advice to avoid Knossos."

"That was Sageleus' guidance."

"I know. I am glad you have him as an advisor. He is a trustworthy one."

She pushed a pile of papyrus out of the way and rested her elbows on the table. "There are few I can trust anymore. I appreciate that you are willing to come here so often and share your news."

"You are not just my family. You are also my High Priestess."

Aria reached over and squeezed his hand. "And staying away from Knossos was enough to give you good trade for the season?"

He nodded. "You know that we run mostly to the east anyway, all the way over to Byblos where Yassib is from." He turned the cup around in his hands. "Those who did not heed that advice have not done so well."

She looked the question at him.

"The word went around the harbor that we should trade only to the east, but one of my friends who has a ship almost as large as mine decided he would sail west instead. He intended to pass by Amnisos and trade at the ports farther west along the coast— Armenoi, Kalami, Kydonia."

"That sounds like a reasonable plan."

"I thought so, too. But it turns out that the Knossians are now patrolling the waters around Amnisos. He was sailing within sight of the coast for easier navigation, and the Knossians attacked his ship. Their ships are equipped with pikes that jut off the prow, for ramming other vessels."

"Holy Mother!"

"They forced his ship into the harbor at Amnisos, where they levied his goods heavily. They would not allow him to leave until he had traded away all that he had brought in, all exchanges that were heavily in favor of the locals, all performed under guard. He lost a great deal on that trip."

"Do they not desire more trade? Why would they force him to barter at a loss?" She shook her head, perplexed. "Now he will not return."

"I do not understand it myself. Their ways make no sense to me. Why attack when they can invite trade with friendliness and enticing bargains?"

Aria tapped a stylus on the table, thinking. "You know I have always had visions."

Ytanos' head snapped up, his gaze scanning her face, his eyes narrowed. "What have you not told me?"

"Perhaps it is time. The more you know, the better."

Reluctantly, she shared with him the vision she had seen that morning so long ago as she lay in Sageleus' bed: the city of Malia under attack, aflame, the townspeople screaming and dying, armed men tearing through the streets.

When she was done, he reached across the table and clutched at her hands. "Your visions always come true," he said, his voice quiet and quavering.

"But I cannot say when."

"This one is not that far away, is it?"

She avoided his eyes, keeping her gaze on their hands, his sunburnt, calloused ones clasping her soft ones, two shades of the honey-brown skin of Ida's children.

"Very well," he said when it was clear she was not going to comment further. "When sailing season opens again next spring, I will spend more time here and less time across the sea in Byblos and the neighboring cities. That way I can deliver the news to you more frequently. If anything bad does happen, you will have warning. Of course, I will be here all winter regardless."

She swallowed. "Thank you." She gave his hands a squeeze then let go, sitting back and poking idly at a stack of clay tablets. "Some days, I wish I did not know how to read or write." He peered at the tablets then back at her, an eyebrow raised in question. "I am tallying the goods we must send to Knossos this time." She shook her head. "They continue to demand more and more, even though the donations are dwindling. The weather has become unpredictable in recent years, which does not help matters. Our crops are not always reliable anymore. But Glymenos does not care, as long as we send full wagons to him. He does not care if we starve."

He twisted around, checking that no one was near the workroom's doorway, then turned back to Aria and spoke in a low voice. "Have you yet discovered who has been sharing oathbound information with the people at Knossos?"

She blew out a breath, her face crinkling into a scowl. "There is a young priest here whose parents are mainlanders, the kind who find Glymenos' ways appealing."

"You think he is the one?"

"He may be. Rhea brought him to my attention. She mentioned that he had been behaving strangely, acting as if he were guilty of some kind of subterfuge. When I asked Lexion to check on him, he told me the young man's parents have traveled to Knossos several times in the past year. Apparently his father is a mainlander with relations in that city. Perhaps the priest is sending messages along with them." She rubbed the crease between her eyebrows. "Many of my people are now suspicious of each other, especially of those with mainland heritage. The situation is starting to affect their work. Even this young man..."

Ytanos scrutinized her face. "You do not believe he is guilty."

"I do not want to believe anyone is."

"But you think it is a man."

She stared at him, taken aback. "What kind of woman would do such a thing?"

"You might be surprised."

Chapter 53

The dining hall was crowded, the full-time clergy and many of the part-timers enjoying the evening meal together. Aria sat with Beli at their usual table at the front of the room. She leaned her elbows on the table, slowly working her way through a bowl of chickpea stew and a small loaf of barley bread.

She was tired to the bone. Over the course of the past Moon she had pushed herself through the Feast of Grapes, the Mysteries, and the autumn planting rites, managed to scrape up another wagon full of tribute to send to Knossos, performed the First Crescent Moon rite, and dealt with the young priest whom Rhea had brought to her attention. Thank the Mothers, his suspicious activity had turned out to be quite mundane in nature. He was sneaking into the city to spend time with a girl, when he was under a vow to have relations with no one. Rather than eject him from the priesthood, as she might have done in years past, Aria chose only to have him ousted from the Agrimi Brotherhood, whose vows he had broken. She had also confined him to the temple for three Moons: no excursions into the city for any reason. Lexion had agreed, as had the priest who was the head of the brotherhood. Other than this transgression, the young man—Dionysios son of Donata—was a good and dedicated priest.

They had few enough new people entering the ranks of the

priesthood these days. Aria did not care to lower their numbers any more unless absolutely necessary. She had asked the people who had attended his hearing—Beli, Rhea, Lexion, and a handful of other clergy—to keep the matter quiet so as to avoid having anyone question the leniency of the decision. She did not want her priests and priestesses thinking that the current hard times were an excuse to break the rules whenever they desired. Besides, keeping a hearing and the resulting decision quiet was a commonplace within the temple, most often simply to spare the person in question from embarrassment. Plenty of good priests and priestesses had stumbled somewhere along the way but had learned to do better afterward.

Now Aria did her best to relax and enjoy the meal alongside her Consort and her fellow priests and priestesses. The tables were full of food, even if it was not terribly fancy, and for that she was thankful. As long as the fields and orchards continued to produce, they would not go hungry, even if Glymenos did thin their herds with his ridiculous demands.

While Aria was enjoying her meal, the steady murmur of conversation in the hall was interrupted by loud voices, bitter and angry. She looked up to see several of her people shifting along their bench so Dionysios could not sit with them. As Aria watched, the young man attempted to find a seat at three different tables. In every case, the priests and priestesses who were already sitting there moved so he could not join them.

Dionysios turned around, seeking any place to sit but finding none. A look of dejection on his face, he crossed the room toward one of the doors. Feeling sorry for him, Aria stood up from her seat. They should not treat him so badly, she thought, simply because he had been weak. At his hearing, he had sworn by the Mothers never to break another vow, his whole body trembling as he spoke the oath, and Aria believed his sincerity.

"Dionysios," she called out, "come sit with us."

The young man's eyes widened, then his face broke into a smile as he rounded the ends of the tables toward where Aria was sitting. A rumble of conversation filled the room as people craned their necks to watch him, commenting to each other, faces full of conflicting emotions. As Dionysios passed one of the tables, one of the other young priests stuck his foot out, and the young man tripped on it, landing hard on the stone floor. The room burst out in harsh laughter and hissing commentary. Aria could not hear the conversations clearly, but the words "mainlander" and "traitor" and "should have been executed" met her ears as brief snatches of speech carried above the general hum of the room.

By the time Dionysios had gotten up, brushed himself off, and made his way to Aria, she was fuming. She motioned for him to sit next to Beli, who happily made room for him. Then she climbed up onto the bench and raised her arms in the goddess posture. The room fell silent, the men and women looking toward their livid High Priestess with more than a little unease.

"By all the Mothers," Aria began, her voice shaking with anger, "is there not enough trouble in the world, but that you must create more by your gossiping? Do truth and honesty hold no value for you? Have you forgotten all your vows?" She gestured toward Dionysios. "This young man is no traitor. His only crime is weakness, for which he has already been punished."

Heads turned, and whispers hissed around the room, but no one spoke loudly enough for Aria to understand.

Dionysios stood up. "Please," he said to Aria, tilting his head up toward her. "Please tell them. I would rather be shunned for something I have done than for something I have not done."

Aria looked him in the eye and saw that he meant what he said. "Very well," she said to him, then turned back to the tables full of people. She raised her arms again, and the whispering stopped as the people waited to hear what their High Priestess had to say. Aria gazed around the room, seeing looks of dismay and disbelief on the faces of her people. That would not do.

"Priests and priestesses of Malia," she said, addressing them as if they were in a formal audience, "Dionysios is one of our temple's clergy. It is true, his parents are mainlanders, but many of you are descended from mainlanders. That does not make you traitors, does it?" She narrowed her eyes, and no one dared speak.

"Dionysios is guilty not of betraying our temple but of breaking one of his oaths. He sneaked out of the temple to lie with a girl when he had taken a vow to abstain until his next initiation within the Agrimi Brotherhood." The room remained silent, the clergy's eyes all locked on their High Priestess as the young priest stood below her, cringing at having his transgressions revealed. "Dionysios has been removed from the Agrimi Brotherhood. He will not be allowed to petition to join them again. And he will not be allowed to leave the temple grounds for three Moons. Lexion is now directly overseeing his priestly work to help him learn the value of abiding by his oaths. Dionysios has been warned that a second infraction will not be dealt with so kindly. I believe him when he says he will do better in the future."

She drew in a sharp breath and looked around the room, only to discover that most of her clergy were looking down now, avoiding her gaze. "I do not always announce the decisions I make in private hearings. Now you understand why. Sometimes it is better to let a priest or priestess learn their lesson without so much embarrassment, as many of you know from personal experience." The people shifted uneasily in their seats. "If you ever want to know the truth about one of these matters, I expect you to come to me directly. Gossip is beneath us, and it harms our temple. Do not put me in the position of having to punish my own priests and priestesses for spreading falsehoods about their fellow clergy." Her face was red, her voice harsh. "And I promise you, if I ever find that any of you have betrayed us to Glymenos and his people, you will not wonder what punishment that person received. You will see it with your own eyes."

When Aria finished speaking, she realized her heart was pounding. Beli was now standing up, offering his hand to help her climb down from the bench. When they were all seated again, Aria found that she had no appetite left. Apparently the rest of the clergy felt likewise. A few of them picked at their food, but most of them got up and left in silence, appropriately chastised. Aria sat there, clutching Beli's hand, until the dining hall was empty.

Chapter 54

They stood between the field and the threshing floor: Aria, Beli, the temple clergy, and the few lay people who had bothered to attend. In the autumn, they had prepared the temple's ritual field and planted the grain: the men in their bull's head masks, the young girls, the pregnant women. The crop had grown throughout the mild, rainy winter, turning green and then golden as the grain ripened. Now it was springtime, and the growing season was done. Spring Equinox had passed. The swallows had returned from their winter sojourn in the lands across the sea to the south.

Aria looked out over the field filled with stubble, the remains of the barley crop the participants had just cut down with their bronze sickles. The temple's main crop, the grain that would sustain the people and fill the stores for the upcoming year, grew in much larger fields in the surrounding countryside. But here, in this smaller field, the labor of the farmer intersected with the work of the priesthood.

Now Aria watched as the people gathered up the sheaves of grain, carrying them in their arms as if they were newborn babes— or corpses. Standing by her side, Beli still brandished a shining bronze sickle, the means of collecting food by cutting down the plants that provided it. Here, in the harvest, life and death met and mingled.

Aria stepped onto the field and collected the last sheaf of barley, the final harvest, standing it on the ground next to the small altar table. As the people gathered around her, their arms full of grain, Aria raised a cup of wine and spoke.

"Hail the Grain Mother!"

"Hail the Grain Mother!" the people responded.

Aria poured a libation, the blood-red liquid spilling onto the field. She handed the cup to Beli and picked up her sheaf of grain, raising it above her head for all to see.

"Hail the Daughter!" she called.

Again the people echoed her words: "Hail the Daughter!"

Beli poured out the rest of the wine, emptying the cup, the dark spot on the ground slowly spreading as the liquid soaked into the soil. For this libation, they had purposely drawn wine from the bottom of the jug, so the cup was full of lees. Where they spilled the wine onto the Earth, the lees lay on the dampened dirt like so much clotted blood.

Aria held her sheaf of barley out in front of her as she spoke. "At planting time the Daughter comes to us, rising up from the World Below with the first green sprouts in the fields."

The people made the sign of blessing, the sign that the Mothers would provide them with plenty, always. Aria wondered if that was enough anymore, simply asking for what they needed and assuming the Mothers would hear and respond. Pushing the thought aside, she turned her attention back to the rite.

"As the grain grows," she said, looking out across the small gathering, "the Daughter walks among us. So long as the crops are in the fields, she is here. But today we strike down the grain."

At her words, Beli held his sickle aloft, its polished metal glinting in the spring sunlight. Next to him, Aria raised her sheaf of grain, holding it upright as if it were a living person.

"When the grain is ripe, the Daughter is fully born into this world. But the very next moment, at the touch of the blade, she dies." As Beli drew his blade lightly across the sheaf, she tilted the stalks over, a corpse lying on the bier of her open hands. "This is the Daughter's birth and death all at once. And so begins her descent back to the World Below."

"Hail Ariadne!" Beli called out.

"Hail Ariadne!" the crowd responded, sending cold shivers down Aria's spine.

Beli set his sickle on the altar and led the people over to the threshing floor, where they laid the sheaves down, spreading the stalks out into a thick layer over the stone surface. The grain from the large fields, the ones that fed the temple and provided for the public feasts, was threshed on broad stone floors by pairs of oxen dragging heavy pieces of timber. This was the most effective way to process large quantities of barley and wheat. But here, next to the ritual field, the people would dance the grain apart from the stalks, as they had done for generations, since their first ancestors came to the island.

Now the people gathered around the threshing floor, Aria and Beli among them. It was always uncomfortable, the first step onto the stone surface. The threshing floor was a doorway to the World Below. Few people dared touch it except during the harvest rites. So Aria went first, with Beli right behind her. Rhea and Lexion followed, then the other clergy and the lay people moved to stand on the grain, the dry stalks crackling beneath their sandals like tiny bones breaking.

Beli began the threshing song. The others joined in, walking forward in a circle, their slow stomping steps keeping time with the chanting.

Daughter of the Mothers
We dance the grain
Thank you for the gift
We dance the grain
Death in life
We dance the grain
And life in death
We dance the grain
Go below, go below
Go below, go below

Come again, come again
Come again, come again
When next
We dance
The grain

As the group moved slowly around in a circle, Aria's gaze swept the ring of dancers. The threshing floor was not nearly as full as it had been in years past, but there were still enough people to do the job. In addition to the priests and priestesses who had served the Malia temple for years, there were a few new participants. Though Aria was glad for the addition to her temple's declining ranks, the reason behind the recent arrival of the new clergy both saddened and angered her.

Apparently dissatisfied with the extent of his hegemony, Glymenos had expanded his control and taken over the city of Tylisos, west of Knossos, a short distance south of the coast. Though the official version was that the wealthy merchants and artisans of the city had welcomed the connection with the larger city and its temple, Sageleus had shared a different story, one of threats and extortion. His story was soon corroborated by the priests and priestesses from Tylisos.

Rather than be forced to endure Glymenos' rule or be executed for speaking out against him, most of the clergy at the sacred house in Tylisos—all of the women and all but a few of the men—had fled. Luckily, they had received help from a local fisherman and his boat, even though sailing season had not yet begun and the weather could still be treacherous this time of year. They had walked to the coast under cover of night and sailed out to sea around Dia, the sacred island, far beyond the patrol range of the ships that guarded Amnisos. They had come back in at Malia and sought refuge in the temple. Of course, Aria had taken them in. By now Glymenos had surely restaffed their sacred house with his own clergy, she thought, her lip curling in disgust. She only hoped he did not feel compelled to come after the fleeing clergy to retrieve them or punish those who sheltered them.

Driven along by the beat of the people's footsteps, Aria stomped the grain. Her mouth had been forming the sounds of the chant mindlessly as her thoughts wandered elsewhere, but now she brought her focus back to the sacred act. She felt the stalks shifting beneath her sandals, stems snapping and seeds crunching with every step. As the heads of barley broke from the stalks and the individual grains separated, the life force of the crop returned to the World Below to await the next growing season.

When the threshing was done, Aria called an end to the chant. The people stopped, then they bent down to gather the crushed stalks from the floor, shaking them to release any remaining grains. Beli cleared the center of the circular area, and the participants piled the stalks there, building a small mound. Later, the stalks would be burned and the ashes scattered on the field to feed the Earth and bless next year's crop.

Now, the people took up rakes and brooms, gathering the loose grain into piles on the stone floor. They divided up into pairs to winnow the grain, one person pouring the seeds from one basket to another while the other person fanned a breeze to waft the chaff away. Aria and Beli worked together, Aria tipping the barley from one basket to the other as Beli used a palm frond fan. Though they were High Priestess and Consort, today they were also ordinary mortals working the harvest, sweating beneath the spring Sun, giving thanks for the bounty the gods and the ancestors had provided.

Once the grain was winnowed, Aria and Beli would set aside the Daughter's portion, to be buried in jars of honey at the corners of the field. The rest would go into storage in the temple for use in certain sacred foods and as seed grain for the next year's planting.

There was no chant for the winnowing, only the sound of the fans buffeting the air and the hiss of the grain spilling from basket to basket, the breath and voice of the crop and the spirits of the dead who blessed it. This was the final step in the harvest, the assurance that the Daughter had returned to her reign in the World Below. She was not dead. The gods could not die. But they could depart, leaving the mortals to their own devices.

Though the Sun shone and the birds sang on this warm spring day, to Aria, the Daughter's departure felt like emptiness. She knew she was not alone in feeling forsaken. The world was changing, and the Mothers could not stem the tide, could not—or would not—protect their children from the onslaught. Aria knew that she and her people had not been abandoned by their gods, not yet, but somehow this time, the Daughter's leaving felt more final, less like a point in the cycle and more like an omen.

Chapter 55

"You will let me in!"

The man's voice rang through the audience hall doors. A moment later, the doors flew open and a short, stocky man marched in with two burly guards at his side.

"My apologies, My Lady," the priest said, hurrying toward Aria where she still sat on the dais after spending the morning helping to settle her people's grievances and allay their troubles. "They would not wait to be announced."

"It is not your fault," Aria said, "that they have no manners." She drew herself up tall in her seat, fighting the impulse to clutch at the arms of her chair. Beli had left moments earlier, their morning's work done, while Aria had remained to ponder the issues of the day. But now her solitude had been broken.

The priest retreated toward the doorway where he took up his position with a second priest and a pair of priestesses. Aria valued the tradition of having a handful of clergy present in the audience room whenever she was present, regardless of the business at hand. As Knossos' influence spread, the behavior of her own townspeople had deteriorated so she could not always count on their respect or civility. Now she was glad she had not yet dismissed the clergy when the last of the people who came to the temple for judgment that morning had left.

"You will call your Consort," the man said, not bothering to address Aria properly or make the salute. "I wish to speak with him."

Aria looked past him to the clergy who flanked the doorway. She caught a priestess' eye, and the woman nodded, understanding the look Aria shot at her. The priestess slipped out of the room as Aria returned her gaze to the man. She squared her shoulders and lifted her chin.

"I will do no such thing. You have barged into my audience hall and disrespected me. If you have business here, you will state it now."

"My name is Mopsos. I have come from the temple at Knossos."

"What has happened to Hedamos?"

"He is no longer with us."

Aria's brow furrowed. "He has left the temple's service?"

The man laughed, a cold, rasping sound. "He has left this world. His appetites caught up with him."

"What does that mean?" Aria asked, though she had a feeling she did not want to hear the answer.

"He took another man's slave woman, spirited her out of her owner's house in the city and took her back to his place to have his way with her. Her owner found them, Hedamos in his cups and both of them in Hedamos' bed, and killed them. But not before he cut Hedamos down to size."

He grasped his crotch with one hand and made a motion with his other hand that made it clear what the slave's owner had done to Hedamos. Aria cringed, and Mopsos snickered at the look on her face. She could not find any grief in her heart for Hedamos, only revulsion at the crudely-told story and the manner in which Hedamos had died. He had probably gotten what he deserved, and she hoped Elli's magic had played into the man's eventual end.

"Hedamos was sloppy," Mopsos said. "I would never let my guard down like that."

Aria looked at him, considering, and decided that what he said was true. He was probably too cold-blooded to do anything that was not dreadfully calculating.

"Oh, I knew Hedamos before he..." He drew a finger across his throat then laughed again, a sound that sent a cold shiver down Aria's spine. "He told me about your visit to Knossos. He said you were quite a fighter." He leered at her, his gaze raking up and down her body, as he elbowed one of his guards to let him in on the joke. Aria's hand flexed, and she wished she had a sword with which to teach him a little respect, then cringed to realize she was stooping to his level, even if only in her thoughts.

"Why have you come here?" Aria said, her voice cold.

"To introduce myself," he said, still refusing to address her properly. "To let you know who will be giving you orders now."

"I am the High Priestess of this temple," she snapped. "You do not give orders to me."

His lip curled up in a sneer. "Very well. You leave me with no choice but to make our new terms known." He gazed pointedly to the side where his burly companions stood. When Aria continued to stare at him, unflinching, the look on his face soured. "Your tribute is due upon the next Full Moon."

"Tribute?" Aria's eyebrows shot up. "You mean donations. Offerings. We have always been happy to share with our fellow temples. These *gifts* are not something we owe, but something we give freely."

"No, woman, I mean tribute," he snarled, taking a step forward, cracking his knuckles. His companions shifted forward as well. "We will allow you to make the next payment at the usual time. But after that, we will require tribute four times a year rather than two."

Aria shook her head. "We cannot afford that, Mopsos. We receive less and less every year. The people do not come to the temple the way they used to."

"That is not my problem." He fingered the dagger at his belt. "I will see to the tribute personally from now on. My associates and I will ensure that the amount is acceptable."

"Oh, you will?" Aria said, refusing to be cowed.

"You understand," he seethed, "that your little temple is safe only because we choose for it to be so. You still sit in that chair only because we allow it. Perhaps I should find out if Hedamos was telling the truth about how much you like to fight before giving in. I like it when they fight," he sniggered.

He took another step toward the dais, his hand wrapped around the hilt of his dagger. His companions moved forward, flanking him. Aria drew back in her seat just as the three men jerked and cried out. Aria's temple guards, called in by the priestess at the door, had grasped the men from behind, twisting their arms and holding them in place.

"You old whore!" Mopsos shouted, fighting against the guard who held him.

"You will behave yourself in my audience hall," Aria snarled, "in my temple, and in my city." She rose from her seat. "Or you will not be welcome here. Is that understood?"

Mopsos jerked his chin up, a look of defiance on his face.

"You will go now," Aria said, her voice ringing with authority.

"We will be back at the Full Moon, and those wagons had better be loaded to the brim," he snarled, tugging against the guard's grip. "May Zeus put you and your infernal goddesses in your place!"

She nodded to the guards, who frog-marched the three men out of the audience chamber. Then she motioned to one of the priests, who approached the dais.

"Have the guards follow Mopsos and his men out onto the road," she said to the priest. "Ensure that they leave the city and do not turn back around when they think we are no longer watching."

The priest hastened from the room, and Aria slumped down in her seat, her heart pounding. She ran her palm across her face, then held her hand out in front of her and realized that it was trembling. Unable to force her mind to work, she sat there for some time, wondering vaguely how such things had come to pass. She could find nothing she had done wrong, nothing Ida's children anywhere on the island had done to deserve this sort of treatment.

At last she could sit still no longer. She rose from her seat, dismissed the clergy from the audience hall with her thanks, and wandered out into the north court. The midday sunshine was a balm, warm on her face and shoulders. At least the Sun-Mother had not deserted her people the way she did in the time of Great

Darkness.

"There you are."

Aria turned to see the Consort striding toward her. "Beli," she sighed.

He crossed the court to stand before her, taking hold of her hands. "My Lady, my Beloved," he said. "The men told me what happened. Are you all right?"

She shook her head. "Mopsos did not touch me... but he threatened."

"I cannot decide whether it would have been better or worse, had I still been there in the hall with you."

She leaned up against him, and he slid his arms around her. His warmth added to the sunshine, reminding her that there was still good and comfort in the world, regardless of what Mopsos and his cronies might try to do.

"Not better or worse," she sighed, "just different. We cannot keep Knossos at bay forever."

They stood together in the sunshine for a while as Aria allowed herself to relax, safe in Beli's arms, at least for a time. When she finally stepped back, he narrowed his eyes at her.

"Our relations with Knossos have changed."

She nodded. "We had best sit down and discuss what can be done to protect our people."

As they turned to go back into the building, the door that led out to the Sea Road opened, and a woman stumbled into the north court, a heavy bag slung over her shoulder.

"My Lady," she said, a little breathless, dropping her bag by her feet. She shook the dust off her skirt and made the salute, though it was obvious from her posture that the effort tired her when she was already exhausted.

Aria hurried over to her with Beli by her side. "Psoreia!" she cried, embracing the woman. "I did not know you planned to visit."

"I am not visiting," she said, looking over her shoulder toward the doorway she had just come through. Her face betrayed anxiety, even fear. "I am returning to my home temple. Please, My Lady, I seek sanctuary."

Aria drew in a sharp breath. "Of course." She looked her visitor up and down. "Let us get you cleaned up and fed. Then we can talk."

A short while later Aria, Beli, and Psoreia sat in Aria's workroom, a platter of bread, cheese, and fruit and a jug of beer on the table between them. Beli poured beer for all of them, and they began to pick at the food, all three of them too anxious to have much appetite. Psoreia had washed and changed into clean clothing, but she looked exhausted, and her face was still lined with worry.

Aria reached over and touched her hand. "Tell us what has happened."

"Knossos has taken over the cave," Psoreia said. "An awful man named Mopsos. He and his men have—" She ran a hand through her hair. "They have taken all the gold and silver furnishings from the shrine, all the sacred objects, and replaced them with simple earthenware ones."

Beli shook his head. "I am sorry. They do not understand where real value lies."

"And they have brought men who stay there and guard the cave."

"Men?" Aria cried. "In residence at Eileithyia's cave?"

"Yes. Not priests, but guards. They rifle through all the offerings people bring and take anything valuable. They leave the shrine with nothing."

"How..."

"By force," Psoreia said, choking back a sob. "When I spoke up the first time, they took my young priestesses away and replaced them with women from Knossos who do not even know the rites. I had to teach them everything."

"You spoke up more than once," Beli said, admiration in his voice.

"Of course I did. But the next time, the guards... they were rough with me, threatened to lie with me against my wishes." Her voice dropped to a whisper. "They used the other priestesses, the ones from Knossos, that way all the time. The women did not dare speak out against them."

Beli sprang up from his seat, his hands clenched into fists. "How can we allow this to happen?"

"What can we do to stop it?" Psoreia said, her voice tired, defeated. "We have no army."

Aria cursed under her breath. "And nothing with which to pay an army, even if we had one." She took a slow drink of her beer, thinking. "What about the ships' guards? The traders pay them to keep the pirates at bay. They have training in these sorts of matters."

"Then who would guard the ships?" Beli asked. "You know as well as I do that word would get around. Knossos would send their own fleet out to attack our ships."

Aria reached her hand out to Beli. Reluctantly, he grasped it and took his seat again. She could feel the tension in him, the anger that threatened to boil over. She knew that anger herself, but right now they needed clear heads if they were to work toward a solution to their problems.

She and Beli spent a short while discussing possible resources for military forces, or at least a greater guard than the temple already had. As distasteful as the idea was to Aria, it was less repellant than being taken over wholesale by the powers at Knossos. While they spoke, Psoreia sat silent, turning her cup around in her hands. At last, Aria and Beli both conceded that there were no reasonable sources of protection for their temple and city, not unless they could find more income somewhere. And with Knossos pressing against their trading relations, there was little chance of that.

With a weary sigh, Aria leaned her elbows on the table, rubbing the crease between her eyebrows. She looked over at Psoreia, prepared to ask her opinion in the matter, but was taken aback at the expression on the priestess's face.

"There is more you have not told us," Aria said, apprehension clear in her voice.

Psoreia drained her cup and dropped it on the table. "You do not want to hear this, but you need to know." Aria nodded for her to continue. "I had to sneak away from the cave shrine in the middle of the night. Otherwise, the guards would have stopped me."

"I am not surprised," Aria said, bitterness rising in her. "What they cannot get through deviousness and manipulation, they retain by force."

"I feared to travel by night. The Moon was out, but so were the marauders."

"We have heard," Beli said, "that the roads are quite dangerous by night these days."

Psoreia nodded. "I only went as far as Nirou Khani last night. My Lady," she said, "they are having serious troubles there."

Aria resisted the urge to clasp her head in her hands. "Tell me."

"At the sacred house, they have had to block up all but one of the doorways on the ground floor. At the one remaining doorway, they have set up a guardroom. One of the younger priests mans it."

"Are they subject to thieving?" Beli asked.

Psoreia stared into her cup, avoiding his gaze. "It is not the gold the offenders are after, at least, not anymore. Nirou Khani has little enough wealth to begin with, especially these days when Knossos takes so much from them."

"Then what?" Beli tilted his head, confused.

"The women."

Beli's hands balled into fists again. This time, Aria joined him in outrage, slamming her hand on the table. "These people are evil!" Psoreia jumped at the sudden sound. "Oh, my dear sister," Aria said, "I am sorry. You are already worn out from facing these horrors yourself." A terrible thought suddenly occurred to her. "They have not touched you, have they?"

"No," Psoreia said. "I arrived after they had blocked the doors and set the guard. But before that—" She swallowed hard. "I spoke with one of their priestesses, who told me about travelers—men— who would come east from Knossos along the Coast Road."

"Seeking shelter? The sacred houses have always offered accommodation to travelers." She paused. "Though an offering of some sort is expected." Poor wayfarers typically helped out in the kitchens or with simple labor in the workshops or fields, while wealthier ones presented goods of some sort in gratitude for the hospitality. No one was ever turned away, no matter how poor they might be, but no guest would dare steal or harm their hosts. Not until now.

"Seeking..." Psoreia blinked back tears. "At first, some of them asked to stay the night, but Nestia told me they were looking for entertainment, not shelter. They attacked the priestesses, acted as if they were slaves for the having."

Aria reached out and squeezed Psoreia's hand. "I do not understand these men. There are brothels in all the cities, with men and women who will happily provide those services for the proper fee—though of course they may also turn away anyone they do not trust to treat them well. And there are still the seasonal festivals, are there not? Why would any man need to use force to obtain sex?" She ruthlessly pushed down the memories of Hedamos in the storage room.

"I understand them," Beli hissed. "They believe women and slaves are property, not real humans, not worth respecting. They do not ask for consent, and they do not pay. They take what they want, like animals."

Psoreia refilled her cup, her hand shaking so badly that the beer splashed onto the table. "At Nirou Khani, they have built strong doors that they bolt at night. I was lucky they recognized me and let me in. They no longer accept lay people as guests, and Nestia told me they have had to turn away priests from Knossos as well due to their behavior. She fears they may have to hire a professional guard if things keep up as they have been, though how they will pay for a guard, I do not know."

Chapter 56

"My Lady!" Rhea cried out as Aria stepped into the corridor from her workroom.

Aria turned to see Rhea grappling with a young man, one of the temple's messengers, some distance down the corridor. She rushed toward the pair just as Rhea tugged a small roll of papyrus from the young man's hands.

"What in the Mother's name is going on?" Aria said.

Just then, Thalamika appeared in the doorway of her scribal workroom. Rhea and the messenger had been standing just outside, in the corridor.

"That is mine," Thalamika said, reaching for the scroll. Rhea snatched it away from the Chief Scrivener and pushed it into Aria's hands.

"I have discovered our traitor," Rhea said, glowering at Thalamika.

"What?" Fingering the scroll, Aria looked back and forth between the two women. Then she realized that the messenger was slowly shifting away. She gripped him by the sleeve and drew him back over. "You will stay right here." She looked at Rhea, puzzled. "You cannot mean..."

"I will tell you everything, but I want witnesses this time. Lots of witnesses."

"Let us all go to the audience chamber, and we will sort this out."

Thalamika folded her arms across her chest. "I have work to do here. She is mistaken again, and I do not have time for this." She set her jaw but would not look Aria in the eye.

The cold, sinking feeling in the pit of her stomach told Aria more than she wanted to know. She shifted so that she and Rhea were blocking Thalamika's way out of the workroom. Then she called across the corridor, to one of the other workrooms. Two priests appeared in the doorway.

"Please assist us," she said. "I have said that Thalamika and this messenger must go to the audience hall, but I fear they are disinclined to obey."

The two men stepped over to the group, and the messenger held his hands up in surrender. "I go willingly. I have only done my job, nothing more. I do not know what is in the scroll. I cannot read."

"And you?" Aria narrowed her eyes at her Chief Scrivener.

"I told you, I do not have time for such interruptions. There is important work I must attend to."

"It will wait."

Aria motioned, and the two priests moved over to where Thalamika stood, flanking her and taking hold of her elbows. She tried to shake them off, but at Aria's orders, they propelled the priestess out into the corridor and down to the audience hall. The messenger followed while Rhea and Aria walked behind the group, keeping an eye on them all.

Along the way, Aria sent a servant to notify Beli and the other temple clergy as well as some of the guards. If Rhea had truly found the conspirator, Aria wanted the whole priesthood to stand in witness. That way, there would be no rumors, no misunderstandings. And if Rhea was wrong, if Thalamika was innocent, she wanted that witnessed as well. But her gut told her that Rhea was not mistaken, not this time.

By the time Aria took her seat on the dais, the audience hall was beginning to fill and the Consort had taken his place beside her. His presence was a comfort and a reassurance, especially since she had no inkling how this situation would play out. She looked out at the faces, her people, the clergy who were still loyal to the old ways — except for those who were not. Though some of the onlookers were waiting silently, more of them were talking with each other in low voices and shooting skeptical glances at Rhea and Aria.

Gathering herself, Aria raised a hand, and the hall fell silent. The priests and priestesses all made the salute, Thalamika included, though her thunderous expression belied the respect the gesture implied. The messenger belatedly raised his fist to his forehead, glancing around nervously.

"My people," Aria said, her voice sounding more confident than she felt, "we are here today to witness the testimony of the Head of the College of Priestesses, the Chief Scrivener, and this messenger." Her gaze swept the assembly. "This is a place of truth, not of rumors. We will discover what has happened so everyone may know. Where there has been no wrongdoing, there will be no punishment, either here or among your ranks." Several of the clergy shifted uneasily as she sought them out and met their gazes. "And now the Head of the College of Priestesses will tell us what she has seen."

"My Lady," Rhea said, stepping forward. "I was in the dining hall when I overheard this messenger speaking with two of the men from the stonecarver's workshop. He was complaining about how often Thalamika sends him to Knossos, and saying that she had summoned him again today with another message to carry." Thalamika shifted forward as if to speak, but Aria raised a hand and gestured for Rhea to continue. The Chief Scrivener held her place, her mouth pressed into a thin, hard line. "He was showing off his scars from fighting off a bandit in Knossos," Rhea said, tilting her head toward the messenger, who was staring down at his feet, doing his best to melt back into the assembled group. "When he left the dining hall, I followed him to the scribal workroom, where Thalamika gave him that scroll to carry to Knossos." She pointed to the papyrus that Aria was still clutching.

Aria looked at the messenger. "Has she spoken the truth?" He cowered, looking around like a cornered rabbit. "Come now, young man, if you have only done your job, you will be in no trouble," Aria said, her voice a little softer. "Please speak."

She motioned for him to come forward. He took two shaky steps, then half-turned back toward the gathered crowd.

"Speak to me, young man," Aria said.

He turned back toward her and swallowed. "I—yes, she told the truth," he said, his voice quavering.

"How often does Thalamika send you to Knossos with written messages rather than oral ones?" Aria asked.

He glanced back over his shoulder at the Chief Scrivener, who offered him an encouraging smile. "Not that often," he said, looking down at his feet.

"I see," Aria said. "How many times since the last Full Moon?"

Again the young man glanced back at Thalamika.

"You do not need her guidance," Aria said, "unless you need help making up a story. Now tell me the truth."

"Four times since the last Full Moon," the young man said, the words tumbling out all in a rush.

Gasps sounded around the hall, and one or two voices murmured, then fell silent. Aria felt Beli's hand on her shoulder, and she realized how tense she had grown. She let out a slow breath, calming herself according to her training. Beli gave her shoulder a squeeze, then his hand lifted from her. Right away she missed the warmth, the connection. Now she was alone again, with a temple full of people counting on her to handle this situation well and not make matters worse.

"We must not jump to conclusions," Aria said. "It sometimes falls to our Chief Scrivener to maintain communication with the other temples. And it is sometimes appropriate to send written scrolls, for security, rather than speaking the message to the messenger and having him speak it to the recipient. Especially in these difficult times. So there may be a perfectly innocent explanation for this." She held up the scroll, now creased from being clutched tightly in her fist. "The way to find out is simple: we read it."

Aria broke the seal and unrolled the small piece of papyrus. She held it up so the gathered witnesses could see that it did, indeed, have a message written on it. As she lowered it, she caught Thalamika's eye. The Chief Scrivener stared back, a look of stubborn defiance on her face, and Aria's stomach lurched. She swallowed hard and pasted a dispassionate look on her face. Then she held the papyrus out at arm's length, since her eyes were not as strong as they had been when she was younger.

"Greetings to esteemed Glymenos," she read out. Hisses and murmurs ran through the crowd. "The donations are down again, but the storerooms still contain gold, silver, and stones. I will send you specific locations soon. I am still unable to obtain the formula for bronze from our Malian smiths, but I will continue trying and send it as soon as I can. There are some within the priesthood who can be turned to your support. May Zeus himself bless you."

Voices erupted around the hall. Some of the clergy surged forward, making for Thalamika, but the two priests who were holding her moved to protect her.

"Enough!" Aria shouted. The room fell silent, with men and women glancing around in suspicion and glaring openly at the Chief Scrivener. "Thalamika," Aria called, "what do you have to say for yourself?"

Thalamika stepped forward and shook herself loose from the priests, who continued to stand on either side of her, close enough to grab her again should she attempt to flee. "I am an old woman," she began, her voice far more feeble than normal. Though she was a good deal older than Aria, Thalamika was still in robust health. "I have been misled, I fear, corrupted by one of our priests." Whispers ran through the crowd. "Odrys." Aria recognized the name, a part-time priest of mainlander heritage who lived in Malia. She could not recall whether he had any family in Knossos. "He has twisted my thoughts so I no longer know what is right or wrong." She wrung her hands, glancing sidelong at her fellow clergy. But none of them were swayed by her act any more than Aria was. They all knew her too well.

"Is Odrys here?" Aria asked, gazing out over the assembly.

"He is not, My Lady." Lexion stepped forward. "He only comes on days when we need him for the rites."

"Very well." Aria thought a moment. "Lexion, please send two of our temple guards, plus one of your priests who knows Odrys by sight, to find him in the city as quickly as possible and bring him back here." Lexion gave a quick bow, then slipped back through the crowd and out the doors. "In the meantime, Thalamika, you will remain in your private quarters."

"How dare you!" the older priestess cried. "I am doing what is best for our temple, so we can be glorious!" She tried to shift back into the crowd, but the people pressed against her, denying her a path, and the two priests took hold of her arms once again.

While Thalamika continued to shout protests, Aria called two of the guards over. She instructed them to escort Thalamika back to her room and stand guard lest she decide to leave. Rhea agreed to ensure that Thalamika's meals were brought to her on time and that she had plenty of water and linens for her comfort. Then Aria dismissed the crowd.

"Return to your duties," she admonished them. "There will be time for gossip in the dining hall. In the meantime, we still have a temple to run. I will call you again as soon as there is more to share."

The hall emptied quickly, the clergy not wishing to have their High Priestess see them gossiping. When everyone was gone, Aria leaned back in her chair and heaved a great sigh. Beli knelt next to her and took her hands.

"You make me proud to be your Consort," he said quietly, lifting her hand to his lips and kissing her knuckles.

"You may not be so proud of me soon," she muttered. "If they have truly done the things it appears they have, you know what punishment I must set down."

Chapter 57

"How many others do you think there are, my Beloved?" Aria asked.

She and the Consort sat in her private quarters, worn out but not yet finished with what had to be done. The guards had brought Odrys in from the city after Thalamika's appearance in the audience hall the previous day. Word had reached the part-time priest that they were looking for him, and he had gone down to one of the harborside taverns, hoping to hide among the crowd there. But the guards had found him, and the priest Aria had sent along with the guards had identified him with certainty.

Once Odrys was back at the temple, facing Aria on the dais with the whole of the temple's clergy watching him, he admitted freely to everything he had done: rifling through the storerooms and ritual chambers to count the valuables, cajoling and eventually bribing some of the temple's smiths in a series of failed attempts to obtain their recipe for bronze. But he insisted that everything he had done had been at Thalamika's behest. She came from an old Malian family, powerful merchants and high-ranking priesthood, while he was a simple man, the son of farmers who had moved from the countryside to Malia during his childhood in order to begin a small business in woodcarving. He was swayed by Thalamika's authority, he insisted, indoctrinated into her way of thinking against his will, and was innocent of any real wrongdoing.

After his testimony, the audience hall had erupted in madness, the clergy shouting for his execution, surging toward him with a hatred Aria had rarely seen within the walls of her temple. She was glad she had left Thalamika under guard in her quarters. Had the Chief Scrivener also been in the audience hall, Aria feared the handful of guards might not have been enough to hold back the swelling animosity of the priesthood. Ultimately, the guards had to spirit Odrys out of the room in order to maintain his safety. He had spent the night in the guest quarters, with a pair of guards at his door and another outside to ensure he did not climb out the window under cover of darkness.

Feeling completely out of her depth, Aria had called on the people she trusted for counsel. Rhea and Lexion had stayed with her in the audience hall most of the afternoon to discuss the situation. Then Sageleus and Ytanos had arrived, offering information about Odrys and his family as well as all the latest rumors and gossip about Knossos from the port. Finally, Beli had drawn Aria from her seat, insisting that she eat and get some rest. They had avoided the dining hall and the press of questions that would surely have surrounded them there, and had taken the evening meal in Aria's workroom, where they had talked over the events of the day until Aria's head swam. Now she sat with her Consort at the small table in her private quarters, their breakfast untouched after a sleepless night.

"I do not think there are others," Beli said. "At least, no others who would go to the lengths these two have."

Aria turned her cup around and around, thinking. "Odrys has no personal ties to Knossos. His parents' farm was halfway between the two cities, or so I am told, but they followed our ways even though they were mainlanders. He oversees the apprentices in their shop when he is not here for his priestly duties. And he performs his work here well."

"So he is not really a supporter of their ways?"

"He is an opportunist, I think. He can see how the world is changing and wants to be in favor at Knossos should they..." She took a gulp of wine, willing away the vision that had reared up in her mind, the image of Malia burning.

"I suspect there are some who will roll over and offer their bellies, if it ever comes to that."

"And some who would force us to roll over, if they could," she spat.

Beli set a hand on top of hers. "Most of the clergy are loyal, and you know that. They are as stubborn as you are." She let a brief smile flicker. Beli knew her stubbornness more intimately than most, endured it more patiently than any other. "And they love you almost as much as I do."

"But there will always be those who want to hedge their bets. Or who have their own agendas."

She stood up and crossed to the window. The Sun had risen on a beautiful day, with birdsong and gentle breezes to taunt Aria as she grappled with the darkness that threatened to take over her world. She turned back to Beli, who was still seated at the table.

"I must determine how to handle these traitors. I must make a decision that is fair and that dissuades any others from attempting similar actions."

"You have known all along what you must do," he said softly. "It was not indecision that kept you awake all night."

* * *

This time, Aria did more than just notify her own clergy. She sent criers out into the city as well. And at Beli's suggestion, she moved the venue from the audience hall to the central courtyard. That had turned out to be a wise choice. The courtyard was as full as it had ever been for any anointing or seasonal rite.

Aria stood on the top step at the front of the loggia with her Consort at her side. She looked out over the crowd and saw every single one of her clergy, including the part-timers, as well as most of the temple's artisans and workers. She saw, as well, many townsfolk, from ordinary laborers to wealthy artisans and merchants. Among them stood Sageleus, Ytanos, and Yassib, looking to her for guidance, just like everyone else who had packed into the courtyard on this fine spring morning.

Aria offered silent thanks that she had called in all the guards and positioned them between the crowd and the loggia. When Thalamika and Odrys were brought out from a nearby doorway to stand on the lower loggia steps, the mass of people pressed forward, shouting obscenities and threatening to kill them then and there. The guards found themselves standing shoulder to shoulder, pushed to their physical limits to hold the angry onlookers back.

The crowd was rowdy, the people talking and shouting and continuing to press against the guards. Concerned that the gathering would soon get out of hand, Aria gave the signal and three blasts of a triton trumpet rang out from the back of the loggia, the sign that this was not just any gathering, but a sacred one. The High Priestess' word was law. The people fell silent and waited for Aria to speak.

She raised her arms in the gesture that turned her from a mere woman into the goddess incarnate. The whole gathered assembly made the salute, holding it in silence until she lowered her arms and drew breath to speak.

"My people," she called out. "We have gathered here today under unfortunate circumstances." She motioned toward Thalamika and Odrys, and all of a sudden the words she had intended to say fled from her mind, leaving only a grieving blankness. The two traitors' faces held no sign of regret or remorse, only resentment and wrath.

Aria looked out across the sea of people, all of them waiting, hanging on her words, expecting her to make things right for them. But the world was right no longer, she feared. All she could do was stave off the inevitable for a short while.

"This priestess and this priest," she said at last, "Chief Scrivener Thalamika and priest Odrys, have betrayed our temple and our people." Aria expected the crowd to shout and cry out, but instead they remained silent. This was a holy rite in a sacred space. No matter how angry they were, they would respect her and their people's ways. Instead of feeling relief at the realization, Aria felt the pressure of responsibility, of generations of High Priestesses who looked up from the World Below to see how she handled this trouble. In the end, there was only one way she could handle it: with honesty, no matter how much that pained her.

"My people, I must tell you, this has never happened before in living memory or in the tales of the generations. No man or woman among Ida's children has dared to deceive and betray their own people in this way." She swallowed. "These two have broken my trust. They have been disloyal to me personally as well as to the temple and the people of Malia. Thalamika was my teacher. I looked up to her." She glanced over at the Chief Scrivener, who tilted her chin up defiantly and refused to meet Aria's eye. "I recommended Odrys to our College of Priests myself after he petitioned me for initiation." The part-time priest kept his gaze resolutely on his sandals now, his hands twisting his tunic-cord into knots.

Aria shot a sidelong glance at Beli, who gave her an encouraging look. She felt a trickle of sweat drip down the side of her face and determined to get this over with. Dragging it out would not make it any less painful.

"Thalamika and Odrys," she said, "have assisted some people from Knossos in plans to thieve valuables from our temple, sacred objects from our shrines and storerooms. The punishment for thievery is recompense for the stolen items, plus reparations in case any of them have been desecrated. If the thief cannot pay, the payment may be worked off in servitude to the temple."

The crowd shifted, people shooting glances back and forth, but no one dared to speak.

"However," Aria continued, "these two have done something far worse as well. They have conspired to steal our temple's formula for bronze and give it to those at Knossos. This recipe is the secret to our blades' reputation wherever our traders go. It is the strength of our trade, our wealth, our glory."

Aria pressed her hands against her sides, fighting the urge to fidget, and drew herself up to her full height.

"There is only one punishment for divulging our bronze

formula to outsiders."

Whispers snaked through the crowd. The guards just below Aria dashed to the side, and Aria realized that Thalamika had attempted to flee, taking the opportunity when the people were distracted. But there was nowhere she could go. A guard blocked the doorway behind her and the crowd pressed in at her front. Cursing under her breath, she writhed against the guards' grip as they held her in place. Aria steeled herself to complete her task.

"These two will be exposed on the mountain to the south. Their blood will not be spilled, for they are neither sacred nor sacrifices. They will receive no burial. Their remains will not be retrieved, but will be left for the wild things."

At this, Odrys began shrieking, crying out his innocence and struggling to get loose from the guards. Murmurs ran through the crowd as the people grew restless, ready for justice to be served. With a quick glance at the Consort for confidence, Aria raised her arms up once again in the goddess pose, and the crowd fell silent.

"The High Priestess has spoken!" she cried out. The triton trumpet sounded three blasts.

Aria directed the guards to take Thalamika and Odrys back into the building, out of sight of the crowd. The people milled around in the courtyard, talking and peering at the doorway where the two offenders had disappeared.

"You will disperse," the Consort called out. "Go back to your homes and your families. Go back to your jobs and your temple duties."

In the end, it took the guards herding people toward the entryways to clear the courtyard. Aria grasped Beli's hand for courage, and together they walked into the room where the guards were holding Thalamika and Odrys. She found Rhea, Orestas, and one of the younger priests waiting there as well.

"We will do the deed," Rhea said. "It should not be the responsibility of the laymen." She tilted her head toward the guards.

Aria watched as the guards bound and gagged the two condemned clergy. Odrys struggled some, but Thalamika stood tall and proud, a scowl darkening her face.

"Glymenos will destroy you," she snarled at Aria before the guards could finish gagging her.

Aria and the others followed as the guards escorted the prisoners out to a waiting wagon. Instead of following the Sea Road toward the coast, they would travel south down the road that led to Mt. Dikte. But they would stop before they reached the cave shrine.

"I know the place," Orestas said. "The mountaintop north of Karphi. The legends say that is where our ancestors took the condemned, tying them down to the large boulders there." He squinted toward the mountains in the distance. "There is still snow in the higher regions. They will not suffer long." He caught Aria's gaze and held it, sharing an understanding: punishment was one thing. It need not be protracted torture.

Loaded with the condemned, the guards, and the clergy, the wagon began its creaking journey southward. Aria watched it go, wrapping her arms around her middle. She did not cry, and that bothered her. She waited and waited for the feeling of remorse, but it did not come.

"You did what you had to," Beli said, steering her back into the temple.

"I wish the gods would not put me in the position of having to do such things."

"I think," Beli said with one last glance toward the wagon that was disappearing into the distance, "it is not the gods who have done this to us."

Chapter 58

"Come, let me help you bathe," Beli said.

Tired almost to exhaustion, Aria dragged herself over to the small terracotta bathtub in the corner of her private quarters. She was naked, having left the blood-soaked cowhide skirt spread out on a table in the storage room to dry. She would go back and fold it onto a shelf in a day or two.

She stepped into the tub, sat down, and began scrubbing the blood off her chest and arms with a sea-sponge. As she washed, Beli poured water from a pitcher to rinse her skin. The cool liquid refreshed her, a welcome relief from the summer heat. She felt like more than just the blood of the sacrificial bull was being cleared away.

She was finally sleeping well again. Though she had appointed one of her trusted priests, an accomplished scribe, as Chief Scrivener shortly after Thalamika's execution, her nights had continued to be troubled for some time. Whether sleep was now coming because her thoughts were calmer, or simply because she was weary in body and soul, she did not care to examine too closely.

"You are counting the years," he said as she stood up and stepped out of the tub.

She turned to look at the layer of bloody water that remained after her bath. "Every Summer Solstice that I slay a bull is one year closer to the day I must do the same to you."

She took the linen towel that he offered and began to dry herself off.

"Another will come after me," he said.

"I know. But though he will be Belisseus, he will not be you."

She sat down on the edge of her bed, picking at the trim on the tunic she had laid out to wear. Too many thoughts crowded her head. She had come to rely on this Consort, to lean on him more than the previous one. She trusted him, shared things with him that she dared not speak to anyone else. With a start, she realized she had fallen in love with him in a way she had not done with any other man, not even Sageleus. What would she do when he was gone and the threat of Knossos still loomed?

Beli sat down beside her. "Glymenos worries you."

"Of course he worries me," she snapped, then regretted her tone. She gentled her voice as best she could, fighting the wave of emotion that the Knossian leader's name always raised in her. "That message he sent after Thalamika and Odrys..." The words caught in her throat.

"He had no right to make those demands."

The message had arrived less than a Moon after Aria had sent Thalamika and Odrys to their deaths on the mountaintop. Glymenos had insisted that Aria had no right to pass judgment over people who were working for him, even if they were clergy in Aria's temple. He had demanded that whenever any situation involving Knossos occurred in the future, she send the people to him for judgment, even if they were Aria's own priests and priestesses. Though the message had not stated it outright, the implication was clear: if Aria interfered with Knossos' ambitions again, her own life would be in danger.

"Do you really think they have someone within this temple who would attack me? Take me down, if Glymenos ordered it?"

He lifted the tunic from her grip and helped her slip it on. "I doubt it. I think, if he had as much power as he blusters on about, he would have taken us over already."

413

"I suppose so," she said, not really believing him.

"Aria, he is all threats. His sails are full of the wrong kind of wind."

She huffed out a laugh at the play on words, but they both knew Glymenos was far more dangerous than a bout of intestinal vapors.

"I have just hired more guards," she said. "They are placing quite a strain on our resources, but I do not think we can do without them."

"Do you mistrust them?"

She thought a moment. "No. I have been careful to select men who have relations among our clergy, so they have a personal stake in the safety of the temple. I was able to recruit a few of the skilled ones who used to guard the ships, but who are old enough that they prefer a less adventurous occupation now, a life closer to home."

"But some of them live here now," he said, gesturing to show that he meant the temple itself and not the larger city.

"Yes. We need at least a few of them within the temple walls at all times. And of course, they take their meals here..." Her voice trailed off, tired.

"We will find a way to pay them and feed them for as long as we need them, My Lady."

Standing, she wrapped her skirt around her hips and tied the cords. "We cannot go back to the way things were before the mainlanders came, and you know it. The guards are here to stay. I fear there is no one left whom I can trust." She stroked a finger down his jaw. "Except you."

They sat down at the little table. Beli poured her some wine while Aria dug a spoon into a bowl of goat stew. She had long since grown used to fasting before rituals. A lifetime of priestessing had taught her stomach not to fight the practice. But the Summer Solstice sacrifice was always hard for her, more so these days. By the time it was over each year, the hunger gnawed at her. She knew it was not really the lack of food that ate away at her gut. But she had to function, had to stand strong against the press of change that threatened to destroy the ways her people had followed for so many generations. If the traditions were lost, if the Mothers were no longer the focus of worship, would the people even be Ida's children anymore?

"Tell me what you are thinking," she said at last when Beli had been gazing at her across the table for some time.

"I am not the only one you can trust."

"Who else?"

"Rhea and Lexion, of course." He took a drink of water, eschewing the wine and the stew since he was fasting for the Dawn-Fire Rite the next morning. "Sageleus. Ytanos."

"That is only four people, and only two of them in the temple."

He shrugged. "That may be all you need."

"Vanadia," Aria added when she remembered her friend at Knossos. The priestess' messages had become less frequent over time, but still they came every now and then, confirming what Aria already knew: that Glymenos and his cronies wished to destroy the island's way of life, destroy the hospitality and the sharing and the compassion and replace them with brutality and domineering power.

"Should we..." She blew out a breath. "I have been thinking about whether we should stop initiating new clergy. Except, perhaps, for those born in the temple. But not outsiders."

"Even if they are from Malia?"

"Yes. That way, we can be more certain of their loyalty."

"I do not think that will solve the problem."

She leaned back, crossing her arms over her chest. "Why not?"

"What if Thalamika and Odrys were not the only ones? What if there are others?"

She shook her head. "No. I cannot—"

"We do not know how much of a network Glymenos and his people have developed, within our temple or any other sacred house on this island. There will always be people who are tempted by the flattery and bribes he offers."

A chill shot down Aria's spine. "We have long shared clergy from one temple to another. For so many generations, it was our strength, the bond that held us all together."

"I do not like to think that it might be a weakness."

"But it is, my Beloved. Just as the sharing of food and goods among the temples has become a weakness."

"That is only because Glymenos has twisted it into something perverse." He gave her a pointed look.

She rubbed her temples, her face creased with discomfort. "We cannot stop him from distorting our ways into awful practices," she groaned.

"You are in pain." He reached out and closed a warm hand around her wrist. "You have been having headaches."

"What do you expect, with all the horrors I must face every day?" She took a long drink of wine, but it did not help. It never did anymore.

Beli sat back and studied her. "I have watched you, my Beloved. These headaches are more and more frequent. But I do not think they are because of the mainlanders, not exactly."

"What else is there?" she said, but she avoided his gaze, peering into her cup instead.

"You are suppressing your visions."

Her head tipped up, and she glared at him. "What if I am?"

"I do not blame you for not wanting to see what lies ahead. But if closing yourself off is hurting you..."

"I am tired," she sighed, standing up and crossing to the bed. "I do not wish to think about this right now."

He joined her, and they lay down together, his arms wrapped protectively around her. "Perhaps your visions could help us determine how best to deal with our problems."

She shook her head. "We cannot change our fate. Once we are tangled in Arachne's web, we cannot escape."

"Then at least we can be prepared for whatever might befall us."

She nestled up against him. "Just for now, I would rather not see what lies ahead. Will you grant me these few moments of peace?"

He kissed her forehead and held her tight as exhaustion dragged her down into a fitful sleep.

Chapter 59

"I will guard you," Rhea said, positioning herself outside the door to the ritual chamber. "I promise, you will not be interrupted."

"Thank you," Aria said, swallowing down a lump in her throat. It bothered her that she felt the need to call on her dearest friend to stand guard while she and Beli undertook a private rite. But there was no one else she trusted enough. The ritual she was about to undertake was sacred. In the past, no one would have dared walk in on the High Priestess and her Consort, or anyone else performing a private ceremony, for that matter.

But Aria no longer felt safe in her own temple. No one had yet breached a sacred space during a rite. But if there were spies in the temple, people working for Glymenos to bring her down, she did not know what they might do. No one guarded the entrances to the building. Clergy and lay people alike came and went as they pleased all day long. The only way for her to feel safe enough to undertake this journey was to have Rhea standing there.

"What have we come to, that we must set a guard on the door of the ritual chamber?" she said, shaking her head, as she sprinkled incense on the coals in the brazier.

Beli set a hand on her shoulder, and she let out a breath, realizing that her heart had been pounding. Now her heartbeat slowed, her body relaxing under Beli's protective touch. Nothing would happen to her while he was here. He would give his life before he let anyone harm her, of that she was certain.

She knelt down and bent over the brazier, inhaling the earthy-sweet incense smoke as the heat from the coals crinkled the skin on her face and chest. This was a familiar act, something she had done more times than she could count in her years as a priestess, both before and after she had taken this office. She continued to breathe deeply until she began to feel light-headed. Then she reached her hand out so Beli could help her stand up. In silence he led her down into the adyton.

She lay down on a blanket there, feeling the stone floor beneath her pressing against her hips and shoulders, solid and stable. The temple was built out of blocks of the island, the Great Mother's body formed into the shape of the people's sacred practices. She lived and worked inside this container made of the Great Mother herself. She pressed her palms against the floor, making a connection with the stone, with Ida, the Mother of her people.

She looked up at Beli, who was kneeling next to her. "Do you think this will help?"

"We cannot know until we do it."

He raised a sistrum and began a slow double beat, a heartbeat rhythm that rattled and hissed, the sound snaking through the darkness. The light from the lamp that burned above in the main portion of the ritual room did not make its way down into the adyton very well, so it made little difference when Aria closed her eyes. Her heartbeat slowed to match the beat of the sistrum. She drew in a deep breath and let it out again, then allowed herself to float on the sound, the rattling beat carrying her along as if it were a giant serpent that she rode on, like a boat slithering over invisible waves.

Then the sound was gone, and she was standing in the familiar cave, the one she had visited so many times since the first Key-Bearer Rite during her year of training with Elli. Once again her bare feet pressed against the warm, soft ground. And there stood the Key-Bearer himself, tall and beautiful, his hand held out to her.

"I have been waiting for you," he said, his bell-like voice

reverberating through the cave as she approached him and took his hand, beseeching.

"I am desperate," she said. "We are... in trouble."

"All will be well."

He squeezed her hand, and all of a sudden they were standing in the ghostly version of her temple, the familiar corridor hazy and lined with closed doors. Golden threads ran back and forth between Aria, the Key-Bearer, and the doors, humming with tension, vibrating with life.

"Which door?" the Key-Bearer asked. That was always his question when she came here.

She thought a moment. When she had discussed this rite with Beli, he had suggested calling on the Daughter, since that was who she met in her very first Key-Bearer Rite. That had not felt quite right to Aria, but she had no better idea, so she had held that in her mind as she began the ritual. But now she felt she should make a different choice. She could not quite remember why, though she thought it had something to do with the moments right before she entered the cave.

"I call on the Great Mother Ida," she said, her voice firm and strong. "I wish to open your doorway."

A short distance down the corridor, a door began to glow. Aria moved to stand in front of it. She reached her hand out, pressing her palm flat against the door. Instantly she was standing on the other side, in the mouth of a cave, but not the same one she had been in moments earlier.

This cave was alive. It smelled of rich earth and cool water. Behind her, the space faded into blackness, feeling at once both tiny and vast in its darkness. In front of her, the cave mouth opened onto the mountains. She was high up, looking out across the jagged peaks that thrust up along the central portion of her island. Bare bones of snow striped the creases along the mountaintops as the wind whistled by.

"Great Mother?" she said, her voice little more than a whisper.

"I am here, my child," came the voice so deep and solid that Aria felt it in her bones as much as she heard it in her head.

"I need your help. We need your help, please, Great Lady. Our ways are under attack."

"And what do you wish me to do?"

"Can you..." Aria swallowed. "I think we are doing the rituals wrong. I think the ones we brought back after the time of Great Darkness are wrong. Or perhaps they are incomplete."

"You think that is so?" came the voice. "But they are not incomplete. They are not broken. They may not be exactly the same as the ones from before, but they are true for your time."

"Then how can so many things be going wrong?" She fought the urge to wring her hands.

"Tell me what is the matter, my child."

"The mainlanders are doing their best to destroy our ways, Great Lady," Aria said, frustrated that a being as powerful as a goddess could fail to see the problems her own children were experiencing. "They teach disrespect of women and children. They value greed and violence over sharing and compassion. I fear they will kill us all if we do not submit to their bidding. They are cruel and wicked."

"This is so. I have seen it."

"Then help me! Show me how to fix what has been broken. Show me the rites and ceremonies that will make them go away, back where they came from, and leave us alone."

Aria stood there in silence for several moments as the wind whistled by the cave entrance. She was sure the Great Mother had not left, for she still felt her presence. A vulture circled nearby then swooped close to the cave mouth before gliding off into the distance.

"That cannot be done," came the voice at last.

"What? No, please, Great Lady, you must help me."

"My child, you have been woven into this fabric, and you must follow the thread to its end. You cannot stop the process."

"But we are falling into darkness!"

"Yes, you are."

Chills ran down Aria's spine. "Then why will you not help?"

"I am helping," came the voice, calm and steady. "This is a

darkness that comes in cycles throughout the ages. You are not responsible for it. None of my children are. But you must endure it."

"If we had clung more strongly to the old ways..."

"That would not have stopped them. Pay attention now."

Aria looked out of the cave mouth, but instead of the view of her island's mountains, now she saw a vast prairie. Across the grassland rode a wave of men on horses, and she knew that these were the mainlanders' ancestors. Just as her people had come from the lands to the north so many generations ago, so the mainlanders also moved from one place to another over the ages. But where her ancestors had been quiet, agrarian people who shared their bounty with each other and blessed the Mothers, the mainlanders' ancestors were a warrior people, moving swiftly through the land and taking what they wanted. Now she saw the horsemen riding down into the mainlanders' territory, but there were no mainlanders there to begin with, only people like the ancestors of Ida's children. Aria cringed as she saw the horsemen setting fire to villages, killing the men and taking the women and children as concubines and slaves. When the vision finally cleared and she could once again see her island's mountains out of the cave mouth, Aria found herself sobbing, her arms wrapped around her middle.

"Why?" she croaked, sniffing back tears.

"It is their time now, for a while," came the voice. "But they will destroy themselves. I cannot tell you how long the darkness will last. That will depend on you mortals. But I can tell you that it will not be forever. It will end."

Aria swiped the back of her hand across her cheek, smearing the tears more than wiping them away. "What if our ways are destroyed? What if I cannot keep Glymenos and his men at bay?" She felt sick at the thought.

"Nothing is ever destroyed, just hidden for a time. You know that. It will all still be here, waiting to be discovered when people are ready for it again."

"And when will that be?" Aria said, wondering how she was expected to maintain the traditions under these circumstances.

Would she be a feeble old woman before Glymenos was finally gone?

"Have patience, my child. The worlds move at the pace of the gods, not of human lives."

And then Aria was back in the corridor, her palm pressed to the door. She drew her hand back and curled it into a fist.

"You must fight for us," she said to the Key-Bearer. "You are the Red Warrior. The Red Champion."

"I am not that kind of warrior, and you know it," he said, his voice soft.

"The world is crumbling around me," she said, struggling to maintain her composure. "How am I to go on if the gods have abandoned us?"

He touched her arm. "We have not abandoned you. We are right here with you. But the cycles of time are greater than we are. We cannot change them, only endure them."

"That is what the Great Mother said."

"And it is true."

Aria drew in a ragged breath and felt the stone floor pressing against her shoulders and hips. When she opened her eyes, she saw Beli leaning over her, silhouetted in the dim lamplight.

"They cannot help us," she said with a sob.

He reached over and took her hand. "Is that really what they told you?"

She shifted, raising herself up on her elbows. "They said we have to endure it. They cannot stop the awful things that are happening."

"So they cannot help after all."

Drawing in a slow breath, Aria sat all the way up and shook her head. "They will never leave us. We are their children. But all they can do is be with us while we endure it."

"That is something, then."

"Perhaps. But just at the moment, I do not find it helpful or comforting."

Chapter 60

Aria suppressed a shudder as the young priest described his experiences to her. Even with Beli at her side, the horror of having been betrayed by someone so dear to her was overwhelming. She looked out from the dais and caught Rhea's gaze, seeing the same revulsion there that she was feeling herself.

For some time, Lexion had been traveling to Knossos on what he called "peacekeeping journeys" whenever the tribute was due. He had managed to talk Glymenos into letting them send more valuables—gold and silver vessels, jewelry, precious stones—and less of the temple's grain, wine, and oil stores and livestock. Aria felt some relief at this, since the temple's food supply had become less reliable in recent years. More and more frequent droughts and hailstorms had done their damage. It did not help that the city was slowly emptying out, many of the locals moving farther east along the coast or leaving the island entirely to start over elsewhere. That meant fewer people bringing donations of either food of finery.

Aria hoped the crops stabilized again before the temple ran out of fancy goods to send to Knossos. They had few extras for the rites anymore. Sometimes they had to shift sacred objects from one shrine to another in order to have what they needed for a particular ceremony. It had not escaped Aria's notice that the valuable objects they were sending to Knossos were among those Thalamika had described to Glymenos in her clandestine messages. But there was no helping it now. It was the gold or the grain, and they could not eat gold.

Now a young priest stood before Aria, telling the tale of his recent journey to Knossos alongside Lexion to deliver the seasonal tribute. The two had enjoyed a feast in the dining hall that evening, but the food had disagreed with Lexion, and he had fallen ill. Not wishing to spend the night in the guest quarters with Lexion as he retched into a basin, the young man had accepted an offer from the Knossian priest whose bed Lexion usually shared when he visited. An abundance of wine had loosened the priest's tongue. Over the course of their intimate encounter, he had bragged to his Malian guest that Lexion had fallen deeply in love with him. The priest insisted that Lexion's love for him had finally brought Lexion to his senses regarding the future of both their temples.

The priest rambled on about how much Glymenos valued Lexion for all the precious information he brought to Knossos along with the offerings, how Lexion had assured Glymenos that the men in the College of Priests would follow his lead when the time came. Apparently what Lexion valued above all was peace, and if that was to be had at the price of his own treason and the destruction of his people's traditions and values, so be it.

When the young man expressed shock at this news, the drunken Knossian reassured him that Lexion was a good priest who only wanted to safeguard his temple so that when Knossos took it over, the change would occur with as little violence and damage as possible. "He is a good peacemaker," the drunken priest had mumbled before passing out.

"I did not know who to go to when we returned," the young priest said to Aria, the look on his face shifting sorrow to anger and back again. "Lexion is my superior. I spoke with one of my brother priests about what had happened, and he told me to go to Our Lord instead, since he is above all the men in the temple."

The Consort had been engaged in a rite that morning, but once he was free and the young priest approached him, he had brought the young man directly to Aria, suggesting that she hear him in the public forum of her audience hall. So Aria had called Rhea and a number of other clergy to witness the young man's words. Now she fought to focus her thoughts, feeling as stunned as if someone had punched her.

"We must hear what Lexion has to say," she said. "That is only fair."

They all waited as a servant went to fetch him. But the servant returned a short time later without Lexion, saying that he had left the temple at first light and gone up into the hills for a ritual hunt with the Ibex Brotherhood. It was now nearly midday. A feeling like a cold stone settled in the pit of Aria's stomach.

"When you spoke with your brother priest about this matter," Aria said to the young man, "how much did you tell him?"

"Everything I have just told you, My Lady."

"And who is this brother you spoke with?"

He named another priest about his age, one who belonged to the Ibex Brotherhood. Everyone knew that particular group valued the old ways and stubbornly maintained their traditions in the face of change. They were not known for being lenient with anyone who broke the Brotherhood's rules, unless Aria demanded it. In fact, they often took it upon themselves to enact justice privately within their own ranks so as to avoid being ordered to be gentler with their judgments.

Doing her best to maintain her composure, Aria dismissed everyone except Rhea, who approached the dais, foreboding clear on her face. When Aria reached a hand out to her, Rhea dissolved into tears, crumpling down onto the edge of the dais and hiding her face in her hands. Aria slid off her chair and knelt on the dais, wrapping her arms around her friend. When Rhea's sobbing quieted, Aria brushed the hair off her forehead and pressed a kiss to the top of her head.

"Is there nothing we can do?" Rhea said, her voice cracking.

"They left at first light," Aria said. "Even our fastest runner could not reach them before..." She choked on the words, falling silent.

"Now what?"

"We wait until they return."

And return they did, but not until late in the day, with two ibexes slung on poles and Lexion's corpse on an improvised litter. They said he had fallen down the mountain while chasing his prey. But his broken and battered body suggested that the fall had involved fists and clubs as well as the rocky outcrops on the mountainside. The men all presented stony countenances when Aria pressed them for the details of Lexion's death. She knew she would never get an honest answer from any of them. They would rather die than betray their fellow members or their traditions.

Shaking despite herself, Aria made arrangements for Lexion's funeral, acceding to a teary Rhea's demand to preside at the rite. Aria chose priests who were not members of the Ibex Brotherhood to prepare Lexion's body, and made them swear by the Mothers that they would be respectful and do the job properly.

"He was my best friend," Rhea said as the priests left to take care of the body. Aria looked the question at her. "Oh, we have not been lovers for years. For a long time we were both too busy, too tired, and in recent times his preferences turned more toward men. But he is—was my counterpart in the temple, someone I could talk to and take advice from. Someone I could trust." She swiped at a stray tear that rolled down her cheek. "Where you have the Consort, I had Lexion."

"We must choose a new Head of the College of Priests, and quickly," Aria said, changing the subject to one more practical and less likely to twist the dagger in her heart more than had already been done.

Rhea shared what Lexion had confided in her about the men in his College: who was good at administration, who was patient and kind, who the other men respected. In the morning Aria would share that information with Beli, who also knew the temple priests well. He would make suggestions to the senior priests, who would approach the likely candidates, and the College would hold their vote. If all went well, the College would have a new Head by sunset tomorrow.

But right now, Aria was not ready to deal with those matters.

The Earth was slipping away beneath her feet and the gods could not—or would not—stop it from going. Aria gathered her friend into her arms, and together they cried.

Chapter 61

A gentle breeze ruffled Aria's hair as she positioned herself on the dock alongside the Consort and a small group of clergy. The smell of salt spray cleared her head as sea-birds circled overhead, crying out their joy at the season, the time when spring begins to wax into summer. Just before dawn, Orestas had sighted the Flock-of-Doves rising in the eastern sky for the first time since the springtime harvest was over: the sign that the sailing season was about to begin. He had lit the fire in the bronze cauldron on the temple roof so that when the townspeople awoke, they would know to make ready for the Blessing of the Ships.

But the aging Orestas had stayed back at the temple while Aria and Beli had made their way to the harbor with their colleagues: Rhea, her newly-elected counterpart Ploteus, a handful of other clergy, servants to carry some of the baskets and the altar table, and Aria's personal guards. Among the group was the Keeper of the Doves and her assistant, who carried wicker cages full of cooing birds for the augury.

They set up on the main dock, Aria going through the motions that were almost automatic after performing the rite for so many years. But her heart was not in it, not this time. When she was a girl, the harbor was packed with fishing boats and trading ships on this day every year, vessels of all sizes pressed close against the docks and filling the water for some distance out from the shore. But so many people had left Malia: fishermen moving farther east along the coast to get away from Knossos, traders relocating either to those eastern cities and towns or to more remote locations: other islands, the Two Lands, Byblos and Tyre. There were ships in the harbor today, of course, Ytanos' vessel among them, but the port was by no means full. Even the gathering of townspeople on the docks was meager by past standards.

As Aria's gaze swept the scene, she noted Rhea's brother and son among the sailors from Ytanos' ship, all standing together on the dock. She could see the family resemblance between the two. When he had come of age, Rhea's son had chosen to leave the temple and join his uncle on board ship. Aria had called on her innermost reserves of strength to support her dearest friend as Rhea had cried on her shoulder about losing her son to the sea. Aria's own son was lost to her as well, though at that time he was still alive, two years into his reign as Consort. So much had happened since then, Aria thought, both good and bad. Now she knew better than to judge her own heartache against anyone else's. We all suffer. We all deserve comfort.

Looking around at the people gathered on the docks, Aria silently thanked the Mothers that this was not a Minos year. In those years, the Blessing of the Ships ended with a flotilla along the coast and a festival that lasted until sunset. Given the sparse crowd, Aria doubted if a flotilla of so few vessels would do more than dampen everyone's spirits. And she worried that even with her cadre of guards, she would be unable to maintain the safety of her people during a city-wide festival.

Still, she had a job to do, and she refused to shirk her sacred duty, even if she could not dredge up much enthusiasm for the task. She had made vows, after all. Her guards hovered nearby as she arranged the items on the altar. She never left the temple without the guards anymore, not even just to walk down to the Sea Temple or the tombs.

While she set out the pitchers for the offerings, Aria watched Rhea out of the corner of her eye. Aria's oldest, dearest friend was working with Ploteus to spread incense on the hot coals in the portable braziers. The smoke billowed up and swirled around the dock before trailing off inland toward the city. Though Rhea was focused on her task, doing the job as well as she always did, Aria knew her friend was also bearing a burden of grief from Lexion's death just half a Moon earlier. Though Rhea smiled at Ploteus as they organized their portion of the rite, the Head of the College of Priestesses avoided looking her counterpart in the eye.

Aria set the last pitcher down and straightened up, scanning the crowd on the dock and on board the boats and ships around the harbor. All her people bore a burden of grief, she realized. If their way of life was not yet dead, it was most certainly dying. They all knew it, whether or not they were willing to say so out loud. She crossed to where Beli was standing in order to take her place for the beginning of the rite, wondering whether her efforts were a waste of time. No amount of ritual could stop the encroachment of Glymenos and his people, she knew. Why, then, should she bother? Were her vows nothing more than empty promises to gods who made no move to help her save her people?

Rhea shifted next to Aria while Ploteus positioned himself beside Beli, the Heads of the Colleges flanking the High Priestess and her Consort. This close, Aria could see that Rhea's eyes were red-rimmed and bloodshot. She could see, as well, that those eyes still held passion and strength in spite of recent events. Rhea squeezed Aria's hand and leaned over to whisper in her ear.

"We must keep to our ways, no matter what happens," Rhea said. "Every moment we continue to praise the Mothers and every grain of wheat and drop of oil we share with our people is a blessing that even Glymenos cannot erase. The three realms bear witness to our devotion."

A shiver ran down Aria's spine. Perhaps not all was lost. Perhaps being saved from the mainlanders' vile ways was not as important as standing firm in the face of that encroachment, refusing to give in even as Glymenos and his people pushed their limits. She would do it right or not at all.

Determined, she raised her arms, drawing up her power, and

the crowd fell silent. The Chief Song-Priestess blew three blasts on her triton trumpet, the sound fading as the wind blew it away. Aria lowered her arms, and Beli drew in a breath, calling out the triple blessing in a voice that carried across the harbor:

By land and sky and sea
Blessed be the Three
By land and sea and sky
By Them we live and die
By sky and sea and land
Beneath Their guiding hand

When he had finished, Aria held her arms out in front of her, palms up, to call to the goddess—not to be overtaken by her, as she might do in other rites, but to bring the goddess' attention to the harbor and the people who depended on her goodwill for their livelihood.

"Posidaeja, Grandmother Ocean," Aria called out, "on whose waves we sail, whose dark depths contain the bounty of the sea and the doorway to the World Below: we invite you to join us today as we mark the beginning of the sailing season. Bless our vessels to safe journeys and our hearts to your service. We honor you, Posidaeja, Grandmother Ocean."

Rhea and Ploteus each took a pitcher from the altar and walked toward the end of the dock, holding their vessels high. As they moved, the Chief Song-Priest and Priestess began the chant, the people joining in until its rhythm washed back and forth across the harbor like so many waves:

Mother of the Waters
Water of Life
Mother of the Waters
Water of Life

When Rhea and Ploteus reached the end of the dock, they held their pitchers out over the sea and tilted them, pouring water into water: the clear water of the island's mountain springs in Rhea's pitcher, rainwater carefully gathered and stored in Ploteus' pitcher, both flowing into the sea that rocked against the docks and rushed along the shore. The streams of water twisted and glinted in the sunlight, sweet water splashing down into saltwater, mingling and becoming one. Posidaeja was the goddess of the sea, yes, but she was Mother of the Waters, all the waters, everywhere.

When they had emptied their pitchers, they made the salute, honoring the sea, then returned to stand by the altar. The chant continued as Aria picked up a small silver figurine from the altar. She took hold of Beli's hand, and together they strode down the dock, their steps keeping time with the chant. When they reached the end, they stopped and turned to face each other, holding the figurine between them, their fingers intertwined.

Aria examined the little statue, the figure of a priestess making the salute, honoring the Mothers. This one was smaller than the offering they usually made at this rite, and it had no precious stones set on it for decoration. But then, the temple was no longer as well off as it had once been. They were lucky to still have silver at all, she thought, wincing at the recent memory of yet another temple artisan—one of the goldsmiths this time—bidding farewell as he left for less tumultuous lands.

Turning her attention back to the task at hand, Aria met Beli's gaze. An understanding passed between them: they would do this well and sincerely, no matter what the people at Knossos said. Together they kissed the shiny little figurine, a token of their people's gratitude for the blessings Grandmother Ocean bestowed. Then, moving smoothly in time with the continuing chant, they turned and tossed the figurine off the end of the dock. It arced slowly through the air, flashing as it twisted in the sunlight, before being swallowed beneath the waves.

The High Priestess and her Consort strode back along the dock, their steps keeping pace with the chant, until they stood by the altar once again. Aria raised her arms, and the people fell silent.

All eyes turned to the Keeper of the Doves and her assistant. They had taken their places in front of the altar, their wicker dove-cages resting atop small portable tables. A slow rhythm began, the Chief Song-Priestess shaking a sistrum in an unhurried double beat, a hissing heartbeat. Soon the people joined in, some of them clapping, some slapping hands on thighs, some stomping their feet on the dock or—for the brave and well-balanced ones—on the floor of a boat.

The rhythm grew in volume and began to speed up until the whole dock was shaking with it, Aria's heart pounding in time as well. When the beat reached a frenzied pace, the Keeper of the Doves and her assistant threw open the lids of the wicker cages. The birds flew up, seven doves flapping wildly up into the blue sky, higher and higher. The rhythm stopped, and the people all waited in silence, watching the birds, as Rhea and Ploteus sought to divine an augury for the sailing season from their flight.

Just as the birds reached a peak and began heading back down toward the dock, a hawk sailed through the air from the west, diving into the small flock and snatching one of the doves in its talons. The doves scattered as the hawk shrieked, swooped around in a circle, and headed back west with its prey.

Aria cast a worried look at the Keeper of the Doves, who shook her head: the birds would not return to the dock to be gathered back into their cages, the way it was usually done. Following Aria's rapidly gestured instructions, the Keeper and her assistant gathered their cages, folded the tables, and moved back from the altar. They would have to wait until after the rite was finished to retrieve any birds that decided to come back. Aria chanced a glance at Rhea and Ploteus, who had both plastered neutral looks on their faces to avoid upsetting the onlookers. Aria did not need to ask them what the dove augury meant. It was obvious even to the townspeople, she was certain.

Moving forward with the ritual as she heard murmurs begin to run through the crowd, Aria called out the old rhyme, the one the sailors used to safeguard their ships before setting out to sea. Her voice rang out loud and clear through the salty air:

A hull to hold the waves at bay
A sail to hold the wind for way

Around the dock and across the harbor, the people repeated the rhyme five times, Posidaeja's number. The words echoed until the only sounds were the waves lapping at the shore and the seabirds crying in the distance. Then Aria motioned toward the Chief Song-Priest and Priestess. The couple began to shake their sistrums and sing the ship-blessing song.

Safely out and safely home
On Posidaeja's waves
All the fish and all the trade
On Posidaeja's waves

After a few repeats, the people began to join in, reluctantly at first, but eventually with their usual enthusiasm. The song spread out from the dock to the boats and ships, the people of Malia calling on Grandmother Ocean for safety and abundance as they plied her waters. While the people sang, Aria and Beli directed the other clergy to take up their containers of herb-water. The water, carefully collected in special cisterns reserved for sacred use, had been steeped with myrtle, rosemary, and hyssop. Now the water filled a collection of bowls, one for each of the priests and priestesses who were participating in the rite.

The clergy gathered in a half-circle in front of the altar, each one taking a bowl of the herb-water and a bundle of hyssop branches that served as an aspergillum. Aria picked up her own bowl, dipping her aspergillum in the herb-water and flicking droplets over the priests and priestesses, blessing them to their task. Then she set her bowl down and stood with Beli as the others moved out. Some of them sprinkled the herb-water on the prows of the ships tied along the dock, while others stepped down into small boats that took them around the harbor, blessing every vessel throughout the port. All the while, the people sang, their voices driving the chant across the dock, across the harbor, into the ocean itself.

The Sun was riding high in the sky by the time the last priestess returned to the dock and set her bowl and aspergillum down by the altar. The Chief Song-Priest and Priestess raised their sistrums, shaking out a rattling hiss to end the chant. Then, at Aria's signal, the Chief Song-Priestess raised the triton trumpet to her lips and blew three blasts. The rite was ended. The crowd cheered briefly, then scattered to return to their regular responsibilities. Some of the ships loosed their moorings from the docks and drifted out, ready to set sail as the new season began.

As Aria was directing the packing of the altarware in a basket for the servants to carry back to the temple, Ytanos came striding down the dock toward her. The look on his face as he embraced her told her that the augury had not escaped his notice.

"I promise you," Aria said when he stepped back from the embrace, "we will work to understand this divination in its fullness. There is no need for panic."

"I am not panicking, My Lady. But I do wish to speak with you — in private, please. Today, if possible."

His serious demeanor shook her. "Come to my workroom after you have taken the midday meal. We can talk then."

He thanked her and headed back down the dock to see to his ship. Unable to shake the sense that her world was beginning to unravel, Aria forced her attention back to the cleanup from the ritual. She could not control the rest of the world, but at least she could ensure that her people performed the rites properly and learned to value the precious things in life.

Chapter 62

"This is not just going to just blow over, you know." Aria pursed her lips, scowling at her brother, who appeared to have taken the midday meal in record time, considering how quickly he appeared at the temple after the Blessing of the Ships was over.

"I am only leaving for a while," Ytanos insisted. "Yassib's family is from Byblos. That will be our base for the rest of the sailing season. We will come back here for the winter, to see if the situation has improved."

"I do not expect anything to change in just one season," Beli said, pouring a cup of beer and handing it to Ytanos. "You saw how many of our people have already moved on to other places where it is easier to do business and live as they prefer."

The three of them were seated around the table in Aria's workroom, Beli next to his High Priestess and Ytanos across from them, all three of them with slumped shoulders and the air of carrying a heavy weight for too long. Aria and her Consort had been discussing the previous day's audiences, which had included complaints from many of Malia's traders about the new tolls on the roads around Knossos. Without special dispensation from Glymenos and his army of bureaucrats and hired guards, every traveler now had to pay to access any of the roads west of Nirou Khani and south of Amnisos. And of course, Aria could do nothing about this development. Then Ytanos had appeared with his own news, and Aria was doing her best to persuade her brother to stay. The last thing she needed was to lose one of the few people she could still count on.

"The tolls do not affect you," she said to him. "You trade by ship."

"I must pay to enter the harbor at Amnisos," Ytanos growled. "Though Glymenos is doing his best to ruin our island's reputation, Ida's children are still well thought of throughout the islands of the eastern sea and among the cities of the easternmost coast. I would like to take advantage of that goodwill for as long as it continues to exist." He took a drink of his beer, scowling. "I fear Glymenos and his people will turn everyone against not just him but the whole island, with his reckless and greedy ways."

"He is a danger to us all," Beli said. "He and the people like him do not understand the value of goodwill. They respect power and nothing else. I have heard people say they are like animals, but I promise you, they are more cunning than the smartest beast."

"No beast hoards food and goods, taking more than it needs and destroying any who try to stop it," Ytanos spat.

"He and his like are unnatural, that is certain," Aria said.

Ytanos narrowed his eyes at her. "There is something you are not telling me. I know that look."

Aria let out a bitter laugh. "Wise men do not ask questions where they do not wish to hear the answer."

"I want to know everything." He reached across the table and set his hand on top of Aria's. "Please, I had rather face the truth than believe a lie."

Aria shot a sidelong glance at Beli, whose look suggested that she should decide for herself whether or not to share the most recent news. For a few moments she stared into her cup, turning it around. Finally she realized that Ytanos was going to hear it sooner or later anyway, and she would rather he heard it from her.

"I have just received word," she said, "that the Mysteries have been cancelled this year."

Ytanos' head rocked back as if he had been struck. "Cancelled?"

Aria nodded. "For several years now they have had trouble with... interruptions. Last year was the worst. They do not wish to go forward under the circumstances."

"What sort of interruptions?" Ytanos asked, looking back and forth between them as if he were afraid to hear the answer.

"Thieving," Beli said with a grimace. "Attacks on the women, both attendees and clergy, as they gather beforehand and after. Disrespectful behavior during the rite itself, disruptions of the ceremony, loud jokes and rude comments. They appear to be more interested in letting the sacred drink turn them into wild animals than in receiving the Mystery. Not all of the mainlanders behave that way, of course, but enough of them... too many of them."

Ytanos gripped his cup, his knuckles turning white. "I cannot believe..." He pressed his lips together until they were a thin, hard line. "Yes, I can believe they would behave in such a way."

"The Mysteries up on the mainland will still go on as far as I know," Aria said by way of consolation.

"Do the mainlanders behave better in their homeland than they do here?" Ytanos asked.

"You know as well as I do," Aria said, "that there is more than one kind of mainlander. The ones who came down from the mountains—Glymenos and his ilk—are the problem. The others are happy to let us follow our ways while they follow theirs. And they still let the old-timers on the mainland, the ones who were there before the horse-riders came, continue with their traditions. But the mainlanders from the mountains, they have other plans. It appears that most of them are concentrating their efforts on our island and ignoring the cities up north."

"For now, at least," Beli said. "I expect they will turn their sights to those cities when they have tired of us."

Ytanos rubbed the back of his neck. "Why have they come here when there are so many of their own cities that they could be taking over?"

Aria gave him a pointed look.

"Our wealth," Ytanos said, blowing out a breath. "Of course. I forget sometimes how the glint of metal can make some men lose their heads."

Aria cringed, thinking of Lexion trying to buy a peaceful takeover with sacramental gold pitchers and silver bowls.

"I occasionally hear rumors," Ytanos continued, "that the mountain-mainlanders have attacked one or another of the cities up north. So they do not have their sights set solely on our island."

"No, but we are first because they want our wealth and our methods of forging superior blades, to make it easier to take over other places." Aria pursed her lips. "They do not understand that we have gained these things over time by sharing and supporting each other, not by taking whatever we want and pretending there are no consequences."

Aria looked over to see Rhea standing in the doorway. "My Lady," the Head of the College of Priestesses said, a look of concern on her face.

Aria motioned her into the room. "You may speak freely," Aria said. "If I cannot trust my brother and my Beloved, then there is nothing left for me in this world."

"A group has arrived from Nirou Khani."

"Excellent!" Aria exclaimed, sitting up straighter and smiling for the first time in several days. "I hope Nestia is among them. Have they already been offered guest quarters and refreshments?"

"It is not that sort of visit. They have... escaped. Under duress."

Aria shot up from her seat. "Where are they now?"

"In the dining hall."

Quivering with tension, Aria took a moment to embrace her brother and wish him well until his return at the end of the sailing season. Then she and Beli made their way to the dining hall, where they found Nestia along with five priestesses and two priests at one of the tables, eating stew and bread with trembling hands. The dining hall was otherwise empty, most of the temple residents having taken the midday meal some time earlier.

The travelers had washed but were still wearing the clothes they had arrived in, dusty from the road. Aria noted that for the most part they were wearing ordinary clothing, nothing that would indicate their status as clergy. They all looked weary and frightened, hunched over and tense. When Nestia saw Aria, though, her face brightened, and she relaxed a little, breaking a smile. At Nestia's request, the priestess next to her shifted over so Aria could sit down. Beli took a seat across the table from them.

"You could have taken your time and changed clothes," Aria said, giving Nestia's hand a squeeze. "There is no rush. The kitchen would have provided you with a meal at any time."

"We had no clothes to change into," Nestia said. Her voice was weary, ragged.

Aria glanced across the table at Beli, who looked as worried as she felt. "Tell me everything," she said to Nestia.

"I told Rhea that we escaped. That is the truth." Nestia's hands shook as she broke a small barley loaf, glancing down the table at her fellow clergy. "We left after dark last night. We had to tie our bed linens together into a rope to climb down from the private quarters on the second floor." Aria gasped. "They had guards stationed at the doorway downstairs so it was the only way to leave without being seen."

"They—who?" Beli said, though his tone of voice suggested that he already knew the answer.

"We have been under Knossos' control, officially, for some time now. But I suppose Glymenos was not satisfied with the way we did things. He sent men to take over our sacred house half a Moon ago."

"Men?" Aria scowled. "No priestesses, of course."

"No, and only one priest. The rest were nothing more than hired guards. Their priest refused even to speak to me. Instead, he took one of my priests as his second-in-command. At least, I think that is what he called him. Most of the time, they spoke their language, not ours, and they used a lot of words I did not know. It all sounded like... armies and soldiers."

"So they even run sacred houses as if they were military installations," Beli said.

"I suppose," Nestia sighed. "I do not know about such things." She fell silent for a few moments, poking at her food, her expression empty.

"I am sorry to press you," Aria said, "but we must know what has happened."

Nestia nodded, looking around at the handful of people she had brought with her. All of them had the wild-eyed look of cattle after a stampede, fearing that it is not yet time to stop running. Nestia herself looked little better.

"This priest from Knossos," she finally continued, "he dismantled the altar in the courtyard."

"He what?" Beli's eyebrows shot up.

"He took the Sun-Mother's altar apart, piece by piece, and sent all the gold and silver back to Knossos to be melted down." Her voice broke and tears glittered in her eyes. "In its place, he erected an altar to Dionysus, calling him the island's Zeus, as if our vine-god is somehow the same as their Thunderer, who claims to be higher than even the Mothers."

"It is a wonder you stayed as long as you did," Aria said.

"I was given no say at all. None of the women were. The new priest treated us like servants. He did not even allow us to lead rituals or tabulate the offerings."

Beli tilted his head. "This priest would not listen when the Head Priestess of the sacred house spoke up?"

Nestia ducked her head, her cheeks reddening. "I did not speak up, at least not beyond the first day or two." She swallowed. "Not after he struck me."

Aria drew in a sharp breath. "He did not do anything worse, did he?"

Nestia shook her head. "We had already heard about what happened when these people took over some of the other sacred houses, the ones south of Knossos along the North-South Road. Glymenos' people... those who fought too hard against their rule, his men simply murdered them." She swallowed. "Sometimes they raped them first, though, both men and women, in full view of everyone else. That is their solution to dissent."

"So you did not dare speak up," Beli said.

"Most of our priests sided with Glymenos' man. These two..." She motioned to the two men in her group, seated just down the table from her. "They were the only ones who did not. So we could not even collect up any altarware, food, or extra clothing without being seen. Though I suppose it is for the best that the men took away our fine ritual garments." She looked down at her dusty clothing.

"So you looked like ordinary travelers on the road," Aria said. "I suppose that is a safer way to journey, these days. Did you not even have a flask of wine for the trip?"

"No. We picked our way along in the dark as best we could, staying back from the road as much as possible. Then at dawn, we found a creek to drink from."

"You are all welcome here," she said. "For as long as you like."

"I would like to join your temple," Nestia said. "To stay."

"Of course." Aria set a hand on hers.

"Two of my priestesses have kin in Gournia, so they and some of the others plan to go on east from here. They wish to get farther away from Knossos."

"I understand."

"And the rest will go south from here to Mt. Dikte and the shrine there, where they will ask to stay and serve."

Beli's brow furrowed. "How is it that the cave shrine on the Mother's mountain has not succumbed to Glymenos and his people?"

Nestia shrugged. "The luck of the gods, I suppose."

"More than that," Aria said, "the cave is not easy to access, unlike your sacred house. It takes a long trek uphill to reach it, and there is nothing else near. And from what I hear, the Head Priestess there has gone to great lengths to send gifts and flattering messages to Glymenos, as if she and her clergy support him."

"But they do not?" Beli asked.

"Of course they do not. But they are wealthy, and they receive many visitors, so they have enough to spare to impress Glymenos with their generosity. When his representatives visit, she and her clergy tell them how the cave is their Zeus' birthplace, and how important the place is to his worship." She made a face, her stomach turning at the thought of having to lie outright in order to safeguard a sacred place.

"We do not have the option of making up tales like that," Beli said, "even if we wanted to."

Aria turned to Nestia then swept her gaze around the table, meeting the eyes of each visitor in turn. "You and your people are welcome to stay as long as you need to recover from your flight. Whenever any of you are ready to go, we will provide you with plentiful provisions as well as clothing. Should you need a wagon, we can offer that as well."

Nestia squeezed Aria's hand. "Thank you. I never expected to come here under such circumstances."

"You are safe here," Aria said. "At least, as safe as any of us are."

Chapter 63

"I understand why you chose this way, but I do wish we could have taken a wagon," Psoreia whispered to Aria as they neared the eastern edge of Knossos.

They had been walking since first light: Aria, Psoreia, and a handful of other Malian clergy, surrounded by their own armed guards. The whole group was, in turn, led and followed along the Coast Road by armed guards from Knossos, rough-hewn, taciturn men whom Glymenos had sent to fetch Aria to his city.

The men had appeared the day before bearing a message from Glymenos, a command summoning Aria to Knossos for an audience with him. Such a thing was unheard of. No one ordered the High Priestess of a temple to visit them, or to do anything else, for that matter. Not wishing to antagonize Glymenos, Aria had reluctantly agreed to make the journey. She had the sneaking suspicion that refusal would have resulted in violence, given the guards' demeanor. They had not given her time to gather any lay advisors from the city with whom to discuss the matter, though she had managed to call on her own priesthood for assistance.

Against everyone's wishes, she had insisted that Beli, Rhea, and Ploteus remain in Malia. Glymenos had not specified that the Consort had to accompany her. And if something happened to her, at least there would still be enough leaders to run the temple until a new High Priestess could be chosen. But she had taken Beli's advice and set out with an armed guard of her own, loyal men who would protect her and her little group no matter what. And she had decided to walk, even though it was such a long way. It would take all day, even if they left before dawn. But if they went on foot, there would be no wagons and no way for Glymenos to complain that they had not brought yet more tribute to him. When Psoreia had insisted on joining the group, Aria had agreed, though not without some unease. It was possible that Glymenos' men would recognize her, if any of them were among those he had sent to take over Eileithyia's cave.

The Sun was curving down toward the western horizon when Aria and her companions finally reached the Knossos temple, exhausted but resolute. Glymenos' guards made them wait outside while their leader went to receive instructions. Aria was thankful they had the shade of a portico to rest in, though she was looking forward to bathing, changing clothes, and having a bite to eat. Her entourage had already finished the food they had brought with them, having their meal on foot as they walked along at midday. They had drained their last flask of wine as well, and Aria's throat was dry. Some plain, cool water would be most pleasant, she mused as she waited.

Soon, the head guard returned and ushered the group into the building. But instead of being taken up to the guest quarters, they found themselves being steered into a small room on the ground floor. Before the door closed, Aria saw two of Glymenos' guards position themselves on either side of the doorway.

Weary from their journey, they all dropped their bags onto the floor and looked around the cramped space. There was nowhere to sit, no bench or stool, and only a pale slanting twilight coming in from the high windows. Aria's guards positioned themselves between her people and the door, but it occurred to her that if Glymenos really wanted them dead, no guard would be able to stop his men.

"I need one of you to go on an errand for me," Aria said quietly to her companions. "One of the women, I think."

"I will do it," Psoreia said, stepping forward.

"That is not a good idea."

"Those men are still at Eileithyia's cave, I am sure of it," Psoreia insisted. "They were sent there to stay. No one here knows me."

"Very well," Aria agreed, reluctant. She tilted her head toward the door. "Tell the guards you need to see the Medicine-Priestess for "women's problems." If you act like you feel bad, I am certain they will believe you. Glymenos' men are frightened by women's cycles, as far as I can tell."

With a sly look on her face, Psoreia drew a small knife out of her bag. She had packed it for slicing up the fruit and cheese she had brought for the midday meal. She slid the blade across her palm, and blood beaded up along the cut. Then she lifted the back of her skirt and tugged the fabric around so she could reach it to wipe her bloody hand. A moment later, her skirt was back in place with a blood stain in just the right spot.

"That should do it," she said. "You are right. These men are superstitious about the perfectly natural things our bodies do. So are some of their women, unfortunately." She glanced at the door. "What message shall I give the Medicine-Priestess for you?"

"It is more along the lines of a request," Aria said quietly. She drew Psoreia away from the others, as well as she could in the confined space. While she did not mistrust any of them, not even the guards, the less any of them knew of her plans, the less danger they would be in. "I need to contact the priestess Vanadia. She has long kept me abreast of the news here. But lately..."

"Do you think something has happened to her?"

"Perhaps she has felt it too dangerous to send me messages." But Aria's gut told her differently. It was not until Lexion's death that she realized a frightening coincidence: Vanadia's messages had stopped coming not too long after Aria had confided in him about her friend at Knossos.

Aria drew in a slow, steadying breath. She would not let fear overtake her, not when she was doing the Mothers' work. "The Medicine-Priestess knows who Vanadia is. I simply want to hear her latest news, whatever she feels I need to know."

"I will be as quick as I can," Psoreia said.

With that, she drew the door open, murmuring about women's problems and turning to show the guards the back of her skirt. They let her pass, shifting uneasily and avoiding looking at her. The door closed again, and Aria settled in to wait.

She could not tell how long they remained in that cramped and stuffy room, some of them leaning against the wall, others giving in to exhaustion and sitting on the floor. The dim twilight that had sifted in through the high windows had long since fled, leaving them with only the flickering flames of two small lamps. Finally the door opened, but it was only the guards. Psoreia had not yet returned, much to Aria's concern.

She saw that two more guards had joined the two who had been standing watch at the doorway. They ushered Aria's group out into the corridor, grumbling when she insisted that her own guards must accompany her wherever she went. The group moved down the corridor, through several small rooms where wide-eyed people watched their passage in silence, and along another passageway. At the end of the corridor, the guards steered them into yet another room.

It was the same audience hall Aria had been in before, with Eileithyia and Lexion and the others. That day seemed an age ago. It was the place where Aria had first laid eyes on Glymenos, seated on the dais with Melena standing behind him, the positions of the High Priestess and the Consort reversed. But today there was no High Priestess. There was only Glymenos, a handful of priests, and a room full of armed men.

"So, My Lady," he sneered, "I see you have decided to obey my orders after all." He threw a pointed look at his guards who surrounded her group.

She gave silent thanks that her clergy and her own guards had the presence of mind to cluster tightly behind her so Glymenos' men could not easily separate her from them. "I accepted your invitation to visit," Aria said, squaring her shoulders. "We want cordial relations with Knossos. We have been sending the tribute on time as you have asked. I was unaware there was a problem."

"Oh, the problem is not with the tribute," he said, "but with your attitude. You are presumptuous, like so many of the women on this island. You do not seem to understand how to be properly respectful. You do not understand who is in charge."

"The cities on this island have always been independent of each other, Glymenos. That is our way, and you must respect that."

"Oh, must I?" he said, leaning back in the chair and spreading his legs out wide in front of him. "I do not think I must. In fact, I think you must respect the might of Knossos." He waved a hand at the burly guards with their gleaming bronze weapons. "From now on, if you want your people to be able to travel safely between Malia and Knossos, you will pay us a special tax." Aria sucked in a sharp breath. "I would hate to hear that your people had been robbed and killed by bandits." He flicked a look toward the guards again.

Aria's hands balled into fists. "Those are not your roads to make such rules."

"Oh, but they are my roads," he said, his voice as cold as ice. "You may have enough guards to defend you and this little handful of your priests and priestesses. But I am certain you do not have enough to protect your temple and your city against my army."

"Army?" Aria said, looking around as if she expected to find ranks of warriors hidden in the shadows of the room.

"We are well-equipped, little lady, and wealthy enough to hire as many more as we wish." He peered at Aria's companions, one after the other. "And another thing. You do not run your temple well enough for our satisfaction. We will send advisors who will help you, who will make sure you are teaching your people the correct values. The proper respect. And of course, they will ensure that you pay your taxes on time and in full as well."

"How dare you—"

"Enough!" He cut her off. "We are done here." He waved a hand, and his guards closed in, shoving the visitors toward the doorway. When Aria's guards resisted, Glymenos' men drew their weapons, so she was forced to let them conduct her group back through the building and out a side door.

They found themselves clustered in the dark beneath the same portico where they had stood upon arrival, with a guard blocking the way back into the building. Aria drew a hand across her face and looked around at her people, their forms hunched and shadowed in the dim light from the torches by the doorway. They were all weary and frightened.

"Apparently we are not welcome here," she said to her companions. "But we cannot walk back to Malia now. So we must make a plan."

Just then, the door opened and Psoreia hurried over to join them.

"I was afraid I would never find you," she gasped as she came to stand next to Aria. She drew in several gulping breaths before calming down enough to speak again. "One of the men from the cave saw me rounding a corner. I thought he recognized me, so I went quickly in the opposite direction. Then I became lost and could not find the room where we were waiting."

Aria set a hand on Psoreia's arm. "You have found us now."

"Yes. Thank the Mothers, I came across a serving woman who had seen you pass, and she told me which way you had gone."

Glancing at the doorway guard and estimating that he was too far away to overhear their conversation, Aria asked quietly, "What did Vanadia have to say?"

Psoreia turned her back to the guard and clasped her hands together, a look of apprehension on her face. "Vanadia is dead."

Aria stared blindly for a moment, a familiar cold sinking feeling settling in the pit of her stomach. "How?" she finally managed to ask.

"They said her body could not contend with the drugged wine in a rite."

"But?"

"But the Medicine-Priestess told me she is sure it is not so. She taught the priestesses how to make those mixtures herself. She told me that those who are opposed to Glymenos, especially women but also some men, have been dying of mysterious causes or simply disappearing for quite some time. They are always replaced by those loyal to him. Many new people are coming over from the mainland, the same kind of mainlander as him, the ones from up in the mountains, with the strange accent."

"I am sure he would like to do the same at our temple," Aria said. She looked around, only to see the guard by the door glaring at her. "We cannot stay here all night. I wager they will remove us if we do not leave soon."

"Do you think we can find accommodation in the city?"

An idea occurred to Aria, and she let out a sigh of relief. "I believe we can. Sageleus' sister lives here. Perhaps she can put us up, or recommend somewhere safe for us to stay. I will happily sleep on the floor if it is in a friendly house."

It took them some time to find the right house. The main streets of Knossos were well lit with torches on the walls and lamps in the windows. But Aria did not know the way, and she feared what might happen to them if they turned down an unlit side street. Finally, they sought the aid of a local man who was on his way home. A short while later, they were on Idomeneia's doorstep, introducing themselves. Aria was relieved that the woman remembered her.

"Not remember you? My brother still speaks highly of you, though his visits are less frequent in these... uncertain times."

Idomeneia ushered Aria's group into her house, eyeing the guards warily.

"I apologize for bringing armed men into your home," Aria said. "I feared for our safety in the temple here if we did not bring our own protection."

"I understand. But we do not have enough beds for all of you."

Eventually they arranged that the guards should sleep on soft pallets in the courtyard while the clergy would occupy the guest rooms. Their hosts arranged to have a generous dinner brought to the guards in the courtyard as well. This suited everyone, since the guards could then drink and game as late as they wished without disturbing anyone else.

After bathing and changing clothes, Aria and the other clergy joined Idomeneia and her son and daughters on the broad, flat roof for a late dinner. A gentle breeze wafted across the rooftops, where so many of the locals preferred to dine, and sometimes even to sleep, in the hottest part of the year. The large table easily accommodated all of them, and the food and wine were as delicious and plentiful as Aria could have wished.

"Oh, we entertain guests regularly," Idomeneia said, assuring her visitors that they were not causing her any extra work. "I am glad to have you here."

Aria shared her news of Sageleus, his business and his friends, as best she knew it. Then they exchanged the latest accounts of life in their respective cities. Though they all did their best to think of cheerful anecdotes, in the end the conversation centered around the problems they faced.

"There is no stopping them," Idomeneia finally said, shaking her head. "We are thinking of leaving for the Two Lands. We know some of the traders who travel to Avaris. Apparently there is a quarter in that city where many of our people have already settled. They have said they will help us find lodging and begin business anew there." She let out a sigh, her shoulders slumping. "Many of our friends have already gone, to this land or that one. The marketplace is now filled with the kind of mainlander who will not listen to a woman, much less trade with her."

Back in the guest room, Aria lay in her bed in the dark, her belly full of good food but her heart full of fear. She stared at the faint starlight through the open window, wishing the gods had given her an easier life in a happier time. But she knew better than to think she ever had a choice. She was doing her best, and if the gods wanted more than that from her, they were going to be disappointed.

She determined to take her people back out on the road as soon as dawn broke. She had brought a few pieces of jewelry, hidden in her travel bag, as a small donation in case Glymenos' summons turned out to be less dire than she expected. She would leave those with Idomeneia as gifts. Then she would return to Malia, where she would bar the doors to any of Glymenos' representatives who dared to show up. They could come, but she would not see them. She would not speak to them or offer them accommodation. And she would have the guards turn them back onto the road again. If they could not get in, they could not take over her temple. It was that simple.

Chapter 64

The Sun had barely risen when Aria found herself shouldering her way through throngs of people who were clogging the Sea Road in the northern part of Malia, all heading toward the harbor, many of them arguing and shouting. She struggled to follow the sailor, the messenger Ytanos had sent to fetch her, across the harbor and down the dock to the spot where his ship was moored. Thankfully, people were respectful of her priestess garb, so most of them made way for her.

"What is such an emergency that I must leave the temple and come to you like this?" she called out to Ytanos as she approached his ship.

Though she cared deeply for her brother, she was annoyed that he had sent one of his sailors to the temple, demanding that she drop everything and come directly to the port. If he had something to tell her, he could come to her workroom as usual, rather than making her fight her way through the harbor crowds. The press of people was unnerving. She scanned Ytanos' busy ship, catching sight of both Yassib and Rhea's brother and son on board, working far more frantically than usual to ready the ship for sailing.

Ytanos crossed the dock to where Aria stood, doing her best to catch her breath and not be angry at her brother's presumption. He took her by the elbow and directed her a few steps away from the bustle of activity that surrounded his ship.

"I have dire news," he said.

The look on his face told Aria that this was no ordinary revelation. "Tell me," she said, steeling herself for the worst.

He tilted his head up, scanning eastward along the coastline, then turned back to her. "Glymenos has hired men, many men, to attack our island's cities. They have already begun, along the far eastern coast."

She staggered back, reeling as if someone had punched her in the stomach. "No."

"Word went around the harbor late last night, when a ship that escaped from Palaikastro made port here before heading off for safer harbors." Aria clutched at his arm, feeling sick to her stomach. "By twilight yesterday, Glymenos' hired brutes had taken Zakros and Palaikastro and were heading toward Mochlos. I expect they have already reached Gournia this morning."

"And we are next." Aria's mouth suddenly went dry.

The bustling sounds of the port broke through her shock, and she looked around. Never before had she seen the docks full of so many people moving so fast. She recognized not just foreign traders who regularly came to the city, but also many of the merchants and artisans of Malia, some of them with children in tow. They were bargaining for space in the harbor's boats and ships, dragging along as many of their possessions as they could carry, desperate to leave, some shouting, some crying, all full of fear. Some small part in the back of her mind told her that there were not nearly enough ships for the number of people who wanted to leave.

"This is your vision coming true," Ytanos said. "It is rumored that Glymenos is also sending men along the Coast Road from Knossos. They will catch us in a vise and crush us. You know what barbarians these people are. You know what they will do."

Aria's blood ran cold. She froze in place, unable to move, the din of the crowd washing over her like the waves that drew the sacred corpses back out to sea. This was the end, come finally as she had always seen, death and destruction worse than the Great Darkness, because this time it was committed not by the gods, but by mankind.

"Come with me," Ytanos was saying as Aria forced her attention back to the harbor. "We are leaving for Yassib's homeland as soon as we are loaded." His gaze swept the length of his ship. "In fact, we are just about ready, thanks be to Posidaeja."

Aria stared at him, her mind a blank.

"Come on board right now," he insisted, tugging at her arm. "You need bring nothing. We will cast off and you will be safe. Yassib and I are wealthy. We can buy you anything you might need." He narrowed his eyes at her. "You can join a temple in Byblos. You need not renounce your vows."

She shook her head, unable to force words to form.

"Please," came another voice, a familiar one. Then Sageleus stepped up from behind Ytanos, and Aria's heart skipped a beat, her breath catching in her throat. He reached out and took Aria's hands. "I am going with your brother. My things are already loaded. Come, I will take care of you."

Aria gazed into his eyes, sorely tempted to fall into his arms and let him sweep her away from all this trouble, all this turmoil. But as appealing as the thought was, she had obligations she could not ignore, sacred vows she refused to break.

"I am sorry," she whispered as tears stung her eyes.

Before Sageleus could make another plea, the hysterical cries of a fisherman who had just come into port met their ears. The man was standing up in his boat, flailing his arms around and yelling, his face wild with horror. One of Ytanos' sailors, who was near the man, listened to him for a moment then raced down the dock to Ytanos, Sageleus, and Aria.

"Gournia is in flames, the man says. The attackers' ships have already left the port and are headed here. They will round the cape soon."

"Then it is time for us to go," Ytanos said. "Get everyone on board. We cast off now." He turned to Aria. "Come on."

"No."

"What?"

"I will not go," she said. She drew in a breath and squared her shoulders. "This is my temple. I will not leave it. I will not abandon my people."

The two men stared at her, baffled.

"I said I will not go." She took a step back from her brother and Sageleus, all the room the crowd on the docks would allow.

"Then this will be your death," Sageleus said, his voice full of sorrow.

"If the gods so will it," she said.

She hugged Sageleus tight, kissed her brother's cheek, then turned and headed back to the temple, resolute. By the time she was halfway up the main road, Ytanos' ship was gone.

Chapter 65

She hurried through the city, dodging clusters of people who were running around in a panic, desperate to determine the safest way out now that the harbor was emptying and word of the impending catastrophe had spread throughout the population. There was a steady stream of people on foot headed south through the city, aiming for the Dikte Road. Full carts and heavily-laden bags and baskets slowed them down, so Aria had to thread her way between the groups, the urgency of the situation stirring her onward. She ran when she could, but found herself stumbling behind slow groups of travelers more often than not. Few people yielded to her now, even though she wore the garb of a priestess and many of them recognized her. Pushing her way through the last cluster of townspeople, she sprinted toward the temple.

She pushed the outside door open and stumbled into the north court, bent over with her hands on her knees, doing her best to catch her breath as people hurried around her, all in a panic. The news had reached the temple, that much was obvious. Now she had to decide what to do. The temple was not built for defense. That had never been needed. Her people were not warlike.

She had just decided to have her most trusted clergy gather up the best altarware when loud shouting echoed from one of the ritual rooms. As she crossed the court, she realized the sounds were coming from one of the men's ritual halls, a space women were not permitted to enter. But when she reached the room, the door stood open. She realized that the rough-looking men who had just pushed past her in their haste to reach the temple's north entrance must have come out of that room.

Peering into the room, she saw the greatest horror she could imagine. There, on the floor, lay her Beli, a gaping wound in his side, a pool of blood beneath him. She staggered over and fell onto her knees next to him, her breath catching in her throat.

"My Beloved!" she cried, scrabbling for his hand and clutching it to her breast.

His deep brown eyes looked into hers, seeing her, knowing her, but when he tried to speak, blood gurgled out the corner of his mouth. Then those beautiful eyes went blank, and he saw her no more.

"No!" she screamed, clutching his dead hand in one of hers and pounding on the floor with her other. "No!" She had barely spoken to him earlier that morning, when the sailor had come to take her to Ytanos' ship, before she had even finished her breakfast. She had kissed him goodbye, she thought, but she could not remember for certain. Had her last words to him been inattentive, hurried? Now he was gone, torn from this world out of time, desecrated...

Her sobbing was interrupted by one of the priests. It took him some time to convince her to let go of Beli's hand. Forcing her thoughts back to the practical, she swallowed hard, standing up and straightening her clothing with shaking hands. She was the High Priestess, and she had a job to do. It did not matter that it was the hardest thing in the world. She had to do it.

"The Consort has died out of time," she said, her voice trembling. "His blood has been spilled, so he is a sacrifice, whether or not that was their intent."

"Were those Glymenos' men?" Orestas asked, his voice strained.

Aria looked over at him where he was leaning against the wall and nodded. A deep gash in his thigh puckered open, oozing dark blood, and his chest heaved as he fought against the pain. Aria's gaze swept the rest of the small group of gathered priests, some young and some old, all of them injured, from blades or fists or both.

"You did your best to protect the Consort from those who would do him harm," she said to them. "But Glymenos has done more than just kill one man. He has sent an army to destroy our city and our temple." The men began to speak, but Aria held her hand up. "Those who can must flee. The marauders will leave no one alive."

Four of the younger priests, beaten and bloodied but still standing, spoke in low voices among themselves for a moment, then crossed the room to Aria.

"We will take him to the sea," one of them said, motioning to the Consort's body.

"The enemy ships will be here soon. You will not be safe."

"Still, we will do it," the priest insisted. He looked at the others, then back at her, setting his jaw. "We will go into the sea with him. Those men will not take us."

With Aria's consent, the men wrapped the Consort's body in linen, soaking up all the blood from the floor and packing the sodden cloth among the wrappings. They did not shy from touching his blood, bane to anyone but the High Priestess. But these men were already dead, even though they still walked. In silence they lifted the Consort between them, moving toward a side door. As they approached the doorway, Aria broke out of her numbed stupor.

"Wait!"

She scrambled up and stumbled over to the men, to her Beloved. Glymenos' men may have killed him out of time, but he was still the Consort. He was still sacred. There were rites to be performed.

With trembling hands she drew the linen back from Beli's face. The priests had closed his eyes and his head was unharmed, so he simply looked asleep. Peaceful. But the pallor of his skin gave the lie to that notion.

Drawing in a slow breath, Aria raised her arms and made the invocation:

By land and sky and sea
Blessed be the Three
By land and sea and sky
By Them we live and die
By sky and sea and land
Beneath Their guiding hand

She stopped, casting about for the right way to do this. He was already dead, but perhaps he was not lost. Perhaps the Mothers would take him in, as they did all their children. Fighting the grief that threatened to constrict her throat, she alerted the Three-and-One that their beloved son was on his way to them:

By the Sun
By the Moon
By the Star of the Sea
Our Fates are woven
Our lives are set
Our time ends when it must
We give ourselves to the gods

Her gaze darted from one to another of the priests who were holding Beli's body. They were all resolute, gripping the winding cloth and ready to do her bidding. They would stand there all day if she asked them to, she was certain. But the danger from the marauders grew greater with every passing moment. Quickly she collected her thoughts and spoke the words she would have said at the right time, in the Minos year.

"All who die live again in the Great Mother." She swallowed hard and continued, her voice cracking as she spoke. "You were a gift at your birth. You were a gift again at your anointing. And you are a gift at your death."

Gazing at Beli's face, she struggled to complete the rite. He was dead, so he could not play his part. She reached out a hand to cup his cheek, still warm against her skin. Then she realized that she would have to say the words for him.

"You welcome the next step on the journey," she said, tears stinging her eyes, her voice barely louder than a whisper. "May the thread of Fate draw you ever onward toward the stars."

She leaned and kissed him one last time, then drew the linen back over his face. Taking a step back, she motioned for the priests to continue on their mission. Bowing their heads to her, they shifted their burden and carried him out the door, heading for the sea.

Slumping back against the wall, Aria blew out a breath and took stock of the room. The triple-footed bronze brazier that contained the sacred fire had been kicked over. The coals were cooling where they were scattered over the stone floor. When she looked more closely, she saw what looked like water among the coals, spots of it on the floor and along the edge of the brazier.

"They pissed on it," Orestas said, limping over to her. "They kicked the sacred fire over and pissed on it. May the Mothers crack their skulls open," he spat.

"Go," she said, her voice breaking as she waved a hand at the remaining men. "Flee while you still can."

After a few questioning glances at their High Priestess and each other, the men began to exit the room, some of them clutching minor wounds or limping. Aria offered her arm to Orestas, supporting him as they crossed the room behind the others. When they reached the doorway, Aria saw that in the short time she had been in the ritual hall, the temple had erupted into chaos. Artisans, servants, and clergy alike were rushing around, shouting, seeking friends and family, collecting up their belongings, deciding which way to run.

"Let us get that leg seen about," Aria said to Orestas, who was still leaning on her arm.

"I fear the Medicine-Priestess has already left," he said.

"Then I will poultice it myself," she insisted. "I studied with her. I know the basics. You cannot flee if you cannot walk."

Chapter 66

Once Aria had seen to Orestas' leg with an herbal poultice and a tight bandage to hold the edges of the wound together, she led him out into the central courtyard.

"Find yourself a walking staff," she told him. "Then get out while you can."

"I will not leave you, My Lady."

"Save yourself, Orestas!"

"I am old. I have seen too much. I will find a staff, and then I will find you again."

He limped off, and she shook her head, forcing her thoughts back to the matter at hand. In a few moments she managed to find Rhea and a handful of other senior clergy. Many of the younger priests and priestesses had already fled, as had the temple artisans, leaving the workshops deserted, projects lying half finished on the workbenches. Feeling numb and lightheaded, Aria gathered her people in the north court and forced herself to focus long enough to share what she knew.

"They are also coming by the Coast Road?" Rhea said, horrified.

"That is what Ytanos told me," Aria said. "Just before he left port."

"The ship..." Rhea clutched at Aria's arm.

"Your brother and your son were on board. They have gotten

away safely."

Rhea let out a sigh of relief.

Aria looked at the clergy who were gathered around her. She met each priest and priestess' gaze in turn, her look resolute and unfaltering. "Tell everyone to take the Dikte Road south into the mountains. It is the only way left. Gather your people and get them out. Now go!"

As the others headed off to find their remaining fellow clergy, Aria and Rhea hurried up to the residential area, taking the stairs two at a time. By silent assent, they rushed to their own rooms to gather up a few belongings. Aria chose not to open the door into Beli's quarters, but she did manage to stuff a few of her clothes and other belongings into her bag. She hesitated for a moment before drawing the sacrificial blade from its box, wrapping it in a scarf, and slipping it into the bag as well. She came out of her room to see Rhea standing at the opposite end of the corridor, her own bag slung over her shoulder.

"Check every room," Aria said. "Make sure they are all gone."

The two of them moved quickly along the corridor, prodding the few remaining clergy to leave. Once the upstairs was empty, they made their way back down to the north court. A handful of people rushed here and there, gathering up sacred objects or searching for loved ones. But the place was largely deserted. A few moments later, even those people had gone.

"I have the altarware from the pillar crypt," Nestia said, breathless, as she crossed the courtyard toward Aria and Rhea with a bag slung over her shoulder.

Just as Aria was about to warn her to leave, she heard the sound of someone pounding on one of the side doors. A moment later, cries rang out from among the corridors, and a young woman stumbled into the courtyard. She was carrying a tiny baby, her tear-streaked face half-coated in dirt, as if she had fallen face-first to the ground.

"They have..." she panted.

"Calm yourself," Aria said. "You are safe for now. Rest a moment, then you can head south on the Dikte Road with the rest of us."

"That is where I was," the young woman said, still breathless. "They... the marauders... they have gone that way."

Aria gazed at her in alarm. "They are following the people up into the mountains?"

"They are killing those who try to take the Dikte Road. No one will even get as far as the hills."

Aria sucked in a sharp breath, fighting to think over the pounding of her heart.

"Look who I found hobbling around the shrine rooms, trying to save the altarware," Psoreia said as she guided Orestas back into the courtyard. He was leaning on a wooden shovel, with an overstuffed bag slung from one shoulder. He and Psoreia tussled for a moment over the bag, but eventually he relinquished it to her. She slung it over her shoulder and looked at the others. "Time to go?"

"The raiders have blocked all the roads," Rhea said. "No way is safe."

They all stared at each other, eyes wide, and Aria could see the panic rising in them. Pushing down her own growing fear, she forced herself to think.

"There is a way," she said after a moment. "You know it as well as I do." Rhea stared at her, puzzled. "How did we sneak out when we were children?" Understanding blossomed on Rhea's face. "Come, let us get out while we can."

Aria herded her small group into the basement, admonishing them to keep silent as she lit a lamp she had snatched up along the way. The young townswoman, whose name turned out to be Themis, put her fingertip in her baby's mouth for him to suck on, to keep him from crying as they went. They moved slowly in the light of the single lamp, picking their way down several narrow passageways crammed full of disused furniture and storage containers. Aria stifled curses as she stubbed her toe on a heavy pot that had fallen over into the pathway and broken into large pieces. They all shifted warily around the piles of stored items, fearful that the least touch might topple a pile of boxes or jars and make enough noise to give them away. Finally they came to a door, its heavy wooden surface coated in dust and cobwebs.

The locking mechanism was jammed. Orestas dug a small knife out of the bag Nestia was carrying for him and hobbled up to the door, leaning on his shovel. It took him some time, but he finally managed to pry the lock loose. Aria held the lamp up to his face, noting that he was pale and sweating, even in the cool basement air. She squeezed his arm in thanks, handed her lamp to Rhea, and motioned for him to move back from the door. Leaning her shoulder against it, she pushed hard until it began to move.

The heavy wood scraped against the stone doorsill, and Aria froze, praying no one had heard. She waited a few moments, then pushed again. This time the door opened enough that a sliver of daylight slanted in through the crack. Distant sounds of shouting met her ears, but nothing nearby. She shoved on the door again, opening it just enough that she could slip through.

Chest-high weeds had grown thick against the side of the building, obscuring the doorway. Apparently the more recent generations of temple children were unaware of Aria and Rhea's secret escape route. Hunching down so the weeds would hide her, Aria motioned for the others to stay put while she stepped outside. The sunlight blinded her for a moment, but after she had blinked for a bit, she could see across the weedy field. The Dikte Road, a short distance away, was empty along the edge of the field, but she could see that closer to the city, alongside the temple's west plaza, a group of marauders was attacking people who tried to leave that way, cutting them down on the pavement and kicking their bodies aside only to brandish their swords at the next group.

The smell of smoke stung Aria's nose, not the delicious scent of woodsmoke from a cookfire or the aroma of hot coals from the smiths' and potters' workshops, but the stench of scorching plaster and burning flesh. Fighting the urge to retch, she stepped back into the basement and motioned for the others to crouch down and follow her in silence. Rhea extinguished the lamp, leaving it on the floor by the door, and the group slipped out the doorway and into the weeds one by one. When the last one was out, Aria pushed the door closed. No sense leaving clues to their route, should anyone come looking.

Orestas had trouble crouching down due to his injury. Even when he bent over, his shovel still stood higher than the weeds. Finally, Aria and Nestia each took one of his arms, supporting him as all three of them moved along together. Rhea ended up carrying his shovel, holding it horizontally so it would not show above the tops of the plants.

The heat beat down on them as they shifted slowly across the field, doing their best to stay hidden. A wasp stung Aria's leg, and she bit down on a cry, forcing herself to keep going. By the time they reached the olive grove on the far side of the field, they were all panting, coated in dust, and streaked with sweat. But Aria insisted that they keep moving. She feared the raiders would come down the Dikte Road at any moment and see them.

Though the dried-out wildflowers in the olive grove were knee-high this time of year, the going was swifter between the trees than it had been in the weed-clogged field. Orestas retrieved his shovel from Rhea and kept up with the others as they moved diagonally through the grove, putting more distance between themselves and the road. On the south side of the olive grove they crossed another field, this one full of barley stubble, then entered a stand of fir trees that sloped up the side of a hill above a small farm. There they finally stopped, dropping to the ground in the shade, panting and wiping sweat from their faces. Themis' baby began to fuss, and she shifted him so he could nurse.

"Has anyone brought anything to drink?" Aria asked, looking around at the members of her group and the bags they were carrying. A flurry of shaking heads confirmed her suspicion.

"I could go down there," Psoreia said, gesturing toward the farmstead just downhill from them. "They must have a well where I could fill... something."

Nestia and Psoreia began rummaging in their sacks, drawing out pitchers and bowls that were meant to adorn sacred altars and shrines, not dip into farmstead wells.

"And what if the marauders have already reached there?" Rhea said. "Or what if the farmers are sympathetic to Glymenos and his cause?"

"We will find water," Orestas said. "The hills are full of streams, even this time of year. But we cannot go back toward the road."

As they all sat staring at the trees, too weary to move just yet, Themis let out a soft groan and doubled over. Rhea moved to sit next to her and set a hand on her shoulder.

"Are you all right?"

Themis shook her head, hunching over her baby where she was holding him in her lap. Her face was pale, though her cheeks sported splotches of bright red.

"He was born late last night," she said, her voice weak.

"You should be resting, not running," Rhea said. She wrapped her arm around the young woman's shoulders. "These are just afterpains," she assured the new mother. "They are not pleasant, but they will pass. The more you nurse your baby, the sooner they will end."

"The midwife ran away when the attackers came," Themis said. "I am not sure she was finished taking care of me, but I could not make her stay, not when..." She blinked back tears. "My baby has not had his milk-and-honey blessing yet. He does not even have a name."

"There will be time for that later," Rhea assured her.

Aria looked at her people, the handful who had followed her out of the temple, and realized she had no idea where they should go next. No plan, no supplies, no safe haven. Her Beloved was dead, murdered, taken from her. Her temple would be in flames soon. She could already see huge billows of smoke rising from the city, beginning to blow inland toward the mountains from the force of the constant sea breeze.

Tears stung her eyes. In just a moment, they were pouring down her cheeks as her body heaved with sobs. Orestas set his hand on hers and gave a squeeze, but said nothing. What words would have made any difference anyway? No one else moved to comfort her, but she did not expect them to. It was all any of them could do right now to hold themselves together. And it was her job to keep them going. But just at the moment, she could not keep going herself. Giving in to the flood of emotion, she let herself cry, let it wash over her for what seemed like ages, until it was all done and she was empty, hollow. Then she drew in a slow breath, wiped her face, and took stock of the situation.

They had no food or drink, but they could find water in the hills. Orestas was right about that. What did they have? She looked around. They were all wearing sturdy enough shoes for the trek, and their clothes would do for this time of year. The cooler air higher up in the mountains would be a relief, in fact.

Nestia and Psoreia each carried a sack of altarware. Nestia's bag looked to be the type most of the priesthood used to carry their belongings in when they traveled, made of good quality linen. But Psoreia's bag—the one she had wrested from Orestas' grip back in the temple—was of coarse canvas, a utilitarian item like a sailor or farmer might use. It occurred to Aria that Orestas had probably snatched it up from one of the workshops, but something about the rough bag with its shiny metal contents pricked at the back of her mind.

She stared at the bag, willing her thoughts to do her bidding, but nothing came. Vexed, she looked up just as Themis' baby let out a soft cry. Then it hit her, as if Psoreia had swung the bag of altarware and sent it crashing into Aria's head. This was what she and the others had seen in the pillar crypt so many years earlier, during the divination after the disastrous Dawn-Fire Rite. Those confusing, disparate visions were all pieces of a single horrific puzzle, all fragments of the Malia's terrible fate. She had known at the time that the visions portended some sort of evil. Now she understood the larger picture they fitted into.

The rough sack full of gleaming polished metal. The heavily-laden ships sailing away from the harbor. The broken bowl in the small, dark room—Aria rubbed at her toe where it still hurt from stubbing it on the heavy ceramic pot. She looked over at Themis as she recalled the description of a woman with a baby, pounding on the temple door.

The visions of the young priestess crying and the merchant's house on fire made sad, sickening sense as the puzzle pieces fell into place. Then her heart clenched as she remembered her own vision, a beautiful young man lying dead on the floor, a gaping sword wound in his side. She had not been able to see his face back then, when she was trying to understand the vision, but now she knew who it was.

My Beloved.

She swallowed hard as the tears threatened to come again. Divination was a tricky business at best, sometimes difficult to interpret until after the fact. In this case, they had not put the puzzle pieces together at the time, and now it was too late, though they had done their best. Then it occurred to her that there was still one piece missing from the current picture. The last remaining vision from that day in the pillar crypt was a group of rough-looking men making their way up the path to the cave shrine at Mt. Dikte.

"No," she said, her voice cracking. The others all turned to look at her. "I am afraid," she said, "that we cannot take the Dikte Road."

"Not even if we go around these farms and join up with it higher into the hills?" Orestas asked. "Then they would not see us from down in the city."

There was nothing left to lose by sharing, so Aria told the others about the divination in the pillar crypt and how she had put the puzzle pieces together. Nestia and Themis had not taken part in that rite. But even those who had been there did not yet understand the import of what they had seen, if the even remembered at all. Aria saw several of them shudder as she listed the details of the divination and they realized they were living those visions.

Nestia fingered the edge of the coarse sack that held the fine altarware, her brow furrowed. "Why are you telling this to us now?" she asked.

Then Aria shared the last vision, the one with the rough men making their way to the cave shrine, and Psoreia let out a choked sob before she regained control of herself.

"The rest of the visions are true," Aria said, "so we must assume that the Dikte Road is no longer safe. We must give the marauders time to make their way to the shrine and..." She swallowed. "They will take all the valuables and do whatever else they desire, and then they will leave. Once they have left, we can take shelter there. I do not expect they will return once the gold and silver is gone."

"We will have to hike through the hills," Rhea said. "East of Karphi, keeping far away from the road so we will not be seen or heard."

"None of you have to come," Aria said, looking each of them in the eye. "You may wait until the raiders have left and then return to the temple if you wish."

"Return to what?" Nestia said, waving her hand toward the plume of sooty smoke that was growing, spreading, drifting farther and farther inland. "And what if some of the raiders stay in Malia, in case people try to come back?"

As they were all expressing their desire to continue toward the Dikte cave, Psoreia put up a hand to silence the group. A handful of burly men, swords in hand, were turning off the road in the distance and coming down the path toward the farmstead just below the trees where Aria's group was hidden. Aria motioned for them all to move deeper into the wooded area.

In silence they worked their way up the hillside, angling eastward away from the farmstead and the road. When Themis' baby began to cry, she shifted him around so he could nurse, though he continued to fuss off and on as they went. Aria prayed he was not loud enough for anyone back at the farmstead to hear. Thankfully, the wind was blowing toward them rather than away, so at least it would not carry their sounds back to the farmstead, though the scent of smoke was growing uncomfortably strong.

Though the trees were thick enough to keep much underbrush from growing, the slope was steep in places. They had to stop frequently to allow everyone to catch their breath, and once to let Themis discard the blood-soaked cloth from between her legs. Rhea fished a linen scarf out of her bag and folded it up for Themis to use as a replacement, then she helped the young woman remove her baby's soiled diaper and replace it with some fabric torn from the hem of her skirt.

While they were waiting for Themis and Rhea to finish, Aria

narrowed her eyes at a spot of blood on Orestas' long tunic. If the blood was showing through his garment, that meant it had soaked through the bandage. He saw her looking and glared at her, turning away and setting his jaw. But when she drew a fine linen shawl out of her bag, he allowed her to wrap it around his thigh, tying the corners tight to staunch the bleeding. There was no time to remove the original bandage and clean the wound, and besides, they had neither water nor medicinal herbs at their disposal.

Late in the afternoon, the smell of smoke grew strong around them, triggering coughs with every few breaths. They stopped on a small promontory and looked out at the land below them, silent, each of them lost in their own thoughts, emotions too strong for words. Sooty, stinking clouds obscured the city of Malia and much of the coastline, creeping up into the hills and casting a grimy pall over the Sun. To the east they could see the ragged remnants of smoke-clouds trailing off from the other cities the raiders had attacked, places where the ashes were now cooling over the corpses of Ida's children and their ruined temples and homes.

Driven by fear and anger in equal measure, Aria and her companions pushed on until it became too dark to see where they were going. Then they all collapsed to the ground, tired and thirsty, falling into a fitful sleep broken by the sound of quiet sobbing in the darkness.

Chapter 67

Aria woke to the sound of birdsong and the smell of stale smoke. Sickly-pale sunbeams dappled the ground between the tree trunks. A pall of smoke still hovered in the sky, thinning the sunlight and turning it wan. Aria looked around and saw that she and the others had spent the night in a cypress grove, Ida's sacred trees growing thick and tall across the hillside.

Stretching out the aches and twinges from walking hard all day then sleeping on the lumpy ground all night, Aria stood and made the salute, praying silently to the Great Mother in thanks for their safety and for the blessing of her sacred grove as their shelter. As the others woke one by one, they saw what Aria was doing and joined in. Nestia finished her prayer and stepped away toward a clump of bushes a short distance uphill, saying that she needed to empty her bladder. Themis woke last, her cheeks flushed. She smacked her lips.

"Is there water?" she asked in a raspy voice.

Nestia came trudging back through the trees, visibly tired but with a smile on her face. "There is a stream just over the rise."

Offering quiet prayers of thanks to every deity they could think of, they all made their way up to the bushes and then back down the far side of the hill to a small stream. The flow was meager but the water was clear and cold. They took their time, cupping their hands and drinking their fill, washing their faces and arms. Briefly Aria considered taking her sandals off and washing her feet, but she decided there was no time for such pleasantries. She would simply have to put up with the dirt and dust for a while, until they found a safe place to stay.

"Now maybe my baby will suck," Themis said, wiping a wet hand over her flushed face. She had curled up next to the stream with her legs tucked under her, trying to get her baby to nurse. He fussed and fussed, turning his head side to side but not latching on.

"Here, let me help you," Rhea said. "I had this problem with my son as well. Sometimes it takes them a little while to learn."

Rhea dripped some water into the baby's mouth from her fingertips. He swallowed, then worked his lips as if he wanted more. With a little wrangling, Rhea and Themis together managed to get him to suck at Themis' breast for a few moments, but then he pulled back and began to cry again. Rhea gave him some more water, shooting worried glances at Aria, who came over to them.

"Has your milk come in yet?" Aria asked.

"I do not know," Themis said. "Is there not... something for him even before my milk comes in?"

"There should be," Rhea said. She pressed a hand to Themis' forehead. "You are fevered. Perhaps that is the trouble." She looked around at the small group. "Do any of you know about midwifing? Anything at all?" They all shook their heads.

"We need to keep moving," Aria said. "Perhaps we can find a farmstead where they can help. For now, let us take as much water as we can."

Her stomach growled as she helped Nestia and Psoreia sort the altarware from their bags. In the end, they left the ceramic items behind—figurines, pitchers, and dishes arranged like a small shrine at the foot of one of the cypress trees.

"Great Mother, take care of these for us," Aria said. "If we come back this way, we will retrieve them, for they are sacred. If not, then they are yours, made from your body, returned to you."

They looked over the remaining vessels, metal that was far lighter in weight than their ceramic counterparts, and also far less prone to break. The pitchers and bowls of silver, bronze, and copper were meant for sacred use on altars and shrines. Perhaps, thought Aria, surviving is the ultimate sacred act.

The group filled the pitchers and bowls from the stream. Then they shared the containers among them, each of them carrying what they could, either in their hands or balanced in a bag. None of the vessels had lids, so some of the water spilled as they made their way back over the rise and farther up into the hills.

"Great Mothers," Rhea said as they began their trek, "please forgive our use of your special vessels in such a way. We are hard pressed just now and are grateful for them."

Keeping to shallow slopes and low mountain passes as much as possible, they made their way slowly south, moving higher up as they went. They were all hungry, but no one commented on the lack of food, since there was nothing they could do about it. Aria's stomach stopped rumbling around midday. Drinking water now made her more hungry rather than less so. This was very different from fasting in the temple, with its peaceful rhythms of daily activity.

As the afternoon wore on, Aria thought they must be nearing Karphi, about halfway to the Dikte cave. So when they spotted a narrow farm road, they made their way toward it. It led up to the top of a nearby hill.

"We should be able to see where we are from there," Aria said. "But we need to stay back from the road, just in case. We do not know how far inland the raiders have come, or how many of them there are."

They picked their way through the woods, fighting with the underbrush, until they neared the hilltop. Raucous laughter met their ears, and they all backed down behind a clump of scrubby holm oaks, holding very still. A few moments later, a trio of burly men came stomping up the road toward the hilltop, laughing and making vulgar jokes about the farmstead they had just raided and the people they had encountered there. One of them punctuated his comments with deep draughts from a flagon of wine. Another kept cramming fistfuls of cheese into his mouth in amounts that muffled his speech. The third was clutching what looked like a clump of glossy black hair in his hand. When the trio shifted as they walked along, Aria saw that the hair was attached to a head, a human head that belonged to a young girl. Drops of blood slung from the hacked-off neck and spattered on the road as the man swung his arm back and forth in time with his steps.

Overcome, Aria bent over and retched, but her stomach was empty. All that came up was bile. When she recovered herself, she realized that several of the others had responded in the same way. They all held still, hunched behind the holm oaks, until some time after the men had crested the hilltop and disappeared on the other side.

"Let me go look," Rhea said at last, her voice low and quiet. "Let me go see where we are."

Aria clutched her wrist. "What if they see you?"

"I was always better at sneaking than you were," Rhea said. "I suspect I still am."

Recognizing the truth of her friend's words, Aria allowed a sad smile. "This time, the consequences will be far worse than just scrubbing floors if you are caught."

Aria and the others watched as Rhea made her way quietly up the hillside, keeping within the shelter of the trees until she reached the top. There, she crept to the edge of the road, staying low, and peered over the other side. Then she moved back into the edge of the trees and stood up, gazing around in all directions. She took her time getting her bearings, then stole back down the hillside to the rest of the group.

"We are not far off from Karphi," she said, flashing a weary smile. "We are northeast of the peak, but if we keep following this series of gaps..." She motioned toward a crease between two hills. "Then I think we will cross the old paths that lead up there."

"Can we take shelter there?" Psoreia asked.

"Possibly," Aria said. "The peak sanctuary there was abandoned after the time of Great Darkness, but perhaps some of the buildings are still standing. It is not a place the raiders are likely to find. Not many of Ida's children still remember it, for that matter."

With renewed energy they set off across the hills, keeping to the low spots and passes as best they could. They crossed two more small streams, still running even this late in the dry season, fed with cool water from springs and snow-melt high in the mountains. At each one, they stopped to drink and refill their vessels, though by the time they reached the second one, late in the day, they were too tired to carry heavy containers of water anymore.

The whole time, they kept their distance from any roads or paths they came across, threading their way through sparse woodland where springy mats of fir needles cushioned and quieted their steps. Several times, they heard cries and the sounds of fighting in the distance. Once, the smoke from a farmstead on fire turned them away from a small valley, forcing them to trudge up a hill and back down the other side before finding their way again.

When they were headed in the right direction again, they came through a mountain pass and discovered another farmstead in the valley below. They stopped within the trees that ringed the area, on the hillside above the farm, examining the setting.

"The farm has been burned," Rhea said, her voice low. "The raiders have come and gone."

"We cannot be certain," Aria said, peering down at the remains of the small stone house with its caved-in, burnt-up roof. "But I do not see any movement. Not even any animals." The barn appeared to be undamaged, but no sheep or goats wandered around it. No sounds of livestock met Aria's ears from the barn or the adjacent pasture.

"The raiders may have taken the livestock," Rhea said. "Driven them back down somewhere for a feast, or whatever it is that people like that do."

Nestia crouched down, narrowing her eyes at the farmstead. "Let me go down there. There may be food." She pressed a hand to her belly.

"It is too dangerous," Aria said, shaking her head.

"There is no one there. No one alive..." Nestia's voice trailed off. Then she squared her shoulders. "I am not afraid of corpses. But I am afraid of starving to death."

"Let me go," Rhea said. "You know I am good at sneaking."

A whispered argument ensued, with Psoreia and Orestas joining in as well. Finally, tired and exasperated, Aria silenced them all with a motion of her hand.

"Nestia will go," she said. "It was her idea."

They quietly emptied Nestia's bag, setting the altarware on the ground at the base of one of the trees. She slung the empty bag from her shoulder and crept out of the woods, making her way slowly down the hillside. The others watched as she clambered across the open space between the woods and a cluster of boulders just up the hill from the burnt-out farmhouse. She reached the boulders and knelt down behind them, catching her breath. Then, just as she stood up to walk down to the farmhouse, a man stumbled out of the barn.

Nestia froze, her head and shoulders sticking up above the top of the boulders, clearly visible should the man turn around. The others watched from their spot among the trees as the man—a burly, well-armed raider—staggered drunkenly over to the fence. He clutched a fence post with one hand to hold himself upright while he used the other hand to fumble with his clothing so he could empty his bladder. By the time he turned around to stumble back into the barn, Nestia had crouched down behind the boulders again. The man did not look up the hillside before entering the barn, but if he had, he would not have seen her.

As soon as he disappeared into the barn, Nestia scrambled back up the hill and lurched into the trees, her breathing ragged. They collected up the altarware from the ground, stuffing it back in Nestia's bag as well as they could without making any noise, and moved on. They did not come across any more farmsteads that day.

As the sky began to darken into dusk, they stopped, dropping to the ground among a few scraggly fir trees on a high hillside. Something had been tugging at Aria's thoughts all day. When she had rested a few moments, the thoughts coalesced into a realization.

"Themis," she said quietly, "your baby has not cried today, has he? And when we stopped, you did not change his diaper, not once today."

The young woman looked over at Aria with a dazed expression. Her face was still flushed, visibly red even in the dimming light, and her eyes were now glassy. The fever had not abated. If anything, it had worsened. "He is a good baby," she finally said, sounding a little confused.

The others turned to watch as Aria moved closer to Themis. "May I see him?"

She reached to draw the blanket away from the baby's face, but Themis clutched him tight against her. "He is sleeping," she said. "You will disturb him."

Rhea shifted over toward them. "Have you nursed your baby today, Themis? I do not recall seeing you put him to the breast."

"I have," the young woman said, nodding. "He is a good baby."

"Yes, he is," Rhea said softly. "He is so lovely. May I have a look at your lovely baby, Themis?"

After some hesitation, Themis allowed Rhea to draw the blanket back from the baby's face. Swallowing hard, Rhea stroked her fingers down the little cheek. The baby's eyes were wide open, unblinking. Its mouth was a small o, gaping and rigid.

"Themis," Rhea said, her voice catching, "your baby is dead."

"He is not!" she cried, clutching the tiny body to her.

Aria shushed her, fearful that even this far up in the mountains, they might be heard. Then she motioned for Rhea to leave Themis alone.

"But the baby..." Rhea said.

Aria shook her head, blinking back tears. "As long as she holds him, she will stay quiet and not give us away. Once we find shelter, we can tend to her and provide the baby with a proper burial. If we do not find food and shelter... and medicine... very soon, I fear she will follow him."

Chapter 68

"Orestas, let me tend to your wound. Change the bandage." Aria
was sitting near him, rubbing the sleep out of her eyes. The thicket
of fir trees they had sheltered in for the night had a layer of dried
needles underneath that made the ground soft enough for good
sleep, especially given how exhausted they all were. But they all
found themselves picking prickly little fir needles out of their hair
and clothing the next morning.

"My wound is fine," Orestas insisted. He tugged the hem of his
tunic down to cover his leg, then hefted a pitcher and took a long
drink of water.

Aria moved closer to him, trying to get a look at his leg. The
wound was on his thigh, and the hem of his long tunic reached well
below his knee.

"Please, My Lady," he said, "leave me be for now."

Taken aback at the formal address under such extraordinary
circumstances, she sat back on her heels and looked the question at
him.

He waved a hand over the wounded area. "The bandage needs
to be soaked loose, I am certain. We have no time for that. And if
you force it off, it will bleed again, and you will make it that much
more difficult for me to walk. I am slowing the rest of you down
enough as it is."

She narrowed her eyes at him. "When we find shelter..."

"You may change the bandage then, My Lady, and tend to me all you like, I promise you." He levered himself up with help from his shovel and a fir sapling, refusing her help.

Once they had all woken, had a drink, and emptied their bladders, they began walking again. Their speed had slowed some the previous day and now, on the second morning after their escape from Malia, they were trudging along at a snail's pace, nursing blisters and sore muscles and doing their best to ignore the pangs of hunger. Aria feared that they would not find shelter before they succumbed to the elements—or starvation.

Themis was heavily fevered, stumbling along with Nestia and Psoreia on either side to keep her from falling. She muttered incoherently from time to time. But most of the day, she just stared blankly ahead, clutching her baby's corpse, her glassy eyes uncomprehending, allowing the others to guide her.

The late summer heat of the coastal regions had given way to chilly breezes the higher up in the mountains they went. At first the cool air was a relief, but now it began to be unpleasant, turning sweaty skin clammy and sifting through their thin summer clothing. They shared the few garments they had brought, wrapping up in layers of tunics, skirts, and shawls with no regard for fashion or custom. Orestas joked that the purplish-black threads in Rhea's shawl that now wrapped around his shoulders emphasized the dark circles under his eyes in a most fetching manner.

Late in the morning, they reached a stream and stopped to drink. Aria mopped Themis' face with a scarf dampened in the cool water, but the young woman was beyond the help of simple comforts such as that. A midwife would know what to do for childbed fever. In any other time, Themis would have stayed in her own home and been tended to properly, would never have fallen ill in the first place. Gritting her teeth, Aria stuffed the scarf back in her bag and began to fill a pitcher with water from the stream.

They did not fill as many containers with water this time. The weight of the vessels in their bags, even empty, was beginning to drag on all of them, but no one could bring themselves to abandon the sacred objects, saved so carefully from the plundering raiders. So they trudged along with their loads, one step at a time.

In the cool air they did not need quite as much to drink as they had at lower elevations. But still, they needed some water. They lugged it along as best they could, stumbling from one tiny valley to the next, moving higher and higher into the mountains.

Not long after midday, Rhea cried out, and they all stopped in their tracks, looking in the direction she was pointing.

"Karphi!" Aria sighed. "Thank the Mothers!"

They could just see the double-peaked stone outcropping, the natural pair of sacred horns that marked the site, over the rise of the next hill. Karphi had been revered by Ida's children for generations, though the peak sanctuary there had long fallen into disuse. Still, it was a possible refuge where they could rest and recover before moving on to the cave shrine on Mt. Dikte.

It took them the rest of the day to work their way over the next rise and up a series of washed-out old pathways on the mountainside below Karphi's horns, struggling with their loads and shivering against the chill wind. Aria began to think that this was a slow, drawn-out version of the execution she had brought down on Thalamika and Odrys. She realized with a start that given a choice, she would not wish it on anyone, not even those two. Finally, as the Sun touched the tops of the western mountain peaks, they stopped, exhausted and disheartened.

"We cannot make it all the way up," Nestia said, shaking her head.

They had already picked their way over several small rockfalls and skirted deep gullies where the rain and snow-melt had scraped the path away. Now just ahead of them lay a large pile of boulders, higher than the tallest of them, blocking the way up the mountain.

"We can rest here," Psoreia suggested. "Then in the morning we can climb over the boulders and keep going."

Orestas narrowed his eyes at the huge rock pile and shook his head. His face was pale, his breathing labored. A patch of bloody fluid had seeped through his clothing, pasting his tunic to the bandage on his thigh.

"You are assuming that there are no more such rockfalls higher up," Aria said, her teeth chattering from the cold. "And that the buildings at the old peak sanctuary are still standing."

"There is shelter over there," Rhea said as she came back around the bend. She had stepped away from the group to empty her bladder when they stopped at the rockfall.

"Shelter?" Aria said, skeptical.

"A small cave. It is deep enough to be a refuge from the wind."

This welcome news gave them all a burst of energy. They moved off the path and made their way across a small bald to discover that Rhea had indeed found them a cave.

It was a low space. None of them could quite stand up in it. But it was deep enough for them all to creep in away from the wind and sit huddled together along the back wall. Aria inspected a few animal bones that lay scattered in the dirt. It appeared that the cave had been unoccupied for a long time, so she did not need to worry about some creature appearing and attacking them. The wild animals were probably smart enough not to wander around the mountains the way Aria and her companions were doing.

They passed around containers of water, each of them taking a long drink. Aria noticed that everyone's hands shook as they lifted the small bowls and pitchers full of liquid. After a short while, Aria stopped shivering. She saw that the others had also relaxed a bit, no longer clutching their garments quite so tight around them. Silently she thanked the Mothers for this small kindness. At least she would not die of cold. Then, as the Sun went down, the cave shifted from dim light to deep shadows and finally to full darkness. They all lay down on the dirty, stony cave floor, huddling together for warmth.

"Maybe tomorrow," Psoreia whispered into the blackness, "we can collect some wood and build a fire."

Though the trees were sparse this high up, there were still enough of them that firewood was a possibility. That is, if they had the strength to collect it.

"What if the raiders see the smoke?" Orestas asked.

"Maybe someone else has escaped from the city and will see it and join us. Maybe they have some food," Nestia said, though her tone of voice suggested that she did not believe her own words.

"What if no one else survived?" Aria found herself saying, then silently scolded herself for suggesting such a thing. She was the leader. It was her job to keep her people going, not to drag them down with her own disheartening thoughts.

"We cannot go back toward Malia," Rhea said. "We cannot be certain the raiders have all gone. We cannot even go back down the mountains. You saw how many of those awful men are still around."

"But we cannot go any farther up," Nestia said. "All those boulders..." Her voice broke off in a quiet sob.

"There is no way out," Psoreia whispered, resigned. "No matter what we do, we lose. The gods have forsaken us."

"I do not think so," Aria said, searching desperately for anything to say to her sister priestess that would not make her even more despondent.

"How can you say that?"

"Perhaps the gods do not wish us to win. Perhaps they simply wish us to do our best in an impossible situation." She was not entirely certain she believed that, but it sounded like something Elli would say, so she thought there must be some wisdom in it.

"The Mothers do not judge us, that much is true," Psoreia said, her voice a tiny bit less sad.

Aria pillowed her head on her arm and let the darkness of sleep fall on top of the darkness of the cave.

Chapter 69

A faint sliver of pale morning sunlight angled in the front of the cave. Aria shifted on the hard stone floor, her eyes fluttering open. The back of the cave was still swathed in shadows as the others began moving and stretching, groaning from aches and exhaustion.

One by one they all woke up, rubbing their eyes and dusting off their clothing—all except Themis. Aria had thought they might bury her baby today, perhaps in one of the little clumps of fir trees that clung tenaciously to the steep hillsides. But as she crept over to check on the young woman, Aria realized that Themis had already followed her tiny son into the Underworld.

Aria sat back on her heels, tears pricking her eyes as she smoothed a strand of hair out of the young woman's face. Her body was already cold. She had died in the night while the rest of them slept.

"Is she..." Rhea began, then pressed her lips together when Aria nodded.

Needing something to occupy her while she worked over some possibilities in her mind, Aria began shifting Themis' body toward the cave wall, away from the others. Rhea got up to help, and between them they soon had Themis and her baby tucked up against the side of the cave, their faces covered with a shawl. When Aria and Rhea sat back down, they were both breathing hard.

"Now let me see your leg," Aria said to Orestas after she had taken a few moments to catch her breath. She crawled over to him, and he stared at her, glassy-eyed, unmoving, still lying on the cave floor where he had slept the previous night. His face was deathly pale, and he did not have the breath left to speak.

"Holy Mother," she breathed as she lifted the hem of his tunic to discover that his entire leg was swollen, mottled purple and black. "Why did you not tell me it was like this?" She pulled the tunic loose from the bandage on his thigh and a foul odor wafted up, turning her stomach. Fighting the urge to retch, she drew the tunic back down. There was nothing she could do now. The wound had overtaken him. If only the Medicine-Priestess had still been in the temple when he had needed care...

Aria sat down hard, her head rocking back against the cave wall. She raked her hands through her hair. "We are..." she began. She swallowed, then forced herself to speak. "We are at an end."

"What if we go back down?" Psoreia said. "We can find a farmhouse to shelter in. There might be food."

"Do you want to be killed... or worse... by one of those raiders?" Nestia hissed. "You saw yourself, they are everywhere. For all we know, they have come to stay, to take over the island."

"We could try going on to the Dikte cave," Psoreia said, not very enthusiastically.

"Even if we could find the Dikte Road," Rhea said, "we have no food. We can barely walk as it is. And we have no assurance that the marauders have not stayed at the Dikte cave, as they have in so many other places."

"What other choice do we have?" Psoreia said. "We cannot stay here. We will starve to death."

Muttering to herself, Rhea rummaged in her bag, drawing out a series of bowls and pitchers and setting each one aside until she found what she was looking for: a lidded wooden box wrapped in a blood-red cloth, with a small ceramic spoon tied on top.

Aria sucked in a sharp breath. "You brought the opium."

"All of it. Yes."

Psoreia folded her arms across her chest. "This is no time for a ritual."

Aria locked eyes with Rhea, whose gaze told her they shared the same idea.

"I do not believe Rhea is suggesting any of our usual rites," Aria said slowly. Her gaze dropped to the box. "Is there enough?"

With shaking hands Rhea untied the spoon from the top of the box and unwrapped the cloth from around it. She raised the box lid to reveal a sticky brownish-black powder, the dried opium ground fine enough that it would dissolve when heated in wine. They had no wine and no way to heat it, even if they had any. But for their purposes, water would be sufficient for swallowing the powder.

"I do not understand," Nestia said, leaning in to get a closer look at the box's contents. "What could we possibly... oh." She sat back, clutching her shawl around her shoulders, nodding reflexively.

Again Aria asked, "Is there enough?"

"I am not certain," Rhea said.

She began measuring the powder out, one spoonful at a time, into a small bronze bowl. The others sat silent, entranced, watching as she counted spoonfuls under her breath. When she was finished, she looked up and shook her head. They all began talking at once, Psoreia insisting they try to make it farther up the path toward the old peak sanctuary, Nestia demanding that they draw lots for the opium, Rhea doing her best to explain how the dosing works.

"Please!" Aria cried out, and the others fell silent. "Do you all understand what we are discussing here?"

Rhea and Nestia nodded, their faces sober, but Psoreia gave Aria a puzzled look.

"You know this can be deadly," Aria said, gesturing to the bowl of opium, "if you take too much. You fall asleep and never wake again."

Understanding dawned on Psoreia. Her face went through a series of contortions, and then tears began to roll down her cheeks. "Yes," she said, "yes, that is best."

"What do you think, Orestas?" Aria leaned over toward the elderly priest, then drew in a sharp breath. She reached out and touched his arm. He did not move. His eyes stared straight ahead.

"Oh no," Nestia said with a quiet sob.

Aria dragged herself back over to Orestas' corpse. She drew his eyelids down, then pulled Rhea's shawl up over his head, covering his face.

"May the Mothers bless and keep you among the spirits of the dead," she said, making the sign of blessing over him.

She was too weary to attempt to move his body, so she left him lying where he was. And now, she found she was too weary even to cry. Her heart was already so full of sadness, there was no room for any more. When she was finished tending to Orestas, she turned back to the others, thinking.

"Rhea," she said, "is there enough opium for three?"

Rhea stared down at the bowl. "Yes, just enough. We have fasted for several days—"

"Against our will," Psoreia cut in.

"Yes," Rhea said. "So it will work quickly and well."

"Very well," Aria said. "You three will take it. We have enough water, I think."

"And what will you do?" Rhea snapped. "Starve to death in a cave full of corpses?"

"No," said Aria. "I have my own way out." She drew an object from her bag, unwrapping the fabric from it with shaking hands until the shiny bronze blade was visible.

Rhea gasped, then swallowed hard. "If that is your wish."

"It is." Aria looked at the others. "Do you two agree?"

They both hesitated before nodding.

"None of us are young," Nestia said. "I have seen things come to pass that I could not imagine in my worst nightmare." She reached out, taking Aria's hand. "I would rather die here, among friends, than chance an encounter with those barbarians out there."

"We do not have any wine," Rhea said, "or any way to heat it, even if we had some. So there is no way to dissolve the powder. We will have to swallow it as best we can with water." She looked the others in the eye, making sure they understood.

Blinking back tears, the four women moved closer together, wrapping their arms around each other. They huddled together, sharing warmth and breath, their foreheads touching, four sacred sisters performing one final rite together. Then they parted, sitting back in their own places, the focused intent of the long-practiced priestess taking over, shifting the exhaustion and the hunger into the background.

They all watched as Rhea portioned the powder out into three small bowls. Aria had expected a flood of emotion, but she found herself strangely numb now, almost as if she were watching herself from off to the side. She focused as best she could, but she felt the Mothers hovering nearby, waiting to overshadow her, the long training of the priestess coming to the fore as she silently asked for the strength she knew she did not have by herself. A warmth descended on her, and she understood that the Mothers would help her, help them all, respect their decision to end their lives in the way of their own choosing rather than at the hands of the marauders.

As Rhea handed two of the bowls full of powder to her sister priestesses, Aria passed pitchers of water around so the three women had plenty within easy reach. The four women sat in silence, contemplating the act they were about to undertake.

After a few moments, Aria began quietly singing. All the priestesses learned the song during their training, though it was rarely used anymore. In recent times, people preferred the simplicity of the triple invocation and poured libations for funeral rites. But long ago, every one of Ida's children left this life by having their soul sung over to the World Below, carried to the place of rest by the voices of the living as they called to the One who held the spirits of the dead in the palm of her hand:

Mother-of-Darkness-and-Stars
Whose body is the World Below
Receive the spirit of one we hold dear
Keep her safe and warm
In the depths of your love

As Aria sang, her three sister priestesses swallowed the powder from their bowls, washing it down with water, coughing as the dusty substance tickled their throats. Then they, too, began to sing, blessing each other on their journey to the World Below, tears flowing down their faces as they released their sorrow — sorrow for each other, for their people, and for their island home.

Soon their words began to slur, their melodies to wobble. One by one they lay down on the cave floor, their voices fading and falling silent. But Aria continued to sing, swaying in place where she sat, the ancient melody swirling around her, echoing from the walls of the small cave. Her voice grew hoarse, but still she sang, forcing the words and the melody out as long as her sisters still breathed. She could not tell how long she had been singing when, one after another, the rising and falling of the women's chests slowed, then stopped. They breathed their last, slipping loose from their bodies, journeying on to a place more peaceful than the island, with its smoldering temples and its cities full of corpses.

For a long while Aria simply sat there, staring at the bodies around her. At last she managed to draw herself out of her stupor, crawling around on her hands and knees, draping shawls and scarves over the women's faces. When she got to Rhea, she stopped, staring at her dearest friend's face. Ter eyes were closed, her expression peaceful.

"You have gone home," Aria whispered. "May the Mothers hold you in their sweet embrace." She stroked Rhea's hair, her eyes misting with tears. "I will meet you there soon, little sister." With a shuddering sigh, she leaned over and kissed her friend's cheek, then she drew a shawl up over the serene face.

With trembling hands she collected the bowls and tidied all the sacred vessels back into the traveling bags, all except the two pitchers that still had a little water in them. She drank from one until it was empty, then tucked it into one of the bags.

Drawing in a slow breath, she reached into the bottom of her own bag and lifted out a small piece of saffron-dyed linen, wrapped up in a bundle and tied with a thin cord. She set it next to the bronze blade on the ground in front of her. With shaking fingers she untied the cord and peeled the sunny yellow fabric from around the precious item it hid: the seal stone she had taken from the Daughter's altar all those years ago.

Chapter 70

She turned the stone over in her hand. It was deep green, still polished to a shine. Onto its surface was carved the image of a priestess dancing, holding handfuls of lilies, a sign that the goddess was upon her. A hole had been drilled through the body of the stone. It was meant to have a cord run through it, to be hung from the bearer's wrist. But she had never worn it that way, not since the day she took it from the Daughter's altar.

Over the years, she had had plenty of opportunities to return the seal stone to its altar, its rightful place in the temple. Many times, she had made her way to the little altar room and stood before the table. But never had she been able to set the stone down, release it from her grip. Perhaps, she thought now, its presence in her life was a reminder of the weight every High Priestess carries, the burden of so much more than just administration and ritual: the lives of the people who counted on her for guidance, support, and protection.

"Great Lady," she said, her voice hoarse from the long singing, "Daughter of the Three-and-One, I cannot begin to express how truly sorry I am. If some other woman had been elected High Priestess, someone more capable... someone who could have talked their way into the good graces of the usurpers at Knossos..." She clutched the stone in her hand, feeling its smooth roundness, its heat as it warmed in her grip. "I know the auguries said I was destined to hold this sacred office. I have done so to the very best of my ability, but it was not enough. I was not good enough. And now our island lies in ruins." She choked back a sob. "I am at your mercy."

Shivering, she gazed around the dim cave at the bodies of the people who had trusted her to lead them. But instead of leading them to the gods, she had led them to their deaths in a shallow cave high in the mountains, a short distance south of her beloved Malia. She hoped against hope that the teachings were true, that the Mothers did not judge their children but only loved them, no matter how profoundly they failed.

Now she gripped the bronze blade, the one sacred tool she had rescued from the temple. With that blade, she and every High Priestess before her had sacrificed their Consorts, their Beloveds. She tilted it back and forth, its honed edge gleaming softly in the faint light. Then she lifted the blade to her throat. It would be a good death.

THE END

Glossary

Pronunciations in this glossary are given in standardized ancient Greek and modern Anglicized form (U.S. pronunciation, not British, since I'm from the U.S.). For some names and terms, there is little to no difference between the two. In those cases, only one pronunciation is given. The Minoans weren't Greek, and we don't know what language they spoke, but ancient Greek pronunciations are probably pretty close to the way the Minoans said their names, so I've gone with that. And of course, some of the character names are Greek (Mycenaean).

The Minoan cities and sacred sites described in this novel are no longer inhabited. Today all you can see of them is ruins, though in some cases, modern cities have been built close by.

The lovely folks at NASA tell us that we should capitalize the names of our Earth, Sun, and Moon the same way we capitalize the names of other planets (Jupiter, Neptune), stars (Aldebaran, Sirius), and planetary moons (Io, Europa). I think it's only right that we show as much respect for our Earth, Sun, and Moon as we do the other celestial objects. So they are capitalized in this book.

Please note: While there is evidence that some ancient people blessed their babies with honey (like the characters in this story do) and fed it to their infants, we now know that's a dangerous practice.

Honey can contain botulism spores. Children who are less than a year old don't have strong enough digestion to destroy those spores, so honey can give them botulism, which can be deadly. Please don't feed honey to your baby or put it on their mouth for a blessing. We can honor the ways of the ancient world without reenacting them detail for detail.

The Seasons: The Mediterranean has a different seasonal cycle from the more northern parts of Europe. Instead of the four seasons that many people are familiar with (spring, summer, autumn, winter) there are two: rainy and dry. The rainy season begins in the autumn. That's when farmers plant their crops. Field crops like vegetables and grains grow throughout the mild, rainy winter and are harvested in the spring—the opposite of more northern regions, where crops are planted in the spring and harvested in the autumn. In the Mediterranean, the summer is the "dead time," when the rain stops almost completely and the temperatures become blisteringly hot. On Crete, the smaller creeks dry up entirely and the water level in the rivers lowers considerably. Then the rains come in the autumn, the ground softens, and the planting begins again. Grapes are typically harvested at the end of the summer to the beginning of autumn, whenever they come ripe locally (late August to early September on our modern calendar). Olives are harvested in very late autumn, typically November, since they need the autumn rains to plump up before they're ready.

The Wine: Ancient people didn't actually stumble around drunk all the time even though their main beverages were wine and beer. Centuries ago wine, like beer, was a good bit weaker than it is now, due to the type of yeast used to do the brewing. People also didn't drink wine undiluted. It was commonly cut with water by a third to a half, and sometimes more. In addition to avoiding drunkenness, this was a way to make the untreated water supply safe to drink—that small bit of alcohol was enough to kill most pathogens that might be floating around in the water.

The Temple: For the purposes of this story, the temple in Malia is organized with the High Priestess as the highest-ranking woman and her Consort as the highest-ranking man. Beneath them are the College of Priestesses and the College of Priests, each one led by a Head Priest or Priestess (referred to in the story as the Head of the College). The High Priestess is elected by the clergy of the whole temple. The Heads of the Colleges are elected by the members of their respective colleges. The Consorts are chosen by divination and may choose to refuse the office. Within the colleges, priests and priestesses can be general ritualists or they can specialize in herbalism, astronomy and the sacred calendar, writing and record-keeping, and other fields. The heads of the various specialties (Chief Scrivener, Chief Sky-Watcher, and so on) are appointed by the High Priestess after consultation with the rest of the clergy.

CHARACTERS
All characters are Minoans unless otherwise noted.

Ariadne [ancient Greek *ah-ree-AHD-nay*, modern English *air-ee-AD-nee*]. A priestess in the temple in Malia. Her friends call her Aria. Her mother is Inia.

Belisseus [ancient Greek *bell-ee-SAY-oos*, modern English *bell-ISS-ee-us*]. The High Priestess' Consort in the temple in Malia. Highest-ranking man in the temple.

Daipita [*dah-ee-PEE-tah*]. Priestess in the temple at Malia. Head of the College of Priestesses.

Dionysios [ancient Greek *dee-oh-NEE-see-os*, modern English *die-oh-NIE-see-us*]. A young priest in the temple in Malia. His parents have mainlander ancestry but he was born on Crete.

Dolios [*do-LEE-os*]. A priest in the temple in Knossos.

Eileithyia [ancient Greek *ay-LAY-thee-ah*, modern English *ee-LEE-thee-uh*]. High Priestess in the temple in Malia.

Glymenos [ancient Greek *glee-MEN-os*, modern English *gleye-MEN-us*]. Consort in the temple in Knossos. A mainlander.

Hedamos [ancient Greek *HAY-dah-mos*, modern English *heh-DAH-mos*]. Layman from Knossos; mainlander. Works for the

Knossos temple as an emissary.

Idomeneia [ancient Greek *ee-doh-MAY-nay-ah*, modern English *eye-doh-meh-NAY-uh*]. A weaver and business owner in Knossos. Her brother is Sageleus.

Inia [*EE-nee-ah*]. A priestess in the temple in Malia. Ariadne is her daughter.

Kaeseus [ancient Greek *kah-ee-SAY-oos*, modern English *kah-EE-see-us*]. Head of the College of Priests in the temple in Malia.

Kailo [*KYE-loh*]. Young man who becomes a Consort in the temple in Malia.

Lexion [*LEKS-ee-on*]. Priest in the temple in Malia. Eventually becomes Head of the College of Priests.

Medea [ancient Greek *MAY-day-ah*, modern English *muh-DEE-uh*]. Priestess in the temple in Knossos.

Melena [ancient Greek *may-LAY-nah*, modern English *muh-LEE-nah*]. High Priestess in the temple in Knossos.

Mopsos [first syllable like the English word "mop": *MOP-sos*]. Layman from Knossos. Mainlander. Works for the Knossos temple as an emissary.

Navila [*nah-VEE-lah*]. Head of the College of Priestesses in the temple in Gournia.

Nestia [*NESS-tee-ah*]. Head Priestess of the sacred house at Nirou Khani.

Odrys [*OH-driss*]. Part-time priest in the temple in Malia. Spends the rest of his time in his family's business in the city.

Orestas [*oh-RESS-tahs*]. Priest in the temple in Malia. Becomes Chief Sky-Watcher in the temple.

Ploteus [*PLOH-tee-us*]. Priest in the temple in Malia.

Presfa [*PRESS-fah*]. Priestess in the temple in Malia.

Psoreia [ancient Greek *psoh-RAY-ah*, modern English *soh-REE-ah*]. Priestess in service at Eileithyia's sacred cave.

Rhea [ancient Greek *RAY-ah*, modern English *REE-uh*]. Priestess in the temple in Malia. Aria's best friend.

Sageleus [ancient Greek *sah-geh-LAY-oos*, modern English *sah-*

gih-LEE-us]. Layman, well-to-do merchant in the city of Malia.

Samara [*sah-MAH-rah*]. Lay woman, merchant in the city of Malia.

Teledike [*teh-leh-DEE-kay*]. Medicine-Priestess in the temple in Knossos.

Thalamika [*thah-LAH-mee-kah*]. Priestess in the temple in Malia. Holds the office of Chief Scrivener.

Themis [ancient Greek *THAY-mees*, modern English *THEH-miss*]. Lay woman who lives in the city of Malia.

Vanadia [*vah-NAH-dee-ah*]. Priestess in the temple in Knossos. She is of mainlander ancestry.

Yassib [*yah-SEEB*]. Sailor from Byblos, a Canaanite town on the coast of the Levant (the area along the eastern Mediterranean coast encompassing the modern nations of Israel, Lebanon, and Syria as well as southern Turkey and the Sinai peninsula). He is Ytanos' business partner and life partner.

Ytanos [*ee-TAH-nos*]. Layman, ship owner, and trader whose home is in the city of Malia. He is Aria's brother.

Yvata [*ee-VAH-tah*]. Medicine-Priestess in the temple in Malia.

Zephyra [*zeh-FEE-rah*]. High Priestess in the temple in Knossos.

DEITIES, PLACES, RITUALS, AND OTHER TERMS

Adyton [*ah-DEE-ton*]. A small section in the corner of a ritual room that is a meter or more below the regular floor level, accessed by steps. Used as a symbolic, man-made cave in rituals. These have been found in all the major Minoan temples and in some smaller villas as well.

Agrimi Brotherhood [*ah-GREE-mee*]. For the purposes of this story, an organization within the priesthood in the Minoan temples, dedicated to the goat-faced Horned God, the male counterpart to the Minoan goat-goddess Amalthea. Agrimi is a name for the wild goats found on Crete.

Alabastron [*ah-lah-BAS-tron*]. A small jar or flagon with a narrow opening, used to store scented oils. Alabastrons were made of ceramic or stone.

Amnisos [*ahm-NEE-sos*]. Minoan port city on the north coast of

Crete, just north of Knossos. This was the port nearest to Knossos, which was located a short distance inland.

Ariadne [ancient Greek *ah-ree-AHD-nay*, modern English *air-ee-AD-nee*]. Also called the Daughter. Minoan goddess of the agricultural cycle and guardian of the spirits of the dead in the Underworld. Her title in this role is Queen of the Dead. Though the Minoan deities do not fit neatly into a human-style family tree, Ariadne is thought of as Ida's daughter and/or as the daughter of all the Minoan mother goddesses.

Armenoi [*ahr-MEN-oy*]. Small Minoan city a short distance south of the coast in northwestern Crete.

Avaris [*ah-VAHR-iss*]. Ancient Egyptian city in the Nile Delta, a major port and trading center.

Belisseus [ancient Greek *bell-ee-SAY-oos*, modern English *bell-ISS-ee-us*]. For the purposes of this story, the ritual name given to the priest who holds the office of Consort in the temple in Malia. Also one of the names of the Minoan god known as the Red Warrior, the Red Champion, and the Lion of Rhea.

Britomartis [ancient Greek *bree-TOH-mar-tees*, modern English *brih-toh-MAR-tiss*]. Also called Diktynna [ancient Greek *DEEK-tin-ah*, modern English *dik-TIN-ah*]. Minoan deer and huntress goddess. She is associated with her male counterpart, the stag-god.

Byblos [*BEE-blos*]. Canaanite port city on the coast of the Levant, in the region that is modern-day Lebanon.

Dia [*DEE-ah*]. Also called the Lady's Island (Dia means "goddess"). Small island off the north coast of Crete, near the port city of Amnisos.

Dionysus [ancient Greek *dee-OH-nu-sos*, modern English *dye-uh-NYE-sus*]. Minoan god of the vine and ecstasy. Born to the mother goddess Ida in her sacred cave at Winter Solstice. Dies with the grape harvest in the late summer to early autumn.

Ear of Grain. Another name for the star Spica in the modern constellation Virgo. For the purposes of this story, the star represents the ear of grain the goddess held during the rituals of the Mysteries; the star's heliacal rising marked the end of the Mysteries.

Eileithyia [ancient Greek *ay-LAY-thee-ah*, modern English *ee-LEE-thee-uh*]. Minoan goddess of childbirth and midwifery.

Flock-of-Doves. The modern constellation the Pleiades. Also called the Bee-Swarm

Gournia [ancient Greek *gorn-YAH*, modern English *GOR-nee-ah*]. Minoan city on the northeastern coast of Crete.

Great Darkness. For the purposes of this story, the euphemism the Minoans use to refer to the eruption of the supervolcano Thera (modern Santorini) in about 1625 BCE, roughly two centuries before this story takes place. The eruption destroyed the center of the island and sent earthquakes and tidal waves out across the eastern Mediterranean, destroying coastal cities in Crete, Greece, Anatolia, and the Levant. The ash cloud covered much of the eastern Mediterranean and hindered the growing of crops for at least a year afterward.

Hagia Triada [ancient Greek *ha-GEE-ah tree-AH-dah*, modern English *AH-yee-ah tree-AH-dah*]. Minoan city near the south central coast of Crete.

Hekaterides [*heh-kah-teh-REE-days*]. Demi-goddesses who sprang from Rhea's finger-marks in the soil at her sacred cave. Associated with sacred dance, the Mountain Mother goddess, and possibly with the production of pottery.

The Horned Ones. The Minoan gods and goddesses who are associated with horned animals: the Minotaur and Europa (cattle), Britomartis and Minelathos (deer), Amalthea and Minocapros (goats) as well as the more ancient ibex god and goddess whose names we do not know.

Iacchus [*ee-YA-kus*]. Dionysus in his form as a youth (in modern terms, we might call him a teenager). He is Ida's torch-bearer, guiding her way into the Underworld to find Ariadne in the story associated with the Mysteries.

Ibex Brotherhood. For the purposes of this story, an organization within the priesthood in the Minoan temples, dedicated to the ibex Horned God.

Ida [*EE-dah*]. Also called Rhea, Earth-Mother, and Island-Mother. Minoan Earth Mother goddess. One of the three Minoan mother goddesses (Ida, Posidaeja, and Therasia) referred to collectively as the Three. Ida represents the land in the three sacred realms of land, sea, and sky. The three mother goddesses plus Ourania are collectively referred to as the Three-and-One.

The Jewel. For the purposes of this story, the name of the star Sirius, on the end of the handle of the Labrys (the constellation Orion).

Kalami [*kah-LAH-mee*]. Minoan city on the northwest coast of Crete.

Karphi [*KAR-fee*]. A prominent mountain peak on Crete about halfway between Malia and Mt. Dikte. A peak sanctuary was located there during early Minoan times, but it was abandoned around the time of the Thera eruption (approximately two centuries before this story takes place).

Knossos [*kuh-noh-SOS*]. The largest of the Minoan cities, located a short distance south of the coast in north central Crete.

Kommos [*koh-MOS*]. Minoan port city on the south central coast of Crete.

Kuretes [*koo-RAY-tays*]. Demi-gods who sprang from Rhea's finger-marks in the soil at her sacred cave. Associated with sacred dance, the Mountain Mother goddess, and possibly with bronze smithing.

Kydonia [ancient Greek *ku-doh-NEE-ya*, modern English *sih-DOH-nee-ya*]. Sometimes spelled Cydonia. Minoan city on the far northwest coast of Crete.

The Labrys. For the purposes of this story, the name of the modern constellation Orion. The Jewel on the end of its handle is the star Sirius. Labrys is the term used to denote the Minoan sacred symbol of the double-bladed ax.

Libation table. A small stone object, square or rectangular, with bowl-shaped depressions in the top, usually placed on an altar or shrine bench. Libations (liquid offerings) are poured into the depressions during rituals.

Lion of Rhea. Also known as the Red Warrior, Red Champion, or Belisseus. Minoan god who is the son of the Three-and-One.

Loggia. Architectural feature of Minoan temples: a ground floor room with one side open to the temple's central court. The location of rituals that were meant to be visible to onlookers standing in the courtyard.

The mainland. Mainlanders. The area that is the modern nation of Greece, which is the mainland directly north of Crete. In Minoan times, the mainlanders were Mycenaeans (early Greeks). For the purposes of this story, the mainlanders who have been there the longest and who respect the Minoans' traditions are Achaeans, and the newer ones from the mountains are Dorians.

Malia [*MAH-lee-ah*]. Minoan city on the eastern coast of Crete. The main location of the action in this story.

Melissae [ancient Greek *MAY-lee-seye*, modern English *meh-LISS-ay*]. Minoan bee-spirit goddesses who guard the spirits of the dead in the Underworld. Ariadne is their queen—the Queen Bee and Queen of the Dead.

Minos [ancient Greek *MEE-nos*, modern English *MYE-nos*]. Minoan god associated with the Moon, the Underworld, and judgment of the dead. For the purposes of this story, the ritual name given to the priest who holds the office of Consort in the temple in Knossos.

Mochlos [*MOH-khlos*]. Minoan city on the far northeastern coast of Crete.

Mt. Dikte [ancient Greek *DEEK-tay*, modern English *DIK-tee*]. Sacred mountain in central Crete, the site of a Minoan-era cave shrine. The cave is called the Diktean Cave, Diktean Andron, or Psychro Cave and is still accessible today.

The Mysteries. For the purposes of this story, the Minoan precursor to the Eleusinian Mysteries, a ten-day-long sacred festival held at Eileithyia's sacred cave and culminating in rituals of initiation. Instead of the myth involving Persephone being abducted by Hades and rescued by Demeter, the Minoan version involves Ariadne voluntarily descending to the Underworld to guard and tend the spirits of the dead there. Her mother Ida comes and fetches her when it is time for her to return to the World Above as the agricultural growing season begins, with Iacchus bringing his torch to light the way.

Nirou Khani [*NEE-roo KAHN-ee*]. Small Minoan settlement on the north central coast of Crete, just east of Amnisos.

Ourania [*oh-RAH-nee-ah*]. Also called Mother-of-Darkness-and-Stars, Mother-of-All, and Great Cosmic Mother. Minoan star-goddess, the sacred embodiment of the universe itself, the cosmos, and space. The Underworld is also her domain, since many ancient cultures viewed the night sky as the Underworld that slips upward above the Earth during the night. She is the One in the phrase the Three-and-One, with the Three being the three Minoan mother goddesses (Ida, Posidaeja, and Therasia).

Palaikastro [*pah-leye-KAH-stroh*]. Minoan city on the far northeast coast of Crete.

Phaistos [ancient Greek *feye-STOS*, modern English *FEH-stos*]. Minoan city near the south central coast of Crete, just east of Hagia Triada.

Pithoi [*PIH-thoy*], singular **pithos** [*PIH-thohs*]. Tall, vase-like containers used to store grain, wine, and oil in Minoan temples. Smaller versions were used to store these staples in Minoan homes.

Posidaeja [*poh-see-DYE-ah*]. Also called Thalassa, Sea-Mother, Water-Mother, and Mother-of-the-Waters. Minoan goddess of the sea. One of the three Minoan mother goddesses (Ida, Posidaeja, and Therasia) referred to collectively as The Three. She represents the sea in the three sacred realms of land, sea, and sky. The three mother goddesses plus Ourania are collectively referred to as the Three-and-One.

Sistrum. A musical instrument, a type of rattle with a handle, a frame with crossbars, and loose pieces of metal on the crossbars that rattle when the sistrum is shaken.

The Three. The three Minoan mother goddesses: Ida, Posidaeja, and Therasia. They represent the three sacred realms of land, sea, and sky.

The Three-and-One. The three Minoan mother goddesses plus Ourania.

The Torch. The star Arcturus in the modern constellation Boötes. For the purposes of this story, this star symbolizes Iacchus' torch in the tale of the Mysteries and its heliacal rising marks the beginning of the Mysteries.

Therasia [*teh-RAH-see-ah*]. Also called Kalliste, Sun-Mother, Fire-Mother, and Fire of Heaven. Minoan Sun goddess. One of the three Minoan mother goddesses (Ida, Posidaeja, and Therasia) referred to collectively as The Three. She represents the sky in the three sacred realms of land, sea, and sky. The three mother goddesses plus Ourania are collectively referred to as the Three-and-One.

The Two Lands. Egypt, a major trading partner for the Minoans. The phrase "The Two Lands" can be taken to mean either Upper and Lower Egypt combined, or the two realms that the Egyptians thought of as making up their world: the desert (ruled over by the god Set and represented by the color red) and the fertile land along the Nile (ruled over by the god Osiris and represented by the color black).

Tylisos [ancient Greek *TU-lee-sos*, modern English *tye-LISS-os*]. Minoan city near the north central coast of Crete, a short distance northwest of Knossos.

Tyre. [Usually pronounced like the English word "tire."] Canaanite port city on the coast of the Levant, in the region that is modern-day Lebanon.

Zakros [*ZAH-kros*]. Minoan city on the far eastern coast of Crete.

Acknowledgments

As with raising a child, birthing a book takes a community. A lot of people helped along the way as I wrote this book, and I am grateful for their support.

First and foremost, I want to thank the members of my online Modern Minoan Paganism group, Ariadne's Tribe, for their constant inspiration. One of those members, Dana Corby, shared her vision that inspired my art for the book cover. Though I have taken some liberties with the details, the overall idea is still hers. Dana is also one of the leaders of the first official chapter of Modern Minoan Paganism, a moderator of our online group, and an invaluable asset to the tradition, with many years of experience as a Pagan leader and priestess.

I'm grateful to another member of Ariadne's Tribe, Emily Reseigh, for sharing her dream-vision of the blessing of the fields in Minoan Crete in the discussion group for one of my online courses. Her description of this ancient rite was moving and inspiring, and led me to write a whole chapter around it.

I'd like to thank my beta readers, who bravely read the manuscript before publication and gave me a great deal of useful feedback: Julie Akers, Shevaa Deva, S. Blake Duncan, Bryan Hewitt, Amanda Holt, J.P. Jamin, Geoff Lundy, D.M. Read, Diana Sinclair, and Catherine Soanes.

I owe a debt to the archaeologists, anthropologists, historians, visionaries, and mystics who have shared their work and their love of the Minoans with the public over the years. From my first "ah-ha moment" in a high school art history class to the latest research and rituals, these people have helped feed my desire to connect with the ancient Minoans, their culture, and their religion.

About the Author

Laura Perry is an artist, writer, and Pagan priestess. The Minoans of Bronze Age Crete have been a passion of hers since a fateful high school art history class introduced her to the frescoes of Knossos. Laura's first book was published in 2001. She continues to write fiction and non-fiction as well as teaching online courses. She also draws and paints Pagan-themed artwork, including *The Minoan Tarot* deck-and-book set and *The Minoan Coloring Book*. When she's not busy drawing, writing, and editing, she enjoys gardening and giving living history demonstrations at local historic sites.

LauraPerryAuthor.com

Made in the USA
Monee, IL
24 August 2023

41583879R10285